TIGER PAW

BY

CHARLES A CORNELL

www.CharlesACornell.com

The Tiger is Unleashed!

Copyright 2012 Charles A. Cornell
ISBN: 978-0615602240
Editor: Caroline Smailes
Cover Artist: Robin Ludwig
Book layout and design: Cheryl Perez

This is a work of fiction. Any similarities between the characters, places or events that take place in this book are strictly coincidental.

To Susan, my soulmate for 35 years, and forever.
Without you, this wasn't possible.

And to my mother, Dorothy, the guardian angel of my creative spirit
who watches over my work

TIGER PAW

1st.
Printing

From the Desk of
Charles A Cornell

#16/25

March, 2012

O nobly-born, when thou art driven by the ever-moving wind of karma, thine intellect, having no object upon which to rest, will be like a feather tossed about by the wind.

—*Tibetan Book of The Dead*

TIGER PAW

Chapter One

New York City was paralyzed four blocks either side of Broadway, all the way from Central Park to Wall Street. What had started as a relatively small Occupy Wall Street demonstration had now grown to over one million people - *one million* very determined people.

People without a clear mission.

Except to be angry.

Very angry.

Fifteen hundred miles away at Denver Airport, waiting for a late flight to Washington DC, Scott Forrester was nursing a Jack and Coke in the Big Sky Bar. It was mid-October and a heavy, early season snowfall in the Rockies had cancelled his earlier flight. The airline had assured him of priority on the next flight out. Conditions were improving and Scott was anxious to get back to DC.

For the past three hours, he'd been glued to the TV screens in the bar watching the desperate scenes unfold in New York City. The Big Sky Bar was filling up fast as stranded passengers came in to catch up with the day's momentous events. New York had descended into chaos and the spiral was far from over. Everyone was developing the same uneasy feeling – this was not going to end well.

In the previous months, Zucotti Park had been the defacto epicenter of the Occupy Wall Street movement. Then it was joined by another camp in Washington Square, and then another in Stuyvesant Square, and then Gramercy Park. But it was a rally in Central Park around 3:30PM Eastern Time that had been the initial catalyst.

As the rally ended, demonstrators had marched aimlessly down Broadway. How far they planned to go, no one really knew in advance. That was the nature of the Occupy Wall Street movement. It was a spontaneous and organic process. The crowd wanted to disrupt the rush hour and that part had come off spectacularly well. But as the march continued south along Broadway, the power of social media had magnified the relatively small scale event into something that defied description.

A few hours into the march, the crowd had grown a whole lot bigger as the power of posts on Twitter and Facebook drew even further support. Out of nowhere, traffic arteries that were usually gridlocked on the way *out* of Manhattan had become gridlocked on the way *in*. Protesters from the Boroughs had found their way into the city by any means possible – the commuter trains, subways and ferries; in cars, vans and school buses; on bicycles and on foot.

CNN was calling the demonstration 'the biggest flash mob in history'. It had emptied stores and offices, bars and restaurants; college classrooms, unemployment lines, homeless shelters; and after linking the tent cities into one and filling the streets en masse, it had then rolled unopposed towards the headwaters of its discontentment… Wall Street.

Finally, as the clock in the bar ticked past 7:30PM Mountain Standard Time, which was 9:30PM on the East Coast, a full six hours after the initial rally had begun in Central Park, every street up and down the entire central spine of New York City was jammed full with protesters.

The sun had set on Wall Street, both literally and figuratively. The narrow streets in New York's Financial District were seething with a volatile mixture of anger and confusion. At penthouse level, in the boardrooms that looked out over Manhattan's twinkling skyline, Wall Street's power brokers were afraid to venture out. They were hiding in their offices, trapped and terrified.

On the TV screens in the Big Sky Bar, media pundits had endlessly debated the origins of the mob. The right wing media had argued they were either a highly organized, union sponsored demonstration or some kind of new communist-inspired anarchy. But the truth was evident as TV cameras scurried through the crowds - there were as many suits and ties in attendance as there were construction helmets and hippie headbands. The placards they hoisted echoed their deep resentment towards the wealthy elite that seemed indifferent to their plight. 'We are the 99%, Too Big to Fail, Too Big to Ignore' – were the words that spoke of the defiance and rage that had boiled to the surface in the face of a nationwide struggle to survive the biggest financial crisis since the Great Depression.

The authorities in New York had reacted slowly, with the usual federal, state and municipal bureaucracies in play. After ten years of figuring out how to handle the tragedy of a collapsing skyscraper, the officials trying to rescue New York City were in the middle of another 'deer in the headlights' moment in the face of something that had come at them in an unprecedented form, and on an unprecedented scale.

When the hammer finally began to fall on the demonstrators, it came down hard.

The TV in the airport bar flashed with *Breaking News*, "CNN has learned that the Governor's and Mayor's Offices have agreed on the emergency steps needed to control the growing demonstrations. In an extraordinary move not seen since the 9/11 attack on the World Trade Center, the Lincoln, Holland and Brooklyn Battery Tunnels, and the Brooklyn Bridge and Williamsburg Bridge, will be closed to traffic coming into Manhattan. The Governor has called up the National Guard to assist the NYPD and Port Authority Police to prevent any more protesters from entering the city. A joint press conference is expected within the hour where additional security measures will be announced. We are already seeing tear gas canisters being used to disperse the crowds in Times Square. The question is: what are they going to do with the hundreds of thousands of people on the streets? They can't arrest them all. Stay tuned as we continue to cover events on the ground with live reports from…"

The noise level inside the Big Sky Bar grew even more intense as arguments for and against the protesters spread among the airport's passengers. It was so loud Scott Forrester couldn't hear his cell phone ringing inside his leather jacket.

Finally, the phone's insistent vibration caught his attention. Caller ID said it was Trish Van Cleyburn.

He stepped out of the bar into the now deserted concourse. He answered, but her reply was drowned out by an incredible din in the background, at her end of the line.

"Can you speak up, Trish?" he asked, trying to cut through the voices and hear what she was saying. "Where are you?"

"New York City."

"*New York City!* Why the hell are *you* in New York City?"

"Something's come up."

"*No shit!* The whole world can see that! But why are *you* there?"

"No... not *that.*"

Demonstrators continued to chant in the background.

"Scott-" she said, struggling to form words into sentences. She was being jostled by the crowd. "Hold on... we're heading into... the World Trade Center Memorial..."

"The World Trade Center? That's just a few blocks from Wall Street. That's where-"

"Yeah, I know... but NYPD closed it off... only place to land a chopper. And a chopper... is the only way to get out of this mess-" A helicopter's rotor wash replaced the jumbled crowd noise around her. She had entered the World Trade Center site, behind police lines. "I'm going to send you a photo."

"Trish... what's going on?"

"Sending-"

The photo was a little muddy. It had been taken by a cell phone and the light was bad. But when the jpeg hit his phone's screen, Scott Forrester recoiled. He gasped, "My god, Trish! *When? Where?*"

"Today. On the dashboard of a car. But not just any car, Scott. A vintage 1955 Mercedes Gullwing Coupe."

"Geez..."

"There were only about a thousand of these cars ever made. They tell me this one's worth over a million dollars. But that's not the point. It's where they *found* the car, Scott... it was on..." Her voice was faint and garbled as the line started breaking up, "...arge in Brook... harbor..."

"Say again, Trish? On top of *what*?"

"A garbage barge... moored off... South Brooklyn Marine Terminal. There's more photos... different place-"

The next set of photos that arrived were in high definition - vivid color, exceptional detail. Professionally taken crime scene photos.

Scott felt his heart begin to race and skip a beat. All he could say was, "Where in *Hell*..."

"Exactly..." The rest of Trish's reply could barely be heard. But it sounded like she said something about a bathroom wall.

"Look Scott, I gotta go-"

She was breaking up again.

"The chopper's ready... if we don't... off in two minutes, we'll be... middle... World War Three. We're... Brooklyn first. Then East Hampton."

"What's in East Hampton?"

"Can't explain everything. Just listen up, Scott. A jet's going to-" He heard the sound of the chopper's door sliding shut. Trish Van Cleyburn was finally able to speak clearly. She was out of breath. "There's no way to get the FBI jet all the way to Denver in time. Take your commercial flight and whatever time you arrive, the jet will be waiting for you on the taxiway at Reagan. When it gets to East Hampton, a police escort will-"

At that point, rotor noise made any further conversation impossible. He heard the rapid acceleration of the chopper's blades as it lifted off. Then Trish's cell phone lost its signal. And the line went dead.

On television, CNN announced that National Guard troops had entered New York City.

With tanks.

Chapter Two

FBI Special Agent Scott Forrester stepped out of the police cruiser into the bone-chilling East Hampton mist, a garment bag in one hand, a travel weary notepad in the other.

A frosty glaze coated the mullioned windows of the Carleton Mansion, an enormous mock French chateau buried deep in a wooded glen. It towered over a circular driveway that was accustomed to greeting Mercedes, Bentleys and Porsches. But now, at 6:00AM on a cold Thursday morning in October, the courtyard was crammed with patrol cars, anonymous black sedans, and the finest Mobile Forensics Lab New York State possessed.

Through the Carleton Mansion's windows, an unholy light cast a sinister welcome through the fog. Scott Forrester's day was beginning the same way every day this week had ended - with a dreary mix of bad weather and bad karma; the sleety rain separating yesterday from today like a bad dream.

He leaned through the cruiser's open window and said, "Thanks for the ride, and the coffee, Deputy."

East Hampton Police Deputy Terence Connelly was a kind-hearted, gray-haired man nearing a long overdue retirement. His typical day consisted of ticketing a spoiled debutante who'd run a stop sign in her Daddy's Porsche Cayenne. Not this. Not frantic calls to every law enforcement agency within a four-hour drive. A nearly uncontrollable media circus outside the main gate. And inside this monument to a billionaire's excess, forensic technicians plying their grim trade.

Connelly asked, "They said you were some kind of expert, Agent Forrester. So what kind of person would do something like this?"

Scott wiped the drizzle from his face. He wished he was back inside the warmth of the cruiser. "Well, Deputy Connelly, let me tell you about 'experts'. At least the ones in my line of work. Every day we barter our prayers with the Devil to get the smallest answers to the simplest questions. But to get the really big answers, he wants us to give him a whole lot more. And right now, this is one 'expert', who's just flat out... *broke*."

Scott looked into the low clouds and shifting fog that hung over the Carleton Mansion's high slate roof and faux turrets. "So what is it I know for sure?" he said. "Let's start with this..."

He pointed to the Carleton Mansion.

"Just look at the sheer *size* of it. The person who had this built, made one *helluva* bargain. You don't have to be an expert to figure that out. So what am I expecting to find inside? I'd wager my soul it's all about the Devil coming to collect his dues."

"Bartering your prayers with the Devil?" Connelly replied, rubbing his fingers over the rosary that dangled from the cruiser's rear view mirror. "That's something no one should have to do. No matter what kind of answer you're looking for, Agent Forrester. So before you go in there... I'd hold onto those prayers. Hold on to them tightly."

The cruiser's window rolled up. The car turned away, its wheels crunching through the fallen leaves, its tail lights disappearing into the mist.

Scott Forrester slung the garment bag over his shoulder and turned towards the steps that led up to the Carleton Mansion's massive entrance. His black leather jacket hid tired slept-in jeans. His dusty black shoes needed a good polish. His pockets were full of credit card receipts for motels he didn't remember sleeping in. And he was hungry. The hasty turnaround at Washington's Reagan Airport meant the FBI jet had taken off for East Hampton stocked with only a few bags of peanuts and a can of warm Coke - the FBI Academy's breakfast of champions.

He climbed the steps and stopped in front of the mansion's double doors, then closed his eyes and took a deep breath. Behind him, as the rustling of the oak trees and cedars echoed with a thousand tiny voices, his thoughts churned memories of ugly sights and sounds, like a stick creating eddies in a stagnant pond.

Whispers in the trees, he thought.

Two days ago, the same whispers, but a different forest. One fragrant with pine. A virgin wilderness in Wyoming's Grand Tetons. The sun's rays descending through equally restless boughs. A murder scene that had nearly vanished; scavengers picking it clean. A hillock of crushed grass, roped off with yellow tape. A chalky white line marking the rock where Charlie 'Silver Moon' MacNabb's rifle had slipped from his hands. Flattened grasses outlining where Deuce Meredith had struggled with his wounds. Two miles down the trail, the tent at their base camp had been painted with human blood. Deuce Meredith's blood.

This had been Scott Forrester's second trip to Wyoming in two weeks. He had returned hoping to find something that had been overlooked. *Something. Anything.* A telltale bend in a blade of grass. An innocuous wisp of cloth stuck to a Scotch thistle's stem. A careless remnant in the wake of a brutal killer's presence, left buried in the soft heath. *Anything.*

The police search had ended, fruitless and barren. Dogs couldn't pick up a scent. He'd left no food behind. Not even a candy wrapper. No campsite. No fires. Indian guides had found some broken ferns he'd tied to his feet, to mask his footprints. But that trail soon went cold.

All that remained were bitter tasting images burned into his mind. And here, in the shadow of a mansion that took the Devil's ransom to build, Scott Forrester could still hear the echoes of that dying hunter's anguish, hoping beyond hope, that inside these doors, it wouldn't be the same again.

He opened his eyes. The eerie glow that was streaming out of the mansion's windows surrounded him.

All of the trails have gone cold.

Six long months.

Mind-numbing hours.

His vision blurred by the dark haze of a phantom's cruelty - a killer FBI Special Agent Scott Forrester had been chasing from one side of the country to the other.

First California. A gift from Hell that had drifted down from a crying sky.

Then Florida. Its shirt-drenching humidity no match for a sniper's bullet.

Wyoming. Howling mountain winds, and two defenseless victims.

And now, it was The Hamptons' turn.

Billionaire Matthew Carleton.

His fifth victim.

Drowned in red wine - a Roman bathtub brooding like an empty marble coffin, its crimson-stained rim setting the high watermark for Matthew Carleton's untimely death.

And *why?*

That was his prayer.

That was the answer Scott Forrester sought.

The Devil be damned.

Chapter Three

The room's ceiling was high and its walls were lined with tall, white marble columns, but as he entered the bathroom, Scott Forrester felt a suffocating and tomblike stillness descending on him.

Forensic technicians were working patiently in absolute and painstaking silence, the violation lingering over them like a sickly veil.

Matthew Carleton had spared no expense: the bathroom was dressed in the finest Italian marble, white for the floors and vanity tops, rose-colored on the walls. The fixtures were gold-plated; the cabinets were rich mahogany. In the room's center sat a large sunken Roman tub, carved from a single block of white Carrera marble, weighing nearly three quarters of a ton. Its gold-plated faucets, shaped like flying swans, peered into an expanse of wine-stained emptiness.

Scott Forrester walked towards the wall directly behind the bathtub. He approached what he had come so far to witness for himself - the sinister proclamation of Matthew Carleton's violent death, smeared across the rose-colored marble. In blood.

The mysterious and indecipherable script was a collection of symbols and lines. Crisply drawn, like calligraphy. But painted with vicious, arrogant strokes.

Ten to twelve inches high, the script stretched across four feet of the wall. The string of symbols ended in a cluster of irregular shapes - a final flourish from the killer's palette.

A bloodied paw print.

It was unmistakable. *It* was undeniable. The definitive connection between Matthew Carleton's murder and the four others that had preceded it in California, Florida and Wyoming.

Scott Forrester felt a pang of fear and loathing biting deeply inside his stomach. The script on the wall advocated the same killer's darkest thoughts. And the last symbol, the bitter tasting image that had been burned into his soul - the paw print – was an illumination of a manic purpose, an icon of evil that the same killer had left behind several times before.

When Scott Forrester had entered the room, the tension could be plucked like a taut violin string. He whispered something. It was barely audible, but it caused the technicians to stop their work and look up.

Special Agent Trish Van Cleyburn broke through the haunting silence, "Okay… but a declaration of *what*?"

Scott's voice hesitated, his thoughts competing with his anger, "It's a shout. His declaration of victory. Captured in the vacuum of time and space."

A voice came from behind them. It belonged to a short, barrel-chested Italian with pudgy cheeks and a thick neck, wearing a snazzy brown suit and a tieless white shirt, "Very poetic, Forrester. But I'm with Van Cleyburn on this. What the hell does a 'declaration' *mean*?"

Trish introduced Scott to the man in the brown suit, "Benito Vincente, Assistant Special Agent-in-Charge, New York Field Office. Special Agent Vincente was the reason I came to New York. I was briefing him on another case when the city decided to take a journey to the wild side. We were just about to get sucked into that vortex when the murder of Matthew Carleton appeared on the radar screens like an incoming missile. And if it wasn't for Agent Vincente, we wouldn't have gotten out of Manhattan last night."

Benito Vincente, mid-fifties, former NY state power-lifting champion, still worked out as hard as if he was thirty years younger. He took the hand of the much younger Scott Forrester and promptly crushed it. "Titus Griffin has high expectations of you, Forrester. And he has a low threshold for disappointment."

Titus Griffin was Scott Forrester's boss at the FBI's National Center for the Analysis of Violent Crime in Quantico, Virginia.

Scott winced, tightened his grip in return, and asked, "You know Titus Griffin?"

Vincente disengaged his handshake, satisfied that Special Agent Forrester wasn't the limp-wristed weakling Titus Griffin had warned him about. "I used to be Griffin's partner. Titus Griffin has a knack of making fifteen years seem like yesterday."

"My life is quickly being filled up with Titus Griffin's yesterdays, Agent Vincente."

Vincente leaned over the now emptied Roman tub. The forensic technicians had taken away carboys full of messy liquid that had been carefully decanted. A hair. A fiber. Something must be in that liquor of death to point them to the person that had done this.

Vincente peered into the tub, as if the echo of the victim's screams could still be heard swirling around its rim, and said, "Oh… it'll get better, Forrester. If I know Titus, he's just warming up."

Vincente then handed Scott a large file. It contained the Suffolk County Coroner's preliminary medical report and a slew of glossies taken by NY State crime scene investigators before Matthew Carleton's body had been removed from the tub. Scott recognized several photos. They were the ones sent to his phone in Denver. "Everyone wants in on this case, Forrester. Carleton was about as big a fish in New York society as it gets… a whale."

Scott shuffled through the Coroner's report like an appraiser viewing a stamp album, pausing with a hushed grunt every time something of value appeared. He pulled out one of the photos and held it in front of the bathtub. "The marks on the body. Carleton was tortured. Hands tied behind his back. Extensive bruising around the neck. A slow, very slow death. Agent Vincente, we will need some uniforms to search the grounds. They'll be looking for a glass or plastic bottle, maybe a dish or bowl, or something similar."

"And why we would be looking for that?"

Scott pointed to a corner of the photo. "The killer's signature mark on the body... a ritual incision that nearly severs the victim's left earlobe. To collect blood. He needed a container to drain it into. To use as an inkpot for the writing."

Vincente flipped open his cell phone, "Okay, Forrester. I'm on it."

Scott then turned to Trish Van Cleyburn. "Does Forensics have a shoe size yet, Trish? He must have tracked wine everywhere."

"He cleaned up."

"He cleaned up?"

"When the police arrived, they found a mop and bucket soaking in red wine and bleach. Guess the killer didn't want to ruin Carleton's expensive rugs on his way out."

"Yeah, he was very considerate, Forrester," Vincente said, the phone pressed to his ear. "If every houseguest were that conscientious, the world would be a much better place to live in."

Scott put the photos back into the file. "Make no mistake, Agent Vincente. This was no ordinary houseguest. Somebody channeled a lot of hatred into this killing. *A lot* of hatred."

"Hatred? Tell me something I don't know. Do the math, Forrester," Vincente added. "There were over a thousand bottles of wine in Carleton's cellar. And every drop, every last drop - all of it – is *gone.*"

"Gone?"

Vincente pointed his latex-gloved hand around the bathtub's rim, "One thing Forensics knows for sure, Forrester... Carleton's wine collection was so big; it couldn't fit in this tub without some serious overflowing."

Scott paused, thinking. "So the killer poured Carleton's wine down the drain? And what would one of those bottles be worth, Agent Vincente? Twenty bucks each? Fifty? A hundred?" Wine was not his expertise.

"Try again, Forrester. But this time, add a zero or two. Two months ago, Carleton purchased a single case of 1961 Chateau Latour at auction for $22,000 and put a note in his computer inventory that said 'picnic wine'."

"*Picnic* wine?"

"Matthew Carleton had the most expensive wine collection ever assembled on Long Island. Worth nearly $10 million by our initial estimates."

"And the killer forced his victim to watch $10 million of rare wine disappear down the drain, bottle by bottle?"

"God, you're smart, Forrester. I wish I was as smart as you. Yeah, he poured it down the drain. Then he filled the tub with what was left... and did his thing."

Scott visualized a bound Matthew Carleton being dunked in red wine; the crimson merlot staining his lips as he gasped; his cheeks blue and his eyes bulging, as he cried out in vain for one last breath of air. "And to a collector like Matthew Carleton... it must have been as much fun as having his fingernails extracted with pliers..."

"He gets it. That's just great," Vincente said, stepping into Trish's space, a little too close for comfort. "You kids can go home now. Send Titus my love."

He rolled his finger up Trish's arm and whispered, "I've enjoyed our time together. A smart country girl like you should transfer to the Big Apple. Give me a call. You'd love it. Wall to wall candy stores."

Twenty-eight-years-old. Model perfect figure. Salon-tussled strawberry blonde hair. Eyes as blue as her faded designer jeans. Trish Van Cleyburn had waded through this kind of macho bullshit before. It had started in the Cincinnati Field Office and then continued after her transfer to Quantico. She had risen up the ranks purely by sweating heavy caseloads, doing meticulous background research, and delivering impressive results. Vincente would have to shop for his candy somewhere else. She might be new at the Serial Crime Unit, but she was no rookie in the FBI.

"Don't underestimate Scott Forrester, Agent Vincente," she hissed.

"I won't, sweetheart. After all, his boss highly recommends him." Benito Vincente swaggered to the door and said, "With the Yankees out of the playoffs, and M1 tanks in Battery Park, what else have I got to do? With a hundred acres of forest outside, I might as well entertain myself by helping the uniforms look for a needle in a haystack! Thanks, Forrester. Thanks a lot!"

Vincente slipped out of the door, gone in a rush of cheap aftershave.

The bathroom descended into silence once again.

Scott approached the rose-colored marble.

He placed a gloved finger a few inches from the killer's last stroke of blood and closed his eyes.

Wyoming. His wilderness survival skills were textbook. Crisscrossing streams. Knowing that snow was on its way. Knowing his trail wouldn't be found - if at all - until springtime.

"That symbol again, Trish. God damn it…"

Taunting him.

Bold. And bloody.

The paw print.

Bitter tasting images.

The marble was smooth and cold. And on its surface, a layer of red blood cells danced to the Devil's tune.

A shout in a vacuum.

The reason FBI Special Agent Scott Forrester lacked sleep.

Chapter Four

From the eighty-seventh floor of the John Hancock Center, the skyline of Chicago was a sparkling array of lights. Far below, against the backdrop of a calm Lake Michigan, a lazy ribbon of traffic curled up North Lakeshore Drive. The last of the city's workers were retreating to the cozy suburbs, thankful that Chicago had not suffered, at least not yet, the same fate as New York City.

It was 9:45 PM.

Dominic Sant'Angello, the forty-two year old President, CEO and principal shareholder of Sigma Venture Capital stood in front of the floor-to-ceiling smoked glass window staring into a quiet night sky. Apart from the radiant glow coming from his laptop and the light from a small brass desk lamp, the office was in darkness.

Sue Lee Chen slipped cautiously through the open office door. "Mr. Sant'Angello?"

It was unusual to find Dominic Sant'Angello so introspective. Her boss wasn't just any successful businessman. He was a financial superstar. But in the past few months, a seemingly endless source of funding had suddenly dried up. Now, the complex set of deals that had been built from a shaky foundation had begun to unwind and Sigma's fate seemed more certain with every passing day. There didn't seem to be any way out of declaring bankruptcy. Dominic Sant'Angello's once invincible investment empire was crumbling.

His hefty frame cast a solemn silhouette against the bright lights of a city he once ruled unopposed. Dominic Sant'Angello looked into the blackness of Lake Michigan and wondered how all this had happened; a 24-

karat gold pen twirling nervously in his fingers like a cheerleader's baton. His always-on, Type-A mind raced through a mental maze created by his risky miscalculations. With every turn there was a dead-end.

What about The Portland Group? he thought. *Dare he tap them one last time?*

Sensing a presence behind him, confirmed by the petit reflection in the window, Sant'Angello turned and asked, "What is it, Sue Lee?"

Sue Lee Chen, Sigma Capital's Vice President of Business Development, had been with Dominic Sant'Angello from the very beginning. She'd suffered the early failures, rejoiced at the 'Hail Mary' moves that had given them their first lucky breaks, and sat side-by-side with Dominic Sant'Angello as Sigma Capital rode the roller coaster ride called the stock market. It had been seven very long years.

Sue Lee inched into the office and peered through the gloom. She steadied herself and took a deep breath. She was there to deliver the latest in a series of bad news messages. Two of their clients - Razorback Software's CEO Deuce Meredith and Liang Wong, founder of Silicon Pathways - were dead. Murdered. And now Matthew Carleton.

Coincidence? Two deaths, maybe. But three?

"Your attorney is holding on Line 4. He wants to know if he has permission to release your correspondence with Mr. Kostelic to the SEC investigators."

Dominic Sant'Angello's pen stopped twirling.

She hesitated to say it - what they were both thinking - but said it anyway, "If you don't co-operate, there's no escaping it. The SEC will indict you for securities fraud."

In the shadows of the flickering light, Sant'Angello's face creased into a burning rage. He thrust the pen forward and snarled, "You tell that fat-assed attorney - those documents are stamped 'Privileged & Confidential'! I'll have the SEC suck my dick in court if he ever turns those papers over!"

Sue Lee Chen knew her boss wasn't kidding. The end game was getting closer. She knew it. The rest of the office knew it. And by the tone of his voice, it would seem that Dominic Sant'Angello had finally realized it too.

"He says his practice never stamped those letters, 'Privileged & Confidential', Mr. Sant'Angello. And no one will testify that they did. He says they're private papers between you and Mr. Kostelic, and legally they're not covered by your attorney-client privilege. He doesn't know who stamped them - or why they thought they could get away with it - but as long as you turn them over to the SEC, he doesn't care."

The expensive pen left Dominic Sant'Angello's hand, smashing dart-like into the Northwestern MBA hanging next to her head. Shards of glass spilled down on the coffee table, showering opened cartons of leftover Chinese food. Sue Lee gasped, dropped her files, and hurried back to her office.

Dominic Sant'Angello's husky six-foot-four frame thundered behind her. "The law?" he yelled. "He's supposed to *protect* me from the law, Sue Lee! That's what I pay that moron for!"

It was a speech his dwindling staff of brokers, who worked in a sea of sparsely populated desks in front of Sue Lee Chen's office, didn't need to hear, but somehow expected would come. As inevitably as death and taxes, Sigma Venture Capital was finished. The few employees that had naively hung on, hoping for some kind of severance package, were polishing up their résumés. Sure, there were a couple of deals still on the table - including the private placement for Whale River Diamond Mines they had to file with regulators in the morning - but there was little hope that one more ride on the roller coaster would help Sigma avoid bankruptcy. Most of them had already decided that when the next paycheck arrived, they would bail and never look back. The glory days of easy money and salary-doubling bonuses at Sigma Venture Capital were over.

"Sue Lee, that legal bloodsucker is helping the SEC dig our graves! So what are *you* going to do about it?"

Sue Lee Chen had always been the voice of reason at Sigma. This wasn't the first time he'd ranted and raved. But Dominic Sant'Angello - whether he would admit it or not - had lived a charmed life. If it weren't for her tireless work - sweating the details after the deals closed and the champagne stopped flowing - Sigma Venture Capital wouldn't have been half as successful as it had been.

She met his venomous rage head on, "Your attorney isn't going to risk losing his license, or become an indicted co-conspirator, to save people like us, Mr. Sant'Angello! Let's face it-" Her next words pierced him like a stake through the heart. "We've lost!"

He yanked Sue Lee by the shoulders and pushed his nose into her face, "That ass-wipe's going to tell the SEC that those letters are 'Privileged and Confidential'! What part of that, Sue Lee, does he not understand? And Sue Lee... tell him if he doesn't fix this, I'll personally sink his new Sea Ray - the one he bought with *my* goddamn money - to the bottom of the lake, with the anchor wrapped tightly around his fag boyfriend's ass! I'll show him what a real man does when he's backed into a corner! Do I make myself clear, Sue Lee?"

Two young brokers - burly college football players on internships - pushed back their chairs and rushed to Sue Lee Chen's side.

Sant'Angello unlocked his grip. She stumbled back, landing awkwardly on her heels. He back-pedaled to his office door, daring the two young bucks to follow. "Don't think I can't handle you! When I was in the Marines, I used to spit out turds like you every Saturday night!"

Sant'Angello clenched his fist and pounded on the glass door. It shook, but it didn't break. "Sue Lee, don't bother me again... until this deal is done!"

The door to his office rattled shut.

Thank God that was over, Sue Lee thought, shaken.

"Are you all right, Ms. Chen? Should we call the police?"

God, no! That was the last thing Sue Lee wanted.

She looked around at the remnants of Sigma's dwindling resources. Nervous hands combed through cold sweat. Tired faces exchanged half-awake looks. Folders closed and were tossed aside in total disgust. The tension in the room had reached DEFCON One.

"I'm going home, Sue Lee. I've had enough of this!"

"Maria… you can't! I need you."

"Look. What he almost did to you, Sue Lee - it's crazy! Don't you see? This guy's a maniac!"

"He's under a lot of stress."

"We're *all* under a lot of goddamn stress! That doesn't mean we're gonna *kill* someone! And it doesn't mean we need to take any more of this bullshit! What makes him think he can talk to any of *us* like that?"

Sue Lee grabbed the stack of files on Maria's desk and pushed them into her arms, "You want to know *what*, Maria? I'll tell you *what*. Money. Cold hard cash! That's right. He's got it in his office! And he's ready to pay it!"

"Says who? *Him*?"

"No. Says… *me*!" The glory days might have gone, but Sue Lee Chen would show them who was still in charge.

One of Sigma's newest and brightest recruits closed her briefcase. "This is a dying cause, Sue Lee."

"*What*? Did you just say what I thought I heard?" Sue Lee Chen replied, staring through the defeat in everyone's eyes. "A dying cause? *No.* I don't accept it! You're going to stay and finish the Whale River deal! Tonight. All of you. *All night*, if we have to! And here's a promise: those who stay… will leave with an envelope of *cash*!"

The buzz in the room stopped cold.

The eternal motivation.

"That's right, people. That's what you want to hear, isn't it? *Cash.* Cold, hard… *cash*. Forget paychecks, with social security deductions.

Everyone who stays tonight and wraps up the Whale River deal with me… gets cash. With no questions asked."

The silence was deafening.

"Now get back to work, people… and make this deal happen!"

• • •

The next twenty minutes passed like twenty hours.

Dominic Sant'Angello spent every second with his face buried in his hands, trying to erase the anger, trying to concentrate on that missing piece of strategy that would get him out of this mess.

How had it turned so sour, so fast?

Seven years was not a long time. But at this rate, it would take until his grandchildren qualified for Medicare to fully recover what he'd lost.

Two hundred and fifty million dollars. In one year. *How had that happened?*

The little black triangle on the digital screen of his desk phone pulsed with an active line. "Not that goddamn lawyer again!" he said out loud.

A red light flashed beside it. It was Sue Lee's intercom.

"It's Mr. Kostelic… on Line 3."

Dominic Sant'Angello was stunned.

"Mr. Sant'Angello, are you there?" she asked.

He rubbed his face. Jiri Kostelic knew he wasn't supposed to call the office, especially on an *open* line.

"Mr. Sant'Angello? Are you OK?"

There was another pause, then, "I'll take it, Sue Lee."

He tapped Line 3 and a voice at the other end said, "Hello? Dominic?"

"Jiri… why are you calling on this line, you crazy bastard!"

"It's about the deal. I have to tell you-"

"You are *supremely* fucked up if you think I'm going to talk to you right now!" Dominic Sant'Angello was never very good at foreplay. "Don't you know the Feds have this line wiretapped!"

"I have to talk to you, Dominic! Right… *now!*"

"The hell you do!"

"I can't do it."

"What the hell are you talking about - you can't do it?"

"I can't do this deal, Dominic. Call me. On *Solara*."

The line went dead.

Dominic Sant'Angello picked up the phone and threw it across the office. He sat back in his chair with both index fingers pointed into his temples like two pistols pressed hard against his head. "That crazy bastard! He's going to screw us all!"

Call him on Solara?

How the hell was he going to do that?

His office phone, his personal cell - both crackled with static from the Fed's wiretaps. He could hear them in the background, munching donuts. The only calls he took were from his wife. "Pick up the kids, I have a hair appointment. Don't forget the Sandemann's on Friday night. They're important people. Don't be late. They don't like people who are late." *Screw the Sandemann's.*

Jiri Kostelic? Call him on Solara? How?

Dominic Sant'Angello, just like Kostelic, had weathered real storms before - maybe not as bad as the one that raged around him now - but with waves that would make lesser men think twice about going back out to sea.

And a type-A mind never gave up.

I gotta get around that wiretap.

There was a way. He just needed to make sure he didn't scare the panties off Sue Lee and Maria in the process.

The imposing figure of Dominic Sant'Angello burst into the trading office. Everyone raised their heads, expecting the worst.

"Mr. Sant'Angello? Is something wrong?"

"No, Sue Lee. Where's Maria?"

"I think she went to the bathroom, Mr. Sant'Angello."

What did he want with Maria?

"It's OK..." he said, as he noticed the concern on Sue Lee Chen's face. "I'm not going to hurt her." Sant'Angello walked through the glass-fronted reception area into the foyer that surrounded the elevators.

Maria Carvelli had only worked for Sigma Venture Capital for eight short months. She'd joined on the downside of the company's current troubles. As a relative of Sant'Angello's wife, she was grateful for any job she could find in a sagging economy. But still, Maria wasn't about to be intimidated by a man like Sant'Angello, for the sake of a crummy paycheck.

"Maria!"

Sant'Angello's towering presence startled the slim, size six girl. Here they were alone, at night, in an empty elevator lobby, eighty-seven floors above the nearest Security Desk.

"Maria, I need your cell phone!"

"What?"

"I need your cell phone!"

"My cell phone?"

He thrust a couple of one hundred dollar bills into her hand. "I need your cell phone... to make a call."

Two hundred dollars to make a call on her cell phone? It was an easy decision for someone like Maria to make. "Just don't call Hawaii, Mr. Sant'Angello. It costs double."

He thrust another one hundred dollar bill into her hands. "It's the Bahamas."

"The Bahamas?" She took the cell phone out of her purse and handed it to him. *Three hundred dollars cash to call the Bahamas? He could call the moon for three hundred bucks as far as she was concerned. Crazy. The man was definitely... crazy.*

"Thanks. You're a doll!"

"Sure, Mr. Sant'Angello. Whatever."

Dominic Sant'Angello jogged down the hall, went into the janitor's closet and placed a 'Closed for Cleaning' sign on the outside of the Ladies Washroom. He took his own phone, found the number for the satellite phone on board Jiri Kostelic's yacht *Solara,* and punched the number into Maria's phone.

It answered on the first ring.

"Jiri?"

"I knew you'd call me back."

"You stupid shit! Calling me like that!"

"But it got your attention, didn't it?"

"I don't need any more hands squeezing my balls, Jiri. What gives?"

"It's dead."

"What's dead?"

"The Whale River deal. It's dead. I just... can't do it."

"What do you mean 'you just can't do it'? You've done it before. This one is just as easy as all the others!"

"I can't do it, Dominic. I'm done. I'm history."

"You're fucking history all right!"

"You're in no position to threaten me, Sant'Angello!"

"This deal is no sweat, Jiri. It's a cake walk!"

"I've got my cake, Dominic. And I intend to eat it. And if you were smart, you'd find a peaceful Caribbean island and a Latin Lolita, and eat it too. Just like me."

"What the hell are you talking about, Kostelic? If it weren't for me, you wouldn't be able to afford a canoe... let alone that fifty-two foot sea bitch you sail on! I need this deal, Jiri! You can't let me down!"

"Right now, as we speak, Dominic, I'm outside U.S. territorial waters. Let the Feds try to find me! It would take a psychic to trace my accounts. It's over, buddy. And my advice to you? Find a place with a friendly banking system and retire to paradise."

"You sleazy... whore!"

"Survival of the fittest, Dominic. Didn't you tell me that? Ironic, isn't it?"

"I'll hunt you down if you screw with me, Kostelic!"

"What ya gonna do, big man? Dangle me overboard and let the sharks nibble at my toes? Screw you! If you had really been that smart, you'd be pledging allegiance to Uncle Sam with your middle finger just like me!"

"You're a dead man, Kostelic!"

"And you're... a fucking loser!"

The line went dead.

Dominic Sant'Angello sent the cell phone airborne. The mirror in the restroom shattered with a loud crash.

There was a knock on the door.

"Mr. Sant'Angello? Are you all right?" Sue Lee's voice was trembling. "Mr. Sant'Angello?"

He stepped into the hallway. His latest outburst was written all over his face. His temples bulged with angry veins.

A security guard was standing beside Sue Lee Chen.

Sant'Angello fumbled his words, "Everything's... OK, Sue Lee. Uh... it's that new secretary... she's in there... crying. Had an argument... with her boyfriend. Guess he doesn't like that she's working late." He was sweating. "But, yeah... who can blame him? She's pretty, and if it were me... I'd want to keep her on a short leash too."

Sue Lee Chen turned her head slowly in the direction of the glassed-in reception area. He followed her eye movements. Behind the etched letters that spelled 'Sigma Venture Capital', Maria Carvelli sat at her computer, typing the Whale River closing documents.

Sue Lee Chen wasn't buying what Dominic Sant'Angello was selling.

She knew it.

He knew it.

The game was over.

Chapter Five

Forensic technicians continued their work combing every square inch of the Carleton Mansion's Executive Wing - a five thousand square foot private enclave within the sixty thousand square foot mansion. The Executive Wing included Matthew Carleton's massive office, a conference room, a billiards room, bar, library, wine cellar, and the bloodstained bathroom suite.

A tiny shard of foreign metal.

A trace of hair.

An out of place thread.

Somewhere in a house as big as a palace, they were sure to find something, Scott Forrester reminded himself. *Nobody can be this careful.*

Scott ran his hand across the grain of Matthew Carleton's seventeenth century ship captain's desk. The scars of four hundred years of European history rippled under his fingers. "A billion dollars in *three* weeks, Trish? Can someone really make that kind of money in *three* weeks?"

"Not only is it possible, Scott, but the Wall Street Journal called it the most daring commodity trade since George Soros shorted the British pound. The Journal attributed Carleton's brilliance to dollar signs encoded in his DNA."

"Now *that* I can believe. Just look around this room… pirates and galleons."

Matthew Carleton's chestnut-paneled office was wallpapered with antique maps and prints from history's golden age of exploration. On the corner of his desk, a polished brass astrolabe – an instrument used by early mariners to navigate by the sun and the stars - slumbered in its velvet case.

Beside the astrolabe, a muzzle-loading pistol with an elegantly carved rosewood handle rested on a mahogany stand.

"Carleton had serious money and serious money makes for serious collections," Scott said, gesturing around the room. "This office is a museum, but it's also a mirror into Carleton's ego – the way he celebrated his DNA. So what do we know about him, Trish?"

Trish Van Cleyburn opened her notepad. "Carleton graduated Harvard Business School, summa cum laude. First job was brokering junk bonds at Morgan Stanley. Very successful. Grew a sizable bank account, then struck out on his own. Had a few lean years, but his venture capital firm, Carleton Securities, finally hit pay dirt with tech stocks and dot-coms, making easy money in a hot market by funding a ton of initial public offerings. Carleton cashed out in 2000 before the dot-com bubble burst and was sitting on a pile so big the Fed asked for a loan. So he turned his attention to manufacturing mortgage-backed securities with gold stamped but phony investment ratings, as well as his bold ventures into commodities, and the rest, as they say, is history."

"That explains it. Pirates and galleons…" Scott mused, carefully lifting the pistol from its stand with his latex-gloved hands. "Fur traders and slavery. An age when this astrolabe and pistol were the essential tools to build a global empire."

"But this…" he continued, pointing to the four flat-panel monitors that comprised Matthew Carleton's trading console, "This is today's equivalent of the astrolabe and pistol. It's the same process of conquest and exploitation, Trish. Just not by galleons… but by electrons."

An FBI Cyber Crime technician had been downloading files from Carleton's hard drive, hoping to find any electronic trail that might uncover what happened that night – what accounts were accessed, what keystrokes signaled an interruption in Carleton's routine; any clues that would point to a financial motive for the grisly murder that followed. The technician demonstrated how quickly the financier could tap into world markets. Pop-up windows appeared one by one, simultaneously quoting stock exchanges from South Africa to Estonia; Thailand to Vancouver.

"Matthew Carleton had a keen instinct," Scott said, pointing at the screen. "An awareness. An understanding. Of where all of *this* began. Call it his DNA. His genetic roots. Call it what you want. Matthew Carleton knew what changes... and what doesn't."

"You're talking in riddles, Scott."

"Look at this map, Trish..." A simple, almost primitive etching hung directly in front of Matthew Carleton's line of sight when he traded at his desk. The map was dated 1664. It had a brass plate below it with the name of a trading outpost on the Hudson River the Dutch had called, 'New Amsterdam'.

"Who would have thought back in 1664..." Scott reflected, "That this odd assembly of one-story wooden buildings planted on a rocky outcrop, would someday give birth to the concrete canyons of Wall Street? Now this is one map Matthew Carleton had to have in his collection. The founding of this colony was one of the defining moments in economic history."

He returned the pistol to its cradle. "Lots of things change, Trish. The length of borders. Who occupies what colored square. But these are just pieces of paper. There are certain fundamentals of human enterprise that don't change over time. And Matthew Carleton understood that."

He paced along Carleton's assembly of cartographic treasures, their elaborate designs decorated with men-of-war and sea serpents, and stopped in front of a depiction of the United States of America as it looked in 1829. "Take this map for example. It shows Alaska belonging to Russia, California to Mexico."

"Okay, I'll bite, Scott. So what fundamentally doesn't change even when the borders move?"

"It created lumber barons and railroad kings. Then Big Banks. Big Oil. Big Steel. Now, it's Big Software. Search Engines. What doesn't change, Trish? Power and control. Lust for money has always been about... power and control. Look around Carleton's office. Pirates and galleons. Gold and silver. Back then, it was about real trading, with real commodities, and real, saber-rattling risk. Not like now. Not the cold calculated transactions of a computer."

Scott returned to the brass astrolabe. "Matthew Carleton admired this era in history. He admired the adventure. The adrenaline rush of conquest. The thrill of empire. Perhaps he wished he could travel back in time to experience it firsthand. Whatever was in his DNA, Trish, this room tells us that Matthew Carleton envied these swashbuckling conquistadors. But it begs the question… was Matthew Carleton an intrepid explorer? Or a brazen pirate? History will be his judge and jury. Our mission… is to find his executioner."

Trish scribbled in her notepad, adding a sketch of Carleton's office to other sketches she'd drawn hours before. Van Cleyburn was a stickler for detail. But Scott rarely took notes, relying instead on a nearly photographic memory. Notes were for later. He wanted to free his mind to capture the essence of murder while it was still fresh and heavy.

Trish looked around the room and sighed, "And despite all of these maps, the one we're looking for isn't on these walls. How did *he* get in here?"

"He's not going to give us a map, Trish. Unfortunately, that's one thing we know for sure."

Scott began to walk up and down the room, along an imaginary rut carved in the office's Chinese carpet.

There were three doors leading out of Matthew Carleton's office - the doorway between the office and the Executive Wing's hallway, another going into the wine cellar, and the third one into the ensuite bathroom. He turned and pointed to the empty space that connected the bathroom door at one end of the office with the wine cellar's door at the other.

"What are you doing, Scott?"

His eyes were peering into the nothingness of the open space between the bathroom and the wine cellar, as if he was watching a ghost.

"A thousand empty bottles, Trish?" he asked. "Think about it. Back and forth... until the wine cellar had been depleted. Carleton was hogtied and beaten, half-dead in the bath. And, methodically, the killer fetched every bottle. And each time, when he returned to his victim, he continued the conversation exactly where they'd left off."

"*Conversation*, Scott? Since when was torture... a *conversation*? Wasn't the reason for Carleton's torture to extract information from him? Account numbers? Business secrets? That's hardly a *conversation*."

"Account numbers? Maybe. But that wasn't the only thing on the killer's mind. The killer took special care to empty *every* bottle in that wine cellar, Trish. Not just a few. He had a purpose for that. He has a purpose for everything. Given the condition we found Carleton's body, the killer would get the information he wanted without all that extra effort. So *why* did he do it? What was the purpose of emptying *every* bottle in Carleton's cellar? I think the manner and brutality of Matthew Carleton's death was as much about the wine."

"The *wine*? He tortured Matthew Carleton over *wine*? But why?"

"Ten million dollars of carefully selected, meticulously catalogued fine wine. Why, Trish? I'll bet, the killer enjoyed the torment. As each unbelievably expensive bottle disappeared down the drain, he debated its merits with Carleton. 'Was this a good year, Matthew?' That *was* the torture, Trish - the torture was treating one of Matthew Carleton's most prized possessions as a commodity, like milk. He turned the screws on Carleton in more than one way."

"They usually do. But *wine*?"

"Notice..." Scott continued, "that none of his antiques were stolen. The astrolabe. The pistol. The maps. These are rare and priceless artifacts. So, robbery was not a motive. There was no damage either. He didn't trash the place. His rage was completely confined. Completely focused. Random vandalism was not on the agenda. And consider the time it must have taken. This killer exhibits great control over his victims - and great restraint within the victims' environment. Pouring rare wine down the drain must have had a special meaning for the killer. For his ritual. And our job is to find out why."

"Great theory, Forrester. I love it," Vincente announced, as he returned from his sojourn outside, a posse of technicians following him with plastic totes of empty wine bottles, each one needing to be checked for fingerprints. "This theory of yours - did you think of crosschecking the empties with his inventory to see if anything was missing?"

"Don't need to," Scott replied. "I know the killer took a souvenir. It wouldn't be right that he wouldn't."

"Well, that's great work, Sherlock. But I think I'll follow standard police procedures and have it checked anyway. That's okay with you, isn't it, Agent Forrester?"

"You're doing your job," Scott said. "I'm doing mine."

Scott pointed to the closed circuit camera just outside the office in the hallway. "Speaking of jobs. If I'd check anything, Agent Vincente - it would be *that*."

"Been there. Done that, Forrester," Vincente said. "The most advanced security cameras available on the market. The company that installed them - Sapphire Systems - did the Royal Palace in Monaco."

"It's only advanced, Agent Vincente, if it works. So?"

"The surveillance video is stored in a data center in Alexandria, Virginia," Vincente replied. "But so far, the footage shows nothing."

"Nothing? Again?"

"As in 'Nada'. But he can't hide forever, Forrester."

"Yeah? Tell it to Miami PD. And the California State Police. So far, I'd say he's done a pretty damn good job of hiding." Scott flipped his notepad open and wrote down a single word - just to make sure Special Agent-in-Charge Benito Vincente knew he'd been here and done that. The word was 'wine'.

"I think we're finished in here, Trish."

"Back to your ivy-covered office to finish your report, Forrester?" Vincente asked, winking at Trish as they turned to leave.

"You have my cell number," Trish replied, without looking back.

"I'll call you, sweetheart," Vincente countered. As he disappeared into the wine cellar with the technicians, he yelled back, "We'll do lunch."

Agents Forrester and Van Cleyburn left the Executive Wing through the hallway that attached it to the main part of the Carleton Mansion. It was a long stone corridor with arched windows on either side that resembled a cloister from a European monastery. Scott glanced outside. The fog was beginning to lift.

"You and Vincente are getting along just fine, aren't you? Smart career move, Scott," Trish said.

At the end of the corridor, they turned a corner to enter the Mansion's Great Room, a two-story cavern-turned-museum dressed with Belgian tapestries and softly lit Italian Renaissance art.

"Why should I worry about Vincente?" he replied. "He's a superficial New York politico, Trish. A Titus Griffin with a Latin rhythm. Fifteen years as Griffin's partner? I wonder how long it took to rub off? Probably fifteen minutes."

"If that's what you're worried about, Scott... don't. There's *no* chance it will rub off on you."

A doorway linked the Great Room to a playroom which was a fantasy world crammed with every imaginable childhood delight. A Noah's Ark of nearly life-sized stuffed animals provided the audience for a room the size of a basketball court. In one corner, there must have been several hundred pounds of Lego and an army of action figures.

"In here..." Trish gestured to the door that led from the playroom into the adjacent media room. Overstuffed sofas were arranged in front of an enormous 152-inch HD Plasma TV. The down cushions of the chenille couch were still indented with the impressions of Lexi Carleton and her three children, curled up by the fireplace watching Disney movies on the night her husband was murdered.

"These walls are acoustically sealed," Trish explained. "It's no wonder Lexi Carleton didn't suspect anything was wrong. You could have an elephant stampede in the rest of the house… and no-one could hear it from in here."

"Really? An elephant on tiptoes is still an elephant."

"I agree. Her alibi does have holes in it. According to her statement, she'd just returned from a business trip to Chicago. She and her three kids - a six-year-old girl and twin eight-year-old boys – collapsed on the sofa with pizza and popcorn, watched some movies. Her maid and personal chef had retired to their quarters at the opposite end of the mansion. Her husband was working late, wrapping up some kind of financing deal."

"Financing deal? Interesting. The elephant in the room no doubt."

"She tucked the kids in around 9:00PM. Hit the sack herself at 11:00PM. The next morning, the maid found Matthew Carleton floating face down in a tub of vintage Bordeaux."

"The time element doesn't match, Trish. All that wine emptied in one night?"

"Well, add that to the list. No witnesses saw the killer enter or leave the estate. There were no signs of forced entry through any windows or doors. No sounds. Nothing to suspect that anything was wrong. No footprints. So far no fingerprints. And this time, no ballistics. Nothing."

"The killer made Carleton's suffering a strictly private affair," Scott mused. "Just him… and his victim."

As they left the media room and walked back into the Great Room, Trish asked, "Don't you find that a little strange, Scott? His wife and kids were left untouched? Cozy and warm, watching 'Beauty and the Beast' while the real beast was marinating Daddy in red wine?"

"Why is that strange?"

"Well… why didn't the killer go all the way? Add the wife and kids to his ritual?"

"You mean a la 'Charles Manson'? No, Trish. The whole 'screw the rich establishment scene' and plaster the walls with their blood - it's not him. This particular killer isn't psychotic. A psychotic killer would leave plenty of evidence behind - a mad, disorganized trail in and out of the house. But there isn't one, is there?"

"And what about Lexi, Scott? I still can't get over the fact she had no clue a killer had invaded her home. Isn't that a little suspicious? Big screen TV's make great babysitters. Her kids are old enough to be left alone, but young enough to be unaware she's gone. She had the opportunity. We just need the motive. Perhaps she was the killer's paymaster? She let him in. She helped him bypass the security system. She helped him move the bottles."

"And if that were true, the surveillance cameras would show her acting suspiciously. Was there any evidence of that?"

Trish shrugged and shook her head. "Not that I know of, from the early indications. But there's still more video to go through. How about Griffin's idea? A contract killer?"

"If a contract killer was working for Lexi Carleton, why do it here?" Scott said. "Under the nose of her children?"

"Wouldn't that be the perfect place? Who would suspect Lexi Carleton hired someone to whack her husband right in her own home? Or maybe - someone else hired him."

"I still don't buy it, Trish. This venue's all wrong for a contract killer. A huge estate to get in and out of, without being seen. Security cameras all over the place. A pro wouldn't take that kind of risk, Trish. Or make this kind of effort. Doesn't it seem to you that every one of these murders has become more complex than the previous one? More difficult? Like this guy is in some kind of contest?"

"Contest? With whom?"

"With himself. This guy *wants* the challenge. He *wants* this kind of buzz. There's a reason he needed to be here, and not somewhere else, to do this. There's a reason he needed to be everywhere he killed. He's sociopathic, not psychotic. It explains the control, the torture and humiliation, the elaborate sadistic drowning. A sociopathic mind would enjoy the planning, the challenge - and the payoff."

"So what are we left with, Scott? If not his wife or someone she hired? A disgruntled employee?"

"How would that connect with the other murders across the country?"

"An estranged relative?"

"Ditto. Let the police check into the obvious possibilities. I don't think they'll find anything. There's a pattern here, Trish and - *damn it* - we're just not getting it!"

They walked out of the Great Room into the Mansion's main entrance foyer, an atrium-like feature with stained glass panels streaming brilliant colors onto a floor inlaid with polished stone. Beneath their feet was a heraldic coat-of-arms.

"A golden bull holding a lightning bolt", Scott said. "How perfect is that? A bull, the symbol of Wall Street. And a lightning bolt, symbolizing the energy and power Matthew Carleton drew from it."

They walked through the Mansion's massive oak doors, into a sun that was battling lingering black clouds. Trish pulled a pack of cigarettes from her Coach handbag and lit up. "So, are you going to tell me about Wyoming or do I need to get my Tarot cards out? Were they tortured?"

"Not by a human being."

"Say again?"

It was another unforgettable scene from the library of faded nightmares indelibly burned in Scott's mind.

An isolated knoll, deep in Wyoming's Bridger-Teton National Forest. Flattened grasses outlined the spot where software millionaire Deuce Meredith had been torn to shreds by a grizzly bear.

"Meredith was wounded. Wounded deliberately. Set up to die a horrible death. His Indian hunting guide, Charlie 'Silver Moon' McNabb, had been felled by a single 7.62mm bullet to the head. His death was instantaneous. Deuce Meredith probably wished he'd been that lucky."

"Who's in charge of the case?"

"We are. The murder occurred on federal land. Lance Caulfield from the Salt Lake City Field Office has it."

"Any leads?"

"State Police and Park Rangers covered every hunting lodge, diner, grocery store, small aircraft landing field. A constant flow of tourists, hunters and backpackers, coming and going. They interviewed local mountain folk, waitresses, gas station attendants, postmen. The whole goddamn state of Wyoming as far as I can tell. Everyone knew I was FBI. Strangers stand out like pimples on a ball of cheese. They could read my eyes. But despite all our efforts, no one has come forward with any useful information. Nothing. It was as if the killer passed through the Wyoming landscape under the same blanket of fog that was here this morning."

Scott wandered over to the Mansion's front windows and peered through the glass. Laser light beams crisscrossed the inside of the window opening.

The best security system money can buy, he thought. *Yeah, right. If only it worked.*

At the far end of the approach road leading into the estate, a dark shadow wound through the woods like a giant sleeping serpent - a thirteen-foot high wall that ran around the entire one hundred acre property. On his way in, Scott had noticed that the sandstone urns lining the top of the red brick barrier were reflecting light from concealed lenses.

"How long is the security perimeter, Trish?"

"Four and a half miles."

"And the laser motion detectors? None of them were tripped?"

"Nope."

"Haven't we seen enough inanimate objects, Trish? Enough barriers of brick and stone. Enough dead-ends. I think it's time we found something with a pulse, don't you?"

"Who do you have in mind?"

Chapter Six

Outside the Mansion's wrought iron gates, reporters and cameramen lent against badly parked satellite vans, looking restless and bored. As soon as the Mercedes E-Class nudged past the State Troopers, the media frenzy began; reporters eager for any morsel of information advancing like a flock of squawking seagulls fighting over a scrap of bread.

Trish squeezed the car through the melee. No interviews. Griffin's strictest rule. As open asphalt emerged, she accelerated past the crowd of disappointed reporters, leaving them in a vapor trail of autumn leaves.

"So, Trish… just exactly how are we going to explain this rented Merc to Titus Griffin?"

"We're supposed to be plain clothes, right? Well, in East Hampton, Scott… this is as plain clothes as it gets."

The Mercedes flew down the country road headed for nearby Southampton where Lexi Carleton had gone to her parents' estate to escape the forensic chaos that had descended on the Carleton Mansion.

A pile of magazines lay in Scott's lap. They contained articles on Matthew Carleton.

Forbes. The New Yorker. Architectural Digest.

Money. Social standing. A palace in the woods.

But Scott selected the National Enquirer. "Matthew Carleton got around, didn't he?"

"You mean his legendary womanizing?" Trish said, glancing over at the tabloid article Scott had decided to read first. "I got the impression it was no big deal. That Lexi Carleton could care less. When I saw her being interviewed by the police, it was like watching a National Geographic documentary, not a Greek tragedy. For someone whose supposed soul mate was brutally killed under her nose, Mrs. Carleton bore her grief very well."

"I can't wait to meet her. She sounds like my kind of suspect." Scott leafed through the notes Trish had made on Matthew Carleton's wife. "Heir to the Stavros real estate fortune. What do we know about them, Trish?"

"The Stavros family has defined the American Dream for the past seventy years. It all started when Lexi's Greek grandfather arrived in New York City in the 1930s, utterly penniless, working one sweatshop job after another before becoming the building superintendent of a slum tenement on the East Side. Ten years later, he bought the building."

Trish's research was thorough, as usual. "Upon his death, his only son, Theodore, Lexi's father, put the family fortune into high gear by expanding the business to office buildings in New York and New Jersey; then golf course communities in Florida and Palm Springs; and his latest ventures, resorts in the Caribbean. The Stavros family has always turned dirt into gold. Lexi grew up as a true blue Long Island debutante…" Trish's voice hid a hint of envy. "Conditioned from an early age to enjoy a lifestyle of entitlement and privilege. I bet her trust fund could feed Brooklyn for the next one hundred years and still have money left over. What was it? What was in that marriage with a cheat like Matthew Carleton that was worth so much? I guess it must be that love *is* blind."

"Justice is blind, Trish. That wasn't love. That was a merger."

• • •

A butler ushered them in.

Theodore Stavros made a brief and perfunctory appearance at the door of his study before the crotchety eighty-year-old delegated the nasty business of receiving the 'policemen' to his sixty-eight-year-old wife, Anastasia, and returned to his butterfly collection.

Lexi Carleton, early forties, in tennis whites the day after her husband had been murdered, entered the chintz-draped morning room a little out of breath. She'd been 'supervising' her children's private tennis lessons. "It's so important for the children to keep to their usual routines," she said, rosy-cheeked and still perspiring, as she flopped into the billowy cushions of the sofa.

The tennis pro passed by the French doors. Scott noticed an unusually satisfied smile on his face. *The children must be making a lot of progress with their swing*, he thought.

Lexi's mother, Anastasia Stavros - a thirty-something wannabe surgically repaired to look better in a photograph than in real life - dispatched the butler to make some tea. When the tea arrived, Trish politely told the old dame, "That due to the sensitive nature of their questions for Lexi, it would be best advised if Mrs. Stavros could take her tea in the conservatory until they were finished."

Naturally, Mrs. Stavros complied. The family matriarch knew how to be discrete.

"They think their daddy is on a business trip," Lexi Carleton remarked, after her mother had left the room. "It's the best explanation right now. They're used to that."

"Of course," Trish said. "We know how hard this must be for you."

Scott paced the periphery of the room, absorbing Lexi Carleton's stoicism from every angle. Lexi Carleton was a strikingly beautiful woman: her hair immaculately coiffed and layered; blonde highlights muting the dark brown of her Greek heritage; her lips sensually round. She wore a mole on her right cheek like a medal of honor from the Imperial House of Versace. Her manner had the cultivation of Cleopatra: regal, self-confident to the extreme, with more than a touch of contemptuous grandeur.

So, Scott thought, *when would Mrs. Carleton tell her children the truth? More importantly, what truth would be told? Perhaps, given the unusually gruesome circumstances, it would be best to frame their father's death as a fairy tale. Daddy was killed tragically: on safari in Africa by a rogue elephant. Or perhaps by an avalanche while skiing with Prince Charles and Prince William in St. Moritz?*

Scott stopped at a table set with fancy linens and family photos, flipped his notepad open and pretended to take notes. "What was your husband doing the day before he was murdered, Mrs. Carleton?"

"He was in New York. It was the day Pegasus BioSciences went public. My husband underwrote the company's initial venture capital. He was there to ring the bell at the New York Stock Exchange."

"And you weren't with him?"

Scott knew she wasn't.

Lexi Carleton threw her head back on the cushions and stared up at the ceiling, her fingers massaging her temples as if she were having a migraine attack. "I was in Chicago."

"You didn't want to share the limelight with your husband? At such a high profile event?"

She sat up, annoyed. "Matthew wasn't the only one with businesses to run, Mr. Forrester. I hold several directorships in my father's companies. I was in Chicago for a Board meeting and returned to East Hampton on Tuesday afternoon."

"And he was in when you arrived home?"

"No. At least I didn't think he was. There was a big party for investors after the market closed on Monday. Bryan and Nicole Riverton are the principals behind Pegasus BioSciences, and friends of ours. He called me in Chicago and said he planned to stay for a few days at the Rivertons' Westchester estate. But obviously something changed his mind. At first, I didn't even know he was in the house."

"What do you mean you didn't know he was in the house? You didn't see him?"

"No. I got a text message. Around 6:00PM."

"He *texted* you? From inside the house? Are you telling us that you didn't actually *see* him?"

"He said he didn't want to be disturbed. If you knew my husband, Mr. Forrester, when he says he can't be disturbed, he can't be disturbed. For any reason."

"He *texted* you? That didn't raise any suspicions?"

"No. And by the way you're looking at me, Mr. Forrester that must sound very strange to you. But that's the way Matthew and I ran our lives. We could pass each other in the street and not notice. We're *very* busy people. He had no reason to talk to me. And I had no reason to talk to him."

"But you *did* talk to him... between the time you arrived home on Tuesday at 5:00PM and Wednesday morning?"

"Yes. He finally did call me. From his office. Just before the kids went to bed. I've said all of this in my statement to the police. Can't you read?"

Scott felt the acid in her voice. The interview had just run over its allotted time on Lexi Carleton's calendar.

Well, isn't that just too bad!

Trish leaned against the French doors and looked across the tennis courts to the frosted beach grass that led down to the ocean. With her back turned and her cup of tea steaming up the glass, she asked, "How was your sex life, Mrs. Carleton? Were you satisfied with it?"

Lexi Carleton squirmed. Her neck became flushed.

Trish moved slowly towards the sofa and sat down. "This is very good tea." She put the empty cup on the table. "Perhaps you would like me to rephrase the question, Mrs. Carleton? When exactly did you and your husband agree that having separate extra-marital affairs was an integral part of your *very busy* lifestyles?"

Lexi Carleton hid behind a well-rehearsed veneer, a decorum instilled from birth. East Hampton, like other tight-lipped upper class villages, readily closed ranks - like the shutting of a steel trap - whenever threatened by scandal. Messy divorces. Financial misdeeds. Teenage pregnancies. Tabloid headlines. East Hampton could find a way out of any indiscretion. Turn any negative into a positive. After all, that's what lawyers and PR firms were paid to do.

Lexi Carleton's psychological immune system had been activated. And as the burden of proof always fell on the accuser, she fought back, "My husband and I have always been happily married. He loved our three children dearly. Neither of us would *ever* do anything to harm them. And if the FBI has any proof to the contrary, Ms. Van Cleyburn, I'm sure my lawyers would love to hear it!"

Trish looked over at Scott.

Lexi Carleton had provided answers to questions they hadn't even asked.

It was time to bring the interview to a close. Scott picked up a photo from the table and as he turned the silver frame over in the light, he asked, "Was there anything in your husband's voice to indicate he was afraid of something… or somebody? That night… or at any time in the weeks before he was killed?"

"Matthew? You've got to be kidding! My husband could stare down a rabid pit bull, Mr. Forrester. Fear and worry were not a part of his emotional makeup."

"Fear is older than the universe, Mrs. Carleton. Everyone has a threshold as far as fear is concerned." Matthew Carleton met his worst fear that night. Scott had witnessed it for himself, on the blood-splattered marble wall. "One more question. Do you know anyone who might have wanted your husband murdered?"

Lexi Carleton paused, her answer carefully chosen.

One word emerged.

Her expression said it all.

"Everyone."

Chapter Seven

The midnight black sedan dodged the potholes of Georgetown's lonely back streets; its windshield wipers in a mad, futile beat to overcome the torrential downpour.

It was 7:00 AM Friday morning.

A brightly colored neon sign appeared like a warm beacon through the heavy rain. It belonged to Archie's, a no-frills, 60's-style diner - a refuge of unfashionable sanity in the middle of the trendy restaurant district of Georgetown.

Archie's tiny parking lot was full. Scott pulled into a nearby dry cleaner's and waited impatiently for the rain to stop. His cell phone rang.

It was the baritone bark of Titus Griffin, "So this time, was it Italian?"

"No, Titus. It wasn't."

"Are you sure it's not a dialect? Sicilian perhaps?"

"It's not even written in the English alphabet, Titus."

"How about Albanian then? They're all over Southern Italy." Street-wise Titus Griffin believed the series of grim murders were the work of a professional hit man hired to settle a few scores. On any given day, there were enough business deals going sour, enough partners being cheated, enough drug deals being scammed, to account for several dozen murders like these. As far as Griffin was concerned, the blood scrawled messages were a warning – a Cosa Nostra-style warning. It was that simple.

"Is Van Cleyburn coming in with you?"

"Still in New York. We have more work to do. I have some theories-"

"Theories? You have some *theories*! I don't believe Matthew Carleton was murdered by a serial killer, Forrester. I don't believe any of them were.

They walk, talk and smell like mob hits. Professional. Efficient. And ugly. *That* is your theory!"

"Why would a professional hit man choose the middle of the Wyoming wilderness to whack someone, when he could have chosen any number of more readily accessible places?"

"I don't know, Forrester. Because he's an outdoorsy type? Carleton's crib on Long Island is surrounded by woods. Deuce Meredith was whacked in the woods. There's the connection. He whacks people in the woods. Find a theory that fits that."

"He's not a hit man, Titus. He's taking these risks because it's some kind of test."

"What kind of test?"

"A test of his skills."

"*A test of his skills?* Bullshit, Forrester! *Absolute goddamn bullshit!* I don't need you turning facts into fiction! I can't spare the resources! I have a file cabinet full of unsolved serial killings by bona fide psychos, just waiting for your *bullshit*! I need you to work up a profile on this hit man, Forrester. Turn your suspicions over to Benito Vincente, to the Racketeering Squad, to whomever - and then move on to something else!"

Scott looked out the car window. The ribbons of drizzle were starting to form into snowflakes. *Shit, it looks like it's going to be an early winter.*

"Are you still there, Forrester? Did you hear what I just said?"

"Sure, Titus. I heard. And I *am* moving on. It's called breakfast."

"Don't mess with me, Forrester. Profile. On my desk. Addressed to Racketeering."

The call ended as abruptly as it had begun.

Scott grabbed his notepad, flung the car door open and dashed for cover. The puddle in front of the rusty paper box was ankle deep. He fumbled for change and stuffed a soggy Washington Post into his black leather jacket. By the time he reached the protection of Archie's metal awning, Scott Forrester looked the way he felt - thoroughly battered by the elements; his short, dark brown hair plastered hard to his head; water dripping everywhere. The diner's aluminum-framed door opened with a familiar creak; a curtain of steamy, griddle-soaked air quickly banished the malicious chill that tried to follow him inside.

Even at this early hour, Archie's Diner was in full swing, its normal busy self, a bustling crossroads in a quiet back street. The restaurant had no social barriers - blue collar, white collar; blacks, whites, Hispanics; all religions, all genders; the inconspicuously well-off mingling with the obviously poor.

Scott looked for an open booth.

Kelly Whelan stood behind the counter with her ever-present coffee pot, oozing the charm that made Archie's meals, part food and part entertainment. "Sorry, hon. We can't serve you. Not until you've changed out of your swimsuit."

It was the kind of reception Scott Forrester expected, and wanted. "Don't you love this time of year?"

"You look like a penguin that's just been through a car wash. Can't you read the sign?"

"Sign?"

"Seat yourself. Find a pond to wallow in, Mr. Penguin."

On the other side of the counter - his spatula chopping at the open-faced grill like a machine - the diner's one and only owner, Archie Karmasian, tended a huge mound of onion-laced hash browns and green pepper scrambled eggs.

Archie recognized the voice behind him, his smooth round face stretching into a broad smile, "I know whatcha mean, Mr. Forrester. That Mother Nature's a bitch." Kelly Whelan dodged bits of egg as the expatriate New Yorker wagged his spatula at the ceiling, mocking an imaginary Heaven. "You're worse than a Joisey loan shark, you whore! One month of decent weatha, and you want it back... with interest! Or you're gonna break our legs! Geesh. I tell ya, Mr. Forrester. There's no justice!"

At Archie's, the owner's wit and wisdom was an integral part of the menu. And everyone who entered Archie's Diner was obliged to make a contribution, however small. Scott Forrester was no exception. "There's always some kind of payback, Archie. That's just the way life is."

"Tell that to my schmuck cousin in Queen's, Mr. Forrester! He ain't paid back nothing!" It was hard to argue with the portly owner's logic.

A booth at the end of the main aisle was empty. Scott hung his jacket on the hook, tossed the Washington Post in a heap on the pleated blue vinyl bench seat, and grabbed a wad of napkins to wipe the cold rain from his face.

The diner's warmth and hospitality wrapped around him. Anyone entering Archie's despondent, dissatisfied, or losing hope, wasn't allowed to stay that way for long - because you checked your blues at the door. It was the house rules.

Kelly filled Scott's coffee mug to overflowing. "Well, I know what to get you for Christmas, hon."

In his damp, jet-lagged state, Scott hadn't a clue what the buxom redheaded waitress was talking about.

She frowned. "You're not awake yet are you? An umbrella. So what ya havin'?"

"Hungry Man's."

"How'd ya like your eggs?"

"Over hard."

"Pancakes?"

"French toast."

Kelly's voice boomed across the diner, "Oooh… hear that Archie? *French toast*! Hey, Archie, wake up! I said… have we got any of that imported *French toast* left?" Kelly was in fine spirits for such a dismal morning. "Would you like red or white wine with that, sir?"

Scott finally managed a smile. That's why he ate at Archie's. You can keep your pretentious cafés, with their fancy chocolate croissants. Archie's

Diner was good, hot, homemade food, at a great price. More than that, it was like stepping into a Saturday morning cartoon - a chubby, ethnic New York expatriate who always had an opinion, and a gang of sassy waitresses that acted as if they were in a perpetual audition for the next sitcom.

"Haven't seen much of you lately. Been sleeping rough or somethin'?" Kelly fingered her chin. The black, day-old stubble on Scott Forrester's face was out of character. The fact that he'd just stepped off the FBI jet was no excuse. But how was she to know?

"You mean this? The 'Colin Farrell' look? It's trendy."

She wasn't impressed. "Look, hon. Take my advice. Keep that up and you'll die a very lonely man. Grunge is out with this lady. I like my men clean-shaven. With a cowboy hat on their heads."

"I hate to disappoint you, Kelly. I don't own a cowboy hat. Still, I do okay without it."

"Sure, hon." She ripped the order from her pad and waved it in Archie's direction. "One Hungry Man's! Overcooked eggs, foreign toast and a bottle of red wine!"

"Red wine?" Archie asked. "Are you sure? With eggs?"

"Okay, make it white. Casanova here won't know the difference."

Scott Forrester smiled. Archie's well-rehearsed floorshow was always worth the price of admission.

He unfolded the soggy Post from its disorganized pile in the corner and took a long sip of hot black coffee as the rain pounded the diner's windows. He opened the sports pages... the Redskins had lost again. Front page headlines... more political gridlock on Capitol Hill. The five-day weather forecast was encouraging... temperatures were set to fall even further.

His cell phone rang again.

It was Trish Van Cleyburn. From New York.

"We have the gatehouse security video."

"Let me guess. The killer waltzed out of a closely guarded estate behind the wheel of Carleton's vintage Mercedes but we don't have a positive image of our killer?"

"Oh, that's where you're wrong, Scott... we have a very positive ID from facial recognition software."

"And?"

"It was... Matthew Carleton. Dry as a bone. Two hours after rigor mortis says he wouldn't be able to shift gears. Okay, I lied. The car's an automatic. The corpse didn't need to shift gears."

"You're shitting me, Trish. You're telling me the killer disguised himself as Matthew Carleton and just drove out the front gate?"

"You must be psychic."

"And then... no one saw him dump a collectible Mercedes roadster on top of a garbage barge in New York harbor?"

"You *are* psychic, Scott!"

Somewhere in the gloom between yesterday and today, the serious flipside of life was waiting impatiently for FBI Special Agent Scott Forrester to punch back in. No matter how much he needed the rest, it wasn't about to let Archie's Diner lull him to sleep.

"Another thing, Scott - Griffin called me and said we need to run a scan on faces in the crowds in New York City. He told me to work a theory that our guy is one of the Occupy Wall Street movement. He wants to see if we can match anyone with known felons associated with the mob. A hit man who hates millionaires and carries a protest sign."

"That is so *not* a theory!"

"I know. But he's the boss. And speaking of mobs, the Governor has proclaimed what amounts to marshal law. He's sent the National Guard into Manhattan. NYPD can't control what's happening. This town is on the verge of civil war. I'll be at the Field Office in the Javits Building. I'll see you Monday, if I'm lucky."

"Watch out for Vincente, Trish. He's got eyes for you."

"No chance. He's a putz. See ya."

The call ended.

"Heads up, soldier." Kelly hovered overhead with his Hungry Man's breakfast. "Three eggs over hard, Canadian bacon and... we had it imported just for you, sweetie pie... French toast."

"Thanks, Kelly."

She caught the frown on his face. "Girlfriend troubles?"

"She's not my girlfriend."

Kelly put the coffeepot on the table and sat down, her inquisitive green eyes trying to break through Scott Forrester's dark clouds. "That's what you've said before. You know you could do much better than her, hon."

Kelly really should have been an actress. That pout was classic Julia Roberts.

He didn't answer. You could cut his funk with a knife.

"Snow," she said, staring out the window. "Can you believe it? In October? I've got a sister that's just moved to Vermont. Loves it there. Says it's beautiful. Even in winter. I might visit her at Christmas."

"Count me out, Kelly. I'm a warm weather kinda guy. Give me Key Largo over Aspen, anytime."

Kelly looked into his eyes. "So when ya takin' me, hon?"

His phone rang again.

Caller ID said it was his younger brother, Jamie.

"Kelly... I'm sorry, I've really gotta take this call."

"Okay, sugar. The Florida Keys? Sounds nice. Not now... right? But someday... maybe?"

Kelly Whelan was Scott's age, early-thirties, with Irish red hair and a lively, expressive smile. Her figure was comfortably full and appealing. She wore a little too much makeup for Scott's taste, but she wasn't dishonest. With Kelly Whelan, what you saw was what you got. And in his current state of on-again, off-again romances, her patient, regularly delivered propositions were definitely tempting. But no matter how he sliced it, she wasn't really his type… whatever 'his type' was.

She picked up the coffee pot and left.

Scott pressed the phone to his ear. "What's up, Bro? Kinda early for you, isn't it? Or have you been up all night again?"

Jamie ignored him. "You coming home?"

"Soon. Gotta check in at the office first."

"You've got mail."

"Have you been hacking into my e-mail again, Jamie?"

"It's my job."

Jamie Forrester. Freelance software programmer. Part-time hacker. Full-time nuisance.

"It's also a federal offence, Jamie."

That never deterred his brother. "She'll like you, Scott," he said.

"Who'll like me?"

"Sarah."

"Sarah? Your friend with that yappy Yorkshire terrier?"

"That's Jennifer. She's not your type. But Sarah's different. She doesn't have pets."

"Jamie, I'm tired of you setting me up on blind dates. If you like them so much, why don't *you* date them?"

"Maybe I will."

Jamie and Scott Forrester had fought over girls ever since they were both in puberty. The two-year difference in their ages was deadly. In high school, Jamie, the younger more outgoing one, stole his brother's dates right from under his nose. Scott couldn't count the number of times he'd gone to a dance with a girl on his arm and then came home alone. Jamie charmed the pants off them. Literally. Jamie had joined the Army after 9/11 and made the Rangers. Then it got worse. The uniform did it every time. Scott was always in plain clothes.

"You haven't answered my question. About coming home."

"Griffin's expecting me back at the office."

"But I replied to Sarah and told her you'll take her to a movie tonight."

"Tonight? No can do. Tell her... tomorrow night. Or maybe next Saturday night."

"Do you want to get laid or not?"

"Jamie, I don't need you to set things up for me! I'm a big boy. I can handle it myself."

"Sure, Scott. That's why you're still single. Just trying to help, Bro."

"You can help, by respecting my passwords."

"Ever heard of a firewall?"

Scott laughed. "That never stopped you before!"

"No, but it would make it more interesting."

"Criminal charges, Jamie. Think about it. Someday, you're going to face criminal charges."

"Sarah... she's hot. You'd better make your mind up... or she's all mine!"

"You can have her, Jamie."

"Seriously?"

"Okay. Tomorrow. A movie."

"Tonight. She's only free... tonight. I'm warning you, Scott, if you don't make it tonight, you'll be resigned to a lifetime of-"

"Tonight. Tell her 7:00. Bye, Jamie."

Well, that was settled then, Scott thought. *Ninety-six straight hours of intensive homicide investigation across three time zones, light naps on redeye flights, eight hours of paperwork; a quick shower, a meal, followed by nodding off in a chick flick, a Starbucks coffee and a final farewell. Goodbye, Sarah. It was nice meeting you. Sorry it didn't work out. Better luck next time. For both of us.*

He picked through his eggs with the fork. His breakfast - like his life and the brutal reality of a vicious killer's victims - had gone cold.

He put the fork down and slumped back in the booth.

Scott's coffee was refreshed, unnecessarily. He looked up. "Don't tell me, hon," Kelly said. "After all that hard work and personal sacrifice on our part, you're not hungry?"

"Sorry, Kelly. For some reason, I've lost my appetite."

Kelly pointed to his plate, "Can I box it for you?"

Scott shook his head. "No thanks. But it looked great." Scott handed her a twenty. "Tell Archie, it's my new diet plan. I just sniff the calories."

"Wish I could do that, hon."

He picked his still soggy leather jacket off the hook and headed for the checkout. On his way out, he paid his respects, "Hey, Archie! If I see that schmuck cousin of yours, I'll tell him."

"Thanks, Mr. Forrester. You tell him. With interest."

Kelly stood behind the cash register with her pouty face and warm green eyes. The twenty-dollar bill re-appeared. "My treat, hon."

Kelly was a nice girl, pretty, with a great sense of humor. But there were too many differences between them, not enough things in common, for it to work out. He was happy to leave it as an unspoken friendship.

"Thanks, Kelly. I'll catch you next time."

"No you won't. Just keep safe, hon," she said.

He returned her warm smile.

As he left, the creaky door blew sleet into his face. Once again, another morning respite at Archie's had slipped into the past.

The diner was Scott Forrester's emotional anchor.

His lifeboat in an ever-raging storm.

Some days, it was the only thing that kept him sane.

Chapter Eight

The ginger tabby rummaged through the unhealthy flotsam of half-eaten sandwiches and half-empty Doritos bags piled up on Jamie's computer desk. A sudden burst of rain pounded the window, spooking the cat. As it jumped from the desk, sheaves of scribbled software algorithms and an ashtray of stale cigarette butts fell on the floor.

A distant thump above him woke Jamie from his sleep. A crack of lightning flashed past the basement window. The monitor flickered as an electrical surge from the storm tripped his computer's backup power. He looked at his watch. It was 12:30AM.

A dialogue box flashed on the monitor. Nun2wise was asking if he was going to rejoin chat. Halfway through typing his reply, the DSL line went dead again, knocking him offline for the third time tonight.

Shit!

He rebooted the modem. The lapse was momentary.

Jamie Forrester had no timetable; no set hours that began or ended. His days were one continuum - the unavoidable necessity of trying to provide a roof over his head. As a freelance software programmer, he plodded waist deep through mindless computer code; as a day-trader, he was whipsawed from one stock market peak to another.

With a few simple keystrokes, the doorway between reality and fantasy re-opened. He logged back in. It was his electronic heroin; a touch of a button and he could rejoin a shooting gallery full of other hopelessly addicted web junkies - chatroom pals, online gaming partners, deliriously self-absorbed bloggers. They shared a common opiate: freedom. Freedom from the shackles of the mundane, frustrating, 'two-steps forward, one-step backwards' world that tried to control their uncontrollable spirits; an imaginary place where ordinary people led extraordinary lives under cloaks of virtual anonymity.

The cost of entry was cheap: a login ID, a password. And a nametag - his avatar, his online persona. Not someone he was, but someone he wanted to be. Someone funnier, smarter and stronger than the person in the mirror. A superhero - more powerful, more intelligent, more virile than real life. Or a carefree fool. The choice was his.

On any given day, Jamie Forrester took a wild and crazy ride; an unpredictable 24/7 existence where competing thoughts and actions determined whether the step he took was forward, or backward. Like Alice stepping through the Looking Glass - whether programmer or day trader, superhero or fool – each day had the potential to shrink him into a thimble, or magnify him beyond recognition.

The message board - WallStreetBuzz.com - knew nothing of the real world called Jamie Forrester. They knew him as 'Jokers_Wild' - a name he'd cobbled together from random bits and bytes.

He logged back into the chat room:

By: Jokers_Wild   (reply to nun2wise)

Too bad. So sad. Cry me a river. That BAMF won't be missed.

By: nun2wise   (reply to Jokers_Wild)

Hey, Joker. That BAMF had a wife and kids. They'll miss him. You should pray for his soul.

By: Jokers_Wild   (reply to nun2wise)

Nun2wise… he'd better pray he cuts the Devil in on his next deal. Or Matthew Carleton won't have any place to hang his pitchfork after a long day haunting widows and orphans!

By: nun2wise   (reply to Jokers_Wild)

You really hate him, don't you?

The word 'hate' had lost meaning with Jamie. It was an overused emotion. He hated washing his hair. He hated the lumps in his bed. He hated broccoli. But Matthew Carleton? It wasn't just that Jamie hated him. He *despised* him with a passion. *Loathed* him. The word 'hate' was too blasé, too pedestrian to describe his feelings towards Matthew Carleton. Hate didn't really express the fury whenever Jamie came across that name.

There was one similarity between Matthew Carleton and broccoli, he thought. Even if it was somewhat superficial. As far as Jamie was concerned, they both deserved to be dipped in hot boiling water, until their insides turned into mush. But it was too late. Carleton was already dead.

By: Vette_Dream   (reply to nun2wise)

Can we please get back on topic! Did anyone manage to squeeze their broker for a piece of the Pegasus IPO?

By: 42EE Kitten   (reply to Vette_Dream)

Me did, honey bun!

By: Vette_Dream   (reply to 42EE_Kitten)

You little ho! What price?

By: 42EE Kitten   (reply to Vette_Dream)

Got a slice of the pie, cupcake. 1,000 shares at the offer price.

By: Vette_Dream   (reply to 42EE_Kitten)

You've got to be shittin' me! Party time at Kitty's house!

By: 42EE Kitten   (reply to Vette_Dream)

In your dreams, Vette Dream!

By: I H8 Brokers   (reply to Vette_Dream)

Got mine on the open… and cashed in quick before the close! Take your profits and run children! This turkey smells old already! Another Carleton P.O.S. IMO. Advice to everyone: day trade Pegasus. Wait til it's oversold and dips, then jump back in again.

By: Jokers_Wild   (reply to I_H8_Brokers)

I got a nice bounce. I'll take a quick 50% to the bank any day of the week. Hey, Broker… is this market starting to turn? Or am I drinking too much aftershave?

By: <u>I H8 Brokers</u>   (reply to Jokers_Wild)

Careful, Joker. IMHO there's no flesh left on this market's bones. This IPO was an aberration. Carleton's usual hype. Besides, Pegasus has nothing in the pipeline beyond Zerotox. The company's a one-drug wonder. All or nothing.

By: <u>freakin screwed</u>   (reply to I_H8_Brokers)

Pegasus is a ten-spot! To da moon baby!

By: <u>Jokers_Wild</u>   (reply to freakin_screwed)

Hey, freakin'... What you smokin' again, man? Broker's right. Pegasus hasn't got a hope in hell of getting FDA approval for Zerotox anytime soon. Why do you think they went IPO? The Rivertons will make out like bandits no matter what the FDA says. And anyone holding when the bad news comes... will kiss their ass-ets good-bye. I'm with Brokers. This one's for day trading. Nothing more.

By: <u>freakin screwed</u>   (reply to Jokers_Wild)

I'm long and strong!

By: <u>42EE Kitten</u>   (reply to freakin_screwed)

You're short and limp!

By: <u>I H8 Brokers</u>   (reply to 42EE_Kitten)

LMAO...!! Good one, Kitty! Meoww!

By: <u>Jokers_Wild</u>   (reply to freakin_screwed)

Don't dream about buying any islands, Screwy. It ain't gonna happen! Is anyone out there bold enough to short this turkey ahead of the FDA announcement on the Zerotox Phase III trials?

By: <u>Gabriel</u>

Fortune favors the brave, Joker.

By: <u>Jokers_Wild</u>   (reply to Gabriel)

Hey, lookie here!... a newbie poster! Welcome, Gabriel. The BuzzBoard needs some new blood. So what's your price target for Pegasus?

By: <u>Gabriel</u>   (reply to Jokers_Wild)

Zero.

By: <u>I H8 Brokers</u>   (reply to Gabriel)

LOL. Sure. You know that ain't gonna happen with Pegasus, Gabriel. So be realistic, how low do you think it will go?

By: <u>Gabriel</u>   (reply to I_H8_Brokers)

Zero.

By: <u>nun2wise</u>   (reply to Gabriel)

C'mon Gabriel... Broker's right. It just went IPO. It's the hottest stock in the market right now! Zero?

By: <u>Gabriel</u>   (reply to nun2wise)

Zero.

By: <u>Jokers_Wild</u>   (reply to Gabriel)

You sure seem confident this turkey's dead.

By: <u>Gabriel</u>   (reply to Jokers_Wild)

It is. They all are.

Chapter Nine

Scott turned off the ignition. The throaty rumble of the car's V8 faded into the night, and with it, the memory of Sarah Vaughn. His evening had started with optimism, and once again, had finished in disaster.

The tree-lined cul-de-sac was quietly slumbering as he shuffled through the leaves to his front door. The screen yawned open. He squeezed into the cramped entrance hall, fumbling for the light switch hidden by a baseball cap hanging on a coat hook.

Scott's nagging hunger was a sad souvenir of an indigestible conversation and an abandoned meal. And his kitchen, a utilitarian galley just big enough to unload takeaway food, was as unwelcoming and empty as his stomach.

He opened the fridge door. It contained a meager picnic of fuzzy green leftovers: chicken chow mein that looked like an eleventh grade penicillin experiment; shriveled lettuce well on its way to the compost heap; moldy cheese. A half-empty jar of spaghetti sauce sat alone, unloved, with no pasta in the cupboard. Everything was either unsafe, incomplete, or a little strange tasting without the proper accompaniment. It was the story of Scott Forrester's life.

Reluctantly, the fridge yielded its one remaining beer.

Scott wandered into the dining room. A mountain of mail had piled up on the faded cherry table. It was useless debris: innumerable bills, all late; worthless solicitations for credit cards; time-consuming coupon books. The only thing of value was a local kid's ad for leaf raking. He rescued it from the rest of the pile and hoped there was a spare fridge magnet left to pin it up.

His small two bed-roomed ranch bungalow was in an unpretentious neighborhood on the outskirts of Georgetown. Built in the late fifties, the house was unspectacular but adequate, furnished in an eclectic blend of post-modern functionality and yard sale bargains; a testament to Scott Forrester's gypsy lifestyle and limited checkbook.

With a beer in one hand, a wad of Ritz crackers in the other, Scott snuggled into the deep curves of his hand-me-down leather sofa, a warm and trusted friend with subtle could-care-less creases and a rich chocolate-brown patina.

The cold beer tasted good.

He closed his eyes and reflected on Jamie's latest attempt to micromanage his love life. He had to admit that when he'd first met Sarah, she had intrigued him with her curious character and boundless energy. Her pretty porcelain face was sensuous and exciting.

The date had started simply enough. Thankfully, she wanted to skip the movie idea. But the evening had ended in a tense, argumentative battle between dissimilar personalities. Apparently, it was too much to expect the spiky-haired, body-pierced student-Goth to enjoy the ambience of the Georgetown Jazz Café. It was like taking a hemophiliac to an acupuncture salon. Fortunately, they had parted ways amicably.

Thanks again, brother Jamie.

Sarah was Jamie's type, not Scott's. It wasn't at all surprising that it would never work out. The snowboarding, pot-smoking Sarah Vaughn was destined to go in directions Scott Forrester would not, and could not, follow.

It was late.

Scott was tired and fed up.

The sofa's leather kissed his cheek.

Exhausted, he fell asleep.

• • •

"You got any more beer?"

Jamie jumped out of his skin. "Don't scare me like that! Don't you ever knock?"

"My last bottle dropped to the floor."

"So that was the noise that woke me up!"

"I'll look in the fridge, Scott said, shuffling into the kitchen, half awake.

The two brothers had inherited their childhood home after their mother, a postal clerk with chronic diabetes, had died of kidney failure in the summer of 2001, just short of Jamie's nineteenth birthday. They never really knew their father. He had died when both of them were very small - Jamie was one and Scott was three, killed in the terrorist attack on the US Marine barracks in Lebanon in 1983.

Scott lived upstairs and Jamie downstairs - in a basement apartment converted from a collection of hobby rooms and storage closets built by their father thirty-five years ago. Jamie's living room had just enough space for a sofa, a stuffed chair and a TV. There was a bathroom and a small kitchen. The largest room, which had been their father's workshop, was an odd combination of bedroom and office. Jamie's bed was against one wall and on the other side of the room, a large farmhouse table doubled as a computer desk. Decor was basic post-military grunge: bookshelves of paperbacks, mostly dark fantasy and sci-fi, and posters of heavy metal bands like Anthrax and Slipknot. And of course, litter.

The house had lingering, bittersweet memories for both brothers. Fatherless Christmas mornings opening presents by the tree. Their mother's struggles to raise two small children while working every shift she could. High school graduations and the drunken parties that followed. The day Jamie left for the Army. And the somber night when he returned home on a medical discharge.

"Got anything to eat, Jamie?"

"We could order a pizza. How was your date?"

"It didn't work out."

"Again?" Jamie said, as he found the webpage for Zombie's Pizza.

Scott popped the lid off two beers. "Why is everything gothic in your life? What happened to Pizza Hut?"

"It doesn't deliver in coffin shaped boxes."

"That makes the pizza taste better?"

"No. But it sure supercharges the stock!"

"Oh, I forgot. The angle. There's always an angle."

"I believe in eating what I invest in, Bro. And don't even think about investing a hundred grand in a pizza franchise - just plunk down a tenth of that for Zombie's stock, and in a few years, you won't need to flip pizza dough for a living!"

"If that were true, why are you still haunting my lower floor?"

"Because I love you?"

"Because you suck at stock picking."

"So, Bro... you and Sarah bombed out?"

"You could say that. I think I'm going to swear off women." Scott wandered over to a poster of Angelina Jolie in her skin tight Tomb Raiders shorts. "All the best ones are taken."

Paper was spitting out of Jamie's printer. Scott plucked the first sheet. He looked it over with a puzzled expression. It was a graph of the first few trading days for the Pegasus IPO. Annotated Bollinger Bands. Stochastic buy/sell signals. Box and whisker points with Jamie's notes added in text boxes. Scott had no clue what he was looking at.

He took a swig of beer, "What's this?"

"Pegasus BioSciences. I would have thought you'd be all over this one, what with its principal backer stuffed in concrete."

"He was *not* stuffed in concrete."

"Oh? Really? And how was he stuffed?"

"I can't tell you, Jamie. It's a case under investigation. You know I can't. Besides, it violates the house rules. I don't talk about serial killers. You don't talk about your stock losses."

"Was it painful?"

"Was *what* painful?"

"Carleton's death. Was it painful?"

"He didn't die in his sleep. Let's put it that way."

"We know that. We just want to know, was his murder *painful*?"

"Who the hell are *we*?" Scott asked. "You got someone living in your closet?"

Jamie pointed to the monitor. "C'mon, Scott... gimme something for the Board."

Scott finished his beer and tossed the empty can across the room. He made a three-point basket. "Murder's always painful, Jamie."

"Tell me something I don't know."

"About murder?"

"Who decides if death is justice?"

"Oh, no... not *this* again." Scott roused the cat onto the floor and sat on the computer table. "Please, Jamie... it's late. Why are we talking about *this*?"

"I've lined men up in my sights, Scott."

"Stop, Jamie."

"They were husbands. Fathers. Brothers. Many who didn't want to be at the end of a bullet. Okay, they didn't look like us or live like us. But they were people. I knew what I was doing. I knew right from wrong. But I still took their lives."

"Jamie - that's what you were paid to do. You were in the Army."

"But I wasn't paid... to *enjoy* it."

"Can we please talk about something else?"

Jamie's outlook on life – negative thoughts about guilt and justice, a morbid fascination with death and retribution – was worrisome. The doctors said it was a manifestation of post-traumatic stress syndrome. Whatever it was, it wasn't healthy. His taste in music: head banging hard rock. The way he dressed: T-shirts with suicidal slogans. The way he acted. The way he talked. The way he thought. Self-defeating. Rebellious. Anti-establishment.

The fact that Jamie Forrester, the tough Army Ranger, had killed people on the battlefield, had to be reconciled with what Jamie Forrester was now... crippled, paralyzed from the waist down.

The things he did in the Army weren't criminal acts, Scott thought. *They were things soldiers had to do to protect themselves and their fellow soldiers. It was warfare, not murder. And Jamie's paralysis wasn't retribution for his transgressions. It was a roadside bomb. An act of war. Jamie's belief that being crippled was somehow 'justice' was insane. For what perceived crimes?*

"So let's talk about Sarah, Scott."

"No, Jamie... something else."

"Why is it Scott... that you can take a perfectly good opportunity to get laid and slam dunk it in the garbage?"

"I told you. It didn't work out." Scott rubbed his hands over his face. "Jamie, let's start this conversation over - I don't want to talk about Matthew Carleton or Sarah Vaughn. And *you* don't want to talk about what you did in the Army, okay?"

"So... what's to talk about?"

"How about... football?"

"Football? Scott, listen to yourself! You want to talk about football? I can't remember the last time you could sit still long enough to watch a football game. Every day you get out of bed, hunt down the most vicious criminals that walk the earth, come home, can't sit through a football game, can't get it up. Don't you see? You're losing it, dude."

"Me? *I'm* losing it?"

Jamie pushed back on his right hand wheel and turned his wheelchair away from the computer. "You think I'm fucked up, don't you? It's not me, dude. It's *you.* You're the one losing the plot. Look at me. I'm trapped in this thing - for the rest of my life! I don't have any more chances. But you do. At least one of us has a chance at *life*. So bring someone home, Scott. And get laid! She doesn't have to be someone who's won Miss America, or even a wet T-shirt contest; if her hair is naturally blonde or she's bald. If she has big boobs or little boobs. Doesn't matter. Just find someone who's as honest as you are… and take it from there. Sarah Vaughn is honest. Most of the girls you find by yourself aren't! Am I right?"

"Do you want another beer?"

Jamie swung his wheelchair in the direction of the fridge. "It's my turn to get it."

The doorbell rang.

Scott went upstairs to answer it. He yelled down, "The pizza's here."

Chapter Ten

It was located at the end of a long, cold corridor on the first floor of the National Center for the Analysis of Violent Crime in Quantico, Virginia - a spartan, windowless room waiting patiently in darkness for the FBI to begin its work.

Scott unlocked the door and flipped the light switch. He was greeted by a musty odor of crumpled burger wrappers and stale French fries. Overhead, blue fluorescent tubes buzzed inside their dingy plastic covers, sending quivering shadows into the room's hollow, barren corners.

The room was large. And its emptiness was stark. A series of whiteboards stood abandoned, smudged with the hastily erased ghosts of long discarded theories. On the back wall, a sea of well-used, pinpricked cork was covered by a flotilla of colorless pushpins, pleading for renewed creativity.

The room's high ceilings yearned to see the sun.

Its bare walls cried out for color and life.

"Oh God! This is *grim,*" Trish said.

"I've been in morgues that were warmer," Scott replied, plunking his armload of files on a coffee-stained desktop. "This room will suit Titus Griffin. It has no heartbeat. No soul."

In the center of the room's yellowed linoleum floor, four battered gray desks were arranged in a zigzag fashion as if a fire alarm had just sounded and everyone had suddenly evacuated. Trish Van Cleyburn, looking like a Sherpa returning from Mount Everest - briefcase dangling from her shoulder, a jumble of FedEx packages under her arm, and a Starbucks coffee in her hand - dumped her stuff on the nearest desk. She ran her finger across its dusty surface, "I've been in haunted houses that were cleaner than this shithole."

Scott's files had outgrown his cramped office. They needed a situation room. And this sad excuse was it. *Thank you budget cuts.*

Scott opened the file labeled 'Matthew Carleton' and took out a glossy photo of Carleton's body floating face down in a crimson bath of wine. He pinned it to the center of the cork-covered wall and took a big step back.

"Tell me, Scott... at what point do you start to get tired of dealing with this serial killer shit?"

"I don't know. It's so long ago, I don't remember."

"Griffin will be here soon. We'd better get busy."

"I can think of better ways of wasting an evening, Trish. Locked up inside a chamber of horrors in verbal combat with Titus Griffin? I've really been looking forward to this."

"He's a pretty smart guy, you know."

"No. I don't." Titus Griffin's transfer to the Serial Crime Unit at Quantico had come as a complete surprise to many in the FBI - including the Unit's star profiler who thought Griffin's appointment was a political decision, not a tactical one.

"C'mon, Scott... he deserves more respect than that. What hasn't Griffin investigated? Loan sharks in Jersey. Money laundering in Miami. Drug cartels along the Rio Grande. The Crips and Bloods in L.A. When it comes to violent homicides and gang warfare, Griffin has few equals at the Bureau."

Whatever Trish Van Cleyburn was trying to sell, Scott Forrester wasn't buying it. "And that means I'm supposed to be impressed? Let's face facts, Trish - so far, Quantico's been an out-of-body experience for this guy. Someone in Washington singled out Griffin for promotion. That's all there is to it. It's the only reason to justify such a boneheaded transfer."

"He's really getting under your skin, isn't he?"

"His approach to profiling bothers me intensely. His investigative style reeks of scorched earth. The Serial Crime Unit's mission is to *assist* local law enforcement - not *roll over* them like the frontline tanks in an armored assault. Titus Griffin doesn't seem to understand that. Profiling demands skill and objectivity, and frankly, I doubt that Griffin will ever have either one. He relies too much on gut instinct, and not enough on science."

"Griffin's seen things most people would prefer to forget," Trish said. "In this business, it seems a good investigator needs to be emotionally detached. And that's something you can't say Griffin isn't."

"And you don't think *I* am? Don't confuse emotional detachment with objectivity, Trish. Don't mistake bravery for insight. If that was all it took, then the 'Hood would be Harvard. No. Pounding the beat in L.A., shaking down shitty little strip joints in Miami, are not the same thing as-" Scott pointed to the photo of Matthew Carleton's naked body. "*That!*"

"You need to give him a chance."

"A chance to do what? To prove himself? He's had that chance. Take Griffin's first case in charge. You remember, don't you? The school librarian in Utah? The madman that conducted sadistic experiments on children?"

Trish sat in one of the bow-shaped metal chairs and leaned back. It creaked unsympathetically. With Scott's words, the cruelness of a child killer's face emerged from the blue shadows around her. She knew where Scott was taking this. A place she really didn't want to go back to.

"Didn't we find his dirt trail at the crime scene, Trish? Didn't we accurately profile his disturbed personality? Pinpoint his behavior patterns? Define his trigger? And just the same, didn't Griffin choose to ignore it all? Said our guy - the one you and I had fingered from the very start - was too mousy, too timid to be a serial killer? Because he used his *gut instincts*. Remember?"

Trish remembered, only too well.

Scott continued, "Gut instinct got Titus Griffin a poor black janitor instead. Some guy who happened to be at the wrong place at the wrong time, and through dumb luck, had guilt written all over his face. Titus Griffin practically castrated the poor bastard during interrogation. Remember that? Then... surprise, surprise! Another little girl was murdered while Griffin had his 'suspect' in custody."

Trish shifted uncomfortably. She knew Scott Forrester was right. "Rookie mistake," was all she could say.

"Shit, Trish! We can't afford any more of Griffin's 'rookie mistakes'!"

Footsteps came down the hall.

"Scott... Keep your voice down!"

Titus Griffin's imposing physique broke the plane of the doorway. "Okay children, recess is over."

A desk groaned under Griffin's husky frame. Six-foot-five, athletic, Griffin wore his street savvy attitude like a tight fitting suit, dominating rooms from the moment he stepped in - steely-eyed glare; jaw muscles rarely relaxed, flexing in and out like bellows, even when his mouth was at rest. Where had this well of insatiable tenacity come from? Some case that remained unsolved? Some grudge he bore? Some criminal that escaped his justice? At least Scott and Trish had agreed on something. The most probable reason was that Titus Griffin was just a mean son-of-a-bitch by nature.

He seldom sat for long. The knee injury that steered the promising running back from the football field at Grambling to law enforcement was still flaring up twenty-eight years later. True to form, he got up and walked towards the photo of Carleton's floating body, slapping a thin file against his thigh.

Griffin aimed the file at the murdered billionaire as if to accuse Matthew Carleton of planning his own premature death. "The SEC and the IRS were about to lay charges against Carleton for securities fraud and tax evasion. But someone else got to him first. Have you found out who?"

Trish looked over at her partner and mentor. There was a pause. *Was Scott going to say something or not?*

Thankfully, he did. "We have a preliminary profile."

"I don't just want a profile, Forrester. I want leads to follow. I want *suspects.*" Griffin's nostrils flared. It was not a good sign. Titus Griffin was not one for long debates. "We're in the FBI, Forrester. Remember? We're in the business of apprehending criminals. That's what we do. We're not in a goddamn lecture hall!" Griffin pushed his face into Scott's. But he said nothing. When he was sure that his silent, angry message had been delivered, he turned his attention to Trish Van Cleyburn.

She cleared her throat and the words came out with a squeaky cough, "We interviewed Lexi Carleton and she has no alibi. Scott thinks…"

"Why don't you let Agent Forrester speak for himself Special Agent Cleyburn?" Griffin always missed the first part of her last name. Whether he did it on purpose or not, she couldn't tell.

Scott stepped in and took Titus Griffin's glare away from Trish, "Lexi Carleton has a combination of sociopathic and narcissistic traits. She's callous, has superficial charm and a grandiose sense of self-worth; lacks emotional response and is sexually promiscuous. You could probably say the same thing about Matthew Carleton. In fact, they were made for each other. Sociopathic personalities make successful businesspeople. Captains of industry shouldn't feel pangs of guilt when closing plants and crushing people's hopes and dreams. It's considered to be part of their jobs. And that's how the Carletons conducted their affairs. At the end of each business day, they were good company for one another."

"Well, that's very insightful, Forrester. Does it get us any closer to a conviction?" Making Scott Forrester feel uncomfortable, in public or in private, had become a regular part of Griffin's daily routine. "Where's the proof that Lexi Carleton hired someone to kill her husband?"

Scott's answer was emotionless and came with a firm conviction, "Lexi Carleton wouldn't want her husband killed."

"And what makes you so sure of that?"

"Because Matthew Carleton was more valuable to her alive than dead. Besides, why would a woman who takes off her tennis shoes before she steps on a carpet and has her maid disinfect her children's toys twice a day allow a crazed murderer to drown her husband in wine under the noses of her precious, sensitive kids?"

"Exactly."

"Exactly?" Scott fired back, "How *exactly* do you mean?"

"So that we wouldn't suspect in a million years that it was *her* signature on the payroll check!"

That remark was Griffin at his superficial worst, he thought, another one of Griffin's out of body experiences as far as Scott was concerned.

"Let's say she did arrange to have her husband killed, Titus," Scott said. "What was her involvement in the other murders? She needs a motive for those as well... and as far as I can tell, she doesn't have one."

Griffin marched back to the lifeless body floating aimlessly in the middle of the cork wall. His voice deepened, "As sure as I'm standing here, Forrester, this murder was *commissioned* and the New York Field Office wants this murder *solved*. And with the help of the IRS and the SEC, we're going to follow Carleton's money trail like it was the Yellow Brick Road. I expect you two cowardly lions to trip over the murderer on the way to Oz. And... *when*, Forrester, not *if*... we find the killer, it will lead to the person or persons who paid him to do it."

Griffin took several stapled pages out of the thin file he had carried into the room. "Tomorrow, the Assistant Director-in-Charge of the New York Field Office will make a statement to the press." He held the pages up, waving them as he talked. "He will announce the formation of a Special Investigative Team headed by Agent-in-Charge Benito Vincente. Its purpose will be to consolidate the efforts of federal, state and local law enforcement agencies, the IRS and the SEC, into a single investigation of the murder of

Matthew Carleton and to expose the conspiracy that lay behind all of these other murders."

Griffin then read from the draft of the press release, "This team will include the resources of the Serial Crime Unit at the FBI Academy, Quantico, Virginia." He gestured to Scott and Trish. "That means you two turkeys."

I thought we were cowardly lions? Scott thought.

Griffin looked at his watch. "The pre-nups are over, children."

"Conspiracy?" Scott asked. "What conspiracy? Where's the evidence of a *conspiracy*?"

Griffin ignored him. "We have less than two hours before the Assistant Director wants our briefing. What kind of profile have you got for me?" He turned his eyes away from Scott. "Cleyburn?"

"We think our suspect is male, between twenty-five and thirty-five years old," she said. "Tall, maybe six foot two. Very physically fit. His murders are carefully planned and he's had top-notch survival training - way beyond Boy Scout level. He's highly skilled in weapons, concealment and evasion. And he avoids publicity. On that basis, we think he's ex-military, and recently so, sir."

Griffin nodded, clearly pleased.

She continued, "Ballistics has confirmed our suspicions. The rifle used to kill Meredith and McNabb in Wyoming was the same one that killed DeAndre Antoin in Miami. The bullets - 7.62mm military-issued rounds – had matching exit markings, showing they came from the same barrel. The suspect's weapon was likely a semi-automatic, silencer-mounted SR-25 sniper rifle - the kind US Special Forces use."

Griffin's face broadened as he turned to Scott. "See, Forrester. Now that's what I call thorough."

"There's more, sir."

"Continue, Cleyburn."

"He knew his victims' behavior and habits. He'd researched the patterns in their daily schedules. He would have stalked his victims for weeks, maybe months. In Wyoming, he hiked over great distances before deciding when and where they should die. So far, it all fits an assassin's profile. A hit man."

"Now that's the kind of job I'm expecting! Good work, Cleyburn!"

"Thank you, sir."

As the senior agent, Scott's name was on the report. He didn't care if Trish was taking the credit. What he did take exception to was her last conclusion - a conclusion he and Trish had debated extensively. She was too eager to echo what the boss wanted to hear. He said, "But paid assassins don't scribble in their victims' blood, *sir*."

Griffin was not impressed, "That's the trouble with you, Forrester. If they don't eat their victims, you don't think they're psychotic! Well, let me tell you, Forrester… walk down any back alley in East L.A. and interrupt a drug deal, and it would be more than your blood dribbling down the wall! They'd sell your dick pickled in a jar for a buck, if they could!"

"Nobody said he was psychotic. You're inferring way too much at this stage of the investigation-"

"Am I? Psychos come in all stripes and flavors, Forrester. So what's *your* next move? Where are *you* going from here, Forrester? What's *your* game plan?"

"I don't believe the evidence is conclusive. Not yet. It needs an expert opinion. We're going to find it. We're going to listen to it. And only then… are we going to act on it, *sir*."

"Well, that's *great*, Forrester. Going back to the lecture hall, are you?" Griffin pointed to a world beyond the room's four walls. "He's somewhere out *there*." Then he cowered in mock fright, "Don't run away from him, Forrester!"

Scott Forrester could handle sarcasm. He could handle the fact that Griffin was a severe taskmaster. What he detested was that no matter how valuable Scott's last contribution had been, it was always relegated to the annals of ancient history in the beat of a bug's wing. And as usual, he had done nothing to deserve it.

Van Cleyburn on the other hand was a nearly faultless match for Griffin's profile of a hard charging agent: intelligent and athletic; edgy and energetic; well dressed and full of spunk. But more than any other attribute, Van Cleyburn had enough experience to be useful and enough inexperience to blindly follow his command. She was Griffin's ideal subordinate.

Griffin closed the folder and walked to the door. "I hope you get it figured out, Forrester. Your profile of this killer. I'll watch my mailbox." He turned for one last dig. "Keep up the good work - you wouldn't want me to make another 'rookie mistake', would you?"

Chapter Eleven

It was a strange place for their first meeting. But there he was, right where he said they would find him: sipping Darjeeling tea at a table for four, in the Garden Café, West Building, the National Gallery of Art, Washington DC.

Dr. Rajeev Chandra wasn't hard to recognize, even in a crowded café. A slightly balding, gray-haired gentleman in his late sixties; well tailored, in a dark brown Brooks Brothers suit, brown Oxford shoes and crisp white shirt. He wore a carefully knotted maroon and cream-striped tie, emblazoned - as he later explained - with the crest of the University of New Delhi cricket team. A beige Burberry overcoat and an old-fashioned umbrella, the kind with a curved wooden handle, hung over the chair beside him. A well-traveled leather briefcase sat quietly at his feet.

The shape of his head was odd: disproportionately larger than the rest of his petite five-foot-four frame and accentuated by a broad bulbous nose and a wide, thick-lipped mouth. In fact, with a cup of tea daintily balanced between two fingers, Dr. Rajeev Chandra might easily be mistaken for a bobblehead doll of the Indian Prime Minister waiting for the guests to arrive at the Teddy Bears' Picnic.

Sitting with the patience and serenity of a monk, his large chocolate brown eyes watched the comings and goings of the busy art gallery with a warm, intellectual curiosity.

"Dr. Chandra? We're sorry we're late. I'm Special Agent Forrester. This is Special Agent Van Cleyburn. FBI."

He nodded politely, returning their handshakes with a limp, almost effeminate grip; plump, rolling cheeks acknowledging his new associates with a shy, refined smile.

The two agents sat down with their Styrofoam cups of stale, no-name coffee. Scott glanced at Chandra's slim briefcase. It didn't look big enough to hold more than a few files and a pad of paper. "Have you received the information you requested, Dr. Chandra? The autopsy reports?"

Dr. Chandra noticed Scott's anxious, wandering gaze and took a sip of tea. "Yes, thank you, Mr. Forrester. I have everything I need."

"If I may be bold, sir... why are we discussing this case in such a public place? You could have arranged to meet us at your office."

"I could have, Mr. Forrester. But where else serves Darjeeling tea within walking distance of the Freer Gallery?"

"The Freer Gallery?"

"Surely you know the Smithsonian's Gallery of Asian Art? It's a very pleasant walk, just around the corner." Dr. Chandra picked up his coat and briefcase. "There are some very important people waiting there for you. People who are anxious to explain what kind of person you're dealing with." He straightened his already straight tie and gestured towards the exit. "Shall we go?"

Outside the National Gallery, a fresh breeze greeted them under clearing skies. "Such a nice autumn day, Mr. Forrester. Looks like the rain has finally gone."

Beyond his stiff-collared first impression, the world-renowned criminal psychologist projected a relaxed and unhurried composure; a soothing gentle demeanor, leaving no doubt he could entice the most reluctant of strangers to share their deepest secrets, over a leisurely cup of tea.

Trish looked impatiently at her watch. It was twenty minutes past eleven and the Freer Gallery was a long, two-block walk on the other side of the red-bricked Smithsonian Castle at the Washington Monument end of the National Mall.

Whoever they were meeting at the Freer, she thought, *and however long it would take... the morning is burning up fast. It better be worth it!*

Chandra was walking with a mild limp. "I can tell you're a very busy young woman, Ms. Van Cleyburn," he said. "You seem to be in such a hurry." Every few strides, she was outdistancing the frail old man. Scott politely stayed by the doctor's side. "Perhaps Ms. Van Cleyburn, it would be more convenient to discuss this matter at another time? At my office, if you prefer?"

Trish stopped, rolled her eyes and turned. Was her impatience that obvious? Scott's expression said, 'slow down and play it cool, Trish'.

She took a deep breath, "We're dealing with a very dangerous mind, Dr. Chandra. If we don't make progress soon, he'll kill again. With all due respect sir, we need answers, and I don't see how a field trip to an art gallery is going to help us. Unless of course, the killer is waiting inside, to confess."

"Well, I'm afraid you won't be getting a confession today, Ms. Van Cleyburn. If that's what you were expecting, I think you will be disappointed."

For the moment, Dr. Chandra had nothing more to offer. The walk down Jefferson Drive continued to be a slow chore, Dr. Chandra using his umbrella as a walking stick, stopping repeatedly, wincing each time, waving his hand to proceed as soon as the apparent pain had passed. "A war injury, Mr. Forrester."

"Vietnam, sir?"

"Indian Army, Mr. Forrester. The Border War with Pakistan, 1967. I was newly graduated - a medical doctor, well before my interest in psychology. In my foolish, idealistic youth, I volunteered. Now, these old bones still curse the shrapnel that is a constant reminder of the promising cricket career I threw away. And for what? I still don't know to this day. The Indian and Pakistani border has not moved one inch, Mr. Forrester. But I have. I've learned to move on. We all must live and learn, Mr. Forrester. Live and learn."

"Indeed, sir."

Dr. Chandra stopped abruptly, wincing in even greater pain, and stumbled back. "You don't mind if we sit here for a while, do you?"

Trish sweetened her smile and said reluctantly, "No, Doctor, not at all." They were a tantalizingly short fifty yards away from the main entrance of the Freer Gallery. Trish was tempted to pick the old fellow up by the scruff of his neck, like a misbehaving cat, and drag him the rest of the way.

Dr. Chandra hobbled over to a park bench. Around them, the sights and sounds of Washington in mid-week resonated through the trees. The noise of jet aircraft echoed like thunder around the vast expanse of the Mall. Police and ambulance sirens blared in the distance. People with cell phones walked by: a businessman barking orders at an imaginary retinue of advisors; a lobbyist cooing politely at the Senator's press secretary, overjoyed that dinner arrangements had finally been made.

A squirrel pranced skittishly between the branches above them, brown leaves crackling as he raced down the tree trunk to the ground.

The three sat in silence for what seemed to be much longer than it actually was. Dr. Chandra had shut everything out: his eyes had closed, his breath was deep and long. He ended his meditation with a sigh. "Ah! Yoga, Ms. Van Cleyburn. It cleanses the mind of its impurities - those unwanted anxieties and frustrations that build up in our bustling society. It expels pain. Refreshes the soul. You should try it some time. It might do you some good."

"She's not used to sitting for this long. And to be honest, neither am I."

"I can tell that, Mr. Forrester."

And that was their answer. This wasn't about an old soldier's gimpy leg. This was about psychology. And patient, contemplative thought. It was Dr. Chandra's way of slowing things down. There was no room for frustrated energy and tangled emotions on the tortuous road that lay ahead. "Yes, Mr. Forrester," he said. "I've read the case notes. Your Mr. Griffin thinks he's a professional hit man? In fact, that's what they all believe, isn't it, Ms. Van Cleyburn?"

Dr. Chandra's network of contacts in the Bureau was extensive. They were all anxious to know what he thought. He paused and looked off in the distance. "I've read your preliminary profile, Mr. Forrester. It's very impressive. It's clear who you are looking for. I don't think you need me."

Scott's chin slumped to his chest. This wasn't what he wanted to hear. His disappointment showed.

"But Mr. Forrester... as I look at you, your face suggests some doubt. Do you doubt your own convictions? How can that be?"

"I think there's something deeper here."

"Deeper, Mr. Forrester?"

"A rage buried inside him. A violence that boils to the surface."

"A rage?"

"There's vengeance and hatred written all over these crimes. It's in the humiliation and torture he uses on his victims. We can't rule out a contract killer. But he would have to be a pretty sick one."

"Then you're suggesting our killer is psychotic, Mr. Forrester?"

"No, of course not, Dr. Chandra. A psychotic killer would react to his impulses and opportunities. He would be triggered by an urge, a compulsion that had to be satisfied. Something would inflame a flaw in his personality and his victims would then be chosen at random. But these victims weren't. They weren't just innocent people who happened to be at the wrong place at the wrong time."

"So, you're confused? Unsure of which road to go down?"

Weary from months of unproductive investigation, Scott Forrester rubbed his eyes and gazed into the sky. "We know he's sadistic, has a chip on his shoulder, and has something to prove. To himself? To someone else? Who knows?"

"He knows."

"Yes, sir. He does."

The squirrel darted about the lawn, jittery and desperate to find a discarded breadcrumb, a tossed apple core. Scott picked up an acorn that had escaped the squirrel's previous searches and threw it to him. The squirrel stuffed it in his cheek, looked at Scott as if to thank him, and scurried back up the tree. Right now, like the squirrel, Scott Forrester would take any small victory, any crumb.

"You could make an argument this guy is proud of what he's doing, Dr. Chandra. He's practicing his craft. A master of the black art of killing. He seems to have selected his victims for some kind of purpose. Call it, his mission in life. Some ultimate goal he has, whatever that may be."

"So, you don't believe he's killing for monetary compensation? You think he's killing for the thrill of it?"

"As the saying goes Dr. Chandra, 'if you want to understand the artist, you have to look at his work'. You've seen the photos. He's totally remorseless, unemotional, detached… a sociopathic killer with a predilection to kill. And keep killing. In my opinion, his ritualistic signature doesn't fit the mold of a hit man. I just can't sell that to Griffin. He's determined we're wrong. He's going for the easy explanation."

"Believe me, I understand. After many years, and many gray hairs, I know it's difficult to disagree with the commonly held view. Departing from the norm is unpopular. It's so much easier to be a part of the crowd. But I must say, the Academy continues to turn out some fine young minds. It's that nagging question that keeps popping into your head, isn't it? The last question that's always the most important one to find an answer to."

Scott knew what Dr. Chandra was hinting at.

"You say he's driven, Mr. Forrester. The question is… what is he driven by? That's what really troubles you, isn't it? Not being able to see what he sees. To walk in his shoes. Not knowing what he feels like at the moment he transforms life into death. Because if you knew, you could answer so many questions."

"It's all about motive, Dr. Chandra."

"Yes, Mr. Forrester. It always is. But that isn't the only reason you sought my guidance, is it? There is other expertise you need on this case... isn't there?"

"Please tell us we've come to the right person, Dr. Chandra."

"Yes, Mr. Forrester... you have."

"Can you make out the writing in the crime scene photos? Is it legible enough?"

"Oh yes, Mr. Forrester. Very legible."

It started out blotchy and crude, like a child's finger painting. In California, *it* was an obscure scribbling. With each new killing, *it* became more definitive, more refined in its brushstrokes. By the time it was Long Island's turn, the script had been inked in a calm, scholarly hand.

"The writing is indeed Sanskrit, Mr. Forrester. The symbols are certainly Hindu ones. That's the real reason you've asked me to help you... isn't it?"

It was a stroke of pure luck that a crime scene photographer at the Carleton Mansion was of East Indian descent. He had recognized the writing as Sanskrit, an ancient form of Hindi, like Latin is to English. He had never been taught to read it. He suggested they find someone who could.

"So our killer is from India, Dr. Chandra?"

"No, Mr. Forrester. I don't believe that he is. But he knows the Hindu religion. He may be a devotee of a Hindu religious group here in the US."

"A group like the Hare Krishnas?" Trish asked.

"They are one of many, many sects in the Hindu religion, Ms. Van Cleyburn. But the Krishnas are strictly pacifist. I doubt he's learned anything from them. He's a student - but not of true Hinduism."

"What do you mean *true* Hinduism?"

"As you said, Mr. Forrester... to understand the artist you must look at his work."

It was time to go. Dr. Chandra gathered up his umbrella and briefcase. As he rose from the park bench, he looked up at the squirrel perched above them as if the previous conversation about a monster on the loose no longer mattered. He pointed the umbrella toward their destination, the Freer Gallery. "I feel rested now. I promise you will be rewarded for your patience, Ms. Van Cleyburn."

They arrived at the entrance to the Smithsonian's Gallery of Asian Art. Dr. Chandra climbed the steps in much less pain. "Mr. Forrester, you are correct in saying the victims were not random. That they were chosen for a particular reason. Indeed, our killer *is* a sociopath. And because of this, his beliefs about right and wrong seem orderly to him; they fit the rules of justice he has created for himself. Yes, these were not crimes of passion, nor crimes of anger. He was very much in control."

"Control of the environment; manipulation and domination of the victims," Scott said. "The modus operandi of serial killers, Dr. Chandra. So why is this particular one so difficult to figure out?"

"Why indeed, Mr. Forrester. You must be tired of asking the same question over and over again. Come with me, my friends, and I'll show you... why."

Chapter Twelve

The Freer Gallery was a gateway between two very different worlds. On the outside, a facade of graceful Renaissance fountains, sky-lit Italianate courtyards and cool pink granite arches. But behind the inviting warmth of its antique cherry doors, lay secrets - ancient mysteries thousands of years old, frozen in time. Persian manuscripts. Chinese silk paintings. Buddhist sculptures. Japanese ceramics. Artifacts soaked in the richness and symbolism of Eastern philosophy, born from the toil of a simpler people from a simpler age, living as one with the beasts of the forest and the heat of the desert.

"Their stories are told in their art," Dr. Chandra said. "Every day was a challenge to survive and prosper." He stood in the shadow of a gilded Buddha. "But they found a way. People in perpetual awe of the world around them. And from whatever ancient distant land, their story is essentially the same."

Dr. Chandra took a firm grip of his umbrella as he steadied himself. "Powerful, mystical, all-seeing supernatural forces governed the fate of Mankind. The Guardians of Heaven, the Demons of Hell, in constant battle, the innocents of Earth caught in the crossfire. And how could they be saved? By following the teachings. The teachings that protected them from evil spirits, led them into spiritual enlightenment, and brought them everlasting peace and eternal life." He touched the foot of the Buddha for good luck. "Are you a religious man, Mr. Forrester?"

"You're the second person in the past week to ask me that."

"Well... are you?"

"Sometimes, Dr. Chandra. When it's important to be. Like weddings and funerals. I'm not a big churchgoer. But it's not the church pew I sit in. It's who I am. It's who I want to be. It's the values I carry with me that count."

"And you, Ms. Van Cleyburn?"

A bronze horse from the Han Dynasty flew into battle with a Chinese knight on its back. Trish looked it over and shrugged, "I've had my fill of organized religion. Can't say I'm a fan of dogma. I was brought up in the Dutch Reform Church in rural Ohio. In high school, my parents didn't allow me to wear a dress above my knees, wear makeup or kiss boys. Let's say I made up for lost time in college."

"Good. A little touch of the agnostic should give both of you an open mind. What do you know of Hinduism?"

There was silence. Either they didn't have an opinion, or thought the one they did have might be politically incorrect. It seemed smarter not to say anything.

"Come." At the end of the exhibit hall was a door. "See what Hinduism is for yourselves. Make your own judgments."

Dr. Chandra led them like a shepherd leading his flock, reaching a sign that said, 'Manifestations of the Divine: Gods and Goddesses of Ancient India. Sponsored by The Portland Group'. Dr. Chandra had arranged to give the FBI a private viewing of the Freer Gallery's star exhibition.

They entered a large, deserted gallery. It had the atmosphere of a temple of worship, their footsteps echoing on bare hardwood floors. Its walls were gray and monotone but the massive paintings hanging on them exploded with vibrant color. In the center of the gallery, bronze statues on sand-colored plinths took light from above, as if Heaven itself was shining down from the ceiling.

Dr. Chandra directed them to a set of three enormous pictures. The first painting had a translucent quality, an inner glow that projected beyond its surface. "Let's start here. What can you see in this image, Ms. Van Cleyburn? What is its story?"

Trish Van Cleyburn, arms wrapped across her chest, stood as if she were daring the god-like figure on the canvas to strike her down for being so unimpressed. "Well, the subject looks androgynous. I can't tell if it's a man or a woman. Boyish eyes. Girlish cheeks. Long flowing robes. He - or is it a she? – has four arms and is wearing a crown with six cobras coming out of the top. He's holding several objects… a shell, a flower, some kind of halo or disk… and a big golden staff. He's standing on water."

"That is all that you see, Ms. Van Cleyburn?" Dr. Chandra said, turning. "And what about you, Mr. Forrester?"

Scott immersed himself in the painting's aura, "I see a strong, powerful god. But one that is also kind. He looks forceful and capable, but also wise. The snakes surround him, but they're not attacking him. They are a part of him. Subservient. Maybe this represents his control over nature… and the world."

"Do you feel protected in his presence?"

"Yes, I guess so."

"You should. And what about the next one?"

Trish shuffled along, devoid of any sense of awe. This was an art gallery. These were just paintings. "Another she-male with long hair, wearing earrings, holding some kind of beads and sitting cross-legged on a fur rug in front of a fountain. The snake theme's here again… this time just one. There's a light beam shining on his head from a flower. I'd say he's some kind of holy man or high priest."

Trish traded places with Scott and whispered on the way by, "What the hell are we doing in here? He's stalling because the people he said would meet us are late!"

Scott whispered back, "He's got his reasons. Have the faith to at least humor him, Trish."

"Maybe he's just a crusty old fart who's wasting our time. Have you thought about that as a reason?"

"Yeah. Briefly."

If Dr. Chandra had noticed their exchange, he wasn't letting on. He continued unperturbed, "Mr. Forrester... what do you think of Ms. Van Cleyburn's 'she-male'?"

"Sorry, Dr. Chandra. We were just comparing notes."

Trish snickered.

Scott resumed his studious pose, "Placid smile. Comforting demeanor. The way he's holding his hands is intriguing. He looks like a source of healing. Is he perhaps the God of Love? Or Peace? Or something like that?"

"Perhaps," Dr. Chandra said, before moving on to the third painting in the set. "This time I want both of you to delve deeper. What do you see in this one?"

Trish shifted impatiently. "What do I see? I see a four-headed mutant rising out of a giant flower like something from 'the Invasion of the Body-Snatchers'. To be honest, Dr. Chandra, it looks like a page from an ancient comic book."

The soft-spoken Dr. Chandra had trouble hiding his annoyance with Trish's glib attitude, "I think, Ms. Van Cleyburn, you're treating these pictures as if they're a lineup of suspects and you're trying to decide which one snatched the old lady's purse."

"Well, Dr. Chandra, my vote's for the mutant. What do you think Agent Forrester? Definitely suspicious. Or maybe it's the one with the most snakes. Snakes have an affinity for the criminal element. Or is it the other way around? I'm never quite sure."

Scott nudged her hard in the ribs. "Come on, Trish... get with the program."

"And what program is that? If you're so smart, what do *you* see?"

Scott had to admit the last painting was a little indigestible. In fact, it seemed pretty far-fetched. "The four heads... each represents..." he said, trying not to stumble over his words without much success, "something like… maybe the four dimensions of life? Birth… death? Love… hate?"

Trish poked back. "You're struggling, Forrester."

"The god is sitting on a water-lily…" he continued.

Dr. Chandra came to his aid. "A lotus flower, Mr. Forrester…"

"A lotus flower. Four arms. Upturned palms. The whole image is beckoning the viewer. Saying… believe in me, and I'll lead you safely into the afterlife."

"And what if you don't follow him?" Dr. Chandra asked.

"I guess you'll drown."

Dr. Chandra smiled, satisfied. His pupil had unexpectedly passed the test. "It seems that Mr. Forrester has a knack for this, Ms. Van Cleyburn."

"You can't tell me… he's right?"

"Well… yes. He is. In a crude sort of way. But for someone who hasn't studied Hinduism, I think he's done very well. It's the way he approached the task. You see, Ms. Van Cleyburn… you didn't 'view' the pictures. You 'observed' them. Clinically. Examined them as a good detective would, sifting through evidence. You have a highly trained mind. And it has been taught to interpret the world as if everything should be put in a Zip-lock plastic bag. Am I not right?"

Dr. Chandra had nailed the essence of Trish Van Cleyburn.

"Mr. Forrester, on the other hand, looked beyond the superficial. He analyzed his feelings as the paintings 'spoke' to him, in his mind's eye. He didn't just 'see' in the literal sense, but viewed them intuitively, interpreting what he saw in a spiritual way. In the end, he had a better appreciation for their intended meaning."

"Which was?" Trish scowled.

"Those three paintings represent one subject. One manifestation. One Supreme Being. You call him God. In India, he is called Vishnu… Shiva… and Brahma."

"How can those *three* very different people be *one* Supreme Being?" Trish asked. "Isn't that a contradiction of terms?"

"Of course it is. To non-believers. But don't most religions contain these kinds of contradictions, Ms. Van Cleyburn? Doesn't Christianity have the Father, the Son and the Holy Ghost?"

"Point taken."

"In Hinduism, these incarnations, called avatars, are of the same ultimate deity. Westerners often equate Hinduism to the multi-deity worship of the ancient Greeks and Romans. It's a common mistake. But it's not the case."

Dr. Chandra approached a statue that stood on a plinth in front of the three paintings. The figure bore the head of an elephant. "This is Ganesh, Son of Shiva. Doesn't Christianity also have a Son of God?"

"The last time I looked, Dr. Chandra... Jesus didn't have floppy ears and a dangling trunk."

"So, Ms. Van Cleyburn, you *do* have beliefs that prejudice your mind. Just like the British in Victorian times. The India they governed seemed pagan to them. The worship of Hindu gods offended their Christian sensibilities. And because of this prejudice, the British were unable to reconcile that Hindus believed, as they did, in the same Supreme Being. Such an enormous misunderstanding, don't you think? Such a cultural chasm. In reality, Hinduism is a religion of supreme tolerance; it welcomes the views of other religions. What kind of world would we live in, if other religions thought the same way? And why else would so many Westerners travel to India to seek spiritual guidance from its gurus and holy men?"

"You mean Westerners... like our killer?" Scott asked.

Dr. Chandra walked over to the painting of Shiva, the God whose countenance of healing and wisdom had left such a positive impression on Scott. "You've heard of bad karma, Mr. Forrester?"

"Heard of it, sir? I've seen it. Felt it. Had enough of it to last a lifetime. Especially lately."

"Excellent! Well then you understand that good karma and bad karma are both derived from the same moral law of cause and effect that Christians also believe in. Look closely at these paintings. In them, you will find the universe's endless cycle of creation, preservation and destruction. I cannot stress more... how important these symbols are throughout the Hindu religion."

Chandra continued, "It is the cornerstone of a Hindu's belief that our destinies are written by our thoughts, words and actions, both in this life and in those we have lived before. And it is karma - the sum of a soul's good and bad deeds – that must be balanced. The internal contradictions must be resolved during your lifetime. If not, you will be forced to start again. Forced to lead - in the next life - a better life than the one you have left behind. This is the purpose of reincarnation. To lead a better life than the one you have left behind. In Hinduism, it is believed this cycle repeats for eternity, until you reach spiritual perfection."

Trish's gaze had wandered and her impatience was hard to hide. She had not come to the Freer Gallery to be lectured on Eastern mysticism. "Okay, Dr. Chandra, this is all *very* esoteric. But we're still FBI agents with a case to solve. Where are the people you promised would meet us here? Will they explain why a dangerous killer gets his jollies plastering someone's brains over a field of wildflowers in Wyoming? Or why he would drown someone in French wine in a bathtub on Long Island? Will they be able to explain that?"

"But Ms Van Cleyburn... you've already met three of them. And if you'd cared to listen, they have already taught you much about your killer."

Trish was done dancing with Dr. Chandra. The time for fun and games was over. "Dr. Chandra, I once worked on a case where a maniac from Indiana believed he'd been abducted by aliens and they'd rewired his testicles. That was the reason he gave for raping and killing six pre-teen girls over a three-year period. He taught me more about serial killers than I ever expected to know. What the hell do these paintings have to do with our serial killer?"

Scott stepped between them.

It wasn't a fair fight.

With a black belt in martial arts, Trish Van Cleyburn could put the good doctor on his butt in a millisecond. But with this verbal sparring, she was bound to lose. "Trish... Dr. Chandra isn't trying to convert us. He just brought us here to think differently. About the evidence. About why the killer is who he is. Maybe our killer thinks he's bringing his victims to Judgment Day, or whatever the Hindu equivalent is."

"There! You see, Ms. Van Cleyburn? Now you see... what a truly open mind can learn?"

"Right now, Dr. Chandra, I'll believe *anything* that takes creeps like that guy in Indiana off the streets."

"*Anything*, Ms. Van Cleyburn? *Anything?* Well, let's try you with this..."

Chapter Thirteen

The final gallery was bathed in a pale semi-darkness; its cavernous gray walls like the interior of a tomb. Three small spotlights tried in vain to fully illuminate a single artwork that rose twenty feet from floor to ceiling, and spanned thirty feet across.

The colossal silk canvas towered over the three solitary figures standing in silence, transfixed by its size and presence. The painting was undeniably the showpiece of the Freer Gallery's exhibition of Indian art, a religious icon never before seen outside of India.

In the dim lighting, the enormous canvas appeared three dimensional, suspended in air. It generated an ethereal energy, a mix of compulsion and foreboding, beckoning at first to draw them closer, then warning them to approach no further.

"It does not seek your admiration," Dr. Chandra said bluntly. "Not in the slightest. It asks – no, it *demands* - your unquestionable fealty. Can you not feel its magnetism, Mr. Forrester? Ms. Van Cleyburn? Its seduction?"

Scott Forrester winced – an immediate, involuntary reaction to the most disturbing images he'd ever seen. A gargantuan black deity with skeletal features, wearing a necklace of skulls, and a girdle made from the severed hands of corpses, was sitting cross-legged in the middle of a battle between two armies of god-beasts, as they attacked, beheaded and devoured each other, in a frenzy of uncontrolled violence.

Villages lay in their path.

Innocent women were raped.

Helpless men were skewered and carved into pieces.

It was a sprawling panorama of suffering and cruelty, executed in the minutest and most graphic detail. Scott could feel the panic of the unfortunates about to be swept up by the demon hordes; their dread as bending bones splintered; their anguish as resistance yielded to defeat, and defeat to death. Its unholiest elements - images of inhuman ferocity and unspeakable depravity - claimed the copyright on horror.

Dr. Chandra tapped his umbrella on the bare hardwood floor and broke the silence. He whispered, as if the painting could hear, "It is said that those who gaze upon her for too long, invite her in. And once she is there, no spell can cast her out."

Trish recoiled, "Oh, my God, Scott. This… is *hideous!*"

No matter where Scott Forrester stood, no matter how far he removed himself from the painting, it produced a sickening sensation - the intense feeling of hovering over a whirlpool, with the compulsion to fall in. It wasn't easy to rationalize why such finely crafted lines of paint on old silk would have such an ugly, hypnotic effect. It was as if cold tentacles of hatred and vengeance were creeping out of the canvas.

"In the early part of the nineteenth century, Mr. Forrester, the sect that worshiped this deity was considered to be so dangerous to the public good that the Indian government ordered their temples closed and their possessions scattered to the wind."

"What is it?"

"You mean… who is it?"

"No, Dr. Chandra… I mean *what* is it?"

"The painting is called 'The Revenge of Dvaipa'," Dr. Chandra said, as he paced its length, hands behind his back, keeping a constant, safe distance from the canvas. He raised his umbrella towards the picture's central figure, "She is Dvaipa. The daughter of Kali, the Goddess of Death and Destruction."

"*It's* a woman?"

Dr. Chandra's words came out slowly, cautiously, "Yes, the Demon-Goddess Dvaipa." He drew a deep breath as if to gain the strength to confront the image before him. "Kali's bastard. A half-caste. Fathered by a demonic Tiger's sperm. Born of Mother Death's tortured labors. The name, 'Dvaipa' in Hindi means... 'from a tiger'."

He pointed to the battle scene at her feet. "Here, she presides over her greatest victory. This once powerful demon-general was no match for her. Slain, she holds his severed head in triumph. And note her four arms. Two of them are human. And two of them are not. They are a tiger's paws. And they drip with her victims' blood."

Dr. Chandra pointed to another figure, in the painting's uppermost left corner, "Here is Dvaipa's Mother... Kali. She is one of Hinduism's most revered symbols. How could the Goddess of Destruction be revered? I know it is hard for Westerners to understand this. She also embodies the Divine Creation... for what is destroyed is reborn. And with rebirth, there comes the dawning of true spiritual knowledge. But here, you see Kali fleeing the canvas in disgust. Showing her revulsion at the slaughter. For these events are an aberration of the truths of Hinduism. She rejects her daughter, Dvaipa... and all that she represents."

Chandra paused, like he did on the park bench, holding his head in his hand as if in pain. Meditating, only for a few seconds. "Again you seek answers, Mr. Forrester. What is *it* you ask? How could such evil possibly be described? *It*... is the defeat of Wisdom by Ignorance. *It*... is the extinction of the bright Fire of Truth by the Darkness."

He turned away from the madness. "Dvaipa was cast out from the Heavens to lead her armies in a constant state of warfare. Here. On Earth. Shunned by the Divine Table of Hindu Gods, equally feared by the Anti-Deities of Hell, she found comfort and solace with Mankind. Because in every nation, in every battlefield scattered across the globe - even here, in the back alleys of America - we can see the evil products of her soldiers' skill."

Trish visibly shivered under the painting's smothering gaze, "There is *no way* - there is *no* amount of money you could pay me - to hang that *thing* on my walls! Not for one single second! It's the creepiest thing I've ever seen. How the hell did it ever end up in here?"

Silhouetted by the gallery's high spotlights, Dr. Chandra turned his back to Dvaipa, and said, "The painting disappeared from public view for almost a century. The sect lost its devotees. But several years ago when an earthquake devastated a remote temple in Indian Kashmir near the Pakistani border, the painting - hidden behind panels and entombed for what the priests had hoped would be eternity - was rediscovered. Her corrupting influence over weak minds was soon re-kindled. One hundred years after the painting first disappeared, she became a national controversy. Should she be restored to her temple? Or should she be burned?"

He paced again, taking a careful look behind him, as if to chase away the demon's vapors. "Mother India is a very respectful, diverse place. She treasures her religious freedoms. And she is also deeply, deeply superstitious. From out of the ruins of her temple, Dvaipa had risen again to take her place alongside the Hindu gods. If the image of Dvaipa was destroyed, there was fear that a catastrophe would befall Mother India. For if Man were to determine her fate, then out of his flames, she would take her revenge."

"That still doesn't explain what *it's* doing in Washington," Trish said.

"Quite right, Ms. Van Cleyburn. It doesn't. The debate over the painting's fate shook India's spiritual community. It was a desperate religious dilemma that required a novel solution. And what better way... than to exile her? Cast her adrift from India's shores. Forever."

"You've got to be kidding!"

"Oh, no... this is not something to kid about. Here you see the Demon-Goddess Dvaipa - like some ghoulish gypsy queen at rest – on the first stop of her perpetual tour of the world's finest art galleries."

"Lucky us."

"Yes, Ms. Van Cleyburn. Isn't it indeed fortunate... that you are so unaware of her religious significance? Fortunate that you can appreciate her... with your agnostic innocence. Unbiased and skeptical. You know nothing of the destructive fanaticism she has bred for centuries. So please... do *observe* her. Observe her, as you so casually observed the others," Dr. Chandra said, spreading his arms. "Enjoy her. In the peace and quiet of these tranquil halls. Enrich yourself with the artist's brilliant craftwork... while ignoring the subject's malevolent message."

Enrich themselves? To Scott Forrester, this experience was about as enriching as the rancid smell of dead flesh in the sickly odor of the autopsy room. It was as much a work of art as the cold, dead expressions staring up at him from the coroner's slab. The painting did *speak*. It spoke the words that murdered hands would write, if only they could protest the presence of evil that had just passed through them. It was a work of art Scott Forrester had seen too many times before.

Dr. Chandra looked tired. He sat down on the solitary cherry bench in the center of the gallery. It absorbed his weight and restored his warmth. "I have made the study of cults... and the criminal behaviors they generate... my life's work. That was the other reason you sought my help, was it not? I am old. And these old bones need your help now. There are rumors the Temple of Dvaipa has arrived in America."

"The Temple of Dvaipa?"

"Yes, Mr. Forrester." His tone had changed - part trepidation, part warning - as if the ultimate truth of the Demon-Goddess Dvaipa was about to be revealed outside the secrecy of her coven. "In the lowest classes of Indian society - those who from generation to generation are condemned to live in grinding poverty until they die - the Goddess Dvaipa finds a receptive audience. She appeals to those who have lost all hope. She becomes their salvation, in a world that has abandoned them. She becomes their guide to a better life. In your simple Judeo-Christian terms, Mr. Forrester, her worshippers are... Satanists."

Still sitting, he pointed towards the black demon-figure glaring down on them, "And there before you… is the savage symbol they revere. Half god, half beast. Tainted with the blood of her many corrupt victories. You see, Mr. Forrester, Ms. Van Cleyburn… the Demon-Goddess Dvaipa is… Revenge Incarnate. And the unholy scythe she wields… the Tiger's Paw."

Trish stepped out of the shadows. "All right, Dr. Chandra, let's agree that this *thing,*" she said, as she grimaced at the portrait of wanton butchery, "Is more than just distasteful to look at. But are you trying to tell us that the act of worshipping a *painting* can coerce people to commit the evil it portrays?"

"No, of course not. Evil needs no gallery of art for people to celebrate it, Ms. Van Cleyburn. That exhibition travels all around us. You've studied religion, Ms. Van Cleyburn… albeit, 'reluctantly'. From the birth of human thought, the sight of a divine apparition was written into scripture. These scriptures gave birth to temples. And then in turn, came the priests to adorn them. From the priests' frailties… comes blindness. From that blindness… comes the will to do good… or in this case, evil."

"Dr. Chandra, this whole discussion is ridiculous. Let's face reality!"

"*Reality*, Ms. Van Cleyburn?"

"Reality!" Trish paced the floor, angry and frustrated. She was searching for something more concrete than mystical incantations. She needed a real world explanation. Something she could put in a Zip-lock bag.

It was a challenge Dr. Chandra had anticipated. The frail old man had positioned her exactly where he wanted her to be. "So Ms. Van Cleyburn, do you believe that evil is simply the absence of goodness… like darkness is the absence of light? Do you think evil is a physical property… like density or electrical current? Something that can be measured by scientists, then controlled and manipulated by human hands?"

Trish had been boxed in by the wily doctor to say *Yes*. But as a trained criminologist, she knew the only answer was… *No*.

Dr. Chandra expected her hesitation. He delivered the decisive blow, "Evil is a spiritual dimension. A dimension of the human mind. It has subtleties we have yet to fully understand. Look again at your so-called 'page from an ancient comic book'. Look into the face of the Demon-Goddess one more time… and tell me, Ms. Van Cleyburn… honestly… can you not see the bestial eyes of your killer?"

"Honestly, Dr. Chandra? I can't. This is a painting. What does this monstrosity have to do with the murders of Liang Wong, DeAndre Antoin, Deuce Meredith and Matthew Carleton? Are you suggesting they were involved in this satanic cult?"

Dr. Chandra was silent. Then he did something completely out of character. The frail old gentleman leapt to his feet, and flung his arms out as wide as he could. He approached the Demon-Goddess Dvaipa as if it were possible for such a small man to grab the massive painting by its edges and shake it from its mount. Then, with arms rigid and outstretched as if they were frozen in a crossless crucifixion, he looked into the vanishing darkness that consumed the gallery's high ceiling, and shouted at the top of his lungs, "I… am the energy of *Her* divine anger!"

Scott was shocked. "Dr. Chandra… are you all right?"

The doctor detached himself from the painting. In his face was a look of wild-eyed possession. He walked back to the bench, his long abandoned briefcase cringing helplessly on the floor. From inside its limp leather body, he pulled out three photographs. Three FBI crime scene photographs.

On the first photo, blood red Sanskrit letters streaked down the walls inside the Carleton Mansion. Dr. Chandra bellowed again, "I… am the energy of *Her* divine anger!" and walked back towards the painting. Without daring to touch its surface, his fingers underlined the Sanskrit writing that was stenciled in large letters below the seated Demon-Goddess.

He repeated the phrase, "I… am the energy of *Her* divine anger!"

The words had been in front of them all the time.

Ancient Sanskrit characters, brittle, but still bright, after two hundred years. They screamed in silence the same message that had been written by the killer... in Matthew Carleton's blood, and the blood of the victims before him.

Dr. Chandra held up the other two photos. One, the previously unknown symbol scrawled on the dashboard of Carleton's 1955 Mercedes Gullwing. The other, a similar shape, etched in blood, on the rocks beside Deuce Meredith's mangled body.

Dr. Chandra pointed to Dvaipa's raised right arm. The killer's message was materializing before them. It was now clear, defined, unrepentant... the bloody Tiger's Paw. The energy of *Her* divine anger.

Finally, Special Agent Trish Van Cleyburn, humbled by the force of his argument, said, "What does all of this mean, Dr. Chandra?"

"It means, Ms. Van Cleyburn, that he's been to India and seen this painting. Not just seen it. Worshipped it. And now, like all of her demonic followers, he's expressing his belief in her unholy power... through *your* victims."

Chapter Fourteen

In the room at the end of the long cold corridor, order had finally emerged from chaos. What was once a patch of dusty, parched earth was beginning to look like a well-ploughed farmer's field. The evidence that comprised Case #479 at the FBI's National Center for the Analysis of Violent Crime – forensic, ballistic, and medical reports; police and witness statements – was now planted on the cork wall in neatly furrowed columns.

Trish Van Cleyburn pushed the final pin into the last of a series of maps that illustrated the killer's suspected movements across the country. Tired and pale, she shut down her laptop and looked over at Scott who was still absorbed in a book he'd been reading for hours. "I've had enough," she said. "I'm going home. You coming?"

"Not yet." Scott rubbed his stiff neck. "I want to finish this." The book, 'The Religious Mosaic of India: From Primitive Origins to Modern Day', had been given to Scott by Dr. Chandra as required reading.

"C'mon, Scott. Get a life! It's 2:00AM. I'm leaving."

The text was dry, but the revelations at the Freer Gallery had energized Scott's curiosity. "Did you know that seven percent of India's population practice pagan religions that haven't changed in over two thousand years?"

"Is that right? Well, seven percent of New Yorkers believe in UFOs. And seven percent of registered Democrats vote Republican. So what?"

"Trish... who insisted we find some 'real world' facts and bring them back in a zip-lock bag? Seven percent of New York City might be a lot of people compared to your hometown in Ohio, but seven percent of a country the size of India is *humongous*. Do you realize that it's *sixty-five million* people! That's three times the size of the whole population of New York

State. And these aren't just any people. These are sixty-five million *poverty-stricken* people. Cut off from the modern world. Not just a single lost tribe on some small Pacific island. *Sixty-five million* people!"

"Okay, Dr. Attenborough... and your point is?"

"Millions of city-dwelling people in India have assimilated MacDonald's and Coca-Cola, and work in globally networked enterprises like software development." Scott flipped to a photograph in the book of the Naga tribe of India's northeastern mountains. "Look at this guy, Trish. He belongs to a tribe that still worships earthquake gods and sleeps every night in fear of attacks from two-headed tigers. He thinks witch doctors can turn people into animals, wears a monkey skull necklace for the magical powers it produces, and believes that the spiritual energy of an enemy's severed head can be transferred into his own. He's a headhunter. In the twenty-first century!"

"So?"

"So... it proves Dr. Chandra was right. There are people in India that are barely connected to the present day. Culturally isolated. Primitive. Think about it. *Sixty-five million* primitive people. That means there is more than just a reasonable statistical probability – in fact, it's almost a certainty – that somewhere in India, the satanic cult of the Demon-Goddess Dvaipa still flourishes."

"Okay, Scott. Then why – after all these hours of reading..." It was time for Trish Van Cleyburn's zip-lock bag to close. "Haven't you found something in that book about the Temple of Dvaipa?"

She was right. There was no mention of a 'Temple of Dvaipa' in Dr. Chandra's text. It was as if India had buried a part of its history that it didn't want to admit it had.

"I don't know. All I know is that the evidence of its existence is plastered around these walls. And if its existence is a given, then the more important question is... why has it come here?"

Chapter Fifteen

There was a rap on the door and a subdued voice asked, "Agent Forrester? Are you in there?" Rebecca Cohen, Titus Griffin's new temp, wasn't sure if the shape she could see through the frosted glass was Scott Forrester or not. He wasn't answering his calls. His cell phone appeared to be turned off. There was a visitor in reception that insisted he speak to Special Agent Forrester. He said it was urgent.

Rebecca was sure she'd seen Scott's car in the parking lot when she came to work this morning.

Scott was slumped over his desk with his arms crossed and his head down. Dr. Chandra's book lay on the floor where it had slipped off his lap. It was now 7:45AM.

Rebecca knocked again. "Agent Forrester? You have a visitor in the lobby."

Scott struggled to the door and as he opened it, Rebecca Cohen recoiled in horror. His shirt was badly wrinkled, his hair was a mess, his chin and cheeks were growing a stiff bristle. She thought a homeless person had invaded Scott's office. In a barely audible grunt, he assured her that was not the case. "It's okay, Rebecca. I've been here all night."

"There's a Mr. Weinberg to see you."

"Do I know a Weinberg?"

"From the Securities and Exchange Commission. Says he needs to talk to you about the Carleton case. He got your name from Benito Vincente at the New York Field Office."

Scott combed his greasy hair with his fingers, and yawned. "Thanks, Rebecca. I need a coffee first. Tell him I'll be there in five minutes."

"I'll put him in Conference Room #6," she said, then mumbled something about the plight of homeless people as she walked back towards Reception.

Scott picked up his notepad and thought, *That's just what I need right now - the SEC!*

The sun was up. The birds were chirping. Another day was starting, and Scott Forrester felt like he hadn't really finished the last one. As he walked down the corridor to Conference Room #6, he tucked in the tail of his shirt and rolled down his sleeves.

The visitor stood up when Scott entered the room. He was clearly not pleased about the delay.

"Are you Forrester?" he asked, in a curt, professorial tone, as if he were scolding Scott for being late to class. Jacob Weinberg looked over his round, wire-rimmed glasses - the kind a tailor in a 1950's B movie might wear – and wondered what the hell the cold October wind had just blown in.

"Hope you haven't been waiting too long, Mr. Weinberg."

Jacob Weinberg was at least sixty-five, maybe seventy years old, about five-foot-seven inches tall, and all of a hundred and twenty-five pounds, soaking wet. He had a weak receding chin line and snow-white, scraggly hair, which was long at the sides and wispy on top. He looked like a Harvard academic - moth-eaten tweed jacket, yellowing white shirt, faded paisley bowtie – and had the attitude to match.

Speaking in a pronounced Boston accent, Weinberg stumbled over his words as if he were tripping down a step, "Your boss – Griffith? Thomas... Thomas Griffith?"

"It's Titus Griffin, Mr. Weinberg."

"He told me you were his man." Weinberg was not impressed with Scott's disheveled state. "Guess you'll have to do."

"I'll do... for *what*?" Scott asked.

"Said you would give me support."

"Support? For *what*?"

"Good God, man! Don't you know?" Weinberg shook his head. "Matthew Carleton's been murdered!"

"I had no idea." *What did this old fart want?* Scott was in no mood for this. Whatever it was.

"Well, Griffin said you did. He said you had some idea. So is he lying?"

"Mr. Weinberg... the FBI has been investigating the murder of Matthew Carleton for two weeks now."

"Well, you'd better get in touch with them. Get up to speed!"

"How exactly can I help you, Mr. Weinberg?"

"Not too quick on the uptake, are you, Forrester? Information. Information that would help with my investigation. I'm not wasting my time, am I? That's why I'm here... information."

"You *are* at the FBI, Mr. Weinberg. But usually, we're the ones that ask for information."

"Of course. Oh, yes. You FBI people think... you think... you're the only ones interested in Carleton? Well I'm here to tell you, you *aren't* the only ones."

An overstuffed pull-along briefcase lay at Weinberg's feet. He struggled to hoist it onto the conference table. The old geezer extracted an armload of brown folders, nearly spilling Scott's foul-tasting vending machine coffee. The first folder on the pile was titled: 'The Structure and Organization of Carleton Securities'.

"I'm briefing Treasury at ten, Forrester. Two years. We've been at this for two years. Treasury. The IRS. I work for the Securities and Exchange Commission you know."

"Yes, I know."

"Uncovered some of it. But not all of it."

"Uncovered some of what?"

Weinberg looked down his glasses again at Scott, then pointed to the papers, "Built a pretty tricky web. Very intricate, you see. Very tricky. Matthew Carleton's companies."

"If you don't mind me asking, Mr. Weinberg, what exactly do you do at the SEC?"

"Do?" Weinberg snickered. "You haven't guessed?"

Scott shrugged.

"I'm a forensic accountant, Forrester."

An accountant?

"Oh. Yes," Scott mumbled. "The Yellow Brick Road. How could I have forgotten Griffin's Yellow Brick Road?"

"Say again, Forrester? Not many brick roads in the Caribbean. I've seen a few. Mainly on Bermuda. Some on Barbados. British you see. They like cobbled streets. Reminds them of London. But this…" He pointed to the pile of folders. "I would say this… is more like a brick wall."

"Follow the Yellow Brick Road…" Scott muttered.

"You're not taking me too seriously, are you, Forrester?"

"Sorry. It's something Titus Griffin mentioned in one of his hissy fits."

"Well, he seems more together than you are, Forrester. Maybe I should be talking directly… directly to him?"

"No. That won't be necessary." This geezer might look old and act odd, but he was better qualified to go off on a tangent than Griffin was. Titus Griffin diving into details he didn't understand was the last thing Scott wanted right now. "I'm the guy you should be working with."

"Well then, Forrester… better pay attention!" Weinberg opened the file 'The Structure and Organization of Carleton Securities', stopping at a diagram that looked like an organization chart, but instead of people's names it had company names. Underneath each company name was a percentage. Double-facing arrows connected the text boxes to each other. "Criss-crossing sources of cash flow," Weinberg explained. "Interlocking equity ownership. Very complex. From an accounting point of view. You wouldn't… wouldn't understand, Forrester."

The matrix of corporate relationships looked like an intricate snakes and ladders game. Weinberg thumbed to another chart, "And here's where the trail ends. The Bahamas… the Cayman Islands… Belize. The banking industry's black… black holes, Forrester."

More pages turned as Weinberg continued, "Yes, Matthew Carleton was an exceptionally gifted scoundrel. A master at manipulating international banking laws. There are only a few inter-governmental agreements between the United States and these Caribbean countries, Forrester. And he knew what these treaties covered, inside and out. He avoided legal pitfalls like a ballroom dancer in a minefield." Weinberg flashed quickly through the rest of the report's charts and accounting statements. "So you understand what was happening, Forrester?"

Scott glanced superficially at the boring charts and numbers, and capitulated. *I think I prefer Indian philosophy,* he thought. "Enlighten me, Mr. Weinberg."

The old man scowled. "Offshore corporations. Property trusts. Investment syndicates. Company A partly owned by Offshore Trust B. Trust B then cross-charged Partnership C, and so on. Almost impossible to follow where the money went. Tax evasion, for sure, Forrester. Solid case for securities fraud. Treasury's looking at money laundering. Pretty… pretty sophisticated corporate accounting. There's plenty of dead-ends. But you can't fully appreciate these dead-ends, can you Forrester?"

"I can appreciate murder, Mr. Weinberg. That's about as big a dead-end as it gets."

"It's… it's such a pity."

"That Carleton's dead?"

"We were that close, Forrester…" Weinberg said, putting his hands in the air, and jerking them downwards. "That close… to pulling down Carleton's shorts!"

Based on what Scott had seen floating naked and face down in a bathtub of wine, he was pretty sure Jacob Weinberg and the SEC would prefer to see Matthew Carleton fully dressed. "Can I have a copy of those documents, Mr. Weinberg?"

"And what would someone like *you* do with them? *You* don't look like you could understand the back of a cereal box, let alone a balance sheet! Do you know... know what unrecorded goodwill is? Lower-of-cost-or-market portfolio valuation? Common stock subscriptions receivable? Or how they apply to my investigation?"

"Of course, I don't, Mr. Weinberg. You're the expert."

"No, Mr. Forrester, I didn't think you would. You'd have to be a Certified Public Accountant with twenty-five years experience in... in analyzing financial statements, securities registrations, to know about Carleton's deferred tax assets, his use of valuation allowances. Or how... how he manipulated accounting principles to... to the payment of inter-company royalties. That's important in this case, Mr. Forrester! Vitally important!"

"I'm sure it is, Mr. Weinberg. And I'm also sure the FBI and the SEC can come to some working arrangement on this. In the meantime, could I ask for a Reader's Digest version? I can assure you, it would be a great help."

Weinberg looked insulted. *"Reader's Digest?* You want Reader's Digest? You did go to university, didn't you, Forrester? You do have a university degree?"

"Two actually. University of Virginia."

"Not accounting, I hope."

"No. Criminology. But the summary would not be for me, Mr. Weinberg. It's for my boss, Titus Griffin. You see..." Scott leaned over and whispered, "He's not too quick on the uptake. I think he got his qualifications by mail order."

"Ah... I see." Weinberg looked satisfied with the explanation. "I know the type."

The briefcase produced a thinner version of Weinberg's report titled, 'Executive Summary - The Securities and Exchange Commission Investigation into Carleton Securities and Related Companies'.

"I think this is what you want."

"It's perfect, Mr. Weinberg."

"Then turn to page 17, Forrester. Appendix C."

Scott flipped to the end of the twenty-page report.

"If the FBI wants to help us, Forrester… this is where you can help. If you find any connection between the companies listed on this page and Matthew Carleton or Carleton Securities, or any of the other Carleton corporate entities that are detailed in my report, please contact me at this number…" Weinberg took out his business card. "If I'm not in, talk to one of my staff."

Scott quickly scanned the Appendix. Most of the company names were unfamiliar to him. Except one… The Portland Group, the sponsor of the exhibition at the Freer Gallery.

Weinberg bundled the files back into the pullalong. "Must be going, Forrester. Treasury at ten, you see. Good day."

And with that, Jacob Weinberg, his investigation in tow, scurried out of the conference room as if he were late for his next class.

Chapter Sixteen

"It's a madhouse out there. Traffic's terrible. And can you believe this weather?" It was 1:00PM. Trish shook the water off her umbrella and shivered. "I didn't know the Indian Embassy was so hard to get to."

A pool of water formed underneath her trench coat almost as soon as she hung it up. "You haven't heard a word I've said, have you? What are you reading now?"

"I made a fresh pot of coffee," Scott replied, immersed in Weinberg's report. "I heard you… it's raining in Washington. Tell me something I don't know. Like the weather in Chicago."

"Chicago?" Trish poured a coffee. "Why Chicago?"

"I booked an FBI jet to take us to Chicago."

"You did *what*? *Why*?"

"It's all in here."

Scott flung the SEC's report on Trish's desk, then recounted his quirky visit from Jacob Weinberg, including the SEC's dead-end Caribbean treasure hunt.

"This guy, Dominic Sant'Angello, is in a world of hurt with the SEC. And Sant'Angello's company, Sigma Venture Capital, has close business ties with Carleton Securities."

Trish picked up the SEC's report and glanced through it. "Does Vincente know about this, Scott?"

"Of course he does. But Vincente has been letting the SEC take the lead. I talked to him about it an hour ago. Vincente was impressed with the way we handled Lexi Carleton. Thinks we should interview Dominic Sant'Angello before he sends in his regular storm troopers."

"When?"

"Tomorrow. We leave at 8:00AM. By the way, where have you been all morning?"

"Suffering in the pouring rain while you've been sitting on your butt, cozy and dry."

"Don't be ungrateful. You're starting to sound like Griffin."

"When you talked to Vincente, did he tell you?"

"Tell me what?"

"That our suspect's on the move."

"Lexi Carleton? Where to?"

"She's coming here. Washington. The day after tomorrow. Private jet. Her own. It's not rented, like ours."

"What's she going to do in Washington?"

Trish threw a brochure into Scott's lap. It was for a charity auction at the Freer Gallery. "The worthy cause is Mother Teresa's Relief Fund for the poor of Mumbai."

"You said something about the Indian Embassy?"

"That's what I've been trying to tell you, Scott. That's where I've been all morning. There's a private reception for the Indian Ambassador before the charity auction starts and Lexi Carleton is invited. It's a big ass event. Tents in the courtyard. Champagne. Lots of big names. Congressmen. Senators. Supreme Court Justices. The diplomatic community. American businesses with ventures in India. So why do you think our little Lexi is going to a reception given by the Indian Embassy?"

"To fulfill one of her late husband's prior commitments?"

"Not even close." Trish's face was like a cat that had caught a very big mouse. "The Indian Ambassador, Sudhir Narayan. He's very suave. Very rich. And a very eligible bachelor. With a habit of kissing and telling. He's been bragging about bedding a certain socialite. Someone we know. Someone who lives in East Hampton."

"How on Earth do you find this shit out, Trish?"

"Female intuition."

"Give me a break."

"When I was in New York City, I had my hair styled at the same salon where Lexi Carleton is a regular. So if you know how to ask the right questions, the rest is easy."

"Lexi Carleton and the Indian Ambassador?"

"Sometimes, Scott, you have to get your feet a little wet if you want to get anywhere."

"Guess I'm going to have to buy an umbrella after all."

Chapter Seventeen

"Is there a point to that question, Agent Forrester?" Adam Wainwright asked, as Dominic Sant'Angello sat glum-faced behind his polished mahogany desk, his muscular weight shifting nervously in the high-back leather chair. Wainwright whispered instructions in his client's ear. Sant'Angello shot back a look that could kill: a mixture of bottled-up hostility and child-like impatience – 'fix this, damn it!'

"You've been very clear from the beginning of this interview, Mr. Wainwright," Scott said. "There will be no discussion of stock trading, venture capital, company finances and the like. Yes, your client has a right to remain silent. And I understand why. But since this virtually eliminates everything he does by his own admission fifteen hours a day, six days a week, it doesn't leave me with much, does it?"

"Everything about my client's business relationships with Matthew Carleton is in the affidavits we have made to the regulatory authorities." Wainwright replied. "In our depositions to the SEC. To the American Stock Exchange. To the IRS. It's all a matter of public record."

"This is a murder inquiry, Mr. Wainwright," Scott said, inspecting the bookshelves laden with photographs and memorabilia at the back of Sant'Angello's office. There was plenty for Scott to soak up, even if Dominic Sant'Angello didn't say another word. "Perhaps, you would prefer to reconvene Mr. Sant'Angello's interview at our Chicago Field Office? And since we need to be back in Washington tomorrow morning, we'd be happy to spend all night playing this verbal ping-pong with you, if you want. So what do you think, Mr. Wainwright? The Field Office? Or here?"

The sun was beginning to set over Lake Michigan. It was already getting late. Adam Wainwright sat down and ran his fingers through his hair. The FBI had held serve on this one. "Ask away, Agent Forrester."

"Trish, it seems Mr. Wainwright doesn't appreciate my approach," Scott replied, intensifying his examination of Dominic Sant'Angello's gallery of memorabilia. "So let's move on with a different line of questioning."

Trish Van Cleyburn looked at her notes and asked, "How often did you visit Matthew Carleton at his home in The Hamptons, Mr. Sant'Angello?"

Dominic Sant'Angello had been warned repeatedly to answer only what was asked and leave out his usual embellishments. He said simply, "Four. Maybe five times."

"So I take it you know your way around Carleton's estate? The grounds? The Executive Wing? His office?"

"It's a big place. Like a fucking fortress." So much for keeping out the embellishments. "Sure, I knew my way around. I knew where his office was. That's where we did business."

"And Matthew Carleton was a pretty aggressive businessman, wasn't he? And looking at you, I'd say you were a pretty aggressive guy too. So, how did you two get along?"

"I can do business with just about anybody, Ms. Van Cleyburn," Sant'Angello said, his eyes wandering over to the curves of Trish's crossed legs. "I mean look at my lawyer." Adam Wainwright knew what his client was about to say. He was used to it by now. "He might be a wimp. But he's a damn fine lawyer – the best that money can buy. That's why I do business with him. That's how business works. I make money. He makes money. We all win."

Sant'Angello continued staring at Trish's sleek, toned anatomy. *He views women as a source of sexual entertainment,* Trish thought. *No problem.* Trish knew how to turn that in her favor. "I just thought maybe you and Carleton, you know, had something going on together... not about money but, uh..."

Sant'Angello nearly exploded, "Do I look...? You gotta be kidding! Me and Carleton? No way! This was strictly business. It was about *money*. Are you saying I was his lover?"

"Four or five visits? Are you sure it was only about money? If it was, then just exactly how much money was involved?"

"You little bitch, we made a ton of..."

Adam Wainwright sprung out of his chair, "Don't answer that, Dominic! I've told them... you don't have to answer any questions about your business dealings with Matthew Carleton." He turned to Scott. "Agent Forrester... you said this was a murder inquiry. Well... it continues to be an inquisition over matters we've already addressed, and do not wish to make further comment on. I'm going to advise my client, once again, not to answer that question."

"No problem," Scott said, his back turned, a framed photo under his eager gaze. "So, let's explore something a little different. Here's a question I think you can handle without violating any rules. Do you like wine, Mr. Sant'Angello?"

Sant'Angello looked puzzled. "What? What kind of trick question is that? I'm Italian. What do you think?"

"Any preferences? White? Red?"

"I said... I'm Italian."

"So you like red wine." Scott put the picture down and moved over to the smoked glass window and its panoramic vista of Chicago at night. "Do you know how much a bottle of 1961 Chateau Latour costs?"

Sant'Angello's face screwed into a tight frown. "How the hell would I know?"

"I just assumed a man of your means would enjoy the finer things in life."

"I'm not the kinda guy to splash out my hard-earned money on expensive bottles of wine. Those kinda guys are just grabbing their crotch and showing off. After you've drunk too much wine, who can tell the difference? So why waste the money? I can think of better uses for it."

Scott made firm eye contact. "Yeah. I agree with you, Mr. Sant'Angello. Expensive wine *is* a waste of money. It's money down the drain… don't you think?"

Trish looked up from her notes.

Sant'Angello was sweating.

"You seem to be a well traveled guy, Mr. Sant'Angello. And for someone who doesn't have any preferences in wine, you have quite an eye for art." The top of Sant'Angello's credenza at the end of the office was adorned with sculptures – Oaxacan folk art from Mexico, ebony carvings from Africa, Inuit soapstone.

Scott walked over and picked up a teakwood statue that had caught his eye from the minute the two FBI agents had entered the room. "So let's change the subject. Can you tell me what this is, Mr. Sant'Angello?" He held the statue up.

"An elephant."

"The head is. The body is a man's. Do you know where it's from and his name?"

"It's from India."

"Ganesh, son of Shiva. A Hindu god," Scott said.

Sant'Angello's face was as rigid as a stone.

"Have you been to India, Mr. Sant'Angello?"

"Yes."

"And the reason?"

"Business."

"Business. That's all?"

"Look out the window, Mr. Forrester. We're on the eighty-seventh floor of the Hancock Building in Chicago! I'm a dealmaker. This office makes deals. Big deals. And I like to get in on deals before everyone else does. So I was in India. On *business*. Outsourcing. Call centers. Scrap metal. Container ships."

Wainwright stiffened. "Dominic!"

"Don't worry, counselor," Scott said, hoisting up the statue of Ganesh, the Elephant-God. "I'm more interested in this. How did you acquire this, Mr. Sant'Angello?"

"The guy that represented me there... he showed me around, we traveled all over, dirt poor places... he gave it to me. It was just a souvenir."

"And how many times did you return to India?"

"A couple. But nothing was doing back then. Too many restrictions on foreign investments. Regulations. Bureaucratic bullshit. That kind of thing. But that was then. And things have changed. A lot. So sue me... I missed some great opportunities."

"Do you still travel to India?"

"I'd love to go back to India. But I can't."

"You can't? Why not?"

"With all this SEC shit flying around my head? What do you think? How would it look, screwing off to India?"

"Did you go to India with Matthew Carleton?"

Sant'Angello squirmed.

Wainwright looked over. This time it was Wainwright's look that could kill. *Keep it simple, Dominic.*

"No," he finally said.

Scott picked up one of the cherry-framed photographs that sat between the sculptures. The picture was of Dominic Sant'Angello, early to mid-twenties, wearing a deep blue uniform and snazzy white cap. The Marines.

"How old are you, Mr. Sant'Angello?"

"Forty-two."

"You still work out?"

"Sure. Play some squash, racquetball. When I have time."

"Racquetball? Gets your adrenaline flowing, doesn't it? Good way to work out your aggression, don't you think? Did you play racquetball with Matthew Carleton, Mr. Sant'Angello?"

Wainwright was ready to pull the plug again. "And your point Mr. Forrester…?"

"Whoa, counselor… since when was a question about racquetball connected to the world of high finance?"

"I'm going to advise my client-"

"Wainwright-" Sant'Angello barked, moving his hand across his lips as if to say *zip it!* "I told you I've got nothing to hide. I'm going to answer his stupid questions… okay?"

Wainwright leaned over the desk. "I'm not a criminal lawyer, Dominic. But I'd advise you to get one. I have a lawyer friend I can recommend-"

Sant'Angello jumped out of his seat and buried his nose in Wainwright's face. "Screw you, Wainwright! I told you… and I'll tell them… I didn't kill Matthew Carleton!"

Wainwright backed off, hands up. This conversation was getting *way too hot*. He pointed at Scott and Trish whose demeanor had never changed from that of two small town librarians on a day trip to the big city. "This is the FBI, Dominic. Go ahead. Let them mess with you. You don't want to take my advice? It's your funeral!"

Trish inched up her skirt and cooed, "We never said you *murdered* anyone, Mr. Sant'Angello. Did we, Scott?"

"No. Not at all. I was just talking about racquetball."

Adam Wainwright hissed under his breath, "They're screwing with you, Dominic."

Sant'Angello sat back down, and rocked back and forth in his chair. They had nothing on him. He would play their game. "What was the question? Yeah, yeah… racquetball. And Carleton. Yeah, I beat him. Twice. Badly."

"Did you enjoy it?" Scott asked, as Wainwright winced again.

"Everyone who knew Matthew Carleton enjoyed beating him," Sant'Angello said. "Because it's something people rarely got the chance to do."

"Because he was always better at doing deals?"

"Because he was a *flaming asshole,* Mr. Forrester... and he needed someone to teach him a lesson every now and again!"

"And did *you* teach him that lesson, Mr. Sant'Angello?"

Wainwright squirmed. "Dominic, please don't-"

Sant'Angello shrugged him off. "I didn't kill the asshole, Mr. Forrester, if that's what you're asking. Okay, okay. Yes, I admit, there were plenty of times when I *wanted to*. He was a giant prick. You know what I mean? Ask anybody."

"I'm asking *you*."

"It's not in my nature."

"It's not in your *nature*?" Scott whistled back.

"No. It's not. Look at me. I'm just a loudmouthed Italian Catholic. With three fat kids. And a wife whose pasta is to die for. I don't go around killing people. That's not what I do."

"Well..." Scott said, as he signaled Trish to come over to the bookcase. "Not any more. Right, Mr. Sant'Angello?"

Trish arrived with pad in hand. But it wasn't her exquisite note taking abilities that Scott wanted. He nodded towards several framed citations on the wall behind the credenza, then leaned into her ear and whispered.

Trish looked surprised, "Are you sure?"

Scott's face said, 'Yes. Definitely.'

Trish Van Cleyburn returned to her chair and retrieved her cell phone from her Coach bag. "Is there somewhere I can make a call? In private?"

Sant'Angello pushed his chair forward and pressed the intercom. "Maria?"

"Yes, Mr. Sant'Angello?"

"One of the FBI agents wants to make a call. She can use Sue Lee's office. By the way, where is Sue Lee?"

"She's off sick today, Mr. Sant'Angello."

"Sick? She's never sick."

Maria Carvelli appeared a moment later at the doorway. "Well, she is today, Mr. Sant'Angello."

Trish followed Maria Carvelli, "This could take a while, Scott. We may not be able to... uh..." As she paused and thought about her excuse, she noticed that Sant'Angello and Wainwright were glued to her every syllable. "We... may not be able to change your flight reservations. But... I'll try."

Sant'Angello sank back into his chair. "Maria, can you get us some fresh coffee?"

"Sure."

Sant'Angello reached into a file drawer and pulled out a bottle of Amaretto. He wiggled the bottle at Scott. "I promised my wife my workday would end at 6:00. So... it's ended."

"Go right ahead. It's your office."

Maria arrived with a tray of mugs and a carafe, placed them on the back credenza and left. Sant'Angello tipped some amaretto into a mug then asked, "Are you sure you don't want any? My fag lawyer doesn't drink... just Perrier."

Scott declined. Instead, he opened the closet where his leather jacket had been hanging, and retrieved his phone. Then he walked back to the memorabilia on the wall. To a V-shaped red crest mounted on a wooden plaque, with an inscription in gold lettering below it. "Fortune Favors the Brave, Mr. Sant'Angello?"

Sant'Angello shrugged. "What are you talking about now?"

"You've forgotten your regimental motto? Fortes Fortuna Juvat... Fortune Favors the Brave."

Scott tapped on the smartphone's screen and searched the Internet. The search returned the answer he was looking for. The crest also bore a large, gold-colored number '3' with a vertical sword running through it. "2nd Battalion, 3rd Marines." He pointed to the citations. "It says you served with distinction - Bosnia, the Persian Gulf, Iraq. Honorable discharge. Letters of commendation for action under fire. Purple Heart. Very impressive, Mr. Sant'Angello. You must be very proud."

"My war's over."

"Is it?" Scott picked up a picture from the bookcase. It was a group shot. In the desert. "And how long were you in the Marines, Mr. Sant'Angello?"

"Seven years."

The photo was taken from a distance. There were about fifteen men in desert camouflage packed tightly together, covered in dust. Everyone was wearing sunglasses and soft boonie hats. Some of them had cigars. They were grinning, having a good time.

Scott scrutinized the picture. It was hard to pick out individual faces. But Sant'Angello's massive frame was front and center. "Operation Iraqi Freedom?"

"We kicked ass. Big time."

"You sure did. Still kicking ass?"

"You mean my business? Tactics are about the same. It's just the weapons that are different."

"Speaking of weapons, Master Gunnery Sergeant Sant'Angello..." Scott said, reading the results of another search from his smartphone, as it directed Scott to the US Marines website. "The citation says you were in MSPF. Says here that MSPF stands for 'Maritime Special Purpose Force'. That's the Marines' version of Special Ops, right? And what kind of 'kick-ass' action did you see in Iraq, Mr. Sant'Angello?"

"Force Recon."

"And it says here... airborne/seaborne rapid assault?"

"The best kind."

Scott kept reading. "Recon behind enemy lines? Enemy strength assessment and surveillance? Maritime interdiction?"

Sant'Angello acknowledged, "Yes. So?"

Scott browsed the picture gallery on the wall. "Did any of those missions involve, you know… assaulting ships and oil platforms? That kind of thing? You know… like knights scaling the walls of a fuckin' fortress?"

Wainwright cringed. With every word, Dominic Sant'Angello was digging his foxhole deeper. Then filling it with his own shit.

The exchange didn't faze Sant'Angello. He just kept on digging. "Yeah, sure. We trained for all of that. But in Iraqi Freedom, we were land-based the whole time. Didn't matter. We saw plenty of action. We took the first rounds of Iraqi artillery fire as US forces crossed over. That picture? That's my Force Recon platoon, the day after we took Baghdad International Airport. Great bunch o' guys."

"Of course," Scott said, picking up another photo of four soldiers – two men and two women, still in fatigues, this time all cleaned up, with big, bright smiles. Sant'Angello had a tight grip on one of the girls. She had dark hair, similar tan fatigues. All of them wore sunglasses. The background was still desert sand. Scott held the photo up. "Who's this pretty lady you're with?"

"My sister. Gina."

"Your sister was in the Marines with you?"

"No. Air Force."

"Pilot?"

"Ground support. Air base defense."

"Wow. A girl who likes to play with big boys' toys? And you're from a big family, Mr. Sant'Angello? Any other brothers or sisters in the military?"

"No. Just me and Gina. She was the youngest of all of us. Brilliant girl. With a great future. She never told me why she enlisted. She joined out of college… just before I finished my last tour."

Sant'Angello's voice suddenly choked, his eyes tearing and his face sinking to his chest, "I came back from Iraq. But…"

Adam Wainwright put a hand on his client's shoulder. "Agent Forrester… Mr. Sant'Angello's sister is an MIA. Afghanistan. Did you ever lose anyone in action, Agent Forrester?"

"Yeah. My father. He was a Marine as well, Mr. Sant'Angello. So I know what it's like to-" Scott paused.

Sant'Angello grabbed the bottle of amaretto, let it glug into his mug and took a big swig. *Genuine sorrow? Or an act?* Scott couldn't decide.

"I remember going through my father's papers with my brother," Scott said. "His war record, his photos… like you have here. We were way too young to understand when he died in the Lebanon barracks bombing."

Trish returned, stiff-lipped. "It's all set, Scott. But everyone… and I mean *everyone*… is pissed."

"Pissed about changing a flight?"

"No, Mr. Wainwright," Scott said. "Pissed about finding a judge this late at night."

"A judge? A *judge!*"

"To authorize the search warrant on Mr. Sant'Angello's home."

Sant'Angello jumped out of his chair and banged the desk with his fist, "*You slimeball!* You don't care about my sister. You've just been stalling to get a search warrant!" Sant'Angello rounded the desk, about to add 'assault with intent to maim' to his long list of hole-digging consequences.

Wainwright stepped in front of him. "On what grounds?" Wainwright asked, restraining his client. "What probable cause?"

"Probable cause, counselor? It's right there… right in front of you, counselor." Scott pointed to the photographs on the wall. "And I'd like to take these back to the Field Office. You'll get them back once they're scanned into our records."

Scott looked Dominic Sant'Angello in the eyes, and in his best librarian voice said, "We began this interview by reminding you of your Miranda rights. And you've been very co-operative, Mr. Sant'Angello. But I'm going to remind you again… that anything you say, can and will be used against you in a court of law."

"*You son-of-a…*"

"I'm sorry to inform your client, Mr. Wainwright, but it's unavoidable. Mr. Sant'Angello will have to accompany us to the Field Office to make a formal statement and answer further questions. We'd like to know your client's whereabouts on specific dates over the past six months. Take fingerprints. DNA samples. That kind of thing. With his permission of course."

"On what grounds? On what *evidence!*" Sant'Angello yelled.

Scott wasn't about to concede his serve. "Your job in the Marines was a pretty important one, wasn't it, Mr. Sant'Angello?"

"I was just another Marine."

"I mean a really, *really* important job," Scott repeated.

"In war, Forrester, they're *all* important."

"One shot, one kill, Mr. Sant'Angello? That's another motto in the Marines, isn't it? But a special motto. A motto few Marines can claim as their own unless they've gone through the same training you've taken and passed with a commendation. The one that's hanging right here on your wall. Perhaps you'd like to enlighten counsel, Master Gunnery Sergeant Dominic Sant'Angello… just exactly *what* was the important job you did in the Marines for seven years?"

Adam Wainwright looked anxious. His face said, 'What had his client withheld from him?'

Sant'Angello sat down on the edge of the desk and put his head in his hands.

"Well, Dominic?" Wainwright asked.

Sant'Angello had willingly fallen into the FBI's trap. A trap he'd then filled with his own shit. Scanned or not.

Sant'Angello removed his hands from his face.

His eyes were glossy and red.

He turned to Wainwright.

"I was a sniper, Adam. And a damn good one."

Chapter Eighteen

The room at the end of the long, cold corridor was a road that led nowhere. There was no evidence that Dominic Sant'Angello possessed a high velocity sniper rifle, either now or in the past. The search warrant executed on Sant'Angello's home had yielded nothing. Scott Forrester had returned from Chicago with little more than a damning military record and a well-developed tension headache.

FBI Case #479, National Center for the Analysis of Violent Crime, Quantico, Virginia.

Columns of unhappy photographs. A wall of visual misery. A grim, unsettling display that was a serial killer's photo-essay on evil. A case that had become the criminal investigator's equivalent of a "Where's Waldo?" picture puzzle.

Scott Forrester's prime suspects had psychological traits consistent with any number of previous serial killer profiles. Lexi Carleton was narcissistic and egocentric, a cold dominatrix. Dominic Sant'Angello was an unexploded grenade waiting for its pin to be pulled. And they were both manipulative, in their own special ways.

But take any sampling of corporate CEOs, slice into any corner of the high-energy entrepreneurial pie, and it would yield a group of narcissistic, egocentric manipulators. Some research even claimed that psychopaths made great CEOs. After all, keeping emotion out of business was Lesson #1 in Success 101.

But it didn't follow that every boardroom was chaired by a potential serial killer. Without a clear motive and without incriminating forensic evidence, the FBI's psychological assessments of Lexi Carleton and

Dominic Sant'Angello were just speculative mumbo jumbo. On their own, they proved nothing.

A vital signpost on the road was missing.

Familiar footsteps came down the hall.

The door opened.

Trish Van Cleyburn entered with a bundle of plastic-sheathed clothing that she hung on the coat stand. "I picked up your tux."

"Thanks," Scott said without looking around, focusing instead on the photographs that retraced the last moments of Victim #1, Liang Wong's life.

Sonoma, California. It was a bright, warm day in late April. Liang Wong, the brilliant, hyperactive founder of Silicon Pathways was an avid balloonist. The conclusions in the coroner's report were medical jargon for an all-too-obvious cause of death. His hot air balloon - its gas cylinder emptied after hours of aimless flight – had floated down to earth and deposited Mr. Wong's dangling body in front of a frightened busload of tourists on a wine-tasting trip to Napa Valley. Liang Wong had been strangled by a noose fashioned from the balloon's guy rope, and his body - hanging below the vivid orange balloon with the Silicon Pathways logo – had descended from the bare Northern California sky like a gift from Hell.

This was the first murder to display the killer's distinctive signature: the sharp vertical incision in the victim's left earlobe. There was also the Sanskrit message written in the resulting blood. A message that had been posted on paper inside the balloon's basket. Scott Forrester now knew what the message said: 'I am the energy of Her divine anger'.

Scott glanced at the whiteboard covered in notes.

'Signature: extracts blood.'

'Ritual message: religious significance.'

The next column of photos on the cork wall: boldly striped cigar boats and spanking white fishing yachts. Row upon row of multi-million dollar floating castles flying the colors of offshore havens like Bermuda and the

British Virgin Islands, their decks laden with preppy crews and scantily clad sun worshippers.

The murder of DeAndre Antoin. Victim #2. In broad daylight. In the marina next to the Miami Heat's stadium in downtown Miami.

It was May. The Miami Heat were on the verge of elimination at home in the NBA playoffs. Boomport.com, one of the Internet's hottest download sites, was a premier venue for new rap music. And DeAndre Antoin, the former used car salesman from New Orleans who'd parlayed a mediocre rap career into a multi-million dollar Internet enterprise, was hosting Miami's rap royalty on the hippest nugget of floating bling on the Eastern Seaboard: the 'Candy Cane', his tricked-out 106-foot Lazzara motor yacht.

The party had been in full swing. DeAndre Antoin was charming his bootiliscious entourage with endless bottles of Cristal champagne. The party had ended when a sniper's 7.62mm round passed through one side of his head and out the other. The assassin had timed his shot to perfection. The Miami Heat game had just finished. Exiting fans were emerging from the stadium and the marina's boardwalk was full to overflowing. By the time the bullet entered DeAndre Antoin's temple, there were thousands of people milling around. Job done, the killer had melted into the panicking crowd.

Miami PD had combed through hours of closed circuit TV records looking for that one 'someone' who seemed totally disinterested in either the result of the basketball game or the aftermath of a precision execution. They'd found no one. A message was discovered the next day on DeAndre Antoin's desk in his office in downtown Miami.

'I am the energy of Her divine anger', it said.

How the hell had he accessed the crime scene after the bullet had found its mark, Scott thought, *to sample DeAndre Antoin's blood?*

The whiteboard screamed out: 'Extraordinary access to his victims – before and after the crime'.

Late September.

The foothills of the Grand Tetons.

Deuce Meredith and his Indian guide, Charlie 'Silver Moon' McNabb.

Ballistics had concluded the same military-issued SR-25 sniper rifle that had killed DeAndre Antoin in Miami had also been used to dispatch Meredith and McNabb in Wyoming. An SR-25 could hit a target up to one thousand yards away. With a noise suppressor mounted on its end, the rifle's muzzle blast would have been negligible.

Perfect for the crowded Miami marina. But why use a noise suppressor in the lonely wilderness of Wyoming, where the nearest human being was more than twenty miles away? Who did the killer think would hear?

A photo showed Charlie 'Silver' Moon's mangled head. It was a quick, sudden, instantaneous death - one moment alive, the next, somewhere else.

Was he meant to die quickly? Scott pondered.

The answer could only be: *Yes.*

Deuce Meredith's face. Frozen in terror. His life ending in mid-scream.

Was he meant to feel helpless when he died? Had the killer enjoyed the suffering that unfolded as the wounded Meredith was mauled to death by the enraged grizzly they'd been hunting?

Again, the answer could only be: *Yes.*

Charlie 'Silver' Moon was in the wrong place at the wrong time. Deuce Meredith was not. Their murders combined preparation with skill; selective targeting with sadistic pleasure.

The notes on the whiteboard: 'M.O.: precise targets. Deliberately planned. Special Ops background. Gratification from victim's suffering'.

And the most recent victim? Victim #5.

The whale.

The bull with the lightning bolt.

Struck down behind his Great Wall of security, the best that money could buy.

Matthew Carleton.

The mock French chateau, buried in East Hampton's woods.

Motion-sensing alarms on a high perimeter wall? Defeated.

Security cameras? Evaded.

The reports from the New York Forensic Investigations Lab, hanging from the wall in neat plastic sheaths.

A photo from the surveillance camera at the gate.

This was the frustrating part. *An elusive presence that left no trace of his movements and no forensic evidence. And an exit from Carleton's Estate crafted like the brushstrokes of a Great Master - driving Carleton's vintage Mercedes Gullwing past unsuspecting security guards, disguised as his victim.*

Scott wrestled with a conundrum: Matthew's wife, Lexi Carleton had no alibi.

Was she the assassin? Careless arrogance?

He thought, *No. It didn't fit the profile of the carefully executed plan.*

Was she the paymaster? His accomplice? he asked himself, annoyed that the obvious might be staring him in the face. *Why had she forfeited her ironclad alibi by not staying in Chicago? Had there been a change of plan? Was she needed in Long Island? To lure her husband back to the chateau where the killer lay in wait?*

Then there was the issue of the wine. Over one thousand empty bottles. It had taken at least forty-five seconds to uncork a single bottle of wine. But that was 'tak time' – the time they had tested when Trish clicked the stopwatch and said, "Go!". Not time as it was, that night in the bathroom, inside the frantic heat of Matthew Carleton's torture. In the rage of a blood-soaked bath, crawling with hate and revenge.

One thousand bottles? Forty-five seconds each? A total 'tak time' in excess of twelve hours?

No one - *absolutely no one* - could transport over one thousand bottles from Matthew Carleton's wine cellar to the bathroom, then uncork them and empty them, in a continuous sequence of forty-five second actions, for twelve hours straight. No one. *Absolutely no one.*

At least not alone.

The killer must have had an accomplice and time, Scott had concluded. *They both had time to savor the moment, to explore their victim's fear. They wanted Matthew Carleton to experience every second as if it would be his last. Twelve hours of last seconds. And it likely had taken a whole lot longer than twelve hours.*

Two days, Scott had concluded.

That was the time between Matthew Carleton's arrival from Westchester until the time he was 'seen' leaving in his Mercedes sports car.

Two days.

Two days of watching Matthew Carleton's expressions as he suffered in the drowning pool. Two days. His accounts accessed. The wine emptied. And then the final ritual – extracting Carleton's blood to paint the rose-colored marble with evil.

Scott looked at the photo of Carleton's naked body, floating face down in a bath of red wine. *Can I feel this killer's satisfaction?*

The whiteboard screamed again in vain.

'Superior knowledge of security systems'.

'Evidence of teamwork'.

'An accomplice'.

'Confident in the plan'.

'Ensures dwell time with the victim'.

'His messages are integral to the result'.

Scott Forrester wasn't sure why he had felt so compelled to add one final solitary word to the whiteboard's list. A word that had been popping in and out of his mind at every bend in this tortuous winding road. It just *seemed* to fit. And for some strange reason, it didn't want to be left out of the puzzle.

The last word he had written was: 'Karma'.

Trish filled her coffee mug. She noticed the recently added word. "Karma?" She asked.

"We've been looking for the obvious, Trish. For the rational. That's not how a sociopath thinks. He's living within a set of rules about right and wrong that he's created for himself. Not the rules that society prescribes. But he's not a maniac. And he's very much in control."

"Sounds like the definition of a hit man to me."

"You and Griffin are not going to give up on that, are you?" Scott said, as he picked up a copy of Webster's Dictionary and handed it to Trish. It was opened to a page with a word highlighted in yellow. "Read this definition."

"Karma?"

"Read it. And think way beyond a hit man."

"Okay. Whatever you say."

"Karma…" she said, as she read from the dictionary, "The totality of a person's actions in any one of the successive states of that person's existence. Thought of as determining the fate of the next stage."

Trish pointed to the photo-essay of a killer's manic rampage hanging on the wall, and asked, "So? What's karma got to do with all *this*?"

"Karma is one of the central tenets of the Hindu religion," Scott replied. "His religion. His deeply ingrained belief system. The well from which he draws his rules of right and wrong."

"*This*…" Trish said, pointing to Liang Wong's corpse, "Isn't Hinduism, Scott."

"He believes it is. I think karma is the link, Trish. The link between *what* he is, and *who* he is. His belief in karma. Its relationship with the Demon-Goddess he worships. The belief system that empowers him. That drives him to kill on her behalf."

"You've lost me, Scott."

Scott pointed to the note on the whiteboard: 'His messages are integral to the result'.

"In his mind Trish, he's living perfectly within the set of rules he's created for himself. Beliefs about right and wrong. Beliefs that *are* orderly. In fact, *beyond* orderly. Perhaps in his mind, they are *ordained*."

"Scott, you're still losing me. Ordained?"

"By Dvaipa. A faith, however misguided, that helps him rationalize everything. A faith that allows him to become detached from his victims and from his actions. A faith that transforms him. He wants to *become* Her divine energy. He wants to *be* the instrument of Her anger."

Scott flipped the dictionary's pages. "Now read this…"

Trish took the book and read the next highlighted definition, "Reincarnation: the Hindu doctrine that the soul reappears after death in another bodily form."

Scott paced the room, "Dr. Chandra said that Hindus believe everyone's destiny is written by their thoughts, words and deeds, in this life, and in those they have lived before."

"Yeah. Okay. That's reincarnation. So?"

"So… reincarnation - the endless cycle of creation, preservation and destruction. All devout Hindus believe that people are reborn. So if that aspect of Hinduism belongs in his set of rules, he must also believe in reincarnation."

"And how exactly does that connect each murder with another?"

"The Hindu law of cause and effect. Through… karma."

"Oh, thank you, Scott. Of course! I see it clearly now. You haven't been buying illegal incense, have you? What trip are you on?"

"No trip. Those that are faithful and deserving are given, by divine intervention, a life better than the one they left behind. Don't you remember Dr. Chandra saying that?"

"Yeah. And I also remember him showing me the ugliest devil-bitch I'd ever set my eyes on. It makes me cringe just thinking about that painting."

"Good. That's exactly the feeling he wants to create. That's exactly the feeling he wants his victims to feel. *That...* that very feeling... is the energy of *Her* divine anger."

"I'm trying to feel it, Scott. Honestly, I am. But I'm not so sure."

"What if the killer believes he can alter his victims' karma at the time of their death?"

"Say again?"

"What if he believes he can send them, not to a better life, but an infinitely worse one?"

"A *worse* one?"

"The messages he writes in their blood. What if they're not intended for *our* eyes, but for *someone else's*?"

"Someone's else's? Who?"

"Someone not of this world."

"I'm sorry, Scott. But I'm totally not connecting with this."

To be sure, it was a concept that even Scott had struggled to put together. Like other occult doctrines, it challenged his Judeo-Christian belief system. But it wasn't inside *his* mind where the answers would be found. It was inside the killer's.

"A lot of the religions of ancient times had similar threads," he explained. "Do you remember the story from Greek mythology of a coin for the ferryman?"

"Scott... if it wasn't in the Bible, they didn't teach it in the Dutch Reform Church."

"Sorry, Trish, I forgot. Well, the Greeks believed that when you died, you took a ride across the river Styx to the underworld where a god named Hades took care of your soul. Before you departed this world and entered the next, you had to pay a ferryman to ensure safe passage across the river to the afterlife. The Greeks cremated their dead with a coin placed over their eyes. A coin to pay the ferryman."

"And how do you get from Ancient Greece to India... with *that*?"

"Paying the ferryman is an analogy, Trish. It represents the cost of passage from one life to the next. It symbolizes how much you have to pay from your earthly experience to redeem yourself in the next world. Every religion has an equivalent of the ferryman. They are guides that lead the dead into the afterlife. Christianity calls them angels."

Scott walked over to the cork wall, a wall full of photographs of death. "Put yourself in the shoes of a devil-worshipper. Can you see the pattern on this wall, Trish?"

Trish shook her head, "No. That's the problem. I can't."

Scott pointed to each victim in turn. "Liang Wong - the balloonist." The next one. "DeAndre Antoin - the party animal." The next. "Deuce Meredith - the hunter." And the most recent. "Matthew Carleton - the wine connoisseur."

His eyes glowed with conviction. "What did they have in common? Find it… and you'll find the killer's motive."

"They were all rich?"

"That's what they had in common, in *life*. What did they have in common, in the *manner* of their deaths?"

"I have no idea where the hell you're going with this, Scott."

"Yes, *Hell* is where I'm going with this. Their wealth provided them with a lifetime of indulgence and excess. Represented by how they spent their money. Somewhere along the way, our killer was wronged. What if this wealth was acquired in a manner that he believed was derived at his expense?"

Trish looked across the column of photographs, "It would explain his hatred and rage."

"Absolutely. And it also says this killer is not just an emotionless, paid assassin, detached from his victims. Because he *knows* these victims. Because they weren't strangers to him. He knew intimate details of their lives. Details that helped him plan their executions. The way they died was very important to him. Because at the moment that he transformed life into death, he was controlling their karma."

"Controlling their karma?" Trish asked, resuming her puzzled look. "How exactly do you *control* someone's karma?"

"In his deviate view of the world, Trish… he wants them to pay back what they owed him. Spiritually. How does he believe he can do that? By delivering them to a place where they will be reincarnated into a life of misery. How does he intend to guarantee that? By altering their karma at the time of their death. His ferry-*man* is not a *man* at all. It's a She-Devil. It's a Demon-Goddess. It's Dvaipa."

Trish took a deep breath, "Scott, I don't know about this new theory of yours. It sounds kind of… well, strange?"

"It *is* strange. I'll admit it. It isn't revenge, as our normal minds perceive it to be. But look around you…" Scott waved his arms at the columns of grisly photos. "*Feel* what he feels. Feel Liang Wong… desperate… pleading… his eyes crying for mercy as the balloon lifts him into the air one final time. Can you *feel* the anguish as he looks down at his estate retreating underneath his feet, as the air is choked from his lungs?"

"Liang Wong's murder was almost surely a hit man."

"It can't be a hit, Trish. This killer wanted *control*."

Scott then pointed to the photographs of a marina full of bobbing super yachts. "DeAndre Antoin. He was never more in his element than when he was hitting on beautiful women. When he was the center of attention. The killer wanted Antoin to attend his own funeral. So what happened to DeAndre Antoin? What happened to his karma, the instant his head exploded in front of his adoring fans?"

"Oh, Jesus, Scott. You've gotta be kidding. That's a stretch."

"It is? Think about Wyoming. He didn't *kill* Deuce Meredith with a silenced bullet. He only wounded him. *Why?* Why did he just wound him, when he so precisely killed Charlie 'Silver' Moon? *Why?* So he could transform the exhilaration of the hunt into Meredith's worst fears."

"Scott..."

"Charlie McNabb was disposed of, Trish. He was erased quickly – an innocent person unconnected to the killer's life, in the wrong place at the wrong time. Coldly dispatched. Eliminated. But Deuce Meredith? No. Meredith was the target. Devoured by a grizzly bear while he was still very much alive."

"Karma?"

"Yes, karma. And then there's Matthew Carleton. Every ounce of wine was delivered with an equal measure of venom. A taste of death in every forced sip. And when the rest of the wine was glugged into the tub, the killer ratcheted up Carleton's pain. He was forced to swallow his own success. And then choke on it."

"And that's *controlling* karma?"

"He wants to watch his victims begin their journey into Hell. He manifests Dvaipa's 'Revenge Incarnate'. He channels the energy of *Her* divine anger and becomes the instrument of *Her* vengeance. The Tiger's Paw."

Scott walked over to the whiteboard. He picked up a red marker and completed the whiteboard. "This case now has a name..."

Four simple words.

Written in bold red letters.

'The Tiger Paw Killer'.

To Scott Forrester, the unknown now had a label.

More importantly, it had a motive.

Chapter Nineteen

The streetlights sent rivers of shimmering gold across the wet surface of Jefferson Drive. The line of limousines snaking their way around the corner of 12th Street blocked the taxicab's progress as it pulled up short of the Freer Gallery. She instructed the driver to stop. As she stepped out, a sudden penetrating gust blew the brightly colored fabric of her sari - a body length dress of embroidered yellow chiffon - against her petite figure. The fluttering ribbon of cloth began to unravel. She straightened it, then leaned through the window of the cab and gave the patient driver a generous tip.

On the corner of Jefferson and 12th, Pradesh Bhandari, hunched over in the bitter cold, handed out leaflets to any passers-by willing to accept them. Few acknowledged his presence. Had she stopped to take one; had she understood that Bhandari's plight was not so far removed from hers; had she moved out of the shadows into the light, then perhaps fate would have been kinder to her.

Instead, she hurried past, rejecting the papers he offered; ignoring his emotionally charged pleas; snubbing the warnings she would desperately need if this madness was going to end.

She dismissed the shivering Bhandari without a second thought, tucking the pale orange headscarf around her cheeks to hide the quiver of her cold lips and the desperation in her eyes.

Outside the Freer Gallery, guests of the Indian Ambassador, huddling under umbrellas in the drizzle, scurried up the steps into the gallery's warmth. A TV interviewer blabbered in the background. A photographer pulled a candidate aside for his camera. But she floated by all of them unnoticed - a faceless shroud absorbed in the rush, clasping two envelopes tightly in her hand against the thieving wind. One contained her invitation. The other, her hopes and fears.

Inside the gallery, she worked her way through the crowd, overlooked by the high society ladies bedecked in Dior and Prada and their important men in Armani. And also by Scott Forrester, who patrolled the entrance waiting for the Ambassador's special guest to arrive.

The woman in the yellow sari had come to the Freer Gallery, forlorn and alone. But she was not without company on her journey. Her ignorance followed closely behind.

• • •

Scott Forrester tapped the earpiece on his com set. "Trish... do you copy?" Distant thunder preannounced the electrical storm that was heading their way. He moved towards the Freer's glass-fronted entrance. The static cleared. "Is this better?"

In the Freer's open-air central courtyard, lavishly decorated marquees had replicated the hospitality of a maharajah's grand palace. The tents' fine fabrics, adorned with exquisite Indian motifs - parades of gilded elephants, gently curving temples, orange-and-black striped tigers - shimmered under a brooding night sky.

Trish Van Cleyburn, wearing a provocative black dress with a plunging neckline, her com set secreted in her clutch purse, sauntered into the Ambassador's Champagne Reception. "Copy. I hear you, Scott. I'm entering the tent now."

A waiter offered Trish a glass of champagne from a silver tray. She took it and moved through the twitter of the crowd, approaching a group in conversation with the patron of the evening, His Excellency the Indian Ambassador, Sudhir Narayan.

Tonight was all about India. Its regal past. Its promising future. Ambassador Sudhir Narayan embodied both. He stood apart from his guests, shunning a tuxedo and white shirt for a sumptuous tunic of gold and red with a pearlescent brocade and a Nehru collar; loose flowing pants; jeweled sandals.

A small group of influential socialites clustered around him like a pack of hungry wolves. A Senator's wife was inquiring about his love of Native American art and the Ambassador's interpretation of its spiritual symbolism when Narayan's attention was diverted by a lone figure in black, holding a champagne glass. He glanced over unconsciously, to the annoyance of the Senator's wife, then handed his glass to an aide and excused himself in mid-sentence.

The spell that bound him to the circle of mindless chatter had been broken. He approached the stunning young woman in the slinky black dress. Trish was caught between leaving and staying. There was nowhere else for her to go.

Sudhir Narayan was movie star handsome: melted chocolate eyes; soft perfect skin, with only the hint of a shadow on his cheeks; satin black hair; and gently rolling eyebrows. Thirty-eight years old, Oxford and Princeton educated - an instant hit within Washington's diplomatic and social circles - and very rich, Narayan was every woman's dream of a tall, dark, romantic stranger.

"My name is Sudhir Narayan," the Ambassador said, as he clasped Trish's hand and brought it up to his lips. With a soft kiss and the look of a king, he added, "A star with jewels for eyes and gold for hair is but a beggar for my attention. I would not be tempted to exchange its radiance for yours. May I ask what name this vision may be called?"

"Tricia... Tricia Van Cleyburn."

He glanced down and noticed the absence of a ring on her left hand. "It would be an honor if you could join me, Miss Van Cleyburn, at my table for dinner. It would seem that several of my guests have been prevented from sharing this evening due to the inclement weather." Flights into Washington were being canceled by the thunderheads forming around the airport.

"That is most kind, Your Excellency," Trish replied.

The prospect of dinner with the Ambassador intrigued her. But there was no doubt Lexi Carleton would recognize Special Agent Tricia Van Cleyburn from their interview on Long Island. It wasn't practical to accept the Ambassador's invitation. It was better that Trish observe them from a distance. "Your offer is very attractive, Ambassador Narayan, but regretfully I must decline."

He gasped. "How can that be?"

"I would not like to be called out suddenly and disrupt your evening." Trish reached into her purse and pulled out an ID badge from George Washington University Hospital and a pager. The pretence of being a doctor was an often-used cover. It allowed her to leave someone's company without the need for any more explanation than an urgent call from the hospital.

"Such a pity, Dr. Van Cleyburn. Perhaps another time?"

"Yes, perhaps."

A peacock swished back and forth in a rose-bordered enclosure outside the marquee. Its iridescent feathers of royal blue and forest green were spread out like a fan. It released a sad call into the night air.

"You see, Dr. Van Cleyburn," Ambassador Narayan said. "Even the peacock laments such a loss."

He was a charmer. *But what would Narayan have said if he knew that Tricia Van Cleyburn was an FBI agent sent to spy on him?* she thought.

As she sipped her champagne on the fringes of the Ambassador's entourage - watching him work his magic on others - she wondered, *Would he still be this charming?*

• • •

In Washington, the media could be as rabid as any media in the world - hungry for a juicy story, a hot personality.

When Lexi Carleton's limousine finally arrived, they were not going to be disappointed. Lexi Carleton sparkled from head to toe. The silver beadwork of her white satin Chanel dress and the 50-carats of Harry

Winston diamonds around her neck and wrist were energized by the paparrazzi's synthetic lightning. She turned her radiance on command, milking every angle for the cameras; the grieving widow had ditched her sulking, marginally cooperative East Hampton attitude for an infectiously photogenic smile.

Scott had learned the minute he had first met Lexi Carleton that she didn't do anything without a good reason. Tonight, that reason was about consuming the limelight, about establishing her agenda, about power. Tonight, Lexi Carleton was going through a living reincarnation. With her husband's body laid to rest, she was Eva Peron arriving in Washington to declare her candidacy for Queen.

Scott spoke into his com set, "She's entering the gallery, Trish. And has quite a group with her - press aides, security."

"Narayan's moving too, Scott. He's just been told of her arrival. His people are leaving the marquee."

Lexi Carleton made her way through the Freer's glass-fronted lobby. As Narayan's party headed towards the dining room, Lexi Carleton and her followers seamlessly joined them.

Will you look at that, Scott thought. *Wasn't that a well-choreographed maneuver?*

As the two groups merged, it was clear in the way that Ambassador Narayan kissed her tenderly on the cheek, and the way Lexi Carleton accepted his arm, they were a royal couple - an Indian maharajah in his red and gold tunic, his Caucasian heiress in flowing silver and sparkling diamonds. The evening was an engineered spectacle. They were ready to be crowned by the assembled minions.

As the group passed by him, Scott moved under an archway. Suddenly, a woman in a yellow sari darted out from behind a display case. She ran towards the Ambassador. His bodyguards reacted, reaching inside their jackets and drawing their weapons.

The woman fell to her knees in front of Ambassador Narayan, clasping her palms together and bowing her head. Her face was hidden by a scarf.

The procession abruptly stopped.

Ambassador Narayan signaled his bodyguards to back off. She presented no threat.

The woman removed the orange headscarf and pulled an envelope from her sash. Scott strained to see her face. She had black hair tied back in a ponytail; in the middle of her forehead was a red bindi, the Hindu holy dot. Everything about her appearance said she was an East Indian woman - the sari, the bindi, the heavy makeup above and below her eyelids. But her skin was not the caramel color of the sub-continent. It was sallow and pale, like an Oriental.

She held the envelope out for Narayan, and dipped her face to the ground. "Lord Narayan… please, I ask for your forgiveness."

Narayan seemed to recognize her. So did Lexi Carleton. He opened the envelope. "My forgiveness?" There was silence as he read the single page it contained.

Several bodyguards ventured down the hall. There were no other threats lurking in the shadows.

"What is this?" he said. "This *blasphemy*? There is no way back for you! You must know that!"

The woman raised her head. She was crying. "Please, Lord Narayan!" Her makeup ran down her cheeks. "I beg you! Please… please… release me!"

Ambassador Narayan tore the letter up and flung it in the woman's face. Shreds of paper scattered around her. "Release you?" Narayan said, as he motioned the group to move forward. "How dare you ask for my forgiveness! Your weakness disgusts me! Your weakness betrays *Her* trust!"

The woman doubled over - holding her stomach in pain - and sobbed uncontrollably. Her shaking arms reached out to retrieve the ripped note. She bundled the tiny fragments of paper to her chest as if somehow they could heal her suffering heart. A bodyguard picked her up like a feather and moved her brusquely out of the way. She fell against the granite wall; her slight frame meeting its hard surface with a thud. She collapsed in tears.

Ambassador Narayan's high society groupies stepped by her, proceeding to dinner as if nothing significant had happened. At one point, it looked like a few of them would shed their indifference and help her. But in the end, a stranger's display of mental illness was less important than their place in line. The incident was a trivial nuisance in an otherwise perfect evening. The group moved on, leaving the woman in the yellow sari curled in a fetal position on the Gallery's cold marble floor.

Security guards carefully worked their way through the remnants of Narayan's procession. They were followed by members of the event staff, recognizable by the neatly typed nametags pinned to their jackets and dresses.

Scott Forrester crossed the hall and flashed his badge. The cordon of security guards opened up. Hovering over the sobbing woman was a pretty brunette in a black velvet cocktail dress. She was giving instructions into a walkie-talkie with a lilting French accent, "It's alright, Henri. We're dealing with it." Her nametag read, 'Christienne Duval, Le Roux-Berg Switzerland'.

"Ms. Duval, I'm Special Agent Scott Forrester, FBI."

The brunette looked up. "Monsieur Forrester, there is no need for your help. The situation is unfortunate, but it is over. The Ambassador was not harmed. He will not be pressing charges."

"Do you know this woman, Ms. Duval?"

"No. I've never seen her before."

"I would like to ask her some questions. Is there somewhere quiet we can take her?"

"I'm just a hostess with the Ambassador's Reception, monsieur. You will have to ask the Gallery's Security."

Trish Van Cleyburn nudged past the guards. "What's going on, Scott?"

"Narayan's got some explaining to do."

The security guards lifted the woman up. The woman was in a world of her own, barely aware of the people around her.

Scott approached her. "Are you all right, ma'am? Are you hurt?" She shook her head, no. "This is my partner, Special Agent Tricia Van Cleyburn. I'm Special Agent Scott Forrester. We're from the FBI. We'd like to talk to you."

When Scott mentioned the FBI, she grew alarmed. "The FBI?"

The woman staggered into the light. Scott looked into her face. She wasn't East Indian. She was either Chinese or Japanese. "The FBI?" The woman repeated, disoriented. "No. No!" Her eyes widened. A sudden fear chased away her shyness. "You… you're not with the FBI. You're with the Temple!"

"The temple?"

"I know who you really are! And what you really want to do with me!" The woman was small and wiry. But strong. She released herself from the security guards' grip and began to backpedal away from them. "You're not from the FBI! You're Narayan's assassins! You're going to kill me, aren't you!"

Trish produced her FBI badge. "Ma'am, please. Calm down."

"Get away from me!" The woman pulled her scarf over her head and started to skip down the hall. "That's not real! They can make anything look real! You're not FBI! I know who you are!" She shed her sandals and ran down a side hall. She seemed to know exactly where she was going.

"Wait!" Scott called out. He and Trish took chase. "We're not going to harm you!"

The woman picked up speed and burst through an emergency exit. It set off the alarm.

Outside on 12th Street, the traffic had eased. The limousines were now parked shoulder to shoulder in front of the Gallery. A traffic cop watched over them, shuffling his feet under a plastic raincoat. It was quiet. A few cabs cruised by. The woman raced past the policeman in an orange and yellow blur. She was fast and agile, the pumping of her legs unrestrained by her loose fitting clothing.

Scott almost closed the gap between them. A taxi screeched to a halt in front of him with its horn blaring. He stumbled onto the taxi's hood with a thump.

The woman hailed a cab going in the opposite direction. Trish caught up with her, reached from behind and put her hand on the woman's shoulder. "Ma'am, please. Please believe us. We really are from the FBI. We really are. We're not going to hurt you. We just want to ask-"

The woman turned and slugged Trish in the face. It was a rapidly executed martial arts move and Trish didn't see it coming. There was no doubt about it. It was an expertly delivered blow, meant to disable. Trish fell backwards. Scott was on his feet in time to catch her.

The cab with the woman sped off. Through its wet rear window, Scott could see the woman's face. She had a look of anguish, an expression of guilt and lingering regret, as if she hoped they were FBI and wanted to talk, but couldn't summon the courage to defeat her fears. The cab turned onto Jefferson Drive and accelerated away. The woman in the yellow sari was gone.

Scott hauled Trish to her feet. Her nose was bleeding. "Are you all right? That was a pretty vicious hit."

"Nothing's broken... I think."

Trish wobbled forward, then her legs gave out. She turned pale and her eyes rolled in their sockets. Scott could see that Trish was struggling to maintain consciousness. "We need to get you to a doctor."

Trish fainted. He carried her back in his arms into the Gallery. The emergency alarm had brought the Gallery's security to the exit. "Call an ambulance!" Scott said. "She may have a concussion."

In the commotion, no one noticed a man in a trench coat carrying a satchel of leaflets, slip by them through the opened emergency doors. Pradesh Bhandari – an outcast, turned away from the Ambassador's Reception because he had no invitation – praised Ganesh for his good fortune. He had prayed to find a way in. And now that his prayers had been answered - he was determined to make the most of the opportunity.

Chapter Twenty

The hallway was bare; its speckled white marble floor a mute witness to a mysterious woman's anguished pleas. The shreds of paper that contained her secret had disappeared from its surface. Either Gallery staff had cleaned them up, or Narayan's bodyguards had returned to do the job for them. Either way, Scott's search was in vain.

A young girl in a white blouse, black skirt, carrying a stack of dishes, pushed through the service door on one side of the Dining Room.

"Where can I find Christienne Duval?" Scott asked.

The girl jumped back, surprised by the stranger in the corridor. "Quelle personne, monsieur?"

"Christienne Duval? She's with Le Roux-Berg Switzerland."

"Christienne Duval? Je ne sais pas, monsieur."

The Ambassador's Dinner was nearing its end.

The double doors to the Dining Room swung apart. A member of the Gallery's Staff buzzed through in a hurry and propped them open. The evening's final event – the Charity Auction - was about to start in the Freer Gallery's adjacent Great Hall.

Scott tried again. "Do you know a Christienne Duval? She works for the sponsor, Le Roux-Berg? Do you know where I might find her?"

The woman huffed. She was busy. *Who was this guy?* The dinner was running late. She didn't have time for his silliness. As she marched towards the kitchen, she glanced over his shoulder, "If you're looking for Christienne Duval, you don't have to go very far, monsieur. Just look around."

Scott turned.

Ms. Duval was standing behind him, a supple silhouette in black velvet, leaning casually against a white marble column, smiling at his impatience. Candles from the Dining Room sent a flickering golden glow through the opened doorway. Her back was arched, like a cat rubbing up against a favorite chair. "So, you have found your fugitive, Mr. Forrester," she purred, holding her hands out, fists clenched, as if ready to be handcuffed. "Here I am... I'm too tired to resist arrest."

Christienne Duval straightened and stepped into the soft light of the candles, her features refined and sensual – long, nut-brown hair cascading gently across her cheeks, down her bare shoulders; her face, a precocious blend of school girl charm and starlet chic; with expansive hazelnut eyes, deliciously curved lips, and eyelashes that played her expressions like a flute.

"I won't take too much of your time, Ms. Duval. I just have a few questions."

"Bien sûr. Of course you do, Monsieur Forrester of the FBI. And why not? A stranger confronts the Indian Ambassador with some peculiar accusations. Then runs amok in the Gallery. Comment épouvantable! How dreadful! C'est un acte de terrorisme, n'est-ce pas?" She giggled and rolled her eyes. "I'm sorry, Mr. Forrester. It's been a very long day."

The waitress returned from her duties in the kitchen carrying a tray of coconut cream profiteroles with chocolate sauce. "Parait bon!" Christienne Duval exclaimed, sniffing the air. "J'adore le chocolat! Can I interest you in dessert, Mr. Forrester? Some profiteroles and coffee? Perhaps that might tempt me to answer your questions."

"That sounds perfect."

"D'accord. I think I can find a table for two. Follow me."

Christienne Duval led Scott into the Dining Room.

Sitting regally at the head table, Ambassador Sudhir Narayan and the merry widow, Lexi Carleton, engrossed in conversation, held court over Washington's movers and shakers. With Trish taken to hospital and their surveillance plan in shambles, Scott welcomed the opportunity to salvage what he could.

Just before they reached an empty table at the back of the room, a diminutive Indian man, wearing a curious floral bow tie, waved a napkin in the air as if he was a tour guide and they had strayed off the prescribed path. "Mr. Forrester! Over here!"

It was Dr. Rajeev Chandra.

Scott acknowledged him, but by doing so put his private tête-à-tête with Ms. Duval in jeopardy, "Dr. Chandra. It's good to see you."

"Please, Mr. Forrester. Come and sit with us. May I introduce my wife… Jasmine?" Mrs. Chandra bowed with her palms flat together, the traditional Indian greeting. She was much younger than her husband, perhaps in her late forties, and slightly taller.

"Aren't you going to introduce us to your companion, Mr. Forrester?" asked Dr. Chandra. "Where have you been hiding her all night?"

"Behind a marble column," Christienne Duval said, smiling coyly as she shook their hands. Dr. and Mrs. Chandra looked puzzled.

"It's an inside joke," Scott added with a shrug.

Mrs. Chandra read Christienne Duval's nametag. "Oh… Le Roux-Berg?" Ms. Duval's association with the evening's sponsor impressed her.

"Oui. I am one of your hosts, Christienne Duval. We are so glad you could come and support this event, Doctor and Mrs. Chandra. We have so many here from the hospital tonight."

"I'm not a medical doctor, Ms. Duval. I'm a psychologist. A criminal psychologist."

Christienne turned to Scott and gasped, "Oh, Monsieur Forrester! You didn't tell me. First handcuffs. And now this! A criminal psychologist? So I must be in big trouble!" Christienne said, smiling.

The Chandras looked even more puzzled.

Scott tried an explanation, "Ms. Duval is helping me with an inquiry."

As enigmatic as Dr. Chandra could be, his wife Jasmine was the exact opposite: a delightfully engaging, gregarious lady. In a singsong voice, as if she were telling a child her favorite Indian nursery rhyme, Mrs. Chandra teased, "We have a saying in India, Mr. Forrester, about men and women... a man and a woman are like two wings of the same bird. How can a man be complete without a woman, since it is not possible for a bird to fly on only one wing? You are making *inquiries*, Mr. Forrester? Is that what they call 'dating' these days?"

Christienne Duval put her hand over her mouth to muffle her giggling. "C'est si drôle! It's so funny!" She played along with Mrs. Chandra. "Scott dear? S'il vous plaît... sit, chéri."

Scott's 'inquiries' appeared to be shelved for the time being.

Mrs. Chandra beamed with delight as the pretty Christienne Duval sat down beside her. In a room full of sour socialites and aristocratic politicians, Dr. Chandra's wife was enjoying the chance to meet someone new, someone with her sense of youth and energy. "How long have you two known each other, Ms. Duval?"

Christienne giggled again. "Let me think. Hmm?" She turned to Scott. "Chéri, how long has it been?"

What the hell? Scott thought. *He'd play along.* "Five minutes?"

"En tout, chéri? I'd say more like ten."

"That depends on how long you were following me down the corridor."

"Touché!"

Dr. Chandra ordered some more coffee. The doctor and his wife were in a jolly mood; it had been an excellent dinner and now with an enchanting couple at their table, it was an excellent *après diner*. "Ms. Duval, I must commend The Portland Group for its sponsorship of this fine Exhibition. Such a wonderful display. It is a joy for the spirit. With The Portland Group's help and generosity, the Indian Embassy has treated us to a welcome taste of our homeland."

"I will make sure Mr. Portland knows how much you both appreciate his support of the arts, Dr. Chandra." Christienne replied.

"Excuse me," Scott said. "But I must have lived the last decade under a rock. Who is The Portland Group?"

"Mr. Forrester…" Mrs. Chandra dropped her coffee cup into her saucer; the fine china chinking as porcelain met porcelain. "You don't know who Michael Wayne Portland is? Or The Portland Group?" He shook his head. "The Portland Group owns Le Roux-Berg Switzerland, the most exclusive fine art and jewelry dealer in the world. Only someone of Michael Wayne Portland's stature and influence could have convinced the Indian government to surrender India's most prized artifacts for this Exhibition."

"I apologize for my ignorance, Mrs. Chandra. Black tie affairs are not my usual hang out on a Friday night."

Christienne Duval looked into Scott's eyes. "What *do* you do on Friday nights, Mr. Forrester?"

She slipped something under his hand. Scott glanced down. It was a business card that read, "Christienne Duval. Spécialiste. La Bijouterie Washington. Le Roux-Berg Switzerland. Sur Rendez-vous Seulement. By appointment only." There was no address or telephone number on the card. Apparently, if you wanted an appointment with Le Roux-Berg you already knew how to do it. He flipped the card over. A phone number was written on the back.

He looked up at Christienne Duval, her eyes asking questions. But before Scott could answer them, a man hurried past, flinging papers from his tatty satchel around the dining room, as quickly as he could. A leaflet flew in front of Christienne's face, surprising her. Scott recognized the man. Loose fitting jacket. Old green scarf. Woolen gloves cut out at the fingers. He was the man who had been standing outside the Gallery making some kind of protest.

"Be warned!" the man shouted at the startled guests.

Scott picked up one of the leaflets. It read, 'A scourge has entered America! Protect your sons and daughters from the evil that is the Temple of Dvaipa!'

Dr. Chandra's face changed from enjoyment to embarrassment. "Pradesh!" he called out. "Pradesh! Not here! This is not the way to do this!"

Bhandari yelled towards the head table. "Tell them why you're letting this happen, Ambassador Narayan! Tell them why you're not working to stop this! Tell America! They must know!"

Security guards converged on him from both sides of the room. His outburst had also triggered Narayan's heavies. They moved to cut off the exits. As the man dodged his pursuers, tables heaved and cups and dishes spilled onto the floor. An Embassy bodyguard drew his gun. A woman screamed. An elderly gentleman in a tux tussled with the scruffy Bhandari, getting in between the weapon and its intended victim. The bodyguard lowered his gun to check his shot. It was getting ugly. Someone was going to get in the way of a bullet.

Pradesh Bhandari was undaunted, eluding his pursuers, yelling and pointing at Narayan, "I see the future of futures. It is cold and it is dark! She is Mother Evil! And you are its Father!"

Ambassador Narayan stood ramrod straight, unflinching, his anger boiling to the surface. An aide tugged his tunic. It was time to go. But Narayan wasn't yielding.

Gallery Security finally corralled the man.

Pradesh Bhandari glared at the Ambassador, "You are an *ardha*-Hindu, Narayan! You preach against the teachings of Krishna! What about *dharma*? What about a*himsa*? Have you forgotten their meaning?"

"Dr. Chandra, what is he saying?" Scott asked.

"He called Narayan an *ardha*-Hindu – a half-Hindu. It's a derogatory term. He questions Narayan's life of duty, his *dharma*; and his obligation to *ahimsa*, the non-violent way."

"You know this man, don't you, Dr. Chandra?"

"Yes. I do."

Bhandari was dragged through the tables, screaming, froth emerging from the corners of his lips. He spat out the words, "You and your Temple will not succeed, Narayan! Goddess Durga will fight your demon hordes!"

In the corner of his eye, Scott saw the glint of a metal blade flash below the waist of one of Narayan's bodyguards. A shot was too public. A shaft of steel could be sunk in without a sound. Scott jumped from his seat to intervene, pushing aside the people in front of him.

Bhandari continued to resist the security guards and broke free. In a rage, he ranted, "I call upon the Avatars of Lord Vishnu to fight her! I call upon Shri Rama... to bend his bow and strike her down with his arrows! I call upon Narasingh... and Vaghadera the Tiger God... to lay their teeth upon the Demon Queen... and tear her apart! True believers, Narayan, await Kalki and the new creation! Not your lies! It will come with a sword and a comet to destroy her! And when she dies, your impurities, Narayan - will no longer be a stain on this Earth!"

The bodyguard saw his opportunity and lunged. Scott threw himself forward, and grabbed the man's wrist. They tumbled onto a table. Scott pinned him, and with his other hand at the man's throat, applied pressure to the jugular vein. As the flow of blood was cut to the brain, the bodyguard fainted, his grip relaxed, and the knife fell to the floor.

Gallery Security came to Scott's aid and subdued the attacker.

Scott dusted himself off and looked towards the head table. Lexi Carleton was long gone and Ambassador Narayan was leaving. Just as the Ambassador was about to disappear through a side entrance, he turned. His eyes bristled with anger as he stared straight at Scott.

The message was clear – 'Don't *ever* get in my way again!"

Chapter Twenty-One

Pradesh Bhandari had been whisked away by Capital Police. The Dining Room was a deserted shambles. The Charity Auction had been cancelled, the Ambassador and Lexi Carleton leaving before the police had arrived. Christienne Duval, Dr. & Mrs. Chandra, and several hundred distraught glitterati had escaped in a procession of limousines and taxis amidst the swirling blue lights of an armada of police cars and the excited flashes of photographers' cameras.

Scott sat exhausted.

The party was definitely over.

His prisoner, a brutish Indian thug with a fat face and a bristly beard was hog-tied with plastic cuffs, sitting alone, emotionless; his shirt bloodied, buttons torn, jacket ripped. It had taken a lot of strength, and more than a few techniques he'd learned at the Academy, for Scott to wrestle the larger man into submission.

Scott knew the drill. He would wait to accompany his suspect to the police station to make a statement. Assault with a deadly weapon. Possibly attempted murder. The difference was just a legal technicality. The intent was the same. It would be the prosecutor's call.

At one end of the Dining Room, two plain-clothes detectives were questioning several guests who had fared the worst in the altercation and wanted to press charges against Bhandari. One of the detectives finished his part in the interview and then walked over to Scott and the prisoner. The detective was talking into a lapel mike. From the shadows of the corridor, another man in a tuxedo appeared. Scott recognized the man from earlier in the evening. He was one of Ambassador Narayan's aides.

"Scott Forrester?" the detective asked. "FBI?"

"That's right."

"Agent McElvery. Secret Service. Embassy Detail."

The U.S. Secret Service was responsible for the protection of foreign embassy buildings and their staff. McElvery took a jackknife from his pocket and lifted Scott's prisoner to his feet. He turned him around and cut the plastic tie.

"What are you doing?" Scott asked. "This man tried to kill someone!"

"And you stopped him. Congratulations."

The suspect rubbed his wrists and scowled at Scott as he was taken away by Narayan's aide.

Scott was furious. "You're just going to let them leave!"

"What else am I going to do? That man..." McElvery said, pointing to the big brute with the bloody shirt, "is an attaché with the Indian Embassy."

Scott was incredulous. "You're kidding?"

"He has diplomatic immunity. The other man he's with? He's the Washington Station Chief for India's State Intelligence Service, a close ally of the White House in the war against terrorism. It's futile to press charges. Besides, no one was hurt."

"You're *not* kidding."

"It would be a lot of paperwork for nothing."

"He tried to knife someone!"

"Yeah? And where's this knife, Forrester?"

Agent McElvery was right. After the scuffle, the knife had disappeared. One of Narayan's quick-thinking heavies must have been watching his partner's back and made sure nothing incriminating was left behind. It was Scott's word against his suspect's.

Diplomatic immunity? More like a diplomatic travesty.

McElvery put his hands in his pockets and walked away. "You did your job, Forrester. Now go home."

Chapter Twenty-Two

The room was bare, with off-white concrete walls. The light from above came from a single bulb housed in a metal shade that resembled a Chinaman's hat. There was a gray table opposite him, and another hard metal chair like the one he was sitting on.

Pradesh Bhandari had been told he was in the First District Police Station, four blocks south of the Air and Space Museum on 4th Street. It was 2:00 AM and he hadn't eaten since midday. His stomach growled. The cuts on his face had scabbed over. His right cheekbone was swollen and tender, and throbbed with a dull pain. His arms ached. There were bruises on his wrists. But his pride and determination were still intact.

The door to the interrogation room opened.

He'd said all that he wanted to say to the police. They didn't understand that this fight transcended the temporal laws of man. Pradesh would take whatever punishment was due. There would be more darkness to face in the days and weeks and months to come. His meditations would see him through the darkness and back into the light. His fight had only just begun. But he was ready.

Scott Forrester sat down in the empty gray chair. He placed the file folder on the table and opened it. Inside was Bhandari's record. He'd been arrested twice before. Both times at demonstrations outside the Indian Embassy. Misdemeanor offenses. Disturbing the peace. Fines, no jail time.

Bhandari, a tall, gangly man, sat silently with his shoulders hunched. Underneath his baggy clothing, he was painfully thin. His face was a construction of skin and bone - collapsed cheeks, sunken eye sockets with a permanently dark rim of skin around them, an angled jaw line. His short, shiny black hair was thinning on top; the hair on the back of his neck and above his ears shaved close to his skin.

Scott glanced at his rap sheet. It filled in the rest of the details. Bhandari lived in Ward Four, a predominantly black, working class neighborhood within the District limits. He was a freelance photographer. He was fifty-three years old. "My name is Scott Forrester, Mr. Bhandari. I'm with the FBI." The man's dark brown eyes were glazed, as if he was in a trance. "Mr. Bhandari?"

Pradesh Bhandari stared into the light. After a moment of silence, he spoke, "If I must submit to your justice, I will do so with strength in my heart and steel in my soul. There is nothing you can do to break me. I will not bend."

"Mr. Bhandari, you're a U.S. citizen. According to your file, you've been a citizen of the United States for the past fifteen years. You must know that you have rights, Mr. Bhandari. Do you think we're going to torture you?"

"There are many ways one man can torture another. *He* tortures me from the moment I awaken each day, until I drift back to sleep at night. Nothing you can do to me could be worse."

"Who tortures you, Mr. Bhandari?"

"The Devil Queen's apprentice… Sudhir Narayan."

"The Indian Ambassador? He's Dvaipa's apprentice?"

Pradesh Bhandari jolted back in his seat. In one brief discourse, an American policeman had named the godhead of evil; the one Pradesh Bhandari vowed to devote the remainder of his life to seeking out and defeating. "How do you know about Dvaipa?" He said, his eyes widening. "Are you one of *them*?"

"Rajeev Chandra told me all about the Demon-Goddess Dvaipa. About the Tiger's Paw. But let me assure you, Mr. Bhandari, whoever *they* are, I am not one of *them*. Durga's shield is my sanctuary. When Kalki rides on his white horse against her armies, I will be a warrior in her cause."

Again Pradesh Bhandari was taken aback. "You know of Kalki, the tenth Avatar of Lord Vishnu?" he said, with a combination of surprise and hope in his voice.

Scott's ploy was working. Bhandari's attention had shifted from whatever meditative state he'd entered to the reality his adopted country's justice system was now prescribing for him.

"He will come at the end of the present eon," Scott added. "Striking evil down with his blazing sword, to bring a new Golden Age upon mankind."

Bhandari jumped to his feet, his skinny face exploding with delight, "You *are* a Hindu! And a believer!" He looked like he was going to reach over and hug Scott.

"No, Mr. Bhandari, I'm sorry to disappoint you. My interest in Hinduism is purely professional."

Bhandari sat back down.

"What do I believe? I believe you are a zealous follower of your faith, Mr. Bhandari. Perhaps a little too zealous. In America, it is your right, your freedom of religion, to believe. However Mr. Bhandari, you walked into a room full of Washington's most influential people, made accusations against the Indian government's highest-ranking diplomat, and nearly caused a riot. Why? What do you think you were going to accomplish with that?"

"You cannot commit to something you don't understand, Mr. Forrester. America must understand first. Understand what the Temple of Dvaipa is, and who her leaders are. Then the American people, and their leaders, can commit to the Temple's eradication."

"I read your leaflet. Who are Rama's Guardians of Deliverance and Redemption?"

"We are a group of true-believing Hindus. Each of us has been touched by an *asura* and seeks to undo its evil."

"An asura… a demon?"

"Yes, a demon. They walk among us."

"Is Narayan a demon?"

"He is Lord of the Demons. He is *Her* servant."

Scott could see in Bhandari's eyes the depth of his conviction. "This Temple - and Ambassador Narayan - what exactly have they done?"

"The Temple of Dvaipa recruits the weak of mind. Too often, Mr. Forrester, the weakest ones are our children. It is through our children they torture us. By taking them from us. Turning them against us. And then molding them into Dvaipa's warriors. We will fight to take them back. Then we will decapitate the serpent's head. She will never steal another child's mind!"

"You've lost a child to the Temple of Dvaipa?"

"My daughter." Bhandari began to weep, his eyes closing tightly and his mouth stretching wide as he broke into tears. "Annika!" he cried with his face to the ceiling. "Annika!"

"How old is she, Mr. Bhandari?"

"Nineteen. Only nineteen." His head fell into his hands.

Losing someone to the influence of a cult or other fanatical group was a difficult situation for law enforcement. It usually started with a missing person's investigation. But once it was known that someone voluntarily joined a cult, proving a crime was nearly impossible. People had the right to choose how they led their lives, protected by the Constitution's freedom of association. Only cases of child abduction or kidnapping under force were prosecutable. The best avenues to rescue wayward youths who had been indoctrinated into cults were victim support groups or the services of specialized consultants in cult intervention. There were plenty of both around. Cults were a booming business. Cult watchdogs estimated there were over a thousand organizations deemed 'a cult', 'occult' or 'New Age' operating in the United States.

"Can you tell me more about how your daughter got involved with the Temple of Dvaipa, Mr. Bhandari?"

"We never forced our Hindu faith on Annika, Mr. Forrester. We wanted her to grow into it, to appreciate her heritage, not be enslaved by it. Perhaps that was a mistake in hindsight. She grew up with an open-mind about other people's religions. In addition to her Hindu relatives, she had friends who were Jews, Muslims, Christians. We didn't mind. Sometimes, she attended their services. We encouraged it. But one day at home," he continued, "she became very agitated when we discussed our Hindu beliefs. She had grown up with them, but she had become argumentative. Stubborn. Obstinate. She knew better than we did. We thought this was adolescent rebellion. We didn't know that a friend from school – someone who had been dabbling in the black arts - had stumbled upon the Temple of Dvaipa and drawn Annika into their clutches."

"Where is your daughter now, Mr. Bhandari?"

"That is it, Mr. Forrester. That is the torture! We do not know! She dropped out of her first year in college, and we have not seen or heard from her since."

"And you believe Narayan belongs to the Temple of Dvaipa?"

"There are many who believe that."

"Do you have proof?"

"No."

"Mr. Bhandari, there was more than one person at the Gallery tonight that preferred you end up in a morgue, rather than jail."

"*They* will do whatever it takes."

"Here is my card. If you feel your safety is being threatened in any way, please get in touch with me."

Pradesh Bhandari took the card. It had Scott's cell phone number handwritten below his printed office number and e-mail. Bhandari looked up. "What is going to happen to me now? I can't afford bail."

Scott folded his file, got to his feet and pointed towards the door. "You're free to leave, Mr. Bhandari."

"I'm free?"

"Perhaps the Indian government and its representatives should not be so harshly judged. The Embassy will not be pressing charges after all. And it would seem - with the Ambassador's persuasion - that the others affected by your conduct at the Freer Gallery have also agreed to drop their charges."

"Narayan does not want publicity. In case it exposes the Temple and its lies to the public and the press."

"Mr. Bhandari, I'm sorry the police and the FBI can't be of more help to you. However, there is someone - a friend - who will make sure you can afford a taxi home."

Dr. Chandra had been listening to Scott's interview from behind the room's one-way glass panel. The good doctor was now waiting by the opened door of the interrogation room.

Pradesh Bhandari clasped his palms together. Again, Ganesh had answered his prayers.

"And Mr. Bhandari…"

The gaunt man glanced back at Scott.

"If it's any consolation… I believe you're right."

Chapter Twenty-Three

Monday morning 6:00AM. Breakfast and the Washington Post. Double-thick blueberry pancakes with real Canadian maple syrup. Imported, as Kelly said, just for him.

At 8:00AM, Quantico loomed in the windshield like a giant microwave welcoming the next leftover. Scott Forrester staggered back into his office, Friday night's chaos relegated to the back pages.

9:00AM. Trish Van Cleyburn called. She had a wicked bruise and a mild concussion. The prescription: a week of bed rest ordered by the FBI's Medical Office, non-negotiable. No one carrying a firearm would be allowed back on the street with double vision.

10:00AM. The 'Phone Call from Hell'.

Titus Griffin.

Like an absentee landlord collecting rent, he could always find a way to make Scott Forrester pay up. "Forrester, I want to see you before you leave." Scott thought nothing of it. That was his first mistake. His second involved a dartboard.

When Scott entered Griffin's office, he was on the phone. He sounded pissed off. Titus Griffin sounded pissed off most of the time. "Tell Morrison that I'm short staffed right now. I can't spare another agent." There was a pause. Griffin motioned Scott in, then the politeness resumed. "Screw Counter-Terrorism, John! Screw Occupy Wall Street! Psychos don't give a rat's ass about either one of them. Doesn't Morrison understand that?"

Griffin pulled three files from his inbox and lined them up as he talked, "Misfits don't wait for written invitations, John! They choke their chickens on little boys' photos. Then they choke the little boys! It's their 'Ying' and their 'Yang'. Do you yo-yos think we can just put them on the backburner like Mama's buttered beans and ham? Well, we can't. So go find some other sucker to staff your 'Surveillance Initiative'! The only airports we're likely to be in, for more than an hour, are the ones with flight delays!" Griffin clicked off his cell phone. "Isn't that right, Forrester?"

Titus Griffin's 'signature' wasn't the citations on the walls or the awards lining his bookshelf - Officer of the Year (National Association of Chiefs of Police), Public Service Award (the State of Maryland), the 2002 Federal Employee Service to America Medal. It wasn't the clean-as-a-whistle, rounded oak desk, with its minimalist inbox and outbox. Griffin's 'signature' was a dartboard opposite his desk that had given him the nickname, 'Bull's Eye'.

The term 'Bull's Eye' had become synonymous with laser-like investigative success. To do a 'Bull's Eye', Griffin-style, was FBI-speak for 'nailing a case' - from the first scrapings of blood off a tiled kitchen floor, to the final verdict in the courtroom. It meant stuffing it. The game-winning touchdown with end-zone celebration. It meant doing it the way Titus Griffin did things.

The story, now written into FBI folklore, had traveled like a surge of electrical current from the staff canteen to the bars where FBI agents hung out, and then out into the Field Offices. Griffin had thrown three darts. The first one had missed the board entirely. The next two landed - one after another - in the bull's eye. From that moment on, Griffin left the two darts stuck in the board.

He never threw any of the darts again. The darts remained in exactly the same positions they'd been thrown: one dart a complete failure, dangling on the office wall; the other two, buried deep in the winner's circle.

The darts became his mantra: no matter how badly someone missed, if you kept your game up, eventually you'd hit the bull's eye. Maybe even twice. It wasn't luck. It was skill and hard work. It was what he expected from himself. It was what he expected of those that worked for him. The objective was always to score a decisive win, not be 'close enough'. Trying didn't count. Hitting the bull's eye did.

Three files sat on the desk, lined up in a row in front of Titus Griffin. He opened the first one and pulled out a stapled three-page memo and held it up. "You know what this is, Forrester?" he asked.

"Of course I don't."

Griffin pushed it across the desk. "Then read it."

The memo's letterhead said, 'Securities and Exchange Commission'.

"It's a complaint," barked Griffin. "That you interfered with the SEC's investigation of a Dominic Sant'Angello. On top of that, Sant'Angello's lawyer, a guy named Wainwright, says you harassed his client. And what did you find with that search warrant, Forrester?"

"Nothing."

"Precisely. Nothing. You were looking for nothing… and you found it. Great!"

"We had probable cause."

"Why didn't you tell the SEC what you were up to? So they could tell you… to *back off*! Because they were going to execute their *own* search warrant! Did you know that?"

"No."

"Right answer. No… again. It screwed up their case, Forrester. Sant'Angello got wise. He circled the legal wagons. Now it will take a battering ram to get into his house!"

"Has that ever been a problem?"

Griffin ignored him. He opened the next file. It contained Scott's request to book the FBI jet to get to Chicago. "Where's the authorized signature?"

"We couldn't find you."

"There are procedures, Forrester. I don't know what the hell they are. But Rebecca does. And apparently you didn't follow them. Now I have some anal-retentive FBI auditor probing my ass. I'm in no mood to have my ass probed, Forrester. Are you?"

"No sir."

Griffin opened the third file and smiled. "I always save the best until last, Forrester."

"If you say so, sir."

"Secret Service. The *Secret fucking Service!* Could it get any better?"

"I saved a man's life."

"You did? Well, there's nothing about that in this report. What it does say is that you conducted a stake out at a diplomatic reception without informing the Secret Service."

"And their point is?"

"It says you roughed up an attaché from the Indian Embassy. Apparently that's set back foreign relations with India by about ten years!"

"That's *bullshit!* And that's not everything that happened. Let me explain-"

"Spilled milk, Agent Forrester! I could give a *rat's ass* about your spilled milk!" Griffin reached over to his outbox, piled high with thick files bound with large red rubber bands. He grabbed the top one and threw it in Scott's general direction. Scott snagged it out of the air. The file was labeled, 'The Kangaroo Man'.

"Five murders, Forrester. In the Interstate 405 corridor from Long Beach to Santa Monica. Prostitutes. Ripped open by what the coroner says was a 'claw-like device'. Witnesses link a man with an Australian accent to three of the crime scenes. Kangaroos when they fight use their sharp front claws to rip their rivals from the neck to the groin. That's what this guy's been doing. They may be prostitutes Forrester, but they didn't deserve to die that way."

Griffin picked up another file and threw it again at Scott. "You remember Special Agent Lance Caulfield?"

"Sure. Salt Lake City Field Office. The case I'm working on. Caulfield took me to a murder scene in Wyoming."

"Well, that's not all that's happening in Wyoming. There are suspicions that a major child pornography ring is operating in the state. Agent Caulfield would like you to profile the owner of a box of pretty disgusting CDs full of kiddie porn. They were found during an arrest in a bar in Jackson Hole. The box was left behind by someone who fled the bar when state troopers were called in to break up a fight. Caulfield has the man's description and would like help finding him."

"He didn't mention anything about that when I was there."

"Too bad."

"Besides, I don't know when I'm going to find the time to get back to Wyoming... or California."

"Funny you should say that. Because... I do," Griffin said, with a huge smile on his face. "Take your pick, Forrester." He pointed to the outbox. "There's plenty more where these came from. I have a file cabinet full of them. And more coming in every day. The pile gets bigger and bigger."

Griffin noticed Scott's eyes wander over to the dartboard. "Yeah, I've heard about my nickname, 'Bull's Eye'. And you know what, Forrester? I *like* it. I like it a lot. To me, it's a badge of honor." He stood up, pulled the rest of the files from the outbox and flung them with a heavy thud onto the desktop. "Look at this *shit*! I want at least one case - just *one* of these cases - solved! You choose. Don't matter to me! Just pick one... and *solve* it!"

"But, I've got one. And *that's* the one I plan to solve."

"I don't need two agents on the same case, Forrester."

"Meaning?"

"Meaning when Cleyburn gets back on duty, she's taking over the Carleton case."

"She can't-"

"She can... and she will! Benito Vincente called me. He wants someone fulltime, on site. And I don't want to send two agents to New York

City. I can't spare the resources. I have to make a choice. And I've made it. And she's it."

"But she doesn't know-"

"Know what, Forrester? How to cause a public disturbance in an art gallery full of influential senators and congressman? How to embarrass the US government in front of a foreign ambassador? How to derail another agency's investigation and scare their suspect away? How to piss the Bureau's money down the drain? What doesn't she know, Forrester?"

"She's not ready-"

"You think you're better than her? Good. That's settled then. Take *one* of these unsolved cases and start working on it! Then bring me a goddamn result... without pulverizing the Bureau's reputation in the process! Now... *get out!*"

Scott threw the 'Kangaroo Man' file on the desk and kept Caulfield's porn case. At least he knew Caulfield and they respected each other.

He marched to the door and looked back at Titus Griffin.

Griffin's nostrils had that characteristic flare.

Scott went up to the dartboard, pulled the two darts out from the bull's eye, and threw them in the trashcan.

"She's not ready," he said.

"The fuck she isn't," was Griffin's reply.

The door slammed shut and the dart that was stuck in the office wall fell to the floor.

Chapter Twenty-Four

He caught sight of his reflection in the bottle-lined mirror; the tequila unable to chase away the haggard stranger that stared back at him with a drawn, blank expression. He tapped his finger on the bar. The bartender poured another shot from a bottle of blue agave. The liquor barely had time to sting his throat.

"You should slow down a touch, Mr. Forrester."

"Nice thought, George. Tough to do."

Even though it was a Monday night, the Georgetown Jazz Café was humming. The club, a mid-thirties era brownstone with an infamous Prohibition past, was a magnet for the cognoscenti of the Capital District.

Scott Forrester sat alone at the bar, feeling as welcome among the club's Bruno Maglis and Louis Vuittons as a brown paper bag that had just blown in from the street; a distant voyeur, abandoned to his own thoughts as he bathed in a tequila haze. *What a jungle,* he thought. *A well-dressed jungle. But a jungle nevertheless.*

Literary agents with fake Caribbean tans prowled the tables like panthers, searching for political celebrities to cozy up to. They lingered only long enough to test the quality of the brandy and the length of the résumé, before moving on.

Starry-eyed congressional interns hustled middle-aged lawyers, a chic clientele with their specialty martinis and portable humidors. Champagne flowed freely with the flash of a platinum credit card - one pair of eyes envious of the size of the wallet, the opposite pair measuring the depth of the cleavage.

A cocktail waitress glanced in Scott's direction - a stunning blonde in a revealing red dress, hourglass figure, sexually confident. Scott had dated girls like her before, designer females that hunted in closely-knit packs. They liked fast cars and hot sex but when they had their fill they would discard a guy like Scott as if he was a pair of uncomfortable high heel shoes. Scott had learned the hard way... that kind of woman was poison for his soul. But still, they were nice to look at.

He watched the blonde meander through the Café's U-shaped leather sectionals. A white napkin was gently placed on a polished black marble table. A slender hand, with a sparkling diamond and sapphire bracelet reached forward, took the glass of merlot, and then placed a tip on the waitress' tray.

The woman, was alone, half-hidden by the high-backed chair. Scott Forrester was tempted. Something whispered in his ear, *Look, but don't touch.*

His cell phone rang. It was Trish.

"Whatever it is," Scott said abruptly, "the answer is... No!"

"What if I'd called to tell you that everything was forgiven, that Griffin wants you back on the case, and that I'm desperate to know your latest theory?"

"I'd say you were lying."

"Yes, I would be lying. I'm flying to New York tomorrow. I called to say I'm sorry, Scott."

"Aren't you supposed to be convalescing?"

"I'm fine. Doctors worry too much."

"I'm pleased for you."

"Look, Scott... you can't keep acting as if you're on a private crusade, some lonely pilgrimage to Tibet to find personal enlightenment. We're supposed to be a team. And I don't mean just you and I. Griffin's a part of it too."

"Griffin's a moron."

"So you keep saying. But frankly Scott, I'm glad Griffin took you off this case. For your sake, as much as mine."

"Well that's gratitude for you - coming from someone who claims to be working with the best mentor she ever had!" Now the tequila was speaking. "But I guess I'm last week's news, aren't I? You and Griffin and Vincente have taken care of that. So you're going to New York City without me? Well, I'll take Tibet over Tiffany's any day. I'm no saint. But you're no Joan of Arc either, Trish."

"Where are you Scott? Have you been drinking? I've never heard you talk like this before."

"As of an hour ago, I went off duty. Let's say I'm celebrating my well-earned new assignment."

"I'm going to let you go, Scott. Why don't you take some time off? You're not drinking and driving, are you?"

"No, Mommy. I'm being a good boy. George here will make sure I get home safe." He took out his car keys and threw them down the bar. George smiled and shook his head.

"Be good, Scott."

"Bye Trish."

Scott punched the phone's off button with his thumb and pulled out another twenty.

"Same again, Mr. Forrester?"

"Same again, George."

As the bottle glugged, a silky hand with a diamond and sapphire bracelet reached from behind and stole the filled glass from the bar. He heard a faint sniff in his ear as a female voice savored the tequila's hot vapor and said, "Mision Reposado? Oui… the vanilla gives it away. Bon choix, chéri." The glass returned to the bar, empty. "Bartender, two more, s'il vous plaît. On my tab."

Scott Forrester turned. His heart skipped a beat. Christienne Duval hovered over his shoulder like a dark brooding angel. She was wearing a slinky black dress that clung seductively to her breasts. Impetuously, he slipped his hand around her waist. She didn't resist. Her body was taut and perfect. Her soft warmth leaned into him.

"Are you following me again, Ms. Duval?"

She smiled, her eyes deep with mystery, "I'm a bit of a devil, aren't I? Following you? Mais non. It seems that I've been stood up."

"What fool would do something like that?"

Two more shots of blue agave arrived.

"C'est bon." She picked up the glasses, her velvety brown eyes pointing towards the leather couch. "Shall we?"

As they sat down in the comfortable softness of the leather, the diamonds on her wrist caught the light with their icy fire. They were breathless in their perfection and beauty. Diamonds of exceptional clarity and quality. Set in white and yellow gold, with deep blue sapphires.

"Exquisite, isn't it chéri?"

Breathless perfection. Just like Christienne Duval.

"It looks incredibly expensive. I wouldn't want to guess."

Christienne giggled and whispered in his ear, "Two hundred thousand dollars."

Scott gasped. But then he asked, with obvious disappointment, "A gift from a rich admirer?"

"Monsieur Portland was supposed to meet me here tonight. But something came up at the last moment."

Scott's eyes turned away.

"Mais non, chéri!" she pouted. "It wasn't a *gift*."

Her reassurance wasn't that convincing. "Two hundred thousand dollars? If it wasn't a gift," Scott asked, "then what was it?"

"My bonus. You don't know much about Monsieur Portland and Le Roux-Berg, do you, chéri?"

Scott looked around at the Jazz Café's clusters of Paris Hilton-wannabe's. "Christienne, this is not my crowd. I'm just here for the tequila."

"Le Roux-Berg is not just *any* jewelry store. Our customers are the wealthiest, the most influential patrons - movie stars, pop stars, heads of state, Arab oil sheiks, CEOs and Senators. We have bijouteries in Geneva, Monaco... Paris, London... Riyadh... Los Angeles, New York. Monsieur Portland is *un entrepreneur fantastique.* Le Roux-Berg of Geneva was a very old-fashioned, family-run business that was nearly bankrupt. Monsieur Portland rescued it from obscurité and grew it from a few stores into twenty-six. Washington is our newest. And on his last visit, he gave me this bracelet. Monsieur Portland est très généreux. I thought I would wear it for him tonight as a thank you."

"He *gave* you a two hundred thousand dollar diamond bracelet?"

"You are *so* suspicious, Monsieur FBI Agent! Do you remember what was on my business card?"

The card was still in his jacket. He pulled it out. It read... *Christienne Duval. Spécialiste. La Bijouterie Washington. Le Roux-Berg Switzerland.*

She took it from him. "You see... *spécialiste.* Well, we are all specialists at Le Roux-Berg. It's Monsieur Portland's way. No fancy titles. But in fact, chéri, I am more than that - I am the Managing Director. Not just here in Washington. For all of Le Roux-Berg's bijouteries in the United States. Our Washington boutique has been open for less than a year... and we have already sold over sixty million dollars worth of jewelry."

"You said... *sixty* million dollars?"

"Oui. C'est ça. We sell only the best. This bracelet? To our clientele, it's just a bauble. Monsieur Portland has many companies within The Portland Group. Les Bijouteries Le Roux-Berg is the largest. Then there is Les Beaux Arts Le Roux-Berg, our fine art auction house. The Exhibition that Le Roux-Berg sponsored at the Freer Gallery has already paid dividends. Les Beaux Arts Roux-Berg has been commissioned by the Indian Government to sell selected works from that collection. It's quite a coup for Monsieur Portland."

"But I thought the Exhibition was on tour?"

"It is. But he has convinced Monsieur Narayan, the Indian ambassador, that the market is right, that now is a good time to sell. Despite what happened, the publicity surrounding the Exhibition has been très excellent. And the items that are sold will continue to tour with the Exhibition. Investors like that. It gives the works even more exposure and caché. Sometimes a piece of art will be sold again by an investor before the tour finishes. Fine art is a *very* profitable business. For everyone."

"What is the Indian Government planning to sell?"

"A few sculptures, most of the silk tapestries and a painting... 'The Revenge of Dvaipa'."

Scott sat up. "*That* painting? It's going to be *sold*?"

Scott felt the soft caress of Christienne's fingers on his face as she drew him close. Her breath was warm. Her eyes were dreamlike. As she kissed him, his nostrils filled with the sweet scent of Chanel.

"I'm tired of talking about Le Roux-Berg," Christienne Duval said.

She was seductive... addictive... a fever with no cure.

The music floated over them like a passing cloud; its notes descending like raindrops.

She kissed him again, her lips glossy and inviting. "Chéri... is there somewhere we can go," she purred gently in his ear, "where we don't have to do any more talking?"

Chapter Twenty-Five

On Sunday, October 23, 1983, in Beirut, Lebanon, an Islamic terrorist detonated a truck bomb with an explosive force of more than twelve thousand pounds of TNT, and took Scott and Jamie Forrester's father, and the fathers of many, many others, from them. It was also a Sunday when their mother died of diabetes related kidney failure. It was a Sunday when they buried her. It was a Sunday when the Army doctors told Jamie he was paralyzed for life. So it must have been on a Sunday when Jamie Forrester stopped believing in God.

Since then, this Sunday was like every other Sunday. Jamie sat with a beer and a bowl of popcorn, watching football. The Redskins' game was languishing into mediocrity. It was late in the fourth quarter and the Redskins were more than two touchdowns away from respectability.

Scott wasn't home. For the third time this week, his brother was out with Christienne Duval. *Scott's a lucky man,* Jamie thought. *And finally, he deserves some luck.*

A faint pinging sound – like a muffled alarm clock – emerged through the crunching of the popcorn. It was an instant messenger alert coming from his computer in the bedroom.

He clicked off the television.

Last week Jamie added a new name to his messenger list… a poster named Gabriel.

He liked Gabriel. Gabriel shared Jamie's hatred for Matthew Carleton. And he knew a lot about Zerotox and Pegasus BioSciences. Whether Gabriel was a rival biotech researcher with a bone to pick, or a disgruntled Pegasus employee, one thing Jamie knew for sure was that Gabriel must have access to information not accessible to the public, to ordinary investors. And he had an axe to grind.

The perfect chat buddy.

But the instant message was from I_H8_Brokers:

I_H8_Brokers: Hey, Joker. Have you heard the latest buzz about Pegasus?

Jokers_Wild: No. What's going on?

I_H8_Brokers: This Gabriel guy has been posting messages to the Board to short Pegasus tomorrow.

Jokers_Wild: So? That's what he was saying over a week ago. The stock's still rising nicely.

I_H8_Brokers: He says it will hit its peak tomorrow, then tank the next day… guaranteed.

Jokers_Wild: C'mon, Broker. You know there are no friggin' guarantees! What makes him any different from any of the other hypsters out there? There's always someone hyping 'long' and just as many betting 'short'.

I_H8_Brokers: This time it may be different.

Jokers_Wild: How different can it be?

I_H8_Brokers: Check it out for yourself. He repeats the same thing in his posts, over and over. People ask him questions. He doesn't give any answers. He just posts the same thing again and again.

Jokers_Wild: Which is?

I_H8_Brokers: You'll see what I mean. Hey, I gotta go. My soup's boiling over! See ya!

Jamie logged into WallStreetBuzz.com and went to its chat room, the BuzzBoard. He searched for messages from 'Gabriel' and a stream of posts flowed on his screen – the past hour, the hour before that, four hours ago, six hours ago.

The first post was 9:45AM.

The message said:

By: <u>Gabriel</u>   (reply to no one)

For those who seek redemption, listen. Those who have stolen from you will pay for their sins with blood from their hearts. Tomorrow, Pegasus will climb a peak and look down upon an abyss. The next day, flames will burn its rotting flesh. Help me light the torch. Join me. Become the energy of Her divine anger.

The BuzzBoard's amateur cryptologists – most of whom were half-crazed soothsayers themselves - debated the message. A consensus was reached on the central theme: the stock price for Pegasus BioSciences would 'climb to a peak' tomorrow and then fall dramatically (the abyss) the following day.

What did Gabriel mean by 'pay for their sins with blood from their hearts'? Subsequent posters asked him that. But as I_H8_Brokers had said, there was no reply from Gabriel.

As a one-time post, Gabriel's words wouldn't register any great seismic waves. The BuzzBoard had its mix of apocalyptic sages and practical jokers. Someone regularly accused the Fed Chairman of being the Son of the Devil. Others believed intensely they were aliens sent to destroy Earth's economy. After some good-natured bantering back and forth, they usually gave up their ranting and went away.

But this time it was different. Very different. The timing and frequency of the posts seemed intent upon reaching as many people as possible. Regardless of when you checked in to the chat room, it was there. The posts came in on cue, every fifteen minutes, like clockwork. 'Those who have stolen from you'. The 'you' was everyone. It was a message for everyone who'd invested in a scam and lost money.

For a software programmer like Jamie, there was something about the rhythm of Gabriel's messages. No variation. No replies. He came to a conclusion. It was a program. The messages were repetitive - a computer broadcast, from a server, like e-mail spam.

So Gabriel, a suspected insider, knew that Pegasus BioSciences was a scam? That meant that the message was more than just a warning to the scammers. It was a gift to their potential victims. Help him light the torch… by shorting Pegasus.

A good friend of Jamie's worked on the BuzzBoard's Compliance Desk. A Compliance Desk was an internal watchdog that monitored posting activity to ensure it complied with the Board's code of conduct. There were no regulatory requirements that drove a Compliance Desk, just the threat of libel lawsuits against the website if the posters got out of hand. About the only punishment the Compliance Desk could dish out was revoking someone's membership and login rights.

Jamie called his friend. "Hey, Steve… have you got a Trojan in your system that's delivering the same post to the BuzzBoard over and over?"

"Yeah, Jamie. We've just shut it down."

"How'd it get in?"

"Beats me. IT hasn't seen anything like it. It walked right in past our firewall, and then put up one helluva fight when we tried to clean it up. Why do you ask? Have you been having trouble logging in?"

"No. Just curious. Can you call me if it happens again? I might be able to trace it for you."

"Sure thing, Jamie."

"Bye."

Jamie's suspicions were confirmed. It was a program. He logged into his online brokerage account. He would short Pegasus tomorrow once the stock peaked as Gabriel said it would. He would then add to his short position during the day. He typed in his conditional sell order. As he did, an instant message from someone on his 'buddy list' popped on his screen.

It was Gabriel:

Gabriel: Chat?

Jokers_Wild: I'm all ears.

Gabriel: How are you Jamie?

Jokers_Wild: How do you know my name?

Gabriel: I know lots of things. Are you with us?

Jokers_Wild: You mean shorting Pegasus?

Gabriel: That. And other things.

Jokers_Wild: What other things?

Gabriel: You think like we do. You can help light the torch.

Jokers_Wild: Who's 'we'?

Gabriel: We could meet. In Georgetown?

Jokers_Wild: You know where I live?

Jamie waited for the reply. Several minutes passed. There was no answer. Jamie checked his DSL line. It was still streaming the chat signal. He initiated a trace. It dead-ended somewhere in the middle of the Caribbean. He tried again:

Jokers_Wild: Gabriel? Are you still there? Do you know a diner in Georgetown called Archie's?

Another minute passed. Then a return message appeared:

Gabriel: Tomorrow, I will rise from the sea and cast a blanket of fire across their souls.

Jokers_Wild: Whose souls, Gabriel?

Again, Jamie waited for a reply.

A reply that never came.

Chapter Twenty-Six

The shark gray BMW Z8 Roadster sped across the causeway connecting mainland Florida with Amelia Island; its top down and its 400 horsepower V8 engine purring as contentedly as its driver. The warm tropical breeze that blew through Nicole Riverton's auburn hair felt so good, so utterly luxurious. Florida's sunshine was the perfect tonic for the frosty atmosphere she'd left behind on Long Island. Nicole was glad to be back in her home state, where warmth was not just a temperature; it was also a state of mind. The icy phoniness of The Hamptons had always given her an uncomfortable feeling of guilt.

High above Amelia Island's thirty-foot sand dunes, seagulls floated lazily in the humid, late October air. In the distance, a billowing swarm of white clouds - the last remnants of a storm that had passed through Northern Florida the day before - hastened their retreat into the Atlantic. The sky ahead was blue and washed clean by the rain.

So much had changed in the past two weeks. The initial public offering for Pegasus BioSciences was supposed to be a triumph for Nicole Riverton and her husband, Bryan. But the murder of Matthew Carleton had turned success into a morbid, hollow victory.

Lexi Carleton had handled Matthew's death in her usual stoic, single-minded East Hampton way. The distance between the somber air of the funeral home and the pampered caress of her country club had been kept to a bare minimum. That didn't surprise Nicole Riverton. What was surprising was that Lexi Carleton was still married to her husband at the time of his death.

There was no doubt that Matthew Carleton was the king of dealmakers - someone who could take a madcap idea and blend it with profit-hungry money to create something out of nothing. Matthew Carleton did it on a scale that was truly sensational, with a speed and frequency that produced extraordinary results. But there was another side to Matthew Carleton. He had an insatiable lust for womanizing - for poking into other people's lives in more ways than one – that made him an unscrupulous, wife-cheating, self-centered bastard. Mourning Matthew Carleton was an extremely brief emotion for everyone involved.

Why had that marriage survived as long as it did, she had repeatedly asked herself. Many people had asked her that. It was a question Nicole thought she now had the answer to. It wasn't love. It wasn't money either. Lexi Carleton didn't need a nickel from Matthew. Her trust fund was big enough to write off the debt of an African country.

Had Matthew known the truth before he died? she thought. *That his prim and proper wife could play the extramarital sex game as well as, if not better, than he could?*

She had often wondered, what really had kept the Carletons together? It wasn't something material like money, Nicole had concluded. Or physical, like sex. It was more insidious than that. No, it was something quite different. Anyone who knew Lexi and Matthew knew they drew energy from the same shared source: power. Raw power.

The political electricity that flowed between them was a wonder of the modern world. It could have made Matthew Carleton Governor of New York, or Senator, or maybe even a legitimate Presidential candidate, if his life hadn't been cut short. Matthew Carleton had been egotistical enough to reach for the unreachable. And Lexi Carleton was still clever enough to milk his seductive political ambitions for her own social gain, even after he was dead.

Nicole Riverton had known the future Mrs. Matthew Carleton, Lexi Stavros, when they were both excitable, naïve classmates in their freshman year at Princeton. Lexi was forever the social butterfly, Nicole the nerdy scientist.

Lexi poured her heart and soul into building her circle of friends, first by sponsoring them into an exclusive Princeton sorority and then nurturing their immature personas like her own garden of rare orchids. Her intentions seemed genuine; the environment inclusive.

Later, Lexi's personality changed. College life became a push me/pull you tug-of-war, with her friends as the rope. Everyone around her felt the new vibe. One week, they were Lexi's closest confidantes; the next, just some passing acquaintance. Lexi seemed more interested in what Nicole and the others were going to do in the future, than what they were doing at the moment. It felt like Lexi was always in a state of calculating her friends' future worth - weighing her options to buy more stock, or sell at a loss. It was a mystery how Lexi's circle had stayed together for so long, on such amicable terms.

After college, the circle's paths diverged. Nicole left Lexi's elaborate ecosystem entirely, to pursue a medical degree at the University of North Carolina. Lexi returned to New York. It was many years later when the two met again. By then, Lexi Stavros had become Mrs. Matthew Carleton. Nicole had married Bryan Riverton. By then, time had increased the distance between Nicole and Lexi - financially, socially and ethically.

The BMW rapidly closed the distance between the causeway and the Riverton's new beachfront home, a seven thousand square-foot, cedar-shingled Cape Cod estate on a prime oceanfront lot. On one side, there were magnificent views of the Atlantic; on the other, the windswept eighteenth hole of Marlin Pointe's perpetually green golf course.

Short of the gatehouse to Marlin Pointe, Nicole slowed the roadster to a crawl and pulled over to listen to the surf. She took off her sandals and walked down to the beach. *The future looked so certain two months ago*, she thought. *Now the only certain thing was that the sun was warm and the ocean would soothe you to sleep.*

The water lapped gently against her ankles as she strolled, the seagulls greeting her lonely presence with their distant cries. The vastness of the ocean was a reminder of how transient one life could be in the grand scheme. The death of Matthew Carleton was now history. It was time to forget and move on. But she couldn't. She couldn't forget how she'd arrived at this place in time. She couldn't forget *who* had helped her get here.

Not so long ago, life had seemed a whole lot simpler. She had been a spunky, middle class Florida debutante, cheerleader and valedictorian on full scholarships; her future husband Bryan, a poor, academically brilliant, handsome son of an Iowa cornhusker.

Was it really seven years since they'd graduated from UNC medical school together? Was it seven years ago that they'd married, without a dime in the bank?

Now, there were no more grueling 24/7 hours as interns. No more menial second jobs to make ends meet. No more struggles to gain recognition in a university environment that seemed more concerned with generating endowments to the football program than making breakthroughs in biotechnology.

Nicole smiled. *Was it seven years since their Friday night ritual? A rented video, a bowl of microwave popcorn, followed by truly passionate sex. Had that sweet memory been buried too, by their newfound riches?*

Nicole picked up a surf-worn shell, the color of fresh snow. *Where had all that simplicity gone?* She rubbed the shell in her fingers. She would keep it – a reminder of the simple pleasures of a simpler life.

Three years ago, a chance invitation had changed everything. That summer had been lazy and hot. They were at the end of their financial rope when they received a surprise phone call. Lexi Carleton had tracked them down. Would they like to spend a weekend with her and Matthew in their new home in The Hamptons?

That was when it all started. When it all changed.

Lexi had that same magnetic pull she had in college - a way of enticing you back into her life when every part of you sensed it was totally the wrong thing to do.

The Carleton's East Hampton home was palatial – its swimming pool was larger than Bryan and Nicole's apartment. It was a fairy tale castle, and the whole weekend was like a dream. *But was it their dream?*

Matthew Carleton had been a charming host - very attentive, as she recalled. It hadn't taken him long to see something inside the mix of medical statistics and biochemistry that laced Nicole and Bryan Riverton's marguerita-soaked conversations. And it hadn't taken him long to became intoxicated with biotech terms he could barely pronounce.

He began to dream a dream.

Their dream. And he wanted to invest in it.

There was no certainty about anything. Research work wasn't like that, they'd warned. There was no straight-line mathematical equation to guarantee that the financial risk he would be taking would ever lead to any reward. Finding a cure for septic shock was the only reward Nicole and Bryan had been working for. Their research had been ground breaking. Septic shock was one of the world's deadliest infections, they'd said, attacking patients when they were the most vulnerable, after major surgery. It invades their vital organs – weakening the brain, the heart, the kidneys, the liver. Once infected, patients have a high mortality rate.

Nicole and Bryan had developed Zerotox, a genetically engineered drug to combat septic shock. Yes, it was experimental, they'd told him. Yes, it was unproven. And yes – definitely, yes - it needed more funding. At that moment, Matthew Carleton became obsessed - obsessed not with the scientific potential of Zerotox, but with its monetary potential.

He had thrown them a lifeline. *Who wouldn't have taken it?* A limited partnership called Pegasus Labs. It would be Matthew's creation. Everything was Matthew's creation. He would hold the majority stake. And why not? Matthew had offered to be their principal source of funding and they had taken it gladly. And true to his word, their overdue bills were paid off. Their hopeless downward spiral into debt had ended. And Zerotox had taken the fast track to becoming a commercial product.

Nicole looked into the endless heavens. High above the sands of Marlin Pointe, a tiny white cross floated effortlessly in the thermals; soaring and diving, looping and rolling. It was like a swooping white quill.

On the grassy sand dune that marked the entrance to the gated estate, a solitary figure turned and waved to her. It was Ezra Tauberman, the Rivertons' neighbor. An eccentric seventy-two-year-old widower, Ezra lived alone in the beach house next door. His hobby was radio-controlled gliders. And conditions on Amelia Island today were perfect.

Last winter - the Rivertons' first in Marlin Pointe – Ezra invited them regularly for dinner. They spent the evenings in deep discussion with him - over their new life, over the family they wanted to start. In turn, he told them about the adventures of a humble general physician from Hoboken, New Jersey who'd spent a lifetime serving the isolated communities of Alaska, and why he exchanged the cold north for Florida's sun.

And they talked about Zerotox.

Today would be the first time since Pegasus stock went public that Nicole Riverton had seen Ezra Tauberman. He looked pleased with himself. With the demand for Pegasus stock at sky-high levels, Bryan had intervened with his brokerage firm to get Mr. Tauberman some shares in the IPO. It was a substantial investment of his retirement funds and Mr. Tauberman had been very grateful.

God, she thought, *please don't let Mr. Tauberman get hurt.* She wanted so desperately to warn him, *Sell Pegasus!* But their lawyers had advised them against it. It would be insider trading. And in Ezra's case, it would be so hard to control what a seventy-two-year-old, painfully honest retiree might say to regulators should his name appear on a list of investors who'd flipped Pegasus for a quick profit before the stock collapsed.

Nicole walked back towards her new BMW. *I must go,* she thought. *Bryan must be waiting for me.*

She sat on a tuft of grass to wipe the sand from her feet and took one last look into the sky at Ezra's soaring glider. It was so hard to forget Matthew Carleton when she and Bryan owed him so much. But she knew she had to. It had only been three years. But in three short years, he'd worked a miracle. When the fledgling Pegasus Labs needed new facilities, he found them. When they needed to hire more research assistants, he told them to hire the best. Funding for clinical trials? No problem. Matthew found it. Everything was going fine... until he wanted human testing of Zerotox accelerated. Matthew was their financier, not their Head of Research. But he could be so persuasive.

"Lingering doubts?" he had asked. "Had they no faith in their own creation? In their talent? The company must move aggressively," he had said. "Find new investors. Expand. Seize the moment, and don't look back."

They were in the middle of difficult experiments to prove the drug's effectiveness. Nicole and Bryan were neophytes in the world of high finance, and Matthew told them repeatedly that the trick to growing a new business - whether it was selling biotechnology or a new flavor of Popsicles - was to push the risk of commercialization into the hands of others.

Historically, startup biotech companies rarely lived up to their promises. Nicole and Bryan Riverton knew that. The medical community would judge Zerotox on its clinical merits, not its potential. They knew that too. That had always been their cross to bear, not Matthew's. The final hurdle of medical proof – where most new drugs fell short of approval – was the FDA's Phase III human clinical trials. In biotechnology research, Phase III was 'make or break'.

But the non-scientist in Matthew Carleton had a different spin on their reality. He was dreaming their dream. Zerotox didn't need a successful Phase III approval, he'd insisted. Not for a successful stock market flotation. He knew a way to make Pegasus Labs prosper, even if Zerotox failed. He called it: monetizing Nicole and Bryan Riverton's intellectual property. With a slight of his financial hand, Matthew Carleton would turn their risk of scientific failure into the common shareholders' price of admission. He said it was the American Way.

And they didn't argue with him. After all, Matthew Carleton was the financial wizard; their first love was science. The process, he told them, was simple. It would start with a pile of documents drawn up by Matthew's lawyers. Then before Pegasus went public, Matthew would solicit something he called private placements.

Soon the company they'd created from nothing more than a few test tubes and a box of computer paper spread its wings into a consulting firm, an independently owned testing lab, and several offshore marketing subsidiaries. Matthew called them 'financial vehicles' - businesses designed to maximize the three founding shareholders' initial investment, and multiply their future wealth.

"New money would come in," he had said, "only if it looked like Pegasus was expanding rapidly."

He had told his investors, "Belly up to the bar, cowboys... and put your nickels down!" And sure enough, with Matthew in high gear, the *serious* money started rolling in. Because if there was ever anything Matthew Carleton did really, really well, it was making the unimaginable appear possible.

Nicole remembered the day when cash began to flood into their bank accounts as if the Hoover Dam had opened its sluice gates. *The money - oh, the sickly sweet money! It had materialized like magic under Matthew's spell.*

Nicole and Bryan had been stunned by where all this money was coming from. Generous salaries. Consulting contracts. Directors' fees. Royalties paid to the Rivertons by the new subsidiaries. Plus a myriad of other services that Matthew Carleton invoiced to the parent company on their behalf. And it was all legal, he had told them.

In less than three years, Nicole and Bryan Riverton went from a leaky rented trailer on the grounds of the University of North Carolina - with a mountain of threatening letters from bill collectors - to two hundred employees, a shiny new headquarters on Long Island, and two well equipped pre-production laboratories in North Carolina and Arizona.

And just as it seemed they couldn't possibly do any better, Matthew Carleton had then sent their dream into orbit. The initial partnership the three of them owned outright - Pegasus Labs - merged with the collection of subsidiaries that had been funded through private placements, to become the newest, the hottest, and the most glamorous company on Wall Street. The stock market had been oozing with venture capital. Greedy mutual funds were begging the market for more IPO's. A mountain of cash was waiting to find the next Apple or Google.

Pegasus BioSciences had been born.

To be honest, they could care less how Matthew Carleton had done it. All they knew was that the money was real... very, very real... and very, very wonderful. And it didn't take a magician to read their bank accounts. In two short years, their net worth had grown to a cool *$350 million dollars*. And they'd owed everything to Matthew Carleton. God knows they hadn't liked him as a person, but as a benefactor, he had been a saint.

Who would want to kill him? And why?

She reflected on the night before his murder. The last time either of them saw him alive. Matthew hadn't seemed concerned that experiments into Zerotox's efficacy had detected a flaw - a toxic side effect that destroyed the immune systems in test monkeys. Suddenly, the probability of Zerotox successfully moving past Phase III was not as certain as they had advertised to Wall Street. In fact, the side effect had put the probability at near zero.

Nicole and Bryan were sweating bullets - not the silver bullets for septic shock they had hoped to invent. But Matthew Carleton had reassured them as only Matthew could. Barely hours after the IPO had sold at fantastic premiums on the New York Stock Exchange, Matthew Carleton had courted its takeover by a large, multinational biotech company.

The day before he died, he'd told Nicole and Bryan not to worry. Rumors of this takeover bid were surfacing. The market was excited. And if they could keep that interest rising before the FDA ruled on Zerotox, and then sell out, they would be home free.

"But what about the little guy?" Nicole had asked him. "People like Ezra Tauberman? What would be left of his investment when the truth about Zerotox came out?"

Matthew had assured them at least some residual value would be left with the acquiring company after they bought Pegasus. The plan was to exchange shares of Pegasus for stock in the much larger biotech company. That company would take the hit when Zerotox failed. When Zerotox didn't pan out - and the Rivertons and Matthew knew it wouldn't – little investors like Mr. Tauberman would have to be patient, but over time, he'd said, they might recoup their initial investment through the other company's stock.

Nicole and Bryan had believed him. He had always said it was the risk the common shareholder took when they bought stock. It was the American Way. And Matthew was never wrong.

At the IPO launch party at the Rivertons' home in Westchester, Matthew had acted as if this had been the plan all along. Financial wizardry. Matthew Carleton. The words were synonymous. He had taken them aside and advised them to sell eighty percent of their stake in Pegasus the very next day.

"Before the takeover? Was that legal?" Nicole had asked.

"Sure," he'd said. "You're just diversifying your holdings, as a prudent hedge against market uncertainty."

That's what Pegasus would report in the SEC filings. It was a defense other founders of start-up companies had made for selling the bulk of their holdings.

"Don't worry," he'd reassured them. "You'll become a lost statistic in the whirlwind of complex share transactions involved in this takeover. It will take the SEC years - if ever - to suspect that Zerotox never really had a chance of being successfully approved. And by keeping a twenty percent residual stake, it will look like you continued to have confidence in the future of Zerotox."

The fact the drug wouldn't work out when the new company took over Pegasus had been a minor issue to Matthew. A risk the other company was taking in the competitive world of mergers and acquisitions, he'd said. So, in his mind, cashing out eighty percent of a whole lot of money a little early was better than keeping a hundred percent of nothing later on.

Even they had understood that.

So, as instructed, they had sold their eighty percent stake and made the killing he'd said they would. And then, the very next day, Matthew Carleton was murdered.

Even in the warmth of the Florida sunshine, it sent a chill up Nicole Riverton's spine every time she thought about what they had done.

Who was Matthew Carleton's killer?

Were Bryan and Nicole Riverton on his list?

It was the very reason she was now seeking the isolation and privacy of Amelia Island.

Second gear growled under Nicole's right hand as she approached the gatehouse to Marlin Pointe. Nicole Riverton felt protected. Security was tight. The guard who checked her ID was no minimum wage rent-a-cop. He was a highly trained executive security agent. The sub's wealthy residents paid well for the best security their kind of money could buy. And that was a lot. It was immensely reassuring. Her husband Bryan was more blasé about the risk. He thought the whole thing was a waste of money. But he would think that. Despite their newly minted wealth, he was still the penny-pinching son of an Iowa cornhusker.

The gatehouse retreated in her rear view mirror. She negotiated a final curve in the smartly asphalted road. Then Nicole Riverton finally reached home. Westchester, New York was nice. Okay, more than nice. It was fabulous, by anybody's standards. But Florida was her birthright. And Amelia Island was as good as it got.

Only two things could make Nicole Riverton feel more at peace: the embrace of her husband, Bryan; and the unconditional affection of their prized purebred Dalmatian, Bailey. Somehow, Bailey had a way to take the most complex problems and simplify them into a walk on the beach. There was no better way to unwind than to combine a glass of cold white wine, the Atlantic Ocean and the soppy looks of a contented dog. For Nicole and Bryan Riverton, that worked every time.

The cobblestone drive that lead up to their beachfront estate marked the last leg of a long and tiring flight from New York City to Jacksonville. As Nicole pulled the BMW into the driveway, Bryan came down the hill from the 18th green on his golf cart. A grin stretched across his well-tanned face. He didn't like losing. Especially to himself. But by his smile, it would seem he had something to celebrate. It was not that long ago that Nicole and Bryan Riverton had to struggle with their last dollar bill to keep a bottle of wine chilled in the fridge. Now they had the finest French and California Chardonnay to choose from, kept in their temperature controlled wine cellar.

The BMW Roadster found its spot in the garage beside the Porsche and the Mercedes. Nicole walked back out into the sunshine, returned his smile and waved.

She closed her eyes and took in the clean ocean air. How could she know that this would be their last moment of shared happiness?

Nicole approached the door leading into the house from the inside of the garage. As she turned the key, Bryan's golf cart mounted the driveway. Nicole Riverton paused on the inside step and looked back. Bryan was still grinning from ear to ear. Perhaps he'd shot a hole in one. Perhaps he was 10 over par. It didn't matter. They'd made it. Finally, after all their struggles, they'd made it. It was theirs. No one... no one... could take it from them. They'd earned it. They'd crawled up a rock face to achieve it... to feel what it felt like to achieve the American Dream. And now, for Nicole and Bryan Riverton, the dream was real.

Nicole turned the key of the door. Bryan's golf cart crossed the boundary between the cobblestone drive and the concrete garage floor.

As Nicole pushed the door open, her world turned to dust.

Dangling from their kitchen chandelier from a rope, the limp, black-on-white polka-dotted form of Bailey's lifeless body hung over a pool of blood.

Nicole Riverton stepped back and gasped. Her eyes could not comprehend what she was seeing. It was *unreal*. She turned, in shock, and met her husband's innocent gaze as he stepped out of the golf cart.

"What's wrong, Nicole?" he asked.

Horror choked back her words.

"Nicole?"

The color drained from Nicole Riverton's face. Her hand covered her mouth. She felt nauseous and faint. She didn't want to look back into the kitchen. Then her eyes moved from Bryan's expression of concern to the white, cross-like shape that silently flew six feet above the cobblestone drive. It floated ever closer to the garage entrance.

"Nicole? For God's sake... *what's wrong?*"

The glider drifted through the garage door like a white ghost in slow motion. It flew over Bryan's head. They looked at it in disbelief. Just before it touched the wall, they acknowledged each other with bewildered eyes. *Something was desperately not right.*

A millisecond later and the garage exploded in a flash of white hot C4. Nicole and Bryan Riverton were torn apart by the blast. Almost instantaneously, heat-sensing detonators inside the house activated incendiary devices embedded in the walls. Plumes of mushrooming orange-red flames burst out of the sliding glass doors, the Palladian windows and the roof - blowing glass and flaming cedar shingles high into the air. The beach house, all seven thousand square feet of it, lit up like a Roman candle. Seagulls squawked in fear as they tried to outrace the shock wave and its incredible surge of heat.

On the top of a solitary dune, a figure dropped the radio control into the grass.

Fire had consumed the Rivertons and their beach house.

It was done.

I will rise from the sea and cast a blanket of fire across their souls.

At the figure's feet, a body lay hidden amidst the sand and grass of Amelia Island. The body of a seventy-two-year-old man.

The figure walked down towards the beach and retrieved a green duffel bag buried under the sand. Out came a wetsuit, a facemask and a snorkel. The figure stripped off its gray wig, floral shirt, beige khaki shorts.

In the distance, the Rivertons' cedar-shingled beach house was a giant funeral pyre that sent a cloud of acrid smoke into the bright blue Florida sky.

The figure entered the surf, the duffel bag of clothes over one shoulder, walked into the water, and disappeared under the waves.

The flames that enveloped the Rivertons' estate converged into a single bright red orgy of heat.

As black smoke filled the gap between ground and sky, Nicole and Bryan Riverton's dream was over.

Chapter Twenty-Seven

The cynics on the BuzzBoard had seen it before, many times. The market was churning sideways. Again. Opportunities were thin. Going long or going short didn't matter. Either way, there were few winning positions; the market was nearly dead.

Jamie needed a winner. He needed one desperately. His trading capital was at an all time low. If he didn't make some profit soon, he'd have to tap into the home equity line he shared with his brother, just to pay the bills.

Second-guessing himself – something he vowed he would never do if he intended to make his living as a day-trader – was beginning to gnaw a hole in his psyche. Shorting Pegasus BioSciences was the only way to give him the winner he'd been praying for. Pegasus was technically oversold, and due for an upward bounce. When it did, Jamie sensed it was reaching a peak, placed his trade in the opposite direction and went short.

Three hours later and the news. A fire in Florida had killed the Rivertons. Pegasus BioSciences immediately tanked. Jamie Forrester was on the right side of the trade. He'd played Pegasus perfectly. With a little help from a friend.

Flush with cash, he was ready for the next big deal:

By: Jokers_Wild   (reply to bizwhiz)

So, whiz kid… what's happening, dude?

By: bizwhiz   (reply to Jokers_Wild)

I'm out of the techs, Joker. The action's elsewhere.

By: Jokers_Wild   (reply to bizwhiz)

Like?

By: <u>bizwhiz</u>   (reply to Jokers_Wild)

Hard assets. Texas tea. All that glitters. You're not still investing in that biotech deadpool are you?

By: <u>42EE_Kitten</u>   (reply to Jokers_Wild)

Hard assets. I like that.

By: <u>Jokers_Wild</u>   (reply to 42EE Kitten)

Keep it clean, Kitty. So it's commodities for the bizkid, is it?

By: <u>bizwhiz</u>   (reply to Jokers_Wild)

It's not the only place to be, Joker. I'm also buying up foreclosed Florida real estate. Taking a sabbatical down south. Real nice. So what's next, you say? Kitty will like this one - Whale River Diamond Mines. Diamonds are a girl's best friend!

By: <u>I H8 Brokers</u>   (reply to bizwhiz)

Whoa, Nelly! The whizbiz is into… diamond mines?

By: <u>bizwhiz</u>   (reply to I_H8_Brokers)

Not just any diamond mines. Canadian diamond mines. In Quebec. It's the new Wild West. Only East, if you know your geography.

By: <u>snorkelman</u>   (reply to bizwhiz)

Parlez-vous francais?

By: <u>42EE_Kitten</u>   (reply to snorkelman)

Oh, I love it when you speak French! Grrrr!

By: <u>Jokers_Wild</u>   (reply to 42EE_Kitten)

Settle down. The kiddies aren't in bed yet. So tell us, bizzywhizzy, what's the deal?

By: <u>bizwhiz</u>   (reply to Jokers_Wild)

James Bay Diamond Mines is already in production, and the diamonds are gorgeous. Whale River has staked a claim next door. The theory is… the diamond pipes extend into their property. Whale River is ready to sample. They intend to do a major survey this spring when the snows melt. They went IPO last month to raise the cash. Get in now, fellow rock n'rollers and ride Whale River when it taps the mother lode!

By: <u>42EE_Kitten</u>   (reply to bizwhiz)

What's the ticker symbol, bizkiss? I'm good to go, as always!

By: <u>Gabriel</u>   (reply to 42EE_Kitten)

Beware of Whale River.

By: <u>bizwhiz</u>   (reply to Gabriel)

What kind of newbie pisses on someone else's parade?

By: <u>Jokers_Wild</u>   (reply to bizwhiz)

The kind that knows, bizzie.

By: <u>bizwhiz</u>   (reply to Jokers_Wild)

Knows what?

By: <u>Gabriel</u>   (reply to bizwhiz)

Knows that Whale River is a scam.

By: <u>bizwhiz</u>   (reply to Gabriel)

You know shit!

By: <u>Jokers_Wild</u>   (reply to Gabriel)

Give him space, biz! He got Pegasus right. And it's more than most of us know right now. This market is dead. Most stocks are road kill. Give him some room. What do you know about Canadian diamond mines, Gabriel?

By: <u>Gabriel</u>   (reply to Jokers_Wild)

Enough to be dangerous.

By: <u>bizwhiz</u>   (reply to Gabriel)

A man of many words, signifying nothing.

By: <u>Gabriel</u>   (reply to bizwhiz)

Most words signify nothing. Action counts.

By: <u>bizwhiz</u>   (reply to Gabriel)

Whale River is where the action is.

By: <u>Jokers_Wild</u>   (reply to Gabriel)

Let's listen to what he has to say. He was right about Pegasus. Who was brave enough to short it? I did!

By: <u>snorkelman</u>   (reply to Jokers_Wild)

I did too! It sure helped that the Rivertons croaked, no doubt about that. But Pegasus had it coming. What's coming out in the press about Zerotox is something special. My snorkel mask's off to you, Gabriel. Got it right? You got it soooo right! Great Barrier Reef... here I come! Thanks! You da man, Gabriel!

By: <u>Jokers_Wild</u>   (reply to Gabriel)

So what's the scoop on Whale River?

By: <u>Gabriel</u>   (reply to Jokers_Wild)

Whale River will only profit those that got in early. Everyone else will lose. The property is bogus. There are no diamonds there.

By: <u>bizwhiz</u>   (reply to Gabriel)

Like hell there aren't, Gabriel! Just wait til the core samples come in!

By: <u>Gabriel</u>   (reply to bizwhiz)

Any core samples coming out of Whale River will be faked.

By: <u>bizwhiz</u>   (reply to Gabriel)

So who would fake them, wiseguy?

By: <u>Gabriel</u>   (reply to bizwhiz)

The late Jiri Kostelic.

By: <u>Jokers_Wild</u>   (reply to Gabriel)

Late for what?

By: <u>Gabriel</u>   (reply to Jokers_Wild)

His own funeral.

By: <u>Jokers_Wild</u>   (reply to Gabriel)

So who's this Jiri Kostelic guy?

By: <u>Gabriel</u>   (reply to Jokers_Wild)

Short Whale River. And profit.

By: <u>snorkelman</u>   (reply to Gabriel)

How do you know this shit, Gabriel?

By: <u>Jokers_Wild</u>   (reply to snorkelman)

What do you care, snorkey? Gabriel's giving us the low down. Let's take this gift and run. He said short Pegasus... and he was right! He says short Whale River... okay, I'm not arguing! I'm shorting Whale River! Gabriel's got the Midas touch. And I'm not fighting it. So... who's with me?

By: <u>42EE Kitten</u>   (reply to Jokers_Wild)

42 big ones sayz I'm in!

By: <u>snorkelman</u>   (reply to Jokers_Wild)

Okay, I'll bite. I'm in.

By: <u>Jokers_Wild</u>   (reply to snorkelman)

See you at the reef, snorkey. I'm in, big time. I have no choice. I need more winners.

• • •

The technicals looked good. Whale River Diamond Mines had run up substantially from last month's IPO price, had quickly backed off on profit taking, and was now on a steady rise to a new high. It was entering classic overbought territory. Jamie could smell the short traders itching to take it down – even temporarily - on bad news.

Jamie pressed the key and felt a ping of anxiety as his order filled. The online confirmation arrived nearly instantly: he'd bought buy put options on ten thousand shares of Whale River Diamond Mines with a six-month expiry.

Buying puts – an aggressive speculation that gambled on a dramatic decline in a stock's value – was a higher leverage strategy than just shorting the stock. Speculators on the right side of the trade would realize a much higher profit than just shorting the stock. But if he was wrong – and the stock kept rising - he risked having his put options expire worthless.

For Jamie Forrester, it was an all-or-nothing gamble. But a gamble he was willing, and needed, to take.

Gabriel – the mysterious newbie whose posts were uncannily accurate - had been right about Pegasus. Jamie didn't care who Gabriel's sources were; whether the deaths of the Rivertons was an accident or not - a gas explosion as the newspapers had suggested. It wasn't Jamie's concern. This was another opportunity to recoup years of losses.

He would go for it. Because if Gabriel was right, Jamie Forrester would net a sixty thousand dollar profit on his put options on Whale River Diamond Mines. It would be an even bigger win than his gains on Pegasus.

And in this game, Jamie Forrester was determined that... the Joker would definitely be wild.

Chapter Twenty-Eight

S cott struggled with the key. The patio door to the walkout basement slid awkwardly with a jerk, knocking the brown bag of Chinese food out of his hands and onto the floor. A stain started to spread across the bottom of the bag. Scott could see Jamie in his makeshift office-cum-bedroom beyond the living room, hunched over his computer screen.

"Damn, Jamie! Can't you hear someone knocking?"

Jamie stretched back in his wheelchair, then pumped his fists in the air. A face that a moment ago was pure concentration was now pure joy. "Cha-ching, big brother! Order confirmed! Now all I have to do is wait. Forget takeout, Scott. The next one's on me! The best Chinese restaurant in Washington! We'll eat until we're sick!"

Scott placed his hands under the soaked bag and gingerly carried it through the living room to the kitchen. He dumped the bag into the sink. "Yeah, I've heard that one before. You got any clean plates?"

"There's paper ones in the cupboard over the fridge."

"So what gamble is it this time? Wireless vending machines? Costa Rican real estate trusts? Fuel oil from fish farms?"

"Canadian diamond mines."

"Jamie, you were always an idiot when it came to geography... diamonds come from South Africa not Canada. You're about eight thousand miles short."

"Try ten thousand short."

"I won't quibble. Ten thousand. Eight thousand. What's a few thousand miles?"

"Try sixty grand."

Scott opened the cartons of Chinese food. "Do you want Szechwan noodles?"

"Didn't you hear me? I said sixty grand, Scott! And no, I don't want any noodles."

"The sweet and sour sauce leaked out. What a mess. Sixty grand of what? Stop talking in riddles."

"Dollars. As in profits. Did you get the foo yung and spring rolls?"

"Of course. Thankfully someone has a real job. Or else dinner would be day old donuts." Scott piled the Chinese food on the paper plates until the plates' design limit was reached. He found chopsticks in a scrambled mess that claimed to be a kitchen drawer.

Jamie accelerated across the hardwood floor. "You haven't listened to a word I've said, have you?" He took a plate of food, wheeled around the counter and headed back to his computer. "Scott, will you please focus! I said sixty thousand dollars. A six, followed by a zero, followed by three more zeroes!"

Scott licked his fingers. "Is there a name for this dream-like masochistic state you're in? What do you call this latest investment theory? The Toilet Plunger Effect? You know... stuff good money down the john and flush? If it gets stuck, throw more in and help it down with suction? So now you're going to make sixty thousand dollars buying Canadian diamonds?"

"Not buying."

"You're stealing them?"

"Yeah, sure. And I'm going to stash them in your locker at the FBI for safekeeping. I'm not buying, Scott. I'm selling."

"But I thought you said the market had bottomed out. And it was time to 'buy like a big dog'?"

"That was yesterday. And that was techs. Today it's diamonds."

"Last year, didn't you lose a bundle shorting sugar futures?"

Jamie paused at the door of his bedroom and gobbled a piece of lemon chicken. "Not futures this time, Scott. Put options. On a bogus diamond mine. You'll see. Whale River Diamonds will begin its descent into worthlessness and I'll be ten thousand shares on the right side of this trade. For a profit of sixty big ones."

"How do you know this isn't another one of your hair-brained ideas?"

"Scott, you know that 'real job' you keep talking about? Playing cops and robbers? Well, I have a real job too. And it's real hard work. It's not easy to find these opportunities. And it's not always easy to capitalize on them. This job is just as hard, just as stressful, and just as skilful as you poking around some dead man's ass."

"Oh, now I get it! Another hot tip from one of those deadbeat chatmates of yours? I'd say that was about as valuable as a fart from a dead man's ass."

"Not this time."

Scott looked up from his dangling noodles. "Yeah, sure." Scott followed Jamie into the bedroom and sat down on the end of the computer table.

Jamie signed back into chat. "He nailed Pegasus. Then the Rivertons got torched. He told us to short it. Most of them ignored him. But anyone who didn't, made out like a bandit! Now he says some guy named Cosmetic or Christ-o-lick, or something like that, will bite the big one just like the Rivertons. And that means Whale River Diamond Mines will be up shit creek without a paddle. Now they're taking notice. He's someone on the inside track. And worth listening to."

When Scott heard Jamie say 'bite the big one', he stopped eating and looked up. The sarcasm disappeared. "Are you saying someone *profited* from the Rivertons' deaths?"

Jamie munched without pause. "Insiders post all the time. Sometimes it's disinformation. Sometimes they employ professional hypsters. But this guy, Scott... he's different. And they think he's a hero. Hot tip? If it makes money, I'll take it! As soon as he goes cold, we'll move on. That's how it works. That's how they make money on us. That's how we'll make our money back from them. It's business. Dirty business, for sure. But if they're going to make the rules, we'll play it their way."

"You've always had a warped sense of what the rules are, Jamie," Scott replied.

"So what else is new? How long are you in town this time?"

Scott put down his plate, opened the bar fridge under Jamie's desk and two beers lost their twist tops. "Don't know. A while."

"You're not going back to New York?"

Scott shook his head, "No."

"You're on the Carleton murder case, aren't you?"

"Not anymore."

"You know what they're saying about Carleton, don't you?"

"Who the hell are 'they'? What have 'they' got to do with it, Jamie? Are 'they' relatives of the deceased?"

"You could say that. Their 'deceased' portfolios."

"Their what? Have you been smoking up again?"

Jamie laughed. "You wish. Now that would put a chill up your spine, wouldn't it? I can see the headlines now… FBI Agent's Home Raided. Police Find Opium Den in the Basement."

"You have no idea what puts a chill up my spine, Jamie. No idea, at all." Scott picked up his plate and chased the last pork ball through the sweet and sour sauce. "So, what are 'they' saying about Matthew Carleton?"

"Why don't we ask 'them'?"

Jamie pointed to the chat in progress on his monitor:

By: 42EE_Kitten   (reply to snorkelman)

Snorky, don't roll it all over. Especially going short! If the market swings the wrong way, all those days clawing back lost profits will be wasted.

By: bizwhiz   (reply to 42EE Kitten)

You know she's right, snorks.

By: <u>snorkelman</u>   (reply to bizwhiz)

You guys have lost your nerve.

By: <u>42EE_Kitten</u>   (reply to snorkelman)

You've lost your memory. And your mind.

By: <u>snorkelman</u>   (reply to 42EE Kitten)

Careful, Kitty. That's in the past. I found it again. Remember?

By: <u>42EE_Kitten</u>   (reply to snorkelman)

Sorry. I forgot, snorky. Hugs and kisses. We luv ya baby. No need to try that again.

"What are they talking about, Jamie?"

"Snorkelman's a retired insurance agent. Lives in Boca Raton. Lost a pisspot on Razorback Software and Silicon Pathways two years ago. Threatened suicide. The Board talked him out of it. He just won big shorting Pegasus. Now he's going to try again with Whale River."

"Did you say Razorback Software and Silicon Pathways?" Jamie's random samples of Internet chat freaks were throwing darts at Scott's cork wall.

And then Jamie hit the bull's eye. "It all revolves around Matthew Carleton and his den of forty thieves - Deuce Meredith and Liang Wong, amongst others. Ding dong, the wicked thieves are dead! Rejoice! Rejoice!"

"Deuce Meredith?"

"Razorback was one of Carleton's greatest scams."

"Liang Wong?"

"Scott, you're doing a terrible job of feigning ignorance. Half the chatboard's made the connection. Surely the FBI has."

Scott scooped up the last grains of fried rice. "So Matthew Carleton was involved with Deuce Meredith and Liang Wong?"

"Don't play me for a dumb shit, Bro. You know he did. Matthew Carleton created Razorback and Silicon Pathways, along with a ton of other companies, from nothing more than the lint between his toes. He made your stiffs rich. And in the process, made himself mega-mega-rich. Then he left poor clods like snorkelman fifty feet down without an air supply. You remember how much I lost on Razorback, don't you?"

He couldn't remember any specific stock Jamie had gambled on. He just remembered that as long as Jamie kept winning, the momentum kept carrying him along. Jamie rolled his winning positions into losing ones then hung on too long. In hindsight, by the time the financial meltdown hit in the fall of 2008, everyone had hung on too long. To what? Dreams of fancy cars and free flowing booze? Snow white yachts bobbing alongside terracotta villas? Carefree days in the tropical sun? 'They' had all hung on until there was nothing left to hang on to. And Jamie had been one of 'them'.

"Do you really want to be reminded, Jamie?"

"Sixty thousand dollars, Scott. A six followed by a zero, followed by three more zeroes! A significant chunk of my losses... delivered... gift wrapped... in one trade. Yes, I'm going to get it back. All of it! And I don't care what cheating scumbag has to die. Don't you see, Scott? Finally... some justice. Some divine justice."

Chapter Twenty-Nine

In the heart of Lower Manhattan, between Wall Street and Chinatown, stands a drab 1960's tower block, its forty-one story concrete façade and zigzagging window slits resembling a giant unmarked lottery ballot. It is the Jacob Javits Federal Building. Housed inside its bland architecture are the offices of the Immigration and Naturalization Service, the Environmental Protection Agency, and the FBI's New York Field Office.

Tricia Van Cleyburn shuffled through a pile of freshly printed crime scene photos that were sprawled on the desk of Special Agent Benito Vincente.

"They're definitely Nicole and Bryan Riverton," Vincente mumbled, gobbling down a hand-stretching deli sandwich.

Trish picked up a photograph showing an incinerated body that was so badly burnt the gender of the victim could not be identified. "How can you tell… from this?"

"It'll take a few days for Forensics to identify the bodies from dental records but we've established that Nicole Riverton was on a flight from LaGuardia to Jacksonville the same day as the fire. A BMW was delivered by valet to Jacksonville airport with her name on it. A security guard saw a BMW enter the estate just before the explosion with a female driver. There's a burnt out shell with a BMW badge in the garage. It's Nicole Riverton."

"And her husband?" Trish asked.

"Jacksonville PD took a statement from one of his golf buddies. He'd finished a round with Bryan Riverton and saw him leave the course just prior to the fatal barbecue."

"Any suspects?" Trish asked.

"None, so far."

"And this?" Trish picked up the photograph of Ezra Tauberman lying in the grass. The old man's eyes were open and his neck was bruised. He'd been garroted.

Vincente pointed to the remote control in Tauberman's hand, "The old geezer was killed and someone took his place. The glider's remote was rigged. With pretty sophisticated electronics. Forensics confirms the explosion was caused by C4. They're typing its origins. Inside the house - incendiary devices. Military grade."

"C4? Remote detonation?" Trish thought, *Forrester was right. This guy's definitely ex-Special Ops.* "Was he seen by anyone?"

"Maybe. But not from the coastal road. Marlin Pointe is oceanfront. Just sailboats and powerboats cruising past. The killer swam to shore. Did his business. Swam back. There's a trail in the sand."

The frown on Trish's face meant she had come to the same conclusion Benito Vincente had already made. "He had an accomplice, offshore. Someone else was manning the helm."

"It's a given. Smells like another hit to me."

"Everything's beginning to link. Matthew Carleton financed the Rivertons' company Pegasus BioSciences. Who did both Carleton and the Rivertons rub the wrong way?"

"And there's this…" Vincente produced a file with his oily finger stains on it.

"Lexi Carleton was in West Palm Beach at the time the Rivertons were murdered?" Trish wondered.

"She arrived two days before the explosion on Amelia Island. Her and Nicole Riverton went to Princeton together. Sorority sisters," Vincente said.

"Two days? It gave her time to go over the final plans with her hired hit man."

"And… we're checking to see if she knows how to pilot a boat." Vincente finished his sandwich, scrunched up the wrapper and tossed it across the room. It bounced off the wall and settled next to the wastepaper basket. "Jacksonville PD are way out of their league on this one, Van Cleyburn. Just like the East Hampton Police. You need to check this out. We need statements from people along the Waterway. Check out the marinas, beach concessions, restaurants, souvenir shops. You know the profile of the man we're looking for. Someone must have seen him. And what about Forrester's theory? This cult thing?"

Trish picked up the photos of the charred crime scene. "If there was any writing on the walls of the Rivertons' home, it's not there now. Because there are no walls." She held up a photo of an incinerated body. "Forrester would like us to believe *this* has a spiritual significance. That the killer did *this* to alter the victim's karma at the time of death - a one way trip to Hindu Hell, escorted by an evil black she-bitch with a tiger's paw."

"And is that what you believe?"

"No, Benito, I don't."

"And are you going to prove him wrong?"

"I'd love to."

Chapter Thirty

Le Roux-Berg's Bijouterie Washington was located in the heart of the Embassy District on a fashionable side street off Connecticut Ave, just a few blocks northwest of DuPont Circle. The jewelry boutique occupied a nineteenth century townhouse with a French mansard roofline and balconies with scrolled iron railings. The building had a storied history, surviving the turmoil of the Civil War, prospering during the Reconstruction from 1866 to 1877, and reaching its peak during the Roaring Twenties as the home of an influential New York lobbyist. But its prosperity slid, along with so many others, during the Crash of 1929 and the Great Depression. Its fortunes were lifted after the Second World War in the post-war boom that saw America rise to the forefront of nations, economically and politically. As La Bijouterie, the building was once again at its zenith, one of many shops in a chic enclave along historic Millionaires Row.

Christienne Duval's townhouse was two blocks away from the boutique. She met Scott for lunch at Le Bistro Fermette, just around the corner. The Bistro's bustling atmosphere was reminiscent of a café on the Left Bank of the Seine in Paris. And when she arrived, the ambience was complete. Christienne was so much more woman than any other woman Scott Forrester had ever known. Cultured, refined and worldly; but at the same time, playful and inquisitive. And so, so beautiful. She shared his love of jazz and blues; preferring a quiet stroll through a museum where they could talk, to the thumping beat of a noisy nightclub. Being around her was the relaxing pause he needed in the whirlwind that was his life - a massage for his soul every time he was with her.

"J'adore Le Bistro Fermette," she mused as their lunch arrived - sandwiches on crusty French bread, and the best onion soup in Washington. "It has a *joie de vie* that is so hard to find in America, chéri. If I close my eyes, it smells like I am back on the Champs-Elysée."

"America has its charms, Christienne. Maybe a little harder to find." Scott countered. "Like my favorite place, Archie's Diner. It's a riot of retro Americana and the people are, well… let me put it this way, not exactly like you would find in here. It's unique, that's for sure."

"A diner? Les hamburgers? C'est si drôle! I would love to go. With you, chéri… anywhere. But I have something to tell you…" She held his hand and squeezed it. "I'm leaving soon for a business trip to Geneva. It's Le Roux-Berg's annual meeting. Then Monsieur Portland wants me to go with him to Paris to meet some of our designers, to review this year's collection. Now you won't be jealous, will you, chéri? Remember, it's just business."

"One of these days, I would like to meet this Michael Wayne Portland. Just to be sure."

"Bien sûr. I can arrange it, sometime, chéri. But you must trust me. With Monsieur Portland, it's strictly professional."

"When are you leaving?"

"The day after tomorrow. I may be gone for a week or ten days, I'm not sure. We will be going to Antwerp to see the diamond merchants as well."

Scott's heart sank. *A week without her?*

He reached into his jacket.

"Qu'est-ce que c'est?" Christienne asked, as he handed her two tickets. "The Washington Capitals?"

"Thank God you're not leaving tonight, Christienne. You have no idea how hard it was to get these."

"Ice hockey? Where they chase a rubber ball?"

"It's called a puck."

"A *puck*? C'est ca… oui, a puck. And then they - comment vous dire - punch up?"

"It's the *joie de vie* that is so hard to find in America."

She laughed. "A bien. C'est ça. Tonight?"

"I'll pick you up. Say 6:00?"

"Magnifique, chéri!" she said, with a kiss.

Chapter Thirty-One

"Has he been here often?" Rosie Moreno asked, as Kelly picked up their orders from Archie.

"Never seen him before."

It was a Reuben sandwich and fries for Jamie. For the guy that was with him - a plain burger, nothing on it, no fries. He wanted the burger pink in the middle. Kelly warned him about food poisoning. He repeated, "A burger. Plain. Nothing on the side. Pink in the middle."

"Sure thing."

Jamie Forrester didn't come to Archie's Diner as frequently as his brother. When he did, he was rarely alone. Most of the people he came with were from the local VFW. There was one in particular – an Iraqi Freedom vet, double amputee at the knees - that Jamie had befriended when he returned from Afghanistan. This guy had helped him work through Jamie's depression when he returned from military service as a disabled person trying to adapt to his new 'normal'.

Kelly didn't know the names of any of Jamie's friends. All she knew was that anyone Jamie brought into Archie's Diner usually seemed anti-social, a little 'distant and twisted'. Today, the usual guy, the Iraqi Freedom vet from the VFW, was nowhere to be seen. The man that was sitting with Jamie was able-bodied. But as far as being sociable? Forget it. He was just like the others. Maybe worse.

This guy was a straight up stiff neck. Dark blue denim shirt. Black T-shirt underneath. Stone-colored khakis with a brown leather belt. By the wrinkles in the corner of his eyes and across his brow, he looked mid-forties. Mousy brown hair - it wasn't lush, but it wasn't thin either. Trim and firmly built, just short of six feet tall. He had a jogger's tan and from the tightness of the shirt, looked like he worked out. A lot.

Rosie Moreno hadn't been working at Archie's very long. But her on-the-job training in man-watching had lasted about two seconds. She understood exactly what the game was from the moment she put her apron on. The waitresses at Archie's had a scoring system that was almost patent worthy. They knew a pig when they saw one and if they thought a regular was an eligible hunk, there was a well-defined understanding of which waitress on which shift was next in line to come on to him. The pecking order didn't need to be written down. It went strictly by seniority.

Rosie, the new hire, knew her place. She would wait until staff turnover moved her up the batting order. Kelly Whelan was the leadoff hitter on Rosie's shift.

"What do you think, Kelly?" Rosie asked.

"Him? Not a chance."

"He's got nice buns."

"That's not what I go for."

"Well, he looks like he has money."

"I don't go for money either."

"So, what is it, Kelly? What is it you go for? And why hasn't he got it?"

"It's the eyes, Rosie. You can tell a lot about a man from his eyes. Sincerity is a hard thing to hide. Phoniness is easy to detect. It's always in the eyes."

"And this guy?"

"He gives me the creeps." Kelly's voice was serious. The usual sarcasm was gone. No comic quips. "Haven't you noticed the way he looks at you, Rosie? His eyes are as blue and as cold as polar ice. In fact, if you ask me… they look dead."

Chapter Thirty-Two

Scott followed Christienne's curves with his lips, stroking, probing, exploring the intense connection with her skin; her wet body pressed tightly to his. The sensual surge of inner heat teased him mercilessly. As she arched her back, the softness of her body slipped in and out of his grasp. Their fire burned hotter than anything he had ever experienced, raging uncontrollably, subsiding only when the apex consumed them.

When the hot embers finally cooled, they drifted into a deep, narcotic sleep.

Scott began to dream.

He dreamt that he and Christienne were walking down a forest path; the trees and bushes on either side were dark and shapeless. The trail ahead was lit by a single candle, carried by a black-robed figure. The figure stopped. A ghostly breath extinguished the candle's flame. The world became a black void, and as cold as the grave. A match was struck and the light re-appeared. But when Scott looked beside him, the path was empty. Christienne was gone.

Scott awoke from his nightmare with a start. He pulled the covers off and jumped out of the bed, naked and in a cold sweat.

Christienne moaned, "What is it, chéri?"

The moonlight through the bedroom window was faint. Scott ducked below the window, then peered carefully over the sill. The yard outside was a ghostly shade of gray.

"Did you hear something, chéri?"

"Ssshh!" Scott said, reaching into a drawer. He pulled out a loaded 9mm Beretta. "I thought I heard something. Something moving outside. Behind that tree."

He held the pistol vertically. A red dot lit up the wall above the dresser as the gun's laser sight broke the semi-darkness.

Christienne's voice trembled. "What is it, Scott?"

"Ssshh!"

"Scott, you're scaring me!" She said, shunting out of bed and onto the floor beside him. She clutched his waist, her naked warmth blanketing his back. "You've been dreaming, chéri."

The trees swayed gently, rustling in a slight breeze. Crispy leaves descended from their branches. Passing clouds hid the crescent-shaped sliver of moon; its flickering light acting like a soft strobe.

Nothing else moved. The darkness was playing tricks.

Christienne could be right. I have been dreaming.

Christienne crawled back into bed. "Chéri, hold me. It was just a dream, chéri. A dream."

Scott put the gun on the dresser and returned to her arms. She kissed him and nestled against his chest. His heart was pounding. *If it was a dream, it was an awful dream.* He looked up into the moonlit blankness of the ceiling, unable to sleep.

A twig cracked outside.

And this time, both of them heard it.

Christienne screamed.

The moonlight was not playing tricks. A hooded figure was peering through the window. A black, faceless silhouette.

Scott jumped out of bed, grabbed the gun and pointed it at the window. The pistol's red dot sighted the target.

Black. Faceless.

The silhouette disappeared below the windowsill.

Like a cat, Scott bolted through the bedroom door and raced through the living room. He reached the kitchen with breakneck speed and pushed the back door open. With two hands gripped tightly around cold steel, he jumped onto the back porch in a crouch. He aimed from side to side, preparing to fire at the slightest movement.

But there was no one there.

Scott stumbled naked towards the maple tree, gun raised at eye level. His palms were sweaty and pulsed with nervous energy. Slowly, he circled the tree trunk, the red dot following the curvature of the bark. One step. Then another. Whoever was hiding behind that tree was about to test his highly trained instincts, trigger-sure reflexes.

There was no one there.

The quiet of the night was disturbed by a rumble. He heard a car's muffler in the distance. The rains of October had swelled the creek that flowed through the ravine behind Scott's house. On the opposite bank of the stream were the backyards of houses on the adjoining cul-de-sac. There was a gap between the houses, and in that gap, a vehicle was parked with its lights out.

It was a large, square vehicle. A van.

Scott descended the ravine and scampered up the other side. The van moved forward, its headlights out. Scott raced towards it.

The van's lights came on in Scott's face.

He grabbed the door handle and pulled it open. The person in the driver's seat recoiled at the sight of a naked man wielding a gun. A pall of dim light reflecting off the instrument cluster revealed the outline of the driver - a figure wearing a hooded sweatshirt.

A laser dot marked the center of the driver's head. The figure cowered in fright. Scott pulled him violently out of the van, pushed him to the ground and put the gun to his chest.

The person screamed, "No! No! Don't shoot! Please don't shoot! I've got money. If it's money you want... you can have it! Please-"

Lights came on around the neighborhood. A man in a dressing gown appeared on a porch, a shotgun in his hands.

Scott reached into the van and turned the interior lights on to see the person's face.

The driver was a teenager.

The emblem on his sweatshirt said, 'Zombie's Pizza'.

Scott was breathing heavily. He lifted the boy off the driveway and pressed the barrel of the Beretta into his chest. "Were you looking into my bedroom window?"

"No, sir! No, sir! I swear! I'm just delivering pizzas!"

The man in the dressing gown, his flashlight wagging back and forth across the grass as he approached, called out, "What's going on here!"

"Take your sweatshirt off," Scott said to the pizza delivery boy.

The kid whimpered in a half sob, "Please, don't kill me!"

"Take your sweatshirt off," Scott repeated, as he relaxed his grip and let the young man go.

The boy removed the top. His voice was shaking, "Here! It's yours!"

Scott took the sweatshirt and tied it around his naked waist, then tucked the gun in the back. "It's okay, Mr. Bremner. I thought this kid was a prowler."

"Scott? Is that you? Scott Forrester?"

"I thought I saw a prowler in my yard. I thought it was this kid." The words stammered out as Scott backed down into the ravine, "It's okay, Mr. Bremner. I'm sorry. I thought he was a prowler."

The young man got to his feet. "Hey, what about my sweatshirt?" he cried out. "I have to pay for a new one!"

Once Scott reached the edge of the creek, away from the prying lights, he pulled the sweatshirt from his waist and threw it up the hillside. "I'm sorry, kid. I made a mistake, okay?" Naked again, he crossed the stream, stumbling through a thicket of thorny bushes and fallen tree branches.

Christienne was standing at the back door wearing Scott's leather jacket, shivering in the cold night air. She held out a T-shirt and a pair of jeans. "I'm scared, Scott. Who was that in the window? Is he gone?"

Scott slid into the jeans, his body racing with adrenaline. He looked back into the twilight. Faint outlines defined the houses. The pizza delivery van had left. The porch light across the ravine was out. Darkness had consumed the subdivision again. And darkness was consuming his thoughts. *Was the darkness still hiding someone?*

"Scott? What should we do? Should we call the police?"

He took Christienne in his arms. She was chilled. They were both chilled. He held her close and the warmth began to return. "It's over, Christienne. There's no-one here."

"Who was that?"

"I don't know."

The air was cold. Sound traveled easily.

There was a noise - the harsh chirp of a drive belt as an engine's starter cranked over.

A muffler rumbled. An engine revved up.

The sound had come from the other side of the house.

Scott let go of Christienne and ran towards the noise, his gun once again drawn.

Scott's house had a rear drive beside Jamie's basement apartment. Jamie's van, equipped with special controls, was gone. He was at a party in Georgetown.

The rear driveway snaked up from the bungalow's walkout basement door through a grove of spruce trees until it met the road. Scott ran through the spruce trees to the end of their drive.

A black van was parked across the street on the grassy verge of a piece of vacant ground. The van pulled out from hiding, cutting the soft turf underneath, then bounced onto the crumbling asphalt and sped away. Its rear wheels caught a patch of wet leaves; it slipped and its back end swung around. Then its tires caught dry pavement and with a scratching roar of rubber and grit, the black van leapt into the night with its lights out.

Scott ran down the road after it, gun drawn. But it was too fast. Scott thought of firing, but decided against it. He kicked the ground. "Shit! Damn!"

He walked back, disconsolate, angry.

Not fear... anger. Rage.

Christienne stood at the kitchen door, trembling, "Scott, should we call the police?"

"No. I didn't get the license number. I didn't see his face. Did you?" Christienne shook her head, no. "Then what description can we give them? Just a guy in a hooded sweatshirt. They'll make the same mistake I did, and shake down some kid delivering pizzas. *Shit!* We can't do anything."

Scott stepped into the warmth of the kitchen, his T-shirt stained with sweat, the gun returned to the waistband of his jeans.

"You must be cold," Christienne said. "I'll make some coffee." She took two mugs out of the cupboard. Her hands were shaking.

Scott looked down at his bare feet. They were dirty and cut from the branches that littered the ravine. "I'm going to take a shower," he said.

He limped from the kitchen towards the dining room, then stopped abruptly and exclaimed, "*Jesus!*"

The dining room was dark, lit only by the stray light coming in from the kitchen. Scott stood in the archway, his eyes frozen straight ahead, focused on a shadowy object in the center of the dining room table.

An object that had not been there before.

His shout caused Christienne to drop the mugs on the counter with a clatter. "Scott? What is it?"

He swallowed hard and pulled out his gun.

How the hell had this thing gotten in here?

He panned the room with his gun, its red laser light darting from wall to wall.

"For Christ's sake, Scott! What are you doing?"

Scott reached for the light switch.

How did this thing get in my house?

He turned the light on. The object on the table stood erect and alone, like a taunting gravestone.

He did this.

Christienne clung to Scott's arm. "You're scaring me, Scott. What is it? Speak to me!"

"Don't touch it!" he said, as he circled the table, transfixed by the object. "Stay here! I'm going to search the house. Don't touch that thing, Christienne. Leave it alone."

"Search the house? And *leave me*? Mais non! You're not leaving me here! I'm going with you!"

"*Stay here*, Christienne. You'll be okay."

"Merde! Non! Je n'arrête pas ici! Scott-"

"*Stay... here!*"

He searched the bedroom. There was no one.

The bathroom was next. The other bedroom.

No one on the top floor.

He crept downstairs to Jamie's apartment. There was no sign of forced entry. In fact, the patio door was still locked. Scott opened each closet; looked behind the small bathroom's shower curtain; in the kitchen; in the furnace room. Anywhere someone might be hiding. There was nothing. Just silence.

Scott returned upstairs. Christienne was curled up on the brown leather sofa, her face gaunt and pleading, "Has someone been inside the house? The prowler?"

"He must have come in through the back door and left the same way." Scott took Christienne into his arms. She crumpled against his chest. The tension of the night released in a flood of tears. He stroked her hair. He pulled her face up. "Christienne... look at me. This is *very* important. Tell me what happened. From the moment I went outside. What did you see? What did you hear?"

Christienne wiped the tears from her cheeks. "You ran towards that big tree. I was afraid. You ran away and I couldn't see you. It was so dark." She sniffled and took a deep breath. "Then I realized. We were both naked. It was cold. I was alone. I didn't know what else to do. I shut the door and bolted it."

"You shut the door? Did you hear anything after that? Inside the house?"

"No. No. It was quiet. I became even more frightened. I was so frightened, Scott!"

"Think, Christienne. Think."

"I remember going into the bedroom, picking up your clothes from the chair. I put your shirt on. Then I looked out the bedroom window. Lights were on. I saw figures. One had a gun. A rifle I think. I saw someone disappear down into the ravine. I was going to call the police. I went into the hall and got your phone out of your jacket, but I didn't have time because I heard shouting, and saw you running back. I didn't know what to do," she sobbed. "I just put on your jacket and came outside. C'est tout. That's all."

He hugged her.

"I was so afraid, Scott! I was thinking… were you all right? Who was that man with the gun?" She began to cry. "Oh, Scott… what's going on?"

"It's hard to explain. I don't want you involved."

"Involved? Have you forgotten the woman in the Gallery? That man with the leaflets? Whatever is going on, Scott… I have been *involved* from the minute I first met you!"

"You needn't be afraid, Christienne."

"Afraid? Of course, I'm afraid. For you, as well as myself. And when you saw this-" she pointed to the object in the center of the dining room table, "I could see the fear in your eyes. You reacted… as if someone had died!"

"Someone *has* died, Christienne. Many someones."

"But it's only a b-"

"No. It's not. It's more than that. It's proof that he was *here* in *my* house."

"You know who that prowler was, don't you? I can see it in your eyes. Who is he, Scott?"

"A killer," he whispered.

Christienne gasped, "A *killer*? Oh my God, Scott! A killer? Who did he kill? Oh, Mon Dieu!"

Scott went into the kitchen.

"Where are you going? *Don't leave me again!*"

"It's alright, Christienne." He pulled open a drawer and took out a large Ziploc freezer bag. "We can't touch *it*. It's evidence. There may be fingerprints."

As Scott approached the object, he could feel it saying, "I'm better than you, FBI Special Agent Scott Forrester."

It was a bottle of wine.

Red wine.

The label was elegant. French writing on a white background. And stained. A dried red bead that dribbled through the words, 'Chateau LaTour 1961' and ended with tiny splatters over the words 'Appellation Contrôlée'.

The stains were blood.

The bottle was from the Carleton Mansion.

It stood silently, defiantly, on the dining room table's cream-colored cloth. Mocking him.

Are you good enough, Scott Forrester?

Are you really good enough... to stop me?

Scott lowered the plastic bag over the bottle's neck and carefully lifted it up. He zipped the bag shut. The bottle and its bloodstains were captured. But the evil it represented was not. He felt the bottle's weight, and with it, the weight of the fear, the weight of the sorrow, the weight of his victims' pain.

Christienne looked into Scott's eyes.

They were on fire.

Chapter Thirty-Three

He had been inside Scott Forrester's house. Walked on Scott Forrester's hardwood floor. *He* had placed a bottle of wine from Matthew Carleton's cellar on Scott Forrester's dining room table. *It* was a middle finger salute, right in Scott Forrester's face.

He drove a van, an older model with a slipping belt.

He was cunning. *He* was stealthy.

But, as far as Scott Forrester was concerned, *he* had made a mistake. A *big* mistake.

The sun rose through the gap between the houses. Christienne was curled up under a fleece throw on the brown leather sofa. She'd refused to go back into the bedroom. Scott was slouched in the armchair; its loose springs poking his back; one eye open, one eye shut; barely asleep, gun in hand, his hand in his lap, his mind full of thoughts. Anger. Rage.

The morning sun broke through the curtains. Scott's cell phone chirped in the black leather jacket Christienne had discarded on the floor beside her.

Few people outside the FBI knew his number. He stumbled out of the chair and crawled across the floor.

The commotion woke Christienne up. She rose with a start, her fear renewed. But seeing Scott, and realizing where she was, she slumped back into the sofa and pulled the throw over her face. "*Merde!*" She mumbled. "Quelle nuit! What a night!"

Scott flipped open the phone, expecting a familiar voice. But he didn't get it.

"Mr. Forrester?"

"Yes."

"FBI?"

"Yes, who is this?"

"You don't know me, but I know you. Sigma Venture Capital."

Scott was still in a sleepy haze. *Where had he heard that before?* "Chicago?" he asked, remembering.

"My name is Sue Lee Chen, Mr. Forrester. I'm Dominic Sant'Angello's Executive Vice President. I wasn't in the office when you were in Chicago. But you left your number. You said if anyone had any information-"

Scott heard her voice choke up. "What's this about?" He asked.

"I know what happened... to Nicole and Bryan Riverton. I know it wasn't a gas explosion."

Her words hit him like a rock. Jacksonville PD were telling the media it was a gas explosion in the hope that it would draw the killer out. That he would take offence that his carefully orchestrated 'work' was being referred to as an 'accident'. They were trying to play to his pride. At some point, even the most hardened killer likes to boast. Only someone who had inside information would know it wasn't a gas explosion.

"Where are you, Ms. Chen? How can we meet?"

"I'm in Washington. And I don't have much time. I think they're following me. I've been able to hide so far but-"

"Name a place. I'll have a squad car there in less than five minutes. I can take you into protective custody."

"*No!* No. I want to meet *you*. And only you. Somewhere away from the police or the FBI. You don't realize how much danger I can put us in if we are anywhere close to a police station."

"I'm not afraid of danger. That's what I do."

"You have no idea, Mr. Forrester... how much more dangerous this can get."

• • •

Trish Van Cleyburn's phone rang. She had just arrived at New York's LaGuardia Airport. It was 7:45AM.

Caller ID said it was Scott Forrester.

"Trish, I need you to come to Washington. Today. It's urgent."

"Scott, what are you talking about? I'm on my way to Jacksonville. My flight's leaving soon."

"I know why you're going. But reschedule it. Stop in Washington first. Do you remember Sant'Angello's VP? The one who wasn't in the office the day we interviewed Sant'Angello in Chicago?"

"Uh, I think so. Somebody named Chen?"

"Sue Lee Chen. She's surfaced. And she has information. She knows it wasn't a gas explosion. I think she knows who the killer is. She's in Washington. She's frightened. And she's on the run."

"Good. Bring her in. Take a statement. I'll talk to Griffin. I'll tell him I asked you to do it."

"You don't understand. She'll only talk off campus. I'm meeting her at noon, at Archie's Diner."

"You and a confidential source? Connected to Sant'Angello? There's *no way*! This has to be done properly, Scott. Officially, it's my investigation, not yours. I need to handle this. You're off the case, remember?"

"Exactly. That's why you need to be here, Trish. Today. And there's something else that happened. Last night. I'll explain it all when I see you."

"Scott, you're sounding crazy again. I don't like what you're telling me. Why now?"

"Because it's happening now, Trish."

"What's happening now?"

"I don't know. That's what I want to find out."

"But I'm about to board a plane for Jacksonville!"

"Delay your trip. Trust me. A few hours… that's all we'll need. Sue Lee Chen is in hiding. Whatever's going on… it's here in Washington. Not Jacksonville. And she sounds like she's inside it."

"You mean the cult thing?"

"A few hours, Trish. That's all I'm asking."

Trish was standing inside the Departure Terminal. The flight to Jacksonville was being called. "You're using psychology on me, Forrester."

"You'll be here? Noon?"

There was a pause. "You said Archie's?" Trish looked at her watch and the Terminal's monitors. She found her flight on the screen. It showed: 'Jacksonville - Now Boarding'.

She sighed, "Damn you, Forrester!"

"Well?"

"Okay... I'll be there."

Chapter Thirty-Four

S ue Lee Chen had been sitting alone in the booth by the door for about an hour. It was almost midday. Archie's regular customers were beginning to trickle in.

Two young men in white overalls, with dried paint on their faces and hands, bantered with their boss over heaping platters of hot biscuits and sausage gravy. In the booth behind them, a young woman in a white blouse and navy blue skirt giggled with her friend as they shared a cup of joe before her big job interview. She flashed a ring proudly on her left hand. With her right palm upturned, her friend read her fortune. The future was bright.

Look at them, Sue Lee thought. *They're all asleep. The whole damn world is sleeping!*

Outside Archie's steamy windows, what was once a quiet and innocuous street was now filling up with people escaping their offices for some fresh air. Transient sunlight shone through the gaps in the brown brick buildings that surrounded the diner. Like a turtle stranded on a rock, sunning itself, Archie's seemed small and insignificant in Georgetown's urban ecosystem.

Sue Lee Chen was about to change that.

She felt in her handbag. A crisp, sealed envelope bulged with secrets - secrets she hoped would set in motion an irrepressible and irreversible tide of truth and justice.

Kelly Whelan handed her a menu. Sue Lee shrugged it off, impatiently checking her watch as she searched the parking lot for the FBI agent she had arranged to meet.

She ordered without making eye contact, "Tuna salad. Oil and vinegar dressing." Even a greasy spoon like Archie's must have a simple tuna salad.

"Sure thing," Kelly said, thinking *Pompous bitch.*

Kelly Whelan spotted Scott Forrester getting out of his black sedan. He entered Archie's with that hurried 'I'm not hungry' look that Kelly had seen many times before; usually when that stuck-up blonde with the perfect hair met him for lunch. This time, he made a beeline for the imperious Chinese woman sitting like a starched shirt by the door. She wasn't Scott's type at all - petit, with taut, shoulder-length black hair, flat-chested, fussy manners – and way too conservative.

"Sue Lee Chen?"

"Mr. Forrester?"

Scott slid into the booth.

Kelly's eyebrows raised. "Coffee?"

"Black."

"What can I get you, Scott?"

"The Special, Kelly."

"Fries or onion rings?"

"Fries," he said in a matter-of-fact tone.

"Heart attack on a plate with fries coming up. And a crushed dead fish salad." Kelly scowled at the Chinese woman, tore off the order, and turned towards the kitchen.

"Are they always like that in here?" Sue Lee asked.

"Like what?"

"Obnoxious."

"Always. That's why I come. But if you feel uncomfortable, we can leave."

"To go to your office at the FBI? No, Mr. Forrester. I told you... no way! This place is perfect. It looks just like in the movies."

Sue Lee glanced around the diner: the faded Yankees pennants on the wall; a signed Mickey Mantle photograph; an old-fashioned covered cake stand on the counter. "You know what I mean? The seedy diner where informants come to spill their guts to the FBI."

She rubbed her arms, as if she were cold. Her Rolex caught the sun and flashed a beam of gold onto the ketchup bottle. The beam of light wobbled as she tried to settle her nerves.

"Movie?" Scott said. "I'd say it's more like a cartoon."

Sue Lee smiled. It was a forced smile. Then she frowned. "I said it, didn't I? I said *informant*."

The lonely stress of the past hour was becoming too much for Sue Lee Chen to contain. She fussed with her blouse, picked lint from her black skirt. Sue Lee Chen - Executive Vice President at Sigma Venture Capital - wasn't used to losing control of what she wanted to say, and how she wanted to say it.

Choking back tears, she reached into her handbag for a tissue, "I knew... I knew it would eventually come to *this*."

Scott studied her face. It had the look of a scared rabbit. "Whatever you're afraid of, Ms. Chen - *whoever* you're afraid of – I promise, you're safe now."

Sue Lee Chen closed her eyes, wishing that were only true. When they opened, tears trickled down her cheeks. "Safe? You have no idea who you're dealing with, Mr. Forrester, do you?"

Scott took an edge-worn notepad from his jacket.

Sue Lee flinched and stiffened. She was emphatic, "Oh, no. You won't need to take notes." She placed the neatly sealed envelope on the table. "Do you remember the woman with the yellow sari and orange headscarf that you tried to help that night at the Freer Gallery? At Narayan's reception? The one who rushed out the emergency exit convinced you weren't FBI agents but Narayan's thugs?"

"The one that nearly gave my partner a concussion? That was some move. That was you?"

"Yes, Mr. Forrester. That was me."

"Why did you ask Narayan to forgive you? Who are they, Ms. Chen?" There was anxiety in Sue Lee Chen's face - that same face of regret Scott had seen peering through the rainy cab window; a face that was still struggling to cross the fine line between holding in a secret, and letting it out.

"I was a fool to think he would let me walk away like that. A fool to think that a simple piece of paper would solve *everything*. And look at me," she sobbed. "Here I am again, trying to do the same thing!"

"You cried out for help to the wrong people, Ms. Chen."

"Yes, I ran away… from the truth."

"But not this time?"

"No, Mr. Forrester. Not *this* time. Hiding from the truth does not change the reality of who I have become, what I have become involved in. I realize that now." She tapped the envelope gently. "And I'm not foolish enough to think that giving you this will solve all my problems. Because it can't."

Kelly arrived with Sue Lee's salad and Scott's coffee. "Your sandwich is still on the grill, Scott. It'll be another minute." She looked Sue Lee Chen up and down: the eyes red and teary, the lips trembling and pale. *Another one of Scott's broken hearted girlfriends?* Kelly thought. *When would Scott Forrester ever learn?*

Kelly knew when she wasn't welcome and left.

Sue Lee pushed the envelope forward. "There's enough in here to indict Dominic Sant'Angello on securities fraud. But the rest is up to you, Mr. Forrester."

"Meaning?"

"I don't want to think that he was involved in the murder of Matthew Carleton."

"But you do think that, don't you?"

She didn't answer.

"How did it start, Ms. Chen? Dominic Sant'Angello and Matthew Carleton?"

She drew a deep breath and as the words finally came out, the release felt good. "Carleton didn't need us. Not at first. There were plenty of investors desperate to throw their money at him. Funny, but in the end, after all that he had done to destroy us, we were all he had left. Especially when the Czech money dried up. We became the only game in town."

"Ms. Chen, let's start from the beginning - how were Carleton and Sant'Angello connected? Were they partners?"

"Not really." She sniffled into the tissue. "But in the end, I guess we were all working for Matthew Carleton. Whether we knew it or not. Whether we liked it or not."

"Then, what *was* the connection between them?"

She batted her softly curved eyes, squeezing another tear onto her cheek, "Jiri Kostelic was the connection."

"Who is Jiri Kostelic, Ms. Chen?"

"He's one of the world's largest gemstone wholesalers. Kostelic owns a few retail stores, but they're just a front. Czech Mafia money. Russian Mafia money. Bulgarian Mafia money. Anyone in Eastern Europe who wanted money laundered eventually found Jiri Kostelic standing in front of the washing machine. He funneled their illicit cash through his wholesale gem trade. Columbian emeralds. Sri Lankan rubies. Sapphires, tanzanite, any kind of precious gem. Even blood diamonds from Sierra Leone. He didn't care. Just because it sparkles, it doesn't mean it's clean, Mr. Forrester."

Sue Lee glanced at the fat envelope waiting by Scott's hand and sighed, then she continued, "At first, it was easy to convert their cash into hard assets, gemstones Kostelic bought directly from the mines and other sources. But eventually there was just too much money coming in. Kostelic was enormously well connected throughout Eastern Europe. And he didn't... no, he *couldn't* disappoint anyone. Some of them were his friends. People he had grown up with on the streets of Prague. Went to school with. That's when his usual money laundering methods ran into trouble. He had a problem."

"What problem?"

"Check it out, Mr. Forrester. He told his clients he was converting their cash into cut stones and jewelry. But if Jiri Kostelic really had the inventory he claims to have on his books, they'd need Fort Knox to house it. What he had started to do was store the money in mining shares, exploration contracts - anything Kostelic could find to turn dirty money into clean, safe money. But he didn't tell his Eastern European 'investors' they were getting paper assets - not the stash of gems they'd been guaranteed. And that's when he turned his problem into Matthew Carleton's opportunity."

"He started funneling his illicit cash to Carleton?"

"To a maze of offshore accounts. Carleton laundered it for him. And for every hundred dollars Kostelic brought in as seed capital, Carleton guaranteed Kostelic a twenty percent return. It was an easy profit for Kostelic and he reinvested it, and then the cycle would repeat itself. Fresh cash. Reinvested profits."

"A perpetual money machine..."

"Until..." Sue Lee paused, picking again at the salad, shuffling through the layers of sliced peppers and cucumbers like an archaeologist at Troy. She examined every flake of tuna as if it were buried treasure. But she didn't find anything worth eating. "You see, Mr. Forrester, when it came to creating companies, Matthew Carleton had this Midas touch. He could turn paper into gold. And as long as his IPO's soared, the source of funding that backed them seemed unlimited."

"But the IPO market became saturated. Share prices started to fall. The money dried up."

"Correct. And Kostelic spent lavishly, on himself and a harem of women, all over the world. But then his Czech friends wanted to cash out. So did the Russians. They'd invested in bad real estate deals and credit default swaps and needed to liquidate the gemstones they thought they'd

deposited with Kostelic, to cover their losses. But Kostelic's inventory of
gemstones was a phantom. He'd invested their money in Carleton's schemes
instead, after his portfolio of mining shares went underwater. He needed a
source of quick cash to pay them back. And he needed it fast."

"And how did that involve Dominic Sant'Angello?"

"By that time, Sigma Venture Capital had built up its own house of
cards. There were more people like Matthew Carleton doing similar things.
Our money pipeline came from the Far East. That's why Sant'Angello hired
me. Relationships count for everything in Asia, Mr. Forrester, and my family
is very well connected. The money came from China, Hong Kong,
Indonesia, Malaysia – new money, oil money, some of it drug money,
especially from Thailand. Like Matthew Carleton, Dominic Sant'Angello
didn't care where it came from. With Kostelic's cash flow starting to dry up,
Matthew Carleton turned to us for funding. We subscribed to his private
placements. And once he found a new source of money with us, he couldn't
be happier. He was like a shark in water: when he smelt fresh prey, he swam
quickly in that direction."

"Was that when people started to die?"

Sue Lee looked away and her face tensed. She put down her fork. She
was done eating. The food had no taste. "Carleton had created his companies
by setting someone up as what he called 'the designated stooge'. Someone
like Liang Wong, an immigrant with a real product but poor cash flow. Or
Deuce Meredith with his hillbilly inheritance and no brains."

"So, they were victims from the start?"

"Carleton created IPO's for them, turned a spectacular profit and
everyone in the game won. Greed greased the wheels and the machine
accelerated. It became a feeding frenzy. Carleton lured in private
placements, created ever more IPO's, even as the market began to tank. He
convinced everyone rising stock prices would never end. Carleton sucked us
all in. Professionals like Mr. Sant'Angello. We should have known better,

but Carleton's schemes were seductive. And no sooner had we started to take bigger and bigger risks with him, he reneged on us."

"How?"

"Just when we got in way over our heads, he dumped his stock – *big time* – and began short selling behind our backs. Driving share prices down."

"No honor amongst thieves."

"Not honor, Mr. Forrester. Co-dependency. How can I explain it? Well, it seemed to us that as long as Carleton was dependant on our funding, it was like several ropes holding up a tent – with one loss of tension, the whole thing would collapse. We felt bound together as one enterprise. We thought we were all *equally* vulnerable." She chuckled again, shook her head and wiped the corner of her eye. "How stupid was *that*? The whole thing was an unholy alliance from the very beginning! A confederacy. And suddenly, when Carleton's process ground to a halt, it got ugly for us. Real *ugly*."

"You mean ugly enough to *kill*?"

"It's all in there." Sue Lee pointed to the envelope. "I knew it was over when Deuce Meredith was killed. When Jiri Kostelic fled to the Bahamas. Now it's climaxed with Pegasus."

"Pegasus Biosciences?"

"It was Carleton's biggest scam. And it was his best: a surefire mega-jackpot of Olympic proportions. And that greedy bastard wouldn't let us in on it! He wanted it all for himself. That's when it really started to unravel for Sant'Angello. Big time. The global financial meltdown dried up our Asian money pipeline. We were left with acres of our own highly leveraged but useless paper, with no place to peddle it. And suckered into Carleton's pyramid schemes, our leverage was untenable. But Mr. Sant'Angello had a plan of his own. He would create his own way out - one last scam called Whale River."

"Whale River Diamond Mines?" Scott said. "In Canada?"

Sue Lee was surprised. "Yes, Mr. Forrester. Does the FBI know about this already?"

"Not officially, Ms. Chen," Scott replied. He knew that his brother had shorted a mining company named Whale River because one of his chat mates had inside information. Some things were beginning to make sense. "So it's another scam? But this time it was yours?"

"Sant'Angello bought prospecting licenses in Northern Quebec, where the world's newest diamond pipes have been found. Kostelic had exactly the kind of expertise we needed. We had to build up the Whale River story. We needed Kostelic to put his reputation behind it. And we needed him to entice his Eastern European speculators into one last investment. That's how Whale River started. And it would become Sant'Angello's undoing."

"How so?"

"Sant'Angello deliberately bought licenses he knew were dry holes - where prospectors had found nothing. They were cheap properties but they were next to successful ones. Sant'Angello needed Kostelic to salt core samples from Whale River with raw diamonds from mines elsewhere. He'd done it before. In Africa. Kostelic knew how to rig the geology to make the samples look like they were drilled at Whale River. Everything was set – we worked up the initial private placements in Chicago, pre-registered the stock on the American Stock Exchange. The next step was Kostelic's. Then just as Sant'Angello was planning a press release to hype the IPO, Carleton got to Kostelic first. Sant'Angello desperately needed Kostelic to 'validate' his core samples - to boost Whale River's potential in the eyes of investors - but Kostelic backed out of the plan and fled to the Bahamas."

"He abandoned Sant'Angello?"

"Kostelic was threatened. Matthew Carleton personally knew some of the Russians who'd invested in Kostelic's cash for gems scheme, investors who hadn't cashed out yet. He knew Kostelic's portfolio was underwater. So he told them that Kostelic might have trouble returning their investment. They were furious. And if they thought for a moment that Kostelic was swindling them, they would have buried him in the garden of his Spanish villa, ass end up. Fear is a better motivator than greed, Mr. Forrester."

"You're preaching to the converted."

Kelly Whelan came by and the conversation stopped. Sue Lee motioned, without speaking, for her plate to be taken away. Kelly complied, with a sneer.

Sue Lee continued, "Then Carleton twisted the knife, straight into our stomachs. He offered Kostelic a sweetheart deal. If Kostelic would abandon his support for Sant'Angello and Whale River, and divert the money he was raising from Eastern Europe to him, he would cut Kostelic in on the Pegasus IPO. Well, Mr. Forrester... that was it. It was a no brainer... a sure fire way for Kostelic to make a big enough profit to pay the Russians back. Kostelic took Carleton's deal and sailed off into his Caribbean sunset. When Sant'Angello pushed back, Carleton threatened to leak information about Whale River to the SEC. Sant'Angello couldn't have that. Our own investors would panic and pull out everything. We needed to finalize our own private placements or the Whale River Diamond Mines deal would be dead. And without Whale River, Sigma Venture Capital was staring straight into the face of bankruptcy. And Dominic Sant'Angello was staring into the cold corners of a jail cell, for securities fraud. We got the deal done without the core samples."

"This isn't just about phony core samples. It's about murder. And the Temple of Dvaipa. They're involved in this somehow, Ms. Chen, aren't they?"

"Yes, Mr. Forrester, it is about the Temple. If it wasn't for me, they wouldn't have-" Sue Lee stopped abruptly. The truth was too much. She broke down.

Scott finished her sentence, "Invested in these schemes? The Temple lost money in these scams, didn't they, Ms. Chen? *Big* money."

Sue Lee turned her head, tears streaming down her face, unable to look him in the eyes.

Scott leaned back. *So, that was it,* he thought. *The deal with the Devil.* "Matthew Carleton..." he said, "in his insatiable lust for money, swindled the *wrong* investors. And the victims? Liang Wong. Deuce Meredith. DeAndre Antoin. The Rivertons. And Carleton himself. All of them. Every one of them. The Temple of Dvaipa is taking apart Carleton's empire, one corpse at a time. And that's the reason you're here, isn't it? You think you're going to be their next victim. You can't go back to Chicago because-"

"Oh God help me!" she sobbed. "If only you understood who *they* are and what *they* really want." Her words were blurred with fear and tension. "Yes, *they* want revenge. And they're going to get it! But I never expected… I never thought… *she* could be that *evil*. And you don't know her like I do. *She*'s so powerful, Mr. Forrester, *so dangerous*."

"Who are *they*, Sue Lee? Sudhir Narayan? Dominic Sant'Angello? And who is *she*? Is she Lexi Carleton?"

Scott's Reuben sandwich arrived.

Kelly's coffeepot hovered to refill his mug.

Everything after that happened in a split second.

Kelly leaned over. The glass of the coffeepot caught the dot of red light that was searching for Sue Lee's temple. The laser refracted through the glass into Scott's peripheral vision. He turned. The red glare vanished. It had moved. It had found its target.

Scott looked into Sue Lee Chen's puzzled face, her expression said, 'What was it? What had the FBI agent seen?'

Scott opened his mouth, but couldn't form the words - the warning - fast enough.

The bullet crashed through the window of the diner and entered the base of Sue Lee Chen's head just behind her ear. It made its lethal exit out the side of her throat and shattered Kelly Whelan's coffeepot. The explosion of glass embedded in Kelly's thigh.

Sue Lee Chen slumped sideways in her seat and dropped to the floor with a thud - her eyes glazed, her mouth foaming with a mixture of air and blood.

Kelly Whelan collapsed in pain beside her.

Then a random spray of shots imploded the windows along the entire front of Archie's Diner - a bullet striking Archie in the shoulder, pushing him backwards into a stack of dishes, the dishes crashing to the floor.

The girl in the business skirt and her fortune-telling friend shrieked with terror as shards of glass from the windows cut their faces, blood staining their white blouses. The apprentice painters made a beeline for the door but were driven back - bullets whistling through the air above them, embedding themselves in the wall with a puff of gypsum dust.

Shots were coming in over their heads, driving everyone to the floor. The sniper's strafing had accomplished its intended effect - complete pandemonium broke out, escape was not an option.

"Trish!" Scott screamed into his cell phone, as he checked Sue Lee's pulse. She was dead.

Trish Van Cleyburn was waiting outside in Scott's black sedan, "I'm on it! SWAT's on its way!"

"Do you have an angle on the shooter?"

"Negative! Can't find him!"

"Look, dammit! Look!"

"I *am* looking!"

A bullet whizzed through the open window space and struck the wall. A woman with a baby panicked.

"Get down! Stay down!" Scott yelled, hunched over, his gun drawn, shuffling through the broken glass towards Kelly Whelan. She had crawled behind the counter. Her leg was bleeding profusely. He found a dishcloth and pulled out the glass shard that was protruding from her leg. She winced. He covered the wound and said, "Press down. It'll stop the bleeding. You're going to be okay, Kelly. Stay here until the ambulance arrives."

She reached out and clutched him tightly around the neck. Her voice was trailing off. He could tell she was going into shock. "Scott, stay with me."

"I can't. I have to check Archie. Stay put. Don't move."

Another volley of shots crashed into the diner's walls. Patiently aimed. Methodically placed. Designed to keep everyone pinned to the floor.

Archie was in bad shape. Scott couldn't tell how close the bullet had come to his heart. His pulse was weak. "Trish... We have people down in the diner. They're badly hurt. What about the shooter? Have you located him?"

"Negative! I can't see where the shots are coming from!"

Archie's frightened patrons huddled under the booths. Scott moved towards the door, keeping his head below table level. He swung the front door open with his foot and jammed a plate underneath it, to hold it open.

Across the parking lot, there was a three-story building - a row of shops and boutiques at street level with two floors of studio apartments and offices above them. Scott scanned the windows but couldn't see anything. He turned his attention to the apartment building behind them. It was a condo, seven stories tall, with wide, open terraced balconies.

"That condo building... those balconies, Trish!"

The laser light from the sniper's rifle skipped in and out of the diner. As its red beam ran across the long counter, Archie's terrified customers anticipated more incoming rounds and let out shrieks of fright.

"I've got him, Scott!" Trish said. "Two floors down from the top, third balcony on the left! Do you see him? Lying prone?"

"Yeah, that's him - call it in!"

Police sirens wailed as a SWAT Team van, escorted by a bevy of squad cars, came into view down an adjacent side street. The van veered into the dry cleaner's parking lot, out of the sniper's line of fire. The van doors opened. A Tactical Team jumped out, gear in hand. The parking lot quickly turned into a staging area and command post.

"What's he doing, Scott? What's he hanging around for? He must know SWAT's arrived."

"He knows."

"He's a fool to stay out in the open like that, Scott. The first police sniper to get an angle on him... and he's smoked!"

"I'm betting that's exactly what he wants!"

"What?"

"He's playing chicken with us, Trish. He's saying - come and get me, if you think you can. But I know you can't. He's waiting until we get set up, then he'll make his exit."

"That's just crazy!"

"He's confident, Trish. And prepared. Like he always is."

Scott picked up a dinner plate from the floor. He held the plate into the space of the diner's opened door. The wandering laser light skimmed the counter top again.

"Come here, baby," he said.

The light found the middle of the plate - as Scott hoped it would – and then stopped moving.

Scott got to his feet, the laser sight of the sniper's rifle remaining perfectly focused on the center of the dish. He slowly eased his body from behind the door jam, his hand and arm outstretched.

He'd guessed right.

He walked out of the diner, holding the plate to one side. As he moved, the laser light didn't wander from its position in the center of the plate. Then Scott moved the plate towards his chest. The light followed - still perfectly aligned in the center of the dish - until the plate was the only thing that separated a killer's bullet from Scott's heart.

He reached the black sedan and stopped. Trish was cowering behind the car's trunk, weapon drawn. "Scott! What the hell are you doing!"

"Tempting fate."

"No shit! But *why*?"

"You'll see." Scott let the plate crash to the ground. The laser light danced across his chest as he moved towards its source. He opened his arms, spreading them wide, as Dr. Chandra had done in the gallery.

He was one bullet away from a sure death.

"Scott Forrester! Are you stark raving mad?!"

"Probably."

"*The hell you are, Forrester!* Speak to me!"

Trish moved from behind protective cover.

The light moved. A bullet shattered Scott's side view mirror, chasing Trish back behind the car's sheet metal. Then the red laser dot returned to the center of Scott's chest.

Scott kept his poise, unflinching, his arms outstretched. "He knows who I am, Trish. And he knows why I'm here. He could have taken me out the second I went in that diner. But he doesn't want to kill me. Not yet. Not on *my* terms. He wants it to be on *his* terms. He wants to maintain control."

"You're a crazy fool, Forrester!"

"I sure hope not."

Scott wiggled the outstretched fingers of his hands, a signal... *Come and get me.* But the laser light stayed still, stayed focused, just left of center on his chest, just a hair-trigger away from his heart.

"He's had his fun, Trish. Are the SWAT guys in position?"

"They're ready."

"Then the next move is up to him."

There was silence. Even the whimpering in the diner had stopped. An eerie stillness descended on the parking lot, all eyes focused on a man with his arms outstretched and a red laser dot on his chest.

"It's your move, bastard. So... *make it!*"

The laser light that had been aimed at Scott's rapidly beating heart, blinked out.

Scott Forrester dropped his arms.

"It's over, Trish."

Chapter Thirty-Five

8:05PM. The search for the sniper had ended. Seven hours earlier at 1:05PM, amidst the bedlam that was Archie's Diner, three police SWAT team sharpshooters had pumped nineteen bullets into a store mannequin. It was lying prone on an apartment balcony, dressed in combat fatigues, with a rusty pawnshop rifle in its fiberglass hands.

The streets had been cordoned off.

A door-to-door search had been conducted.

In a well-rehearsed ballet of Kevlar body armor, laser-sighted assault rifles and battering rams, an army of black clad intruders had invaded the condo building like a cloud of alien bees. And what did the SWAT Team catch? A few stoned students smoking up on a worn Persian carpet. And an elderly shut-in whose contribution to the chaos in the center of Georgetown was to go into coronary heart failure.

It was a disaster zone. And like all good disasters, the media swarmed like the media knows how to swarm. The top-of-the-hour headline was: 'Police and FBI will not confirm or deny that an Al-Qaeda terrorist was to blame for this unprovoked attack. One dead, seven wounded...' And as the tabloid-style frenzy grew, the network spin increased. 'Could this be a new Beltway Sniper? The FBI is not discounting that possibility at this time'.

Scott Forrester sat in the driver's seat of his black sedan, door open, feet on Archie's pockmarked asphalt, his head down, his mind unable to process any more visual stimulus.

Trish handed him a coffee. Not from Archie's - its coffeepots had been victims of the sniper's bullets - but from an enterprising sandwich truck that was making the most of the opportunity: servicing an exhausted SWAT

Team, and the thriving ant colony that was the Washington media.

"Forensics will find something in that apartment, Scott."

"Why should they find something there… when they haven't yet found anything, anywhere else?"

"We've finally gotten close to him. That's gotta count as some kind of progress. He's going to make a mistake. It's just a matter of time."

"*I* was the one who made the mistake, Trish. I should have brought her in like you told me to. I knew he was in Washington. So why did I think I could protect her?"

"What are you talking about? You *knew* he was in Washington?"

Scott explained the events of the previous night - the nightmare of the man in the hooded sweatshirt and the black van with the slipping drive belt.

"And you didn't call it in?"

Scott's confidence had been shaken by the heat of combat, "I didn't think it was… conclusive enough."

"Is this…" Trish asked, angrily pointing to the yellow police tape surrounding Archie's Diner. "*Conclusive* enough?"

"I'm not on this case, remember?"

"Scott… *open your eyes!* Look around you!" Plainclothes detectives and uniformed police were still taking statements. Lights from the TV cameras bathed the street. "Right now, I'd say you *are* the case!"

Scott put his head in his hands. "God, I wish I wasn't."

• • •

"I'm here to see Kelly Whelan."

The night nurse looked up from her desk, peered over her glasses and frowned, "Visiting hours are over."

Scott flashed his badge. "I need to ask her some questions."

"And I need my patient to heal."

"That's what these are for," Scott said, holding up a bunch of flowers. "It won't take long."

The nurse stood up. "You policeman are a pain in the ass."

"FBI."

"Okay, you FBI are a pain in the ass. Sign in. Then Room 14-C. Second right. First room on the left."

The hospital corridors were semi-lit and the floor sent out a dull echo underfoot. A mechanical voice resounded in the distance, "Dr. Sheldon, emergency. Dr. Sheldon, emergency…"

Kelly Whelan had drifted off to sleep. Scott placed the flowers on the top of her bedside table. She stirred, then her eyes slowly opened, "They're beautiful. Thank you."

The stage makeup she wore for her performances at Archie's Diner was gone. For the first time, he could see the freckles on her cheeks, the unadorned softness of her skin, the purity of her Irish green eyes.

"I must look awful," she said, as she primped her ragged hair. It still had its natural tumbling flow and radiant Celtic warmth. She sat up and patted the bed. "You don't have to go, do you?"

He nestled in beside her. "How are you?"

"Sore. Tired. But tomorrow, they say if there's no sign of infection, I can go home. Did they…?"

"Find him? No."

Kelly reached for his hand. "Scott, why have you never told me that you work for the FBI?"

"Because Kelly, when I come into Archie's, I leave that part of my world behind. At least for a little while. Usually it works. But today, it followed me through the door. I'm so sorry about what happened. I'm so glad you're okay. That's the most important thing."

"And Archie? How's Archie?" She choked up. "Please don't say that he's…"

"No." He clasped her hand tightly. "He's in intensive care, but he's going to make it."

She sank into the pillow, "Oh, thank God!"

"He took a pretty nasty hit. The bullet missed a main artery. It embedded in the fat tissue under his collarbone. His biggest danger was from shock and loss of blood. We got to him just in time."

"Fat tissue? Guess his Hungry Man's Special has a purpose after all."

"It's good to see you smiling, Kelly."

"It's good to see you, Scott Forrester... period." She pulled herself up, took his hand and gently walked it to her lips. "Thanks for being here." She kissed his hand, then leaned forward and kissed him on the cheek, her lips lingering near his. It felt good. An unexpectedly, good feeling. But he withdrew, and that startled her. She looked very disappointed.

Christienne Duval had left on her European business trip that morning, before the sniper's bullets strafed Archie's Diner. And after what had happened today, he so desperately wanted someone to hold him tightly and say that everything was going to be alright. But that someone was Christienne, not Kelly. *Maybe he shouldn't have come to the hospital?* he thought. *But how could he not? It wasn't fair to Kelly that he shouldn't come to see her. But maybe it wasn't fair that he had.*

Scott stroked Kelly's hair. She smiled. "Kelly..." he said, as her eyes glistened. "You never stop trying, do you?"

"That's right, Scott Forrester. I'll *never* stop trying."

His cell phone rang. She tugged at his black leather jacket. "Give me that. You're off duty."

"Kelly... I'm *never* off duty."

It was his brother, Jamie. His voice sounded distressed, "Scott... God Scott, where have you been? You have to come home. Right away!"

"Jamie... what's wrong?"

"I don't know what they're going to do to me, Scott! You've got to come home! You've got to help me!"

"Who are *they*, Jamie?"

The phone went dead.

"Jamie?... Jamie?..."

Chapter Thirty-Six

The midnight black sedan raced into the cul-de-sac. There had been desperation in Jamie's voice, "Scott, you've got to help me!"

Tall maples rustled in the darkness, their boughs nearly devoid of leaves; scrawny fingers reaching into the moonlit night sky. At the back of Scott's darkened bungalow, a bright light shone from Jamie's basement apartment. Scott could see activity inside the house. Silhouettes of people moving in and out of the bright light. Shadows that scampered away from Scott's oncoming headlights as he slowed the car.

People were outside his house. Lots of people. And cars. Unmarked. Unmistakable. Drab full-sized sedans with dull wheels. Parked irregularly on the driveway, as if they had arrived in haste.

And a van. With a familiar shape - like the van Scott Forrester had chased, naked, down the street.

What the hell was going on?

Scott's sedan clambered up the driveway and ground to a halt. Someone approached with a flashlight and shone it into the car. Scott grabbed his badge from his jacket and stepped out. The figure looked him up and down with the beam of light.

Scott shielded his eyes and said, "Get that out of my face! What's going on here? Who the hell are you?"

"You'd better come inside, Forrester. They're waiting for you."

"Who?"

"Griffin for one."

"Titus Griffin is *here*?"

"You poor son-of-a bitch. Your brother's landed feet first in a pretty big pile of shit and personally, if my boss was Titus Griffin, I wouldn't want to explain why."

Scott could see the hulking silhouette of Titus Griffin in the kitchen window. Another car pulled into the cul-de-sac and a woman got out. It was Trish Van Cleyburn, her phone to her ear. "Forrester's just arrived." She brushed by Scott without looking at him. "Aren't you coming in, Forrester? Griffin isn't pleased."

They walked into the kitchen – straight into the glare of Titus Griffin.

"So glad you could join us, Forrester," he said with a grunt.

"What's going on, Titus? Where's Jamie?"

"Downstairs."

Two clean-shaven, stern-faced young FBI agents came through the living room and headed for the front door. One of them was carrying Jamie's computer tower, wrapped in plastic. The other had a box full of books, papers and CDs.

Footsteps clunked up the stairs from the basement. A man entered the kitchen, wearing a dark blue denim shirt with a black T-shirt underneath and khakis with a brown leather belt; mid-forties, mousy brown hair, about six feet tall, athletically built, with a jogger's tan. The most noticeable feature was his eyes. They were blue. And as cold as polar ice.

"This is Special Agent Spencer Brant," Griffin announced. "White Collar Crime Unit, New York Field Office. Assigned to the SEC. Agent Brant has been monitoring a particular Internet chat room called WallStreetBuzz.com. Ever heard of it, Forrester?"

"Vaguely."

"Vaguely? That's what I like about you, Forrester. You do everything *vaguely*. Did you know your brother is a regular contributor to that chat room? Like every night regular?" A file sat on the kitchen counter. Titus Griffin opened it. "He calls himself *Jokers_Wild*. Cool, huh?"

"What has Jamie done?"

Griffin turned to the agent with the ice-cold eyes, "You tell him, Agent Brant."

As soon as Brant opened his mouth, Scott Forrester knew his brother was in big trouble, "We've been monitoring the traffic on that site for evidence of insider trading. Especially in the shares of two companies - Pegasus BioSciences and Whale River Diamond Mines. Did you know your brother bought and sold stakes in both of those companies, Mr. Forrester? Did you know he actively traded those shares, including going short and owning put options?"

"I didn't think it was illegal to own stocks in America, Agent Brant. My brother's a day trader. That's what he does for a living. Now cut to the chase... what have you got on my brother?"

"Don't screw with me, Forrester," Brant said. "You know as well as I do that it's illegal to trade on information that should be available to the public, but isn't. It's called insider trading."

"Let me, Agent Brant..." Griffin said, taking the baton, and looking like he was about to shove it up Scott Forrester's ass. "Your brother made substantial profits trading Pegasus BioSciences. The fact that two company executives, Bryan and Nicole Riverton died, certainly helped. They were murdered at their beach home last week. Their company was financed by Matthew Carleton. He was murdered the day after he attended a party at Bryan and Nicole Riverton's Westchester mansion to celebrate Pegasus going public."

"So? There must be plenty of other investors who profited on Pegasus without knowing someone was going to be murdered. That's all circumstantial."

"Circumstantial? Is that what you call this?" Griffin picked up a file that been sitting on the kitchen table and pulled out SEC records of Jamie Forrester's stock transactions. "Did you know your brother lost a lot of money in the stock market in the past several years?"

"He had a run of bad luck."

"No kidding. But what has interested the SEC – and now is very interesting to *us* - is how many of these trades involved companies financed by Matthew Carleton. And if you read your brother's posts to this chat board..." Griffin pulled out another sheaf of papers, transcripts of Jamie's Internet chat, "it would appear your brother didn't like Matthew Carleton very much. In fact, and I quote... 'this bastard should roast in Hell for what he's done to me...' Threats like that are not taken lightly by the FBI, Agent Forrester."

"What are you suggesting, Titus? Jamie's a hothead. He's not a murderer! For Christ's sake... can't you see? He's a cripple!"

Griffin pulled another paper from the file, "This is an affidavit from a Guillermo Reyes, a punk with a criminal record and ties to Columbian drug lords."

Oh shit! Scott thought. *Another one of Jamie's weirdo friends no doubt?*

"In his affidavit, Mr. Reyes says he carried fifteen thousand dollars in cash and deposited it in a Bahamian bank account, not just once, but on two occasions. He says he did it for Jamie Forrester. The first deposit was the week before Matthew Carleton was murdered. And the second - last week - before the Rivertons were incinerated in their multi-million dollar home. Sounds like some kind of payment to me, Agent Forrester. For services rendered? What do you think? Totally *circumstantial*?"

Agent Brant added, "Did you know that Guillermo Reyes was a regular on WallStreetBuzz.com under the alias of 'The_Bandito'? He's also on your brother's 'buddy list' in Windows Messenger. We've been intercepting their one-on-one chats. Makes for very interesting reading."

"So?"

"So, I posed as one of your brother's Internet buddies and met him at Archie's Diner. You must know Archie's Diner... or thanks to you, what's left of it. I circulated a picture of Guillermo Reyes. The waitresses recognized him. Your brother had lunch with Reyes many times. Pretty *circumstantial*, huh?"

"Where is Jamie? I want to see him!"

Titus Griffin's smug smile stretched across his jaw line like an archer's bow, "We thought you might come around to seeing it our way, Agent Forrester."

• • •

Jamie's apartment was in the process of being stripped clean of its books, computer equipment, trading records and chat printouts. Scott found Jamie by the patio doors, drooped in his wheelchair. He was pale, his eyes were gaunt and his brow was sweaty. If his legs could bounce with nervous energy, they would. But they couldn't. The only alternative Jamie had was to tap on the sides of his wheelchair in a jungle rhythm, beating time with his accelerated heartbeat.

When he saw Scott, he perked up, "Scott! Jesus, Scott!" He started crying.

Scott knelt down beside him, cradled his brother's head in his hands and whispered. "It's okay, Jamie. It's okay. They don't have anything. You've not done anything wrong. We'll get you out of this..."

Jamie sobbed.

"Tell me you haven't done anything wrong, Jamie." Scott pried Jamie's fingers from hiding his face. "Look at me. Calm down. Take a deep breath. And tell me you haven't done anything wrong."

Jamie's face, gripped by tension and fear, couldn't lie. "I don't know, Scott. I don't know..."

"Jamie... listen to me. Did they read you your rights?" Jamie nodded his head, yes. "Then you don't have to say anything more. Look at me, Jamie."

Jamie looked up and sniveled.

"What have you told them?"

"It doesn't matter. They don't believe me. What are they going to do with me, Scott?"

"Don't worry, Jamie." Scott could feel the ominous presence of Titus Griffin and Spencer Brant looming over them. "I know a good lawyer. We'll work this out." He whispered again into Jamie's ear, "What's this about a guy who says he carried money to the Bahamas for you? Is that true?"

Jamie whispered back, "It's not what they think."

"Jamie… what the hell were you doing with that kind of cash?"

"I had to pay off some debts."

"What kind of debts?"

"Gambling."

"Gambling debts? You don't go to casinos."

"Internet gambling."

"Internet gambling!" Scott checked the volume in his voice and whispered, "Don't tell me that, Jamie. Don't tell me you've been suckered into Internet gambling!"

"I was desperate, Scott. You know how much I needed the money. I checked them out. It was a site that pays off. I just wasn't very lucky, that's all."

"*Thirty thousand* dollars? I'd say that was more than just unlucky, Jamie. I'd say you were conned! But why deposit cash in the Bahamas?"

"I owed more than thirty thousand dollars. Guillermo told me he knew the website's owners. He said he could cut a deal for me. If I paid cash into an offshore account, they would reduce the amount I owed them. He told me he could take the cash to the Bahamas and deposit it for me. He's a friend, Scott. He helped me out of a jam."

"He helped you twice, Jamie?"

"I didn't have all the money they wanted, Scott. Not all at once. They put pressure on me. I had to make some kind of initial payment or…"

"They threatened you?"

"Yes."

"Why didn't you tell me?"

"Oh yeah, sure! And you - *Mr. FBI Agent* – as if you would listen to *me*?" Jamie looked over at Griffin and Brant. "Those goons would have come here sooner, wouldn't they, Scott? If I told you I was involved with these people, what choice would *you* have? You would have turned me in yourself!"

The question hit Scott in the face like a pail of cold water, "Jamie... how could you say that? I'm your brother!"

"You're also an FBI agent, Scott. An FBI agent! You guys take some kind of oath, right? Swear some kind of allegiance to each other. You *would* have turned me in, Big Bro. You're just too... too..."

"Honest?" Scott pulled his fingers through his hair. *God, Jamie. What is this all about? You're in trouble. Real trouble.*

Scott got to his feet and approached Special Agent Brant. "I assume you've exercised a legal search warrant?"

Brant nodded, yes.

Then Titus Griffin, wearing latex gloves, picked up a book that was in a tote – a book with a raven-black leather cover, with a boldly embossed title in silver lettering. He flipped through its well-used pages, reading in silence the margin notes inked in Jamie's handwriting. "Interesting topic for a day-trader, Forrester."

Jamie shot back, "There's plenty of stock-promoting pickpockets out there! You see them on TV in their slick, preachy suits! The talking heads. The CEO's with company lies to sell. The accountants who would fire someone for stealing a pencil at the same time as they fill their offshore accounts with the shareholders' embezzled cash. They profess to live goody-two-shoes, pure-as-snow lifestyles. It all comes unglued – the lies, the deception - when they're caught scamming widows and orphans! Guys like that jerk-off Matthew Carleton!"

"Jamie..." Scott said. "Keep your mouth shut!"

"I know my rights, Big Bro. And I have the right to call Carleton an asshole if I want to!"

"You're a smart kid," Griffin said. "So how does *this* book help you trade stocks?"

"*That*?" Jamie paused. "I guess you could say… *that* helps keep things in perspective."

"Perspective?" Griffin read some of Jamie's margin notes. "A book like *this* gives a stock trader *perspective*? Did you know your brother had a copy of this laying around the house, Forrester?"

Griffin handed the book to Agent Brant who took it over to Scott, but wouldn't let him touch it.

"Jesus, Jamie!" Scott exclaimed as he read the silver lettering on the cover. "What the *hell…*"

The book was 'The Satanic Bible'.

Brant placed the book back in the tote. "My guys in the van will download your brother's hard drive. We've already got a pretty solid case for insider trading. Maybe money laundering. Depends on what else we find out about that thirty thousand dollars."

Scott looked at Titus Griffin. *There was more wasn't there?* "What have got, Griffin? You've got nothing!"

Griffin shrugged, his jaw muscles flexing again, "You tell me, Forrester. Conspiracy? Murder? I told you we'd follow the money. Let's see where your brother's money leads us before we decide on that. Like Agent Brant says, it depends on Jamie… how much he co-operates."

Scott was stone-faced, resolute, "Jamie's not done anything wrong!"

"That's up to a grand jury to decide, Forrester."

Footsteps thudded down the stairs. Trish Van Cleyburn handed Griffin an object in a large Ziploc plastic bag.

Griffin looked it over, surprised. "Where did you find this, Cleyburn?"

"In his car."

Griffin studied the bloodstained bottle of wine. "Is this what I think it is?" Griffin handed the bottle back to Trish. "Get Forensics on it."

"And we also found this in Scott's bedroom…"

It was an official looking report with the SEC's seal on its front cover. Spencer Brant flipped through the document. If it was possible, his eyes grew even icier. "This is highly restricted information. How did you get this, Forrester?"

Griffin took the report and flipped through its pages, "Answer Agent Brant's question, Forrester. Explain what you're doing with an SEC document addressed to the Treasury Department containing a summary of their investigation into Carleton Securities?"

"That report was given to me by an SEC investigator." Scott answered. "Not just any investigator. The *Chief* Investigator on the Carleton case. He came to my office at Quantico."

"The Chief Investigator?" Brant asked. "Was in your office?"

"Yeah. He was. A guy named Weinberg. Jacob Weinberg. He explained the whole thing to me. He was looking for any information I might have on Matthew Carleton. It was inter-agency co-operation. Jamie had nothing to do with it."

Agent Brant frowned; his face painted with skepticism, "Weinberg?"

He doesn't believe me? Scott thought. He continued, "Yes. Weinberg. He was in Washington to brief the Treasury Department and asked for my help."

Spencer Brant laughed and shook his head.

"What's so funny about that?" Scott asked.

Brant looked at Titus Griffin with a smirk, then answered in his anally retentive tone, "Jacob Weinberg was in your office? Jacob Weinberg? He was in Washington to brief the Treasury Department? I find that a little hard to believe, Forrester."

"Why not?"

"I'll grant you the first part of your story, Forrester. Yeah, at one time, Jacob Weinberg worked at the SEC. But he doesn't anymore." You could cut Brant's smugness with a knife. "Because he died... *five years ago.*"

Chapter Thirty-Seven

It was three days before Thanksgiving and Scott Forrester had received two pieces of bad news. The first was a call from Christienne Duval from Paris. The Board meeting in Geneva had gone well. But after this week's meetings to review jewelry designs in Paris, she'd been asked by Michael Wayne Portland to go to Moscow to inspect a property he was considering buying. Apparently, the nouveau riche of Russia couldn't wait any longer to spend their millions in one of his exclusive Bijouteries and were fed up with flying to Paris to do it. She said her trip had been extended by at least another ten days because Portland wanted to close the deal quickly so they could start renovating the new site into a boutique for the Russian capital.

Another ten days without her? That was cruel enough on its own. The second piece of bad news came in the form of a note that Rebecca Cohen handed him, which was in Titus Griffin's handwriting, and read simply, 'My office. Now!'.

Thanksgiving or not, the mood inside Titus Griffin's office was not exactly festive.

"Forrester, this is Agent Corey Hamilton from Internal Affairs," Griffin said.

Hamilton was a rangy, tall black man in his late thirties. He was wearing a gray-pinstriped suit, white shirt, cobalt blue tie and shiny black shoes. As Scott entered, he didn't get up, barely made eye contact.

Hamilton was sitting in one of three low back chairs with forest green leather seats and dark-stained oak legs. The chairs creaked; a consequence of age and wear and a characteristic of old oak that was highly prized by antique collectors and directors of Hollywood vampire movies. The chairs were perfect companions for the tortuous conversations that had become the hallmark of visits to Titus Griffin's office.

Hamilton was holding a file in his lap. Two files of similar thickness, size and color sat on the desk in front of Titus Griffin. Griffin pushed one of them forward. "Take this and take a seat, Forrester."

Scott glanced at the infamous dartboard. The two darts had been replaced. They were back in the bull's eye. Despite his heroic efforts, the legend of Titus Griffin's darts carried on.

Agent Hamilton opened his copy of the file. "We all know what happened the day before yesterday at Archie's Diner. I'll spare you the details. And Titus has filled me in on the other incident..." Hamilton produced several documents from the file, "at the Freer Gallery. The Indian Embassy's letter of protest. The Secret Service report. Then there was the ill-timed search warrant that lead Dominic Sant'Angello's lawyer to write this... and lead the SEC to write this..." One by one, reports and letters found their way out of the file and onto Titus Griffin's desk. "I'd love to hear your side of the story."

"That's easy, Agent Hamilton," Scott said. "Every one of these so-called 'incidents' occurred within the boundaries of my duties as an FBI agent investigating the Carleton case-"

"A *former* investigator on the Carleton case," Griffin interrupted. "I distinctly remember taking you off that case, Forrester. Didn't I?"

"Agent Forrester, let's move on to more recent events." Hamilton's file yielded more paper. "Let's start with Sue Lee Chen. Why didn't you let Agent Van Cleyburn handle the interview of Ms. Chen?"

"Sue Lee Chen insisted on meeting only with me. She refused to meet at a police station or an FBI office. She said it would be dangerous unless I agreed to her terms. At the time, I believed her. And I didn't want to scare her away. She was an important lead. Agent Van Cleyburn was with me, as back up. I didn't engage in anything that she wasn't a part of."

Griffin clasped his meaty fullback hands together and placed them on top of his copy of the documents, "Sue Lee Chen came out in the open all right. She came out in the open and took a 7.62mm round to the head. And it was on *your* terms that the patrons of a diner in Georgetown had to pray for their lives. And what was that stunt you pulled? Walking out of the restaurant, exposing yourself when a sniper was still shooting at anything that moved?"

"I know this killer. I know how he thinks. I took a calculated risk."

"You *know* this killer, Forrester? That's interesting. He never fired a shot at you, did he?" Griffin looked cryptically at Hamilton. "And why not?"

"What the hell are you insinuating?"

"If you *know* this 'Tiger Paw Killer', then what's his name, Forrester? His last known address? Do you have a description good enough to put out an APB? Well, I can answer that for you..." Griffin banged the table with a flat palm. "No! You don't! We have no idea who he is, or why he's doing what he's doing. Unless-"

"Unless what? Sue Lee Chen's letter corroborates everything I've theorized. The connections between Sant'Angello and Carleton. Her involvement with the cult and Sudhir Narayan-"

"I'm going to stop you right there, Forrester!" Griffin's nostrils flared. "I'm going to stop you right there. This is a theater of the absurd, Forrester. *What* letter?"

"What do you mean, 'what letter'?"

Griffin repeated, "I mean exactly *what* letter are you talking about, Forrester?"

What letter? What game was Griffin playing? The letter. The letter inside the bulging envelope. The letter Sue Lee Chen called the key to a grand jury indictment. The letter that explained the connection between Narayan and the Temple of Dvaipa. *What letter? They must be joking.*

Agent Hamilton picked a piece of lint from his pinstriped sleeve, "Here's the bottom line, Agent Forrester. Crime scene investigators found no letter inside or outside Archie's Diner. There is no letter, Agent Forrester. Just a dead woman with a 7.62mm round in her head."

"You're lying!"

Griffin piled it on, "So why didn't you wear a body wire, Forrester? Then we'd have your conversation with Sue Lee Chen on the record."

"I didn't have time-"

"How convenient! Because if you had worn one, we would have irrefutable testimony in Sue Lee Chen's own words to corroborate this story you keep telling us. As it stands, she's laid out on a slab. And she's not talking."

They couldn't find the letter?

"Agent Forrester..." Hamilton pressed, "have you any evidence at *all* to prove Ms. Chen's allegations about a connection between an Ambassador from a friendly power and a cult that we don't even know exists, except in your theories?"

Scott Forrester looked past Hamilton's shoulder, through the office window. The November sky was a uniform gray; the trees were barren; there was an emptiness inside and outside the room. "I didn't have time for a body wire..." He stuttered. "The procedures... The logistics... I just didn't have time..."

Agent Corey Hamilton, like a veteran prosecutor who had backed a witness into a corner and wouldn't let him go, asked, "Did you know that Agent Van Cleyburn was headed to Jacksonville to investigate the murders of Nicole and Bryan Riverton?"

"Yes."

"And yet you diverted her to Washington, didn't you?"

"What are you driving at?"

"She was going to Florida. There's lots of sand, wind and water in Florida, Agent Forrester. And evidence at the crime scene that was bound to deteriorate with the weather. Then there were the transient witnesses – like tourists and boaters – who would be leaving the area to God knows where."

"What are you saying? That I obstructed justice? She didn't have to come to Washington. It was *her* call."

"*You* were the one that gave her the compelling reason to change her plans, Forrester. Sue Lee Chen was the reason. She's now a *dead* compelling reason." The creaky oak chair that Hamilton was sitting in groaned as he leaned forward, "The night before the sniper killed Ms. Chen, you claimed you had seen an intruder at your home."

"It's not a *claim*. It's true! And I'm not the only one who saw him!"

"Yes. Your girlfriend. And why hasn't this Christienne Duval come forward to make a statement?"

"She left for Geneva and Paris. She's the Managing Director of the US office of a Swiss company. She went to Switzerland for a Board meeting. Now she's travelling to Moscow."

"How very convenient, Forrester," Hamilton said. He produced yet another series of papers. "We'll look her up when she gets back. Assuming she does come back. But in the meantime, we have this…"

Griffin's chair squeaked like a pack of rats. He smiled. "I like this part the best, Forrester. It just keeps getting better and better. Man, you are one crazy, fucked up dude!"

Scott started to shake.

Hamilton stood up and asked Scott to do the same. "Are you packing, Forrester?"

Scott nodded, yes.

"Then I'd ask you to put your arms out." Hamilton removed Scott's Smith & Wesson from the holster inside his jacket and handed the gun to Griffin.

Griffin took out the gun's clip, opened a drawer and dropped it in, then said, "Sit down, Forrester."

Hamilton picked up the next set of papers from the file. "One of your neighbors - a Mr. Gary Bremner - said he saw you in the middle of the night pointing a gun in the face of a pizza delivery boy. Is that true?"

Scott's head fell into his hands.

"We traced the kid. He corroborated everything Mr. Bremner told us, including the undeniable fact that while you were terrorizing an unarmed pizza delivery boy, you were butt naked."

"Now that's worthy of one of your famous theories, Forrester," Griffin chortled. "That really is."

"Well, you're not getting one, Titus. So keep it in your pants!"

Hamilton read through the delivery boy's statement, "The kid was thinking of pressing charges, but said the way you looked at him, in his words, and I quote… 'I don't want this guy coming after me, when he gets out of jail. He looks like the kind of guy who carries a grudge, and wouldn't think twice about popping me. It's not worth the hassle to file charges.' And when we told him you were an FBI agent, he didn't seem any more reassured."

"And this is the part I liked…" Griffin added. "He asked us whether it was a new FBI technique to intimidate suspects by taking our dicks out!" Griffin sat back in his creaky chair and laughed. "Forrester… this has gotta take the cake! I mean, really… what kind of *sick* dude are you?"

"Is that what this is all about? You think I'm nuts?"

"Then there's this…" Agent Hamilton took a photo from the file and put it on the desk. It was a photo of a wine bottle in a plastic bag.

Oh, shit!

Hamilton kept the pressure on, "You told Agent Van Cleyburn that you intended to turn this bottle in to Forensics. So why didn't you? Let me guess… you didn't have time?"

Griffin opened a drawer and took out a familiar report. It had the unmistakable cover of a Serial Crime Unit psychological profile. It was Scott's profile. Of the Tiger Paw Killer. Griffin plunked the report on the desk. "Ex-military?" he said. "Highly skilled in weapons? We know he uses a semi-automatic silencer-mounted SR-25 sniper rifle. And recently you added the following… likely to have experienced a major life trauma, such as a death or a failed marriage, that may have lead the subject to become involved in *satanic* cults or practice *satanic* rituals. Motive may be revenge connected with investment losses associated with the victims' companies."

"Jamie?" Scott leapt out of his chair and banged his fist in front of Griffin. "He's a *cripple*... you moron!"

"Who are you protecting, Forrester?"

Scott pulled his fist back, but Hamilton grabbed him and pushed him down into the chair. "Your brother..." Hamilton said, as he held Scott by the shoulders, "is an ex-Army Ranger sniper. He knows how it's done. You can't deny that he's a bitter individual. And who wouldn't be? He's paralyzed for life. He's lost a ton of money on the stock market, then compounded it by gambling and losing more. And rather than turning to God - or his brother - for guidance, he reads the Satanic Bible. Do you want to read the comments he made in the margins of that book?" Hamilton held out another piece of paper but Scott turned his head away. "Let me read some of it for you..."

Scott swatted the pages out of Hamilton's hand, "For God's sake, my brother's a *cripple*! How in hell can he be the killer? He can't even walk!"

"Forrester..." Griffin barked. "This time, it's my turn to propose a theory to you. Someone has the skill and motivation, but not the means? So he trains an accomplice. Perhaps one of the vets he hangs out with. Perhaps another investor like himself who lost money and has a shared ideology, shared religious beliefs – if you can call them that – and also has the same warped urge for revenge?"

"Now who's in the theater of the absurd?"

"*Really*? It's that unbelievable?" Griffin was enjoying this. "You've heard of John Lee Malvo, haven't you?"

"Of course I have!"

"Seventeen years old. At a very impressionable age. Tutored by a forty-one-year-old Army veteran, John Allen Muhammad to treat humans as if they were deer in hunting season. The Beltway Sniper. Two people. Not just one. Even you must see the parallel, Forrester."

"Jamie isn't like either one of those two."

"No? Okay, then there's always Theory B. Our perp can't execute his plans without help. He's crippled right? So he hires a contract killer to do what he can't do himself. He makes cash payments to secret accounts in the Bahamas and then... bang, bang, you're dead." Griffin waited for a reaction. But none came. "I'm not surprised you don't see either of these possibilities, Forrester. He *is* your brother. And blood does run thicker than water."

"Speaking of blood, Titus, then how do you explain blood written messages in a language my brother doesn't read or write? How does that evidence connect with my brother?"

"Let's pretend for a moment that I agree with you about something. Let's say I believe you, when you talk about this cult. So let's say your brother is a member."

Scott had had enough, "If you have proof that my brother was involved in those killings, then charge him! If not, then get the fuck out of his life!"

Agent Corey Hamilton sat on the edge of the desk and made his closing argument, "Your brother posted bond this morning on charges of insider trading and surrendered his passport. And we're going to do both of you a big favor by giving you some time off to help him prepare for court."

"Time off?"

Griffin's arm reached over the desk. "Give me your badge, Forrester. Effective immediately, your FBI privileges have been suspended. I'm placing you on paid administrative leave."

"On what grounds?"

Hamilton pronounced sentence, "Conflict of interest. The on-going investigation of dereliction of duty."

Griffin closed the proceedings, "And Forrester... don't leave town. We'll be watching."

Chapter Thirty-Eight

A searing ninety-degree heat baked the deck of the 'Coral Queen'. Winston Billings sipped his rum daiquiri, thankful for the strong offshore breeze. Overhead, the island hopper from Fort Lauderdale - a flying boat that delivered high rollers to Paradise Island's casinos - cut its engines and floated down to the turquoise seas of Nassau harbor.

The winter tourist season in the Bahamas was getting nicely into gear after a difficult summer of drenching tropical storms and the near miss of a Category 4 hurricane. The harbor bustled with activity. An enormous cruise ship, recently arrived from Port Canaveral, was disgorging its passengers into Nassau's straw markets. White-sailed catamarans were bringing exhausted but happy divers back from the reefs.

Tomorrow was his last day on the job. After thirty-four years of faithful service to the Royal Bahamas Police Force, fifty-nine-year-old Detective Inspector Winston Billings was retiring.

And even though he was a single man with no wife or children to support, it had still taken all of those thirty-four years, through careful savings and fortunate real estate investments, to buy the 'Coral Queen', the seven-year-old Hatteras sport fishing boat that would soon double as workhorse and home.

The 'Coral Queen' was his retirement present to himself, fulfilling a lifelong promise to cruise the isolated cays of his native Bahamas in something other than a police patrol boat - chartering deep-sea fishermen when he felt like it; pampering him as live aboard captain when he didn't.

The seaplane taxied into its berth across from the sun-bleached jetty terrace of the Parrot Bay Restaurant. It was 6:00PM and time to savor the island's coconut rum, taste victory at the blackjack tables.

In the distance, a gray Bahamian Navy ship limped sadly into port, a rusty poor cousin to the smart-looking US Coast Guard cutter, a fast DEA pursuit vessel, that followed. Despite Nassau's voluptuous appearance and enticing nightlife, everything was not as pristine as it seemed in Winston Billings' island paradise.

As the 'Coral Queen' bobbed in the wake of a ramshackle ferryboat plying Nassau harbor, Winston Billings reminded himself that in just one more day, the seedy side of Bahamian life would be someone else's problem.

Three slips down from the 'Coral Queen', crystal clear water flapped against the footings of a pier where a precocious boy was inching closer to a seven-foot, unguarded drop off the end of the dock.

"Joey! Don't get too close to the edge! Joey, did you hear me? I told you not to get too-"

"Ease up on him, honey. He's only six," Kendall Baker said, as he tugged at his wife Tracy's arm. "What do you expect a little boy to do? There's a whole new world out there to explore. He's okay. Let him have some fun."

The boy's naughty smirk dared her to stop him. Below, at the ocean's surface, a swarm of pinkish jellyfish had been swept by the tide into a still pool between a million dollar yacht and the dock.

"Daddy, if I fell in there, would they eat me?"

The boy's father caught his wife's expression in the corner of his eye. It said, 'Don't you dare tell him any more stories about the dangerous creatures that live in the sea!' From the moment they had landed in the Bahamas, little Joey had developed an instant fascination for everything under the water. It came as no surprise to his father - the boy was fearless, to the point of being reckless; behavior that had his conservatively raised Midwestern wife, Tracy in fits most of the time.

And why shouldn't his son enjoy himself? Wasn't that the reason they were in the Bahamas? To enjoy life? Warm breezes. Sun-kissed beaches. Sailing. Snorkeling. Pink jellyfish.

But Tracy Baker had drawn the line at casinos. Kendall had lost enough money gambling on what their broker had told them were 'safe long term investments'. Including the mutual fund that was supposed to have paid for Joey's college tuition by now but was trading at just twenty cents for every dollar they'd invested. Thanks to the stock market, they couldn't afford to lose any more money, especially on the roll of a dice.

For now, their worries had evaporated. Nassau was leisure in its purest and most stress free form - the kind of holiday the Bakers needed after a difficult two years struggling to get back on their financial feet.

"They won't eat you, Joey. But if you fall in, they'll sting... and it will really hurt!"

Joey grinned impishly at his parents, took another step closer to the edge and got down on his knees. The jellyfish looked delightfully goopy. He could just imagine slipping one down the back of that old lady's swimsuit - the one that yesterday seemed to complain about everything. It wasn't his fault he couldn't tell a riderless wave board from a shark - sending people scurrying when he ran out of the water screaming hysterically. Her bitching had really spoiled his fun.

"That's close enough, Joey!" his mother warned.

The sly toddler quickly changed the subject. "Can we get an ice cream?"

"Sure!" said Dad, remembering the ice cream seller next to the rum store with the free tastings.

"Honey... that's his third ice cream today! It's going to create problems when we get back home."

"Well, Mom... can we?" Joey pleaded.

It had been such a perfect day. Reluctantly, Mom agreed.

The sun hovered over the horizon, getting ready to sink below the sapphire blue waters. As the Bakers turned their backs, a thirty-two foot Hunter sailboat slipped into the harbor searching for the rented mooring it had departed from earlier in the day.

Sam McAllister, standing at the bow, with his wife Fiona at the helm, took down the sails and scanned the all too similar rows of slips.

Sam and Fiona McAllister, natives of the Chesapeake Bay, were expert sailors. Their brand new Hunter sailboat was on its maiden voyage from their oceanfront retirement home in Jupiter, Florida. The boat entered the congested marina and gently slowed down. "Son of a bitch! It looks like someone has taken our spot!" he said.

"Are you sure you're looking in the right place, dear? All these quays look the same to me."

The sailboat drifted into Tamara Powell's view as she enjoyed the gentle evening breeze with her husband of two days on the outdoor terrace of the Parrot Bay Restaurant. She looked up from her plate of crab's legs as the McAllister's yacht appeared with the setting sun at its back.

"Isn't that just gorgeous, Keyshaun!" She said, reaching for her camera. "I've got to take a picture! It's so beautiful!"

Keyshaun Powell looked out across the harbor. His steak could wait. It was another wonderful Bahamian memory. His new wife was right. "Hey, hon. Why don't we ask someone to take our picture? That sailboat would make such a great background."

An elderly woman, sitting alone at the next table, had been admiring the two lovebirds all evening. He looked like a football or basketball player - tall, muscular and fit; smooth ebony skin; gold chain and expensive tropical shirt. She was also tall - a shapely Nubian princess, with a bright orange bikini that glowed like sunshine under her white beach sarong. They were a chic and sophisticated couple. *And yes*, thought the elderly lady, *it would make such a delightful picture.*

"Can I help you?" she asked.

"Would you? That would be so sweet."

"It would be my pleasure. You're such a handsome couple."

"Why, thank you," Tamara Powell said, taking Keyshaun by the hand. They cuddled together by the washed gray cedar railing, their photogenic smiles beaming into the camera.

"I bet you're on your honeymoon, aren't you?"

"Yes, ma'am. We are."

"I thought so. Are you a football player?"

"Baseball, ma'am."

"I thought so! What team?"

"Baltimore Orioles, ma'am. Right field."

"Oh, I've never met a baseball player before! Can I have your autograph?"

"It would be my pleasure, ma'am."

• • •

Joey Baker unhooked himself from his mother's hand and ran back down the pier.

"Joey! Where are you going?"

"I lost my flippy-flop, Mommy!" The little boy raced back to fetch his fluorescent green rubber sandal.

"Joey, be careful! Don't run!"

"I won't, Mommy!" He didn't slow down. The boy reached his flip-flop and put it on, but instead of returning to his worried mother, he wandered to the end of the pier to look at the jellyfish again.

"Joey!"

That boy would be the death of her! she thought.

"Joey, come back here! Right now!"

Joey Baker sat down on the dock, his two hands cupped under his chin, looking into the setting sun. The waters glistened with a magical, sparkling iridescence.

Tracy Baker trotted down the pier, determined to scold her mischievous child regardless of how innocent his father thought he was. That boy was taking them for a ride and she was going to put a stop to it before his naughtiness ruined their holiday.

"Is that a pirate ship, Mommy?"

Direct sunlight shone into his mother's eyes. She stepped back into the shade to see what Joey was looking at.

A double-masted sailboat was entering the harbor, traveling very fast, its topsails fully unfurled.

Joey repeated his question, "Mommy, are there pirates on that boat?"

Kendall Baker caught up to them, the glare of the sun fully in his eyes. Then he saw it too - a large, rapidly approaching, teak-decked yacht with a dark navy blue hull and a blue bimini top over the stern. Kendall Baker wasn't a sailor - he was a feed store manager from Topeka Kansas - but whatever the boat's captain was doing, Kendall Baker knew something wasn't right. The sailboat was racing headlong into the channel, straight for docks crowded with other sailboats, powerboats, and cruisers. If the captain didn't slow down, a lot of expensive toys would soon be in his way.

"Joey, come away from there!"

Once again, the boy was walking dangerously close to the end of the pier. His mouth gaped open. He pointed to the sailboat's mast, "Is that a pirate flag, Mommy?"

Tracy Baker ran towards her son and grabbed his hand before he almost stepped off the pier. She squinted, and said, "I don't think so, Joey. Pirate flags are black. That one's white."

"It doesn't look like a flag, honey," her husband said. "It looks like... someone's T-shirt."

"But Daddy… it's got a pirate face on it!" The little boy meant a skull and cross bones, like the pirate flag he wanted his parents to buy him at the souvenir store.

"Kendall, that's the strangest looking flag I've ever seen. That red patch on it looks hand painted. What is it?"

"Beats me, hon. Maybe it's some kind of distress signal."

"Isn't that boat going too fast, Kendall?"

Sam and Fiona McAllister's idling Hunter sailboat was about to cross in front of the larger yacht's path.

"Look, Daddy! It's going to hit that boat!"

Fiona McAllister wasn't aware they were about to be broadsided. Fortunately her husband Sam had recognized what was about to happen. He ran along the gunnels, yanked the helm wheel hard to port and pulled the diesel engine's throttle hard forward. The Hunter reacted swiftly to his command and swung violently about.

As it whisked by them, the advancing yacht's wash pushed the two boats apart.

"You crazy bastard! Didn't you see us!" Sam yelled.

As the yacht passed within inches, Fiona McAllister caught sight of the boat's lone occupant, dangling over the back. She let out a terrified scream.

The rogue sailboat rushed past the pier where Kendall and Tracy Baker, and their six-year-old son Joey, stood. It was on a collision course with the cluttered marina.

Its aft deck came into view. "Mommy… what happened to that man's legs?"

"Oh, my God!" Tracy Baker shrieked, covering her son's eyes. A legless body was strapped to the back of the sailboat, tied to the chrome rails with nautical rope.

"Is that real blood, Mommy?"

Kendall Baker ran down the pier shouting as loud as he could, "Hey! Hey! It's going to crash!"

The patrons of the Parrot Bay Restaurant were too far away to hear him. "Hey! Hey! That boat's not gonna stop!"

The rampaging yacht, the fifty-two foot Bahamian-registered 'Solara', was not the product of some tipsy captain's careless inattention. The double-masted sailboat careening headlong into the heart of the marina was instead the pilotless coffin for the blood-soaked body of its owner, Jiri Kostelic.

A small fishing skip jutted out from its slip; its owner cleaning out a bait box into the waiting mouths of a flock of seagulls. The runaway sailboat made glancing contact with the much smaller vessel, tipping the man forward, almost knocking him overboard. "Hey, you idiot! Slow down!"

As the yacht charged forward undeterred, a Sea Ray took the first direct hit. There was a sickening crunch as two hulls buckled and cracked. But the impact couldn't deflect the fully trimmed 'Solara' from its initial course. The stiff offshore wind blew new life into her aimless sails and the yacht's heavily anchored bow lurched towards the exposed Parrot Bay Restaurant.

The whole marina became acutely aware of impending disaster. Foghorns blared a warning: the 'Solara' was like a jousting knight on an armored seahorse galloping recklessly towards the packed quayside terrace.

For a brief moment, Tamara Powell was mesmerized. *What was it? It couldn't be what she thought it was, could it?*

The people cramming the terrace of the Parrot Bay Restaurant froze, glued to their seats, unable to process the image and connect it to reality.

Suddenly, the reality took hold. They scattered in all directions, tripping over each other, knocking over tables. Glasses and dishes crashed to the terrace's gray weathered planks. The elderly spinster who had so kindly taken the Powells' picture, fell to the deck. Keyshaun Powell grabbed his wife and yanked her off her feet.

Chaos erupted. The tropical evening air filled with the sounds of panic and fear. The gasps and shrieks merged into a single collective scream as the 'Solara' made impact. Its full weight was concentrated on its front edge. The ship's bow tore effortlessly through the terrace's wooden railings and ploughed into the foundations of the quay. Its teak deck splintered. Its fiberglass hull cracked wide open.

The yacht's bowsprit skewered the elderly woman.

People fell into gaping holes, screaming.

The sailboat's masts groaned as the whiplash strained its guy ropes. Its sails flapped and billowed; the leading jib detaching from its coupling. The tail wash that had upset the McAllister's Hunter rushed along the hull and mounted the pier. After what seemed like an eternity, the force of the impact dissipated. The lunging yacht had come to a full stop and was taking on water from an enormous top-to-bottom gash in its bow. The 'Solara' was beginning to sink.

The screaming also stopped, replaced by the cries and moans of the injured. Keyshaun Powell cradled his new bride in his arms. Tamara's leg was bleeding nastily from a scrape against the cedar railings, but other than that, she was mostly unhurt. Keyshaun thanked the Lord for giving him his athletic ability. Without it, they might both be dead.

Further down the harbor, Joey Baker stood quietly by his mother's side. Tracy Baker pressed her hand against her mouth, trying to stop her sobbing, tears streaming down her face.

Little Joey looked up at his mother and said, "Mommy, what happened?"

That was the moment that Detective Inspector Winston Billings put his retirement plans on hold.

Chapter Thirty-Nine

There was a rap on the patio door. A young woman holding a box peered through the glass, the wind biting into her porcelain face. Her cheeks were red and the gel in her spiky hair looked frozen. It was Jamie's student-Goth friend, Sarah Vaughn – Scott's ex-blind date with the infectious laugh and boundless energy whose conversational style had turned an evening at the Georgetown Jazz Café into a verbal judo match.

She hopped from one foot to the other, shivering. "Well… aren't you going to let me in?"

Scott opened the door and wrested the box from her hands. The label said it contained a laptop computer.

Jamie wheeled into the room. Sarah gave him a long lingering kiss on the lips. She pointed to the box she'd brought in. "This was on sale. It has more RAM and a faster processor than the one you spec'ed out. I got deals on a desktop and a laser printer too. They're in the car."

Jamie was all smiles. "You're an angel, Sarah."

"What's this all about, Jamie?" Scott asked. "New computer equipment? Where are you getting the money from?"

"Chill, Bro. Where else? Credit cards. Don't worry, when the bills come in, there's always our home equity line."

"Jamie, whatever small amount of equity we have left in this house, we're going to need it, to pay your legal expenses."

"Yeah Bro, but we're going to need computers too. You don't think I'm going to let them throw me in jail without putting up a fight, do you?"

"Your lawyer says it'll never come to that. You can plea bargain. Pay a fine. Probably get probation. You were a small investor. And a victim."

"We've all been victims, Scott. Haven't you been watching TV? New York City? Oakland? Just yesterday, Chicago? There's a whole world of victims out there. I'm fighting for more than just myself."

"Jamie... this is no time to appoint yourself People's Hero."

"Why not? Isn't that what the Occupy Wall Street movement is all about? The People taking back a democracy that's been stolen from us?"

"This isn't about Occupy Wall Street at all, as much as you might want it to be, Jamie. And it could get much uglier than just insider trading."

"You don't honestly believe those FBI goons have a hope of pinning a murder wrap on me, do you?"

"No. But they can bankrupt us trying."

"So? I'm going to fight it! Are you going to fight *with* me... or *against* me?"

"Shit, Jamie. You know the answer to that."

"Boys! Can we just get along, please? Who's going to help me bring in the other stuff?" Sarah asked, looking directly at Scott.

"Stay here and get warmed up, Sarah. Hey Jamie, get off your pulpit and make her a coffee and a sandwich. She must be hungry. I'll get the rest of the stuff from her car. " Scott started up the stairs to get his coat.

"A coffee and a sandwich? Is that it?" she said. "Don't tell me you guys have forgotten what day it is?"

Their days had blurred into one. In the current circumstances, time didn't seem to have any relevance.

Sarah took off her long black trench coat and wind-battered wool scarf. "You did forget, didn't you? Having all these sales didn't give you guys a hint?"

Scott stopped halfway up the stairs and realized. "It's Thanksgiving? Today?"

"Oh shit..." Jamie said. "I guess we did forget."

"Well, thankfully for you, someone else didn't. There's a cooked turkey, wrapped in foil, inside a cooler on the back seat of my car. I figured even if you guys had thought to buy one, it would either still be frozen or burnt. There's also a bag of potatoes and vegetables, already peeled and ready to go."

Scott looked into her porcelain face and smiled. "I didn't know you could cook."

Sarah Vaughn put her hands on her hips and scowled back. Black mini-skirt over black pantyhose. Chrome-studded leather belt. Tight black T-shirt that said, 'I Take Medication for Your Safety'. Nose ring. Lip ring. Four piercings in one ear, three in the other. "I'm not just a pretty face, Scott Forrester."

• • •

It was the best Thanksgiving dinner Scott Forrester had eaten in so long he couldn't even remember.

"Hey, guys. It's been fun," Sarah said, as she bent over to kiss Jamie. "But I've gotta go. Some of the girls have stayed in town to prepare for tomorrow's Occupy Wall Street rally at the Washington Monument. I promised to help."

Sarah put on her trench coat.

Scott kissed her on the cheek. "Sarah… thank you. It was great. Really special."

"You guys look after yourselves. If there's anything else I can do, call me."

"You're my angel, Sarah," Jamie said.

She responded with a hug. "You're a devil, Jamie. A cute devil. Take care, guys."

As she opened the patio door, the November wind roared back in. Scott watched her rusty Jeep Wrangler skid backwards up the slippery drive. "You've got a pretty solid friend there, Jamie."

"Thanks to you."

"Me?"

"Yeah… you dumped her. I got her on the rebound. Told you I would."

Scott grinned. "Jamie, what are we going to do with you?"

As Jamie rolled into the bedroom, he replied, "Well, you can start by helping me set up the new computer stuff. We've got work to do."

"Work? Now?"

"Yeah. That dead Chinese chick's last will and testament. You know… the infamous letter at Archie's that disappeared off the face of the Earth. We have to begin somewhere, Bro. The fight starts right here. Right now."

Scott helped his brother unpack the computer gear and connect the power cords. Once he was up and running, Jamie knew exactly where to go. His physical disability had some annoying limitations but once he was on the Internet, his mobility was second to none.

Jamie entered search terms into an online database and when the information came back he exclaimed, "Bingo! Just what I thought. Check this out, Bro."

"Where do you find this stuff, Jamie?"

"C'mon, Scott. What do you think I do all day? Without research, you won't get past the first hour as a day trader. By the time you listen to those talking heads on TV pumping their favorite stocks, the real money has already been made. But for anyone willing to pay to subscribe to this website, it's a data mine deeper than a West Virginia coal seam. Which reminds me - I need to call someone in West Virginia."

"West Virginia?"

"He can dig even deeper than *this*-"

This were the detailed electronic records behind every private placement that had funded Matthew Carleton's illicitly conceived companies. And the names of those who had participated. Before an IPO, the Securities and Exchange Commission required disclosure of a company's obligations to the early investors and venture capitalists that had bought into sweetheart deals in exchange for pre-IPO financing. Deals that gave them options to buy stock at below market pricing, or the ability to convert their debt into shares at a discount. Deals that were no doubt described in the bulging envelope Sue Lee Chen had deposited on the table at Archie's Diner before a 7.62mm sniper round took away her own chance to fight back.

"Is that who I think it is?" Scott asked, as he scanned the financial disclosures on Jamie's monitor. His brother had drilled into mundane SEC filings and dredged up a Who's Who of names associated with the FBI's biggest serial killer investigation. "The Portland Group?"

"Believe it, Bro. The Portland Group had a big piece of Carleton's private placements. So did Narayan Holdings of New Delhi, India. Sound familiar?"

Scott whistled through his teeth.

Jamie's new printer worked overtime dumping the data. "See Bro..." he continued. "Dominic Sant'Angello's Sigma Venture Capital. Jiri Kostelic's Global Gem Importers. It's all here: when they invested... how much they invested... how much they were exposed."

"And what about these companies?" Scott asked, as the screen scrolled down the list of investors. "Strange names."

"They're offshore trusts. Look at where they're incorporated. P.O. Box numbers - in the Bahamas, Bermuda, the Cayman Islands; in Belize, in Liechtenstein. They're dead ends, Bro, as far as I can tell. We won't get any further with these. Not on this website. Maybe not on any site."

"Dead ends? In the Caribbean? That guy who impersonated Jacob Weinberg, he mentioned offshore trusts run by Matthew Carleton that dead-ended in the Caribbean."

"Geez, Scott. Look at this-"

"What is that, Jamie? It's meaningless to me."

"The private placement investors. They didn't sell."

"So what does that mean?"

"Any insider that wants to cash out after an IPO has to file notices with the SEC. This becomes public information. So selling is the one thing they can't hide. Serious stock traders like me look for insider selling as a 'tell'.

Selling can be innocuous, or it can be a big red flag. A flag that something fishy is going on. Time to bail. But take a look at these records. The insiders who owned Silicon Pathways stock - The Portland Group, Sigma Venture Capital, Narayan Holdings - they *never* sold any of their shares."

A few keystrokes later and Jamie saw the same pattern again. "Let's try Razorback Software. Sure enough, Bro. Deuce Meredith's angel investors not only didn't sell, they *added* to their positions. They exercised their options. They bought more stock. They subscribed to further private placements. By the time these guys were done, I'd say they were majorly exposed. In real deep."

"How deep?"

"To the tune of tens of millions of dollars. Each. Maybe even more."

"And that means, that when these stocks eventually tanked, they took a bath just like everyone else?"

"You got it, Bro. But then look at the trading pattern for these offshore trusts. The ones we suspect Matthew Carleton created to cover his tracks. They didn't buy more. In fact, they cashed out. Right after the companies went IPO. They sold right at the top. Every time. Like clockwork. So what did they know that the others didn't?"

"They knew what Matthew Carleton knew."

"Bingo. You win a prize."

Scott dug into Jamie's printer tray. He looked again at the trading records. The pattern was now clear. "Matthew Carleton didn't warn his partners that he was selling. The same people that bankrolled the deals in the first place. He betrayed them. Sue Lee Chen was right. He defrauded The Portland Group. Ambassador Narayan. And Dominic Sant'Angello."

"You're catching on, Bro."

"Except..." Scott added. "That what Matthew Carleton didn't realize was that he was swindling the *wrong* kind of people. Because the bath he would finally take... was the last one he ever would."

Chapter Forty

"Scott, I can't talk with you. You know that."

"Trish, it's important. Pretend I'm someone off the street with information that might help your investigation."

"Scott, you're more than just 'someone off the street'. And you know it. Do you want me to get fired?"

"Where are you, Trish? New York?"

"Maybe."

"C'mon, Trish. Stop playing games!"

"Yeah, yeah. Okay… I'm in New York. So what?"

"Did you find out who was impersonating Jacob Weinberg?"

"Scott… you're not listening to me! I couldn't tell you that information even if I knew."

"Okay, okay. I'm just telling you to dig deeper into the stock transactions between Matthew Carleton and The Portland Group. And a company called Narayan Holdings out of New Delhi, India."

"Narayan?"

"Yes, that's what I said. Narayan Holdings."

"Scott, I don't work for you anymore, remember?"

"Trish, that's irrelevant. I'm giving you a great lead!"

"Hold on."

Scott could hear her talking to someone in the background. She was whispering, "It's Forrester. He says-" And then the conversation went faint.

"Trish? You still there?"

She came back on the line. "Scott, you're not thinking of conducting your own investigation, are you? Internal Affairs and Titus Griffin would string you up by your nuts on the front lawn at Quantico, if they found out you were pretending to conduct some kind of official FBI inquiry."

"Yeah, yeah, I know. But I'm just a private citizen, exercising my rights. I'm just asking questions. And trying to get answers. But if you follow these leads, and my suspicions are correct, then Internal Affairs and Titus Griffin will have to eat the biggest, fattest crow I can find."

"Sure. But until then, I don't have to talk to you."

"Suit yourself."

"I will." And she hung up.

Chapter Forty-One

Dr. Rajeev Chandra's office was inside a three-story townhouse in the vibrant neighborhood of Scholar's Village, seven blocks from the infamous Watergate complex and within walking distance of George Washington University's Dept. of Psychology. His home was built in the Second Empire style popular during Ulysses S. Grant's presidency. Railings and steps approached a mahogany front door through two smooth, extra tall white columns. Leaded sidelights adorned the entrance. The red-brick front was topped by white-painted dormer windows and a gray slate roof edged by a wide white cornice. Overall, the townhouse had a wedding cake facade.

The building occupied a prestigious space within the University District of Washington. But it was more than just a business address or a residence. It was a scholar's sanctuary, a focal point of philosophy and thought within the academic community.

Mrs. Chandra greeted Scott Forrester at the door with her customary prayer-like bow and ushered him through the entrance hall into Dr. Chandra's office. "Would you like some tea?"

How could he refuse?

Dr. Chandra's office was like a Victorian London reading room. Built-in oak bookshelves climbed the full height of a thirteen foot ceiling. A profusion of leaded glass doors preserved a treasure trove of antiquarian books. By the tall windows, a Victorian desk with rich mahogany grains sat atop an East Indian Agra rug - a carpet that was lush and rich, patterned in deep plums and greens with a border of meandering flowers in ivory and red. Dr. Chandra's office was very much like its owner: it conveyed a calm grace, an intriguing importance, and a spirit of quality and dignity.

The oak floorboards announced Scott's entrance.

"Ah, Mr. Forrester! I'm so glad you could join us," Dr. Chandra said. "May I introduce my good colleague, Detective Inspector Winston Billings of the Royal Bahamas Police."

A tall, sun-weathered black man with gray temples and a smile like Bahamian sunshine stood up from where he had been sitting, in a leather wingback chair next to the fireplace. "Mr. Forrester, my pleasure." He extended his hand. "Dr. Chandra says we have much in common. And there is much to discuss."

Scott had been surprised by Dr.Chandra's sudden and somewhat cryptic invitation to his home. "We do?" he said, as he shook the man's hand. It had an iron grip. Winston Billings was dressed in a white, open neck short-sleeved shirt and slate gray pants. Scott could tell by the tone in his voice – a simplicity punctuated by authority and experience - that Detective Inspector Billings was a deliberate, methodical and studious man.

Much to discuss?

"Gentlemen... tea has arrived," Dr. Chandra said.

Mrs. Chandra entered, put the tray down on her husband's desk and left. She closed the thick library door behind her, trapping the sound of ticking clocks inside.

The three men sat for a moment cradling their Darjeeling tea, its warm mist rising from their cups into the chilly library air. Then Dr Chandra spoke, "It's been my privilege over the years to consult with several police forces in the Caribbean, Mr. Forrester. And in particular, with Inspector Billings. He has invited me to help on many of his fascinating cases. And as far as I can tell – unless he admits otherwise - he has solved them all."

"Dr. Chandra has a way of putting his colleagues on a pedestal, Mr. Forrester."

"Yes. I know," Scott said, sipping his Darjeeling tea. "But once you're on that pedestal, Inspector Billings, it's hard to keep your balance without Dr. Chandra propping you up. There's a method to his madness."

"Indeed, Mr. Forrester." Winston Billings pulled a file from a black leather attaché at his feet. Inside the file was a photo. "This is what Dr. Chandra tells me we have in common…"

It was a photograph of the inside of Jiri Kostelic's yacht. The photo showed a bloodstained message written across the yacht's polished teak cabinets.

"A funeral invitation from the Devil?"

"The day after the Solara sailed into Nassau harbor was supposed to be the day I would retire from the Royal Bahamas Police, Mr. Forrester. But *this* changed my mind…" Inspector Billings pulled out another photo. This one showed Jiri Kostelic's legless body draped over the Solara's stern.

As he looked again at the killer's handiwork, the feeling in Scott's stomach returned. "The victim's legs?" he asked.

"Reef sharks, Mr. Forrester." Billings produced a map of the Bahamas from the file. "He found a place with privacy… and time. And an abundance of Caribbean gray reef sharks. He applied a tourniquet above the knee to stop the blood flow. To keep his victim alive as long as possible. I believe he took Jiri Kostelic to the Spiral Cavern, an underwater haven near Walker's Cay… here, in the northern Abaco Islands." Billings pointed to the map. "It's a popular place for divers. They can witness a feeding frenzy we call the Shark Rodeo. Up to one hundred reef sharks at a time, Mr. Forrester. As large as three meters long, circling for food. Food in the form of Jiri Kostelic, with cuts on his legs to attract them… assuming we could ever find his legs to prove it."

"Kostelic was a diver, as well as a sailor?" Scott asked.

"Yes, he was. An expert diver. Dr. Chandra says you *know* this killer. That you understand him."

Scott Forrester finished his tea and placed the cup and saucer on the desk. He wandered over to the bookcase, deep in thought. He focused his mind on the body of water where Jiri Kostelic had met his ugly fate – a fate the Devil had prescribed for him. "Jiri Kostelic appreciated the beauty of the

Bahamas, Inspector Billings, as any sailor or diver would. But not this time. This time, the killer wanted his victim to experience the Bahamas as a place of terror."

"You *do* understand him, Mr. Forrester," Billings said. "Then, it's settled."

Scott Forrester pushed the ghostly images of a blood-soaked turquoise sea aside, and informed Inspector Billings, "Dr. Chandra misrepresents the assistance I can provide you. I've been suspended from the FBI. Perhaps if you had been here a few weeks earlier, I could have helped you more. But not now."

Dr. Chandra had been sitting quietly during the discussion. "But Mr. Forrester, you are mistaken. It is not *you* who have come to help *us*. It is *we* who have come to help *you*."

"With all due respect, Dr. Chandra," Scott replied. "You can't risk your reputations by involving yourself with someone suspended from the FBI. And how can I possibly be of help? If you want my help, all I can do is refer you to Agents Vincente and Van Cleyburn at the New York Field Office."

Winston Billings pressed the fingers of his hands together and rested his chin on his thumbs. "Ah, the New York Field Office. I don't find the FBI's *official* attitude to be very helpful to my investigation, Mr. Forrester."

"You've already contacted them?"

"Twice in fact. The last time was yesterday. I had forgotten what a cold place New York can be in November, Mr. Forrester. And I got a very cold reception."

"But these photographs? The writing? They are conclusive of a connection-"

"Oh, yes. They took everything I came with. And I'm sure they filed it appropriately. But they treated me as if I was a FedEx courier. Not their equal. Not their partner in apprehending a sadistic killer. Agent Vincente was very clear. I was to return to Nassau and wait. The FBI's Caribbean Liaison Officer in Miami would contact me. *Liaison Officer?* I can assure you, Mr. Forrester... *that* is unacceptable to the Royal Bahamas Police, and to the Bahamian government. Does the FBI think the only job the Royal Bahamas Police has, is to patrol the beaches to protect American tourists from pickpockets?"

"These photographs prove otherwise."

"Precisely, Mr. Forrester!"

"Did the New York Field office tell you, Inspector Billings... that these killings point to a conspiracy?"

"They didn't have to. It's simple physics."

"Physics, sir?"

"When I was in high school my first love was physics. But since there's not much call for nuclear power plants and atomic particle accelerators in the Bahamas, Mr. Forrester, I pursued a career in the police force. Police investigations are just physics... on a human scale. For every action, there is an equal and opposite reaction. Apply terror and what do you produce? Fear. A conspiracy? Of course there is a conspiracy. There was far too much organization involved in this killing to be the work of just one man."

"Apply greed... and you produce revenge."

"Dr. Chandra said you would understand what I'm dealing with, Mr. Forrester. What we are *both* dealing with."

Scott looked over at Dr. Chandra. His face portrayed a serene determination. "So what have we got here, Dr. Chandra? A disenfranchised Yankee. A Bahamian physicist turned cop. And an Indian philosopher. Sounds like a perfect combination to me. So... where do we start, Inspector?"

Winston Billings sipped his tea. "I think I have some pull with Interpol. And I understand you may need some influence with Bahamian banking regulators?"

"Mr. Billings, at this stage, any help is better than no help at all."

Mrs. Chandra interrupted their discussion with a firm rap on the door. "Rajeev, there is someone on the phone. He says he must talk with you urgently."

"Now? I'm in the middle of a meeting."

"Rajeev, I can tell from his voice, this can't wait. He can't stop talking. If he doesn't take a breath soon, I'm afraid he will asphyxiate himself!"

"Is this one of my patients?"

"No, Rajeev. But what he's saying sounds very important."

"Who is he?"

"He says his name is Pradesh Bhandari."

"Pradesh?"

"And he says his daughter has been found. She has escaped."

"Annika Bhandari has escaped? From the Temple?"

Chapter Forty-Two

Heroin is Baltimore's primary drug of abuse. The proportion of Baltimore's residents that need treatment for heroin addiction is fifteen times the national average. Which means there's a shitload of pushers in Baltimore. A shitload of pushers guaranteed that the Temple of Dvaipa could procure Jacqui Antoin's drug of choice as easily as filling a prescription at her neighborhood pharmacy.

Jacqui's death would have been another forgotten statistic in Baltimore's drug overdose records if it hadn't been for the courage and perseverance of her friend and fellow hostage of the Temple, Annika Bhandari, a nineteen-year-old girl Jacqui only knew by her abbreviated first name, Anna.

Anna Bhandari.

It was Anna who brought Jacqui Antoin to the Emergency Department of downtown Baltimore's Sacred Heart Hospital.

It was Anna that helped Jacqui Antoin find the detox unit of the nearby New Freedom Treatment Center.

Anna saved Jacqui Antoin's life.

Because Anna Bhandari had seen enough, had done enough, and had felt ugly enough, to know that the path that she was on would lead to the same fate as Jacqui Antoin.

It was enough to break through the evil.

It was enough to cause Anna Bhandari to seek out Rama's Guardians of Deliverance and Redemption.

It hadn't been easy. It wasn't as easy as just walking off the street into a drug treatment center. The Temple's 'handlers' were not as compassionate and trusting as the doctors and nurses of the Sacred Heart Health System.

Anna and Jacqui were not just free to walk away.

From the moment they joined the Temple of Dvaipa, its authoritarian regime, its isolation, its mind control, had sapped them of their will to think for themselves. The Temple's doctrine was a soporific liquor of addictive mystical deception mixed with drug-induced carnal rituals.

It had made them slaves.

Jacqui Antoin, former prostitute, junkie and thief had escaped death because Anna had been by her side. They had sworn an oath of sisterhood; an oath to escape the insanity that consumed them. And escape they did.

Now Anna Bhandari had found sanctuary in the suburban Baltimore home that was the Guardians' safe house. The Guardians' psychologists and therapists were free to work the healing Anna Bhandari so desperately needed. It was the kind of healing that a 7.62mm bullet prevented Sue Lee Chen from receiving in her own moment of need.

Scott Forrester and Dr. Chandra entered her bedroom. Anna Bhandari looked anxiously at the visitors, curled up in a fetal position in the center of a mound of pillows on her bed. She was cuddling a teddy bear. As she squeezed the bear, it looked as if she wanted to disappear through the wall into the next room.

A short, balding man with glasses rose from a chair by Anna's bedside. "My name is Dr. Anderson," he said, quietly. "Anna is very fragile. The guilt she feels over what she's been a part of, is overwhelming. The residual effects of the Temple's indoctrination still threaten her sanity. Go ahead with your questions, but please be careful."

Scott Forrester and Dr. Chandra sat down in the folding chairs by her bed.

"Anna, do you know why we are here?" Dr. Chandra asked.

"Yes," was the meek reply.

"We need your help," Dr. Chandra said softly. "To learn as much as we can about the Temple of Dvaipa. It's very important. So we can help the others that are still in their grasp."

"Yes. I... want... to help them," she said.

Dr. Chandra's tone was warm and reassuring, but he knew their questions would probe her deepest fears. "You told Dr. Anderson that you and Jacqui were being prepared, that you were about to 'step through to the next spiritual plateau'. What does that mean?"

As Anna replied, her eyes were staring into a void between the strangers' shoulders, into a space where only Anna Bhandari had been - where Anna Bhandari had vowed she would never return. "We were told... we were the chosen ones."

"Chosen? To do what?" Dr. Chandra asked.

"Priestess..." she said, cringing into the pillows, as if the word 'priestess' had escaped into the room, and was dangerous. "We were chosen... to become a priestess... in the Great Temple."

"The Great Temple?" Scott asked. "Do you know where this Great Temple is, Anna? Is it here, in the US?"

"No... it's in the clouds. Soon it will descend with *Her* throne, and *Her* earthly form, so *She* can preside over mankind."

Dr. Chandra whispered in Scott's ear, "You see, my friend, the cult's teachings are still very strong. If we were not here – if she were not in this safe house – she might easily be drawn back into the cult. The Temple still holds a perverse comfort for her, a sense of belonging. It will take time to break the bonds of their brainwashing."

Dr. Chandra intercepted Anna's far away gaze and asked, "Anna, you became frightened enough to escape. Why? What did they want you to do?"

"They..." Her eyes began to water. "They said *She* would descend when we had collected enough..." She shivered; her face revealing the torment of the terrible images dancing in her head.

Scott sensed Anna's struggles. She was trying to let go of her secrets, like Sue Lee Chen had tried before her. "Anna," he said. "What did they want you to collect?"

"Careful, Mr. Forrester..." Anderson warned.

Scott understood the discomfort Anna was feeling. But no one had been able to reach inside a Temple coven and pry open its secrets. They *must* know more. But they also knew the risks they were taking with Anna's state of mind.

Scott remembered the interview he'd had with Anna's father in the cold interrogation room of the First District Police Station on 4th Street. Pradesh Bhandari had said that Anna had grown up in a tolerant household and had many friends from different religious backgrounds.

They needed to break through the barrier the Temple had erected inside Anna. Scott Forrester decided to try an unorthodox approach. He asked, "Anna, will you pray with me?" Then he began, "Yea, though I walk through the valley of the shadow of death..."

"Mr. Forrester!" Dr. Anderson said, objecting to Scott's tactic. "This could be very damaging to her!"

Scott understood Anderson's protest, but continued regardless, "I will fear no evil. For thou art with me; thy rod and thy staff, they comfort me..."

Anderson repeated, "What are you doing, Mr. Forrester? This will confuse her. Please stop!"

But Anna had responded to the prayer, tears streaking down her cheeks. She moved out of the pillow-strewn corner of the room and began to pray with him. She looked up into the ceiling and raised her hand, as if she were reaching for a light. A light of hope. A light of deliverance.

Together, they finished reciting the 23rd Psalm, ending with, "And I will dwell in the house of the Lord forever."

Scott's tactic had snapped Anna out of her trance. Her eyes now contained the spark that had been Anna Bhandari before the Temple had taken her away from everything she had known and loved. The goodness that was still inside Anna had increased the distance between her and the Temple's power. Scott extended his hand, and as she took it, he could feel the yearning in her grip.

"Anna, I know this is very hard for you. You don't have to answer this question if you don't want to."

"I want to. I *need* to. And if this will help the others... then, yes... I will tell you."

"What did they want you to collect, Anna?" Scott asked.

Her grip tightened as she chased away her fear. "Blood, Mr. Forrester. They wanted us... to collect blood."

"Whose blood?"

"The blood of *Her* enemies."

"Was it Jacqui Antoin that took blood from her brother as he lay dying on the deck of his yacht in Miami, Anna?"

"Yes. She told me how much she hated her brother. They told her she needed to take his blood and offer it to the Goddess Dvaipa. He had been her pimp. Did you know that?"

"Yes, I did."

Scott Forrester knew Jacqui Antoin's history from her brother's case files. Their mother had died in a drive-by shooting in New Orleans when Jacqui was fourteen. She and her brother became destitute. They had never known their father. Jacqui Antoin's prostitution was the way her brother DeAndre paid the bills while he worked as a used car salesman during the day and rapped in clubs at night. Jacqui disappeared from Miami two days after her brother's death. She didn't attend his funeral.

Anna Bhandari pulled herself into Scott Forrester's arms and curled up against his chest. "He beat her," Anna said.

"But Jacqui is safe now, Anna," Scott replied. He could see Anna's gaze drifting back into the darkness that was still torturing her soul. "To help the others escape, we need to know as much as possible about the evil people who are doing this. Anything you can remember will help us."

Dr. Chandra whispered in Scott's ear, "Anna is stressed to the hilt with unresolved questions and conflicting beliefs. You can see it now in her eyes. She's beginning to shut down. It's her brain's defense against stress."

Dr. Anderson added, "Mr. Forrester, Anna looks very tired. She will need more rest. She's making good progress, but there is no need to push her."

"Anna..." Scott asked gently, "can we come back and see you tomorrow?"

Anna cuddled her bear. "Yes... Yes, I would like that."

• • •

It was late morning on Day Two of their stay at the safe house run by Rama's Guardians. Anna Bhandari had suffered a major relapse in the night, hallucinating and shrieking in fear, over people in the room that only she could see. Dr. Anderson had heavily sedated her. She was still sleeping.

Scott and Dr. Chandra were waiting in the kitchen for their next opportunity to interview her, hoping they could get even further insights into the secret practices of the Temple of Dvaipa.

Overnight, Scott had become very anxious. They desperately needed the FBI's help. Not for his sake, but for the sake of the innocents who had been cheated of the promise of happiness by the evil of the Temple.

He finally got through to Trish Van Cleyburn after repeated attempts. "Trish, I found Jacqui Antoin."

There was a pause.

"Yes, DeAndre Antoin's sister. She's in a detox unit at the New Freedom Treatment Center in Baltimore."

Trish's reply sounded irritated, not grateful.

"How do I know?" Scott continued. "I just do, let's leave it at that! Yes, I know there's a material witness warrant out for her. But listen... she's in great danger. She's involved with the Temple of Dvaipa. That's why I'm calling. We need to put her into the Witness Protection Plan. Immediately. There's no time to waste. Before they find her."

Dr. Chandra looked up from his cup of tea.

"Damn!" Scott said. "That bitch hung up on me!"

"Mr. Forrester, do you think the Temple will pick up Anna and Jacqui's trail?" Dr. Chandra asked.

Scott finished his third cup of coffee. "It's a distinct possibility. If I'm correct and Ambassador Narayan is at the top of the Temple's organization, we should expect anything. Narayan has powerful friends in powerful places. It's worth trying to get Jacqui Antoin into Witness Protection. But even so, there are ways to penetrate that program if you have the right connections."

"And Anna?"

"Anna is a gold mine of damaging evidence against the cult. For now, I think she's safer with us."

Dr. Anderson stepped into the kitchen with good news. "Anna's ready to see you again," he said.

As Scott Forrester and Dr. Chandra entered her bedroom, Anna was sitting up eating cereal. She looked happy, relieved, calm.

"Anna..." said Dr. Chandra. "You look wonderful!"

"For the first time in a long while, Dr. Chandra, I've been able to sleep without waking every few minutes in fear that *She* was in the room with me."

Her eyes were doe-like and uncorrupted, full of a spirit that was once again fresh and young and innocent. "I know that the 'absolute truths' the Temple taught me are fiction. That my faith in Dvaipa and my obedience to the cult's leaders will not bring the rewards they claimed."

Anna was curled up in the pile of pillows, but this time she was the one in control - the visions in her head were not controlling her. "You asked me what I could remember. Well, I remember a man who said we were going to leave the country. For the Great Temple. And that was when my fear was unbearable. I was afraid I would never see my parents and friends again."

"Anna..." Scott asked. "Do you remember this man's name?"

"They called him Bakasura."

"Bakasura?" Dr. Chandra wondered out loud.

Anna continued, "Yes, he was a very peculiar looking man. He had a large nose and a moustache. His eyes were very far apart. One of them didn't look in the same direction as the other."

"It was a glass eye?" Scott asked.

"Yes, Mr. Forrester. He always seemed very nervous and sweated a lot. The rest of the Temple's leaders had trouble accepting him. It was like he was a part of the group, but then again, he was not. He was allowed to come and go as he pleased. Sometimes we would never see him for weeks."

Dr. Chandra grabbed Scott's arm and whispered, "Bakasura. That name is interesting," he said. "Bakasura was a demon in Indian mythology; a giant that lived in a cave. A king and his army tried to fight the giant but were defeated and the king's army was slaughtered. It was left to the villagers to make peace with Bakasura. So each day they sent him food and a human sacrifice. In some legends, Bakasura transformed himself into a bird. A crane. A man with a glass eye would look like a bird, and in Hinduism, it is common to believe that someone was once an animal in a past life. Bakasura must be a name the Temple gave him – a stage name, like in a play."

"More like a horror show, Dr. Chandra," Scott said. He turned back to Anna and asked, "Do you know where this man called Bakasura went when he left the house?"

"One night, I got out of bed and slipped into the kitchen for something to eat. I was very quiet so they wouldn't hear me. I heard Bakasura talking on the phone in the next room. He mentioned something about a hole and mountains. I didn't understand what he was saying. I was sleepy and still a bit drugged."

"A *hole*? And mountains?"

"I remember someone in the next room calling him by another name. Maybe, it was his real name."

"What name?"

"They called him Chester."

"Anna, this is very important," Scott said. "Please try to help me. You said a hole and mountains? Do you remember anything else he said about this hole or these mountains? Anything that would indicate where the mountains were?"

"No. But I thought he said something like Yao Ming."

"The basketball player?"

"It was late. I was sleepy…"

Yao Ming? A hole? A mountain? Scott thought. *And a man named Chester?* It was an unusual name. *A man with a large nose and moustache? And a glass eye?* It bothered Scott. It had made a connection with him. Then Scott Forrester realized how everything fit together!

"Anna…" he asked. "Was he tall?"

"Yes, very tall."

"Anna…" he said. "Think, Anna. Not *Yao Ming*. Was it… *Wyoming*?"

"Yes!" she said. "Yes, Mr. Forrester! It *was* Wyoming."

Chester.

Wyoming.

The hole in the mountains.

It was like holding the final piece of a jigsaw puzzle, but holding it the wrong way round. With a simple turn, the piece's true position had been found.

Dr. Chandra was still mystified. "A hole in the mountains… in Wyoming, Scott?

"Yes, Dr. Chandra… the town of Jackson Hole! And I know a Chester in Jackson Hole, Wyoming. Because I met him. A tall man with a moustache and a glass eye. The man Anna is describing is someone I know very well… because I interviewed him. Chester Franklin. The owner of Pine Ridge

Lodge. The last place anyone saw Deuce Meredith and his guide, Charlie 'Silver Moon', alive."

Chapter Forty-Three

The phone rang on Lance Caulfield's busy desk at the FBI's Denver Field Office. "Hello?" he mumbled, his mouth full of sandwich.

"Lance?"

"Just a minute," Caulfield said, swallowing. "Forrester? Scott Forrester? What can I do for ya, buddy?"

"The murders of Deuce Meredith and Charlie MacNabb. There's been a new development."

"Keep talkin', Forrester. And I'll keep eatin'."

Lance Caulfield was a stocky, clean-shaven, and straight-talking agent; a massive six-foot-four, two hundred and sixty pounds, and for someone pushing sixty-years-old, still had arms like a gorilla. He always wore a cowboy hat and a string tie to work, dress code be damned; loved the high mountains, and in particular Wyoming's backcountry.

After ten grueling days combing the towns and valleys of the Grand Tetons together, Lance Caulfield had grown to like Scott Forrester. Lance Caulfield didn't make friends that easily and didn't take kindly to fools. Scott Forrester was no fool. Whatever Scott Forrester had to say, Lance Caulfield would listen. Scott Forrester had earned a full measure of his respect.

It only took two words to re-establish their common ground. Those words were, "Chester Franklin."

Lance gulped. "You know about Chester Franklin?"

"I know he's a member of a Hindu cult."

"Is that what *it* is?"

"*It? What* is *it?*"

"I tried calling you. But your office said you were on some kind of administrative leave. Are you sick or somethin'?"

"Yes, I'm sick of something. Something by the name of Titus Griffin."

"That asshole put me on to… um, I have a note here somewhere… a Trish Van Cleyburn in New York. Know her?"

"I'm acquainted with her. She's on the Carleton case."

"Well, she's useless. Says she can't come see *it* for three friggin' days! Three days? Somethin' about goin' to Florida. Can you believe it?"

"Come where?"

"Wyoming. Jackson Hole. Isn't that why you're callin'? How soon can you get here, Forrester? I need someone like you to take a look and tell me what the hell *it* is." Caulfield tossed the remains of his sandwich in the wastepaper basket. "And this time… don't forget to bring a warm coat!"

• • •

In the early 1800's, a 'hole' was a term used by trappers to describe the high, broad valleys of the Rocky Mountains. Trappers would come down from their isolated cabins to 'holes' like Jackson to sell their furs, buy supplies, drink copious quantities of liquor, and avail themselves of the local womenfolk.

By Thanksgiving, a blanket of fresh snow, eight inches deep, had covered the 'hole' that the town of Jackson occupied at the base of Snow King Mountain. The ski slopes of the Grand Tetons now had a base of twenty-one inches of loosely packed snow. Total snowfall had already reached fifty-five inches, well on the way to the season average of four hundred and thirty-five inches. It was more snow than Scott Forrester ever wanted to see for the rest of his life. And it was cold. Twenty-six degrees Fahrenheit at the base of Snow King Mountain. Eleven degrees Fahrenheit at the summit.

Pine Ridge Lodge was located seventeen miles south of Jackson Hole, near the junction of the Snake and Hoback Rivers. Pine Ridge Lodge was exclusively a hunting camp and this time of year it was closed.

Its owner, Chester Franklin, was not a native of Wyoming. He hailed from Omaha, Nebraska and settled in Wyoming as a property developer - an old school, 'Warren Buffet'-style investor, putting his money in ventures he could understand, like rental properties, small office buildings and hunting camps. Chester Franklin had a reputation as an upstanding member of two far-flung communities – Jackson Hole, Wyoming, his summer home; and in the winter, Fort Myers, Florida.

But Chester Franklin was also a pedophile.

And Chester Franklin was also dead.

Killed by two 9mm bullets to the back of his head. Fired at close range, while working in the office of his modest, fairly spartan apartment within Pine Ridge Lodge. The first shot was fired as he was sitting upright at his computer downloading child pornography; the second, as ballistics analysis had confirmed, entered his head while his face was slumped on the keyboard. This second bullet was 'just to be sure' - unnecessary to the outcome, but indicating the mark of a professional.

Scott examined the blood-splattered, glassless shell that used to be a computer monitor before it was shattered by the first bullet that exited Chester Franklin's head. "Any witnesses, Lance?"

"No. He lived alone," Caulfield explained. "The staff had left for the season. Franklin was scheduled to fly out of Salt Lake City for Tampa three days after he was killed. We might not have found him until spring if it weren't for one of the cooks. He'd returned from illness to collect his last paycheck and found this..." Franklin's body had long since been removed from the apartment, but the photo Lance showed Scott Forrester was clear enough to confirm that Chester Franklin, a tall man with a glass eye, was Anna's Bakasura.

Scott looked around the room. The walls were varnished pine, plainly and efficiently decorated with photos of Wyoming's wildlife. And there was very little evidence that anyone had taken any interest in searching through Chester's papers and desk drawers. "Chester Franklin knew his killer, Lance."

"Forrester, we figured all that out by ourselves. As far as we can tell, Franklin let him in. They talked. Franklin got on the computer, and when his back was turned... thup, thup... in the back of the head."

"So what did you bring me here for?"

"*It's* in there, Forrester. In his bedroom. Hidden in the closet. Please tell me you know what the hell *it* is, Forrester."

Scott Forrester entered Chester Franklin's bedroom. It was as nondescript as his office. A closet door opposite the bed was open. The clothes that were hanging inside had been parted. Behind the clothes, there was another doorway - a secret entrance that led to a hidden room, almost as large as the bedroom itself.

As soon as Scott entered, the reason Lance Caulfield had requested him to come to Wyoming became painfully obvious. "Jesus, Lance! What in God's name-"

"I thought you'd be impressed."

Every wall in the entire room was covered. Every square inch. Posters. Drawings. Pictures. Photographs. In a wayward hunting camp deep in the Wyoming wilderness, Chester Franklin, a pedophile, had created a shrine to the Demon-Goddess Dvaipa.

And at what appeared to be an altar - flanked by candles and strange half-human, half-animal statues – a wall-sized reproduction of the painting, 'The Revenge of Dvaipa' reined over the hidden room like a doorway to Hell.

"I take it, Forrester, you know what all *this* means?"

The walls were papered with pictures from Hindu mythology, most of them about the demon Bakasura. Terrified villagers offered cattle and human sacrifices to keep peace with the giant. Fierce battles raged between the Hindu Gods and Demons. And intermingled with depictions of Hindu legends were pornographic photographs of children, mostly of East Asian and Oriental descent, in various stages of pedophilic violation.

But clearly the focal point of the room was the grisly image of the Demon-Goddess Dvaipa. The altarpieces were still in place - a curved silver knife in a gold and silver scabbard, a chalice and a leather-bound book. "We haven't touched a thing, Forrester. We needed someone to see it, just as we found it, before Forensics took the room apart."

"You did the right thing."

Scott put on a pair of latex gloves. He picked up the leather-bound book. The front of the book was embossed in gold leaf with the title, 'The Asura Ghita'. And it was heavy. The weight of a century of malcontented souls pressed down on his hands. He could feel the heat of cruelty and revenge emanating from inside.

"The Asura Ghita," Scott said, as he opened the book to the frontispiece with its ink-sketch depiction of Dvaipa. "It says the translation is, 'The Song of Demons'."

He gingerly turned the faded pages. Like the title page, the body of the book contained passages written in two languages - one side in Sanskrit, the other, in English.

He passed the book to Caulfield, "Read the first sentence on this page for me, Lance. Read it out loud. I want to feel what it is like to hear these words... inside a room like this."

Lance Caulfield obliged. "I am the energy of Her divine anger."

Scott looked into the eyes of the Demon-Goddess as the image came to life with the utterance of her commandment. The terror and violence of the painting ignited with cruel brilliance, just as it had done with the original in the Freer Gallery. But this time - with degrading images of children beside her, crying out for their salvation - the sadism filled the air with its stink.

Caulfield read through the first few pages of the book, then stopped. The more he'd read, the more his face had grimaced with the unease of a simple but learned man who had never read of such unspeakable things. "What is all of *this*, Forrester?"

"It's the instruction manual, Lance."

"Instruction manual? Instructions for *what*?"

"What else? Evil."

Chapter Forty-Four

Pine Ridge Lodge was no backwoods cabin, draped in dusty spider webs and sprayed with dingy lighting. Not at all. Chester Franklin knew his market. The Lodge was immaculate. Five-star. The finest food. The finest furnishings. Expert hunting guides. Expensive after-hunt cognac. Secret stashes of banned Cuban cigars hidden behind the bar.

At the front desk, the Lodge's guest book was a veritable Who's Who of American prestige and influence, from Wall Street to Hollywood, from Capitol Hill to West Palm Beach. Pine Ridge Lodge was an exclusive retreat for the wealthy and privileged. As Scott Forrester thumbed through the entries in the guest book, he found the name of software millionaire Deuce Meredith.

"Chester Franklin was not a victim of the Tiger Paw Killer. He was killed by someone else," Scott said.

"How can you be so sure, Forrester?"

"Because Chester Franklin died without trauma."

Scott wandered from the registration desk over to the information board on the other side of the lobby. It displayed survey maps of the Wyoming Range, the Bridger-Teton National Forest, and further to the south, on Wyoming's border with Idaho, the Snake River Canyon. A notice board to one side contained Forest Ranger advisories and weather reports, and testimonials and photographs from the Lodge's wealthy clientele - photos of unshaven hunters holding the heads of their limp prey, mainly bighorn sheep, elk and moose; the occasional mountain lion and grizzly bear. The notice board was glass fronted and locked.

"Chester Franklin's death was quick and instantaneous," Scott continued. "This was an assassination, pure and simple, clean and quiet. The Tiger Paw Killer likes to dwell on his victims, act out rituals of torture and revenge. Leave cryptic messages. That's the clearest indication it wasn't him. No bloody message near the body."

"So who then?" Caulfield asked.

"I think Franklin's killer had been a guest here previously. He knew Franklin and knew his way around. I would start by interviewing people who stayed at Pine Ridge Lodge in the final weeks of the season. See if they noticed a male guest, arriving alone, who seemed to have an unusually friendly relationship with Chester Franklin."

"Another pedophile? Meeting up with Franklin to swap porn?"

"Possibly."

"We finally tracked down that guy who left a box of porn CDs in that bar in Jackson Hole. He said he bought them from Chester Franklin."

"Don't restrict yourself to just his pedophile connections, Lance. Chester Franklin let his guard down. I believe he telegraphed something the cult didn't want him to do or say, and they sent someone to silence him. He may have reached a limit that most sane people won't cross and wanted out of the cult." Scott reflected on the killing of Sue Lee Chen at Archie's Diner. "But the option of turning your back on the Temple doesn't appear to be available."

"How deep was Chester Franklin into this cult-thing?"

"As deep as it gets. Anna Bhandari explained to me how Chester Franklin - or as she knew him, Bakasura – provided the logistics that moved the Temple's followers from one ritual event to another. He seemed to be their travel agent, purchasing agent, and agent of whatever evil schemes paid the rent. He was an organizer and facilitator."

Scott looked over the photos and testimonials in the display case. "From the looks of his guest book, Pine Ridge Lodge was an entry ramp where the Temple could cruise the superhighway of America's powerful elite. And I would wager this lodge became a focal point on that highway. A way station where important people could connect with the Temple through one of its main intermediaries, Chester Franklin. He was a broker of deals, and always on the go. Track his movements and you'll probably find that. We know the Washington/Baltimore area was one of his hubs because of the Temple's recruitment of Anna Bhandari and Jacqui Antoin. I'll bet New York City was another. And try the West Coast - San Francisco, Los Angeles."

"That's uncanny, Forrester," Caulfield said. "We've already confirmed Franklin was a regular traveler under different aliases between those cities. How on Earth did you know that, Forrester? You're a goddamn genius."

"No. Not a genius, Lance. Take the psyche of this pedophile, mix it with membership in a Hindu devil-cult with national ambitions, and just extrapolate from there."

"If this killer was sent to silence Franklin, why didn't the killer try to cover up the evidence of Franklin's cult connections? The secret room? The altar? Nothing in there was disturbed as far as we can tell."

"Chester Franklin had a natural talent for keeping secrets," Scott explained. "That was his vocation - that was the service he provided to the Temple. I'm guessing he kept his secret life well hidden from them. The simple answer is... the killer the Temple sent to silence him didn't know. Because, if the Temple knew about that room, Lance... I can assure you... they would have burned this whole lodge to the ground. The last thing the Temple wanted was having that manuscript end up in the hands of the wrong people... people they can't control. People like us."

"We're getting close to the source of his child pornography, Forrester. It's a porn ring we think Franklin was a major player in. I'd like you to stay and help us."

"Well, I'm not supposed to be in Wyoming, remember? If Titus Griffin found out, Lance, you'd be looking through a different doorway into Hell than this one."

"Okay, Forrester. I understand. But how about playing it like this? You weren't here. You were *never* here."

Scott thought through the opportunity. To clear his name. To help his brother. "I guess I can't get into any more trouble than I'm already in."

"Then it's a deal."

Lance turned to leave. Scott took one last look at the photographs: the hunting trips, the testimonials. Then something stood out. He pressed his nose against the case, straining to pick out a faint detail in one particular snapshot. "Hey, Lance... wait a minute! Have you got the key that unlocks this case?"

"I think so. Why?"

"This photo - the one with the two hunters and a mountain lion - take a look at this..."

Lance Caulfield peered into the glass.

"Do you see what I see, Lance?"

"Sure. Two hunters and a dead mountain lion."

"No. Not that. There. That object in the background behind their heads? And look at their letter. These hunters were here the same week Deuce Meredith and Charlie MacNabb were murdered."

Special Agent Lance Caulfield squinted through the glass at the photo. There was an odd black shape in the sky behind the hunters. It didn't belong. "Well, I'll be hotdamned-"

Scott Forrester felt the hairs on the back of his neck tingle. A knot formed in the pit of his stomach. "We never understood, Lance, did we? We could never figure out how the Tiger Paw Killer got *into* the Bridger-Teton Forest without being seen by anyone. Or how he got *out*. We never knew how he arrived in Wyoming in the first place. We interviewed the staff at every private airfield; at public airports in Jackson Hole, Yellowstone and Idaho Falls; but we missed some airfields, didn't we, Lance?"

"Well, I'll be hotdamned..."

"We never checked..."

"The military ones."

"Looks like a Black Hawk, doesn't it?"

"Damn right. And I should know that shape. Cos' I flew inside enough of them in the Army."

"What's a military chopper doing around here, Lance?"

"Don't know. But damned if I'm not going to find out! It's got markings. We can take the photograph to the Sheriff's Office in Jackson Hole, have them blow it up and check it out. And we'll take the letter. See if these hunters can tell us if they saw it. I'll get the keys to unlock the case."

The knot in Scott Forrester's stomach tightened.

Two smiling hunters. A dead mountain lion.

A military helicopter in the clear blue sky over Wyoming's Grand Tetons. The bitter tasting images crystallized. *He was lowered into the forest by chopper. No signs of entry. He tracked his victims. And when he was done, they came to pick him up. Gone without a trace.*

Caulfield returned with the key.

"It was so simple, Lance. In fact it was so simple, it wasn't even obvious. The killer of Deuce Meredith and Charlie McNabb had a lot of people helping him. They provided the means. They found the targets. They enabled him to carry out his work. Not just Meredith and McNabb, the others too. All of his victims."

Lance Caulfield plucked the pin that held the photo onto the notice board and placed the new evidence in his hands, "Yeah, Forrester. *Now* it's simple. *Now* it's obvious. But answer me this, genius... who the hell are *they*?"

Chapter Forty-Five

"Are you sure I should be doing this with you, Lance? Wouldn't you be better off on your own?"

"It's no big deal, Forrester. You're just doing your job. That's all."

"My job? My job is to be at home in front of a Redskins game, eating pizza, remember?"

"Do you think, that after we get through *that* gate, that anyone will even admit we've been here? Whether you're suspended... or not?"

That gate... was the entrance to Harry S. Truman Air Force Base, home to the 73rd Space Wing of the U.S. Space Command, ten miles north of Cheyenne, Wyoming.

The 73rd Space Wing was not the home base for pilots in a U.S. interplanetary fighter squadron. It was the headquarters for one hundred and fifty nuclear-tipped Minuteman III intercontinental ballistic missiles.

It was also home to the 22nd Helicopter Flight.

Caulfield's car approached the airbase's security gate. Lance flashed his FBI badge at the heavily armed guard. "Caulfield. FBI. Colonel Johnson is expecting us."

Colonel Bradley Johnson was the Commander of 73rd Space Wing. The guard looked at Caulfield's credentials, then spoke into his walkie-talkie. Instructions were sent back. "Go to the building on the left. Park your vehicle in the enclosure, check your weapons, and enter the screening room."

In the post-9/11 world, Air Force security screening involved a full body X-Ray and fingerprint verification. Fortunately, the Air Force's database couldn't pick up Scott Forrester's suspension from the FBI.

"Lance, I thought you said no one will even admit we've been here? After this screening, they'll be able to count how many pubic hairs I have!"

"Stop your gripin', Forrester. I got you in, didn't I?"

They advanced through the layers of the base's security screening and reached Colonel Bradley Johnson's office. His aide ushered them in.

The 73rd Space Wing's ballistic missiles were deployed in hardened silos controlled by twenty underground launch centers spread out over a twelve thousand square mile area of eastern Wyoming, western Nebraska and northern Colorado. Colonel Johnson, a poker-faced man with a tight-to-his-head brush cut and immaculately turned out uniform, was separated from World War III and global nuclear holocaust by a few simple launch codes and a push of twenty fat, red buttons.

"What can I do for you, gentlemen?"

Lance Caulfield produced a photograph, a blowup of the one they took out of the display case at Pine Ridge Lodge. "Do you recognize the markings on this chopper, Colonel?"

Colonel Johnson knew all of the insignia in the 27th Air Force to which the 73rd Space Wing belonged. He identified it quickly. "Yes, that's one of ours. What's this about, gentlemen?"

"Do you know what one of your choppers was doing in the skies over the Bridger-Teton National Forest on the 20th of September this year, Colonel?"

Johnson straightened his tie. "I'm not sure I understand why you would want to know that, Agent Caulfield. Has one of my crew done something wrong?"

"That depends."

"Depends on what?"

"It depends on what they did on the 20th of September. And why."

"Well, that's not very specific. We like being specific in the Air Force, Agent Caulfield. It prevents us from, you know, accidentally doing the wrong thing."

"Like pushing the wrong button?" Scott said. "That wouldn't happen here, would it? Not under *your* command."

Colonel Johnson handed the photograph back. "I suggest you work through the appropriate channels, Agent Caulfield. At the Air Force Office of Special Investigations in Washington. This base and its personnel are off-limits to civilian investigators. We are a 'Top Secret' facility."

"Whoa! *Top Secret*? That's mighty impressive, Colonel. Scott - we'd better skedaddle outta here! I guess Colonel Johnson would rather be a goat than a hero, as far as the FBI is concerned. But whatever the Colonel wants..."

Lance Caulfield, to Scott's surprise, put his cowboy hat on and rose to leave. Scott looked at him with an expression that said, 'After all that fuss getting in here, Lance, we're going to leave? So soon? What gives?'

The tall cowboy stopped at the door, paused and looked back at Colonel Johnson, "Well, Colonel?"

Johnson moved nervously in his chair, strumming the desk with his fingers. "Sit down, gentlemen. Perhaps we can work through your issues. Then agree on an amicable course of action."

Caulfield smiled. He placed his cowboy hat on Johnson's desk, sat down in the chair again, took a cigar out of his jacket pocket, and rolled it between his fingers.

"This is a no smoking facility, Agent Caulfield."

"You don't mind if I chew on it, do you Colonel Johnson? Helps me think."

"No, Agent Caulfield. I guess not. Go right ahead."

Caulfield didn't say another word. As the seconds ticked by like minutes, Colonel Johnson became increasingly uncomfortable, as if he was the one that should be conducting the interview, rather than the other way around.

After what seemed like forever, Colonel Johnson broke the stalemate, "What did you mean Agent Caulfield, when you said, 'goat or hero'?"

Lance Caulfield shuffled the cigar from one side of his mouth to the other, then pointed it, soggy-end forward, at the Colonel. "We'd like to see the logbooks of that chopper, Colonel Johnson. Let's start with say, the 20th of September, and then the preceding and subsequent two months. While you're at it, we'd like to know what personnel were on board. And their missions. You know, that kind of thing."

Colonel Johnson chuckled, then his officially polite face turned from laughter to sneer, "You know I can't give you those records, Special Agent Caulfield."

"Why not?"

"Because they're classified military documents! That's why!"

"Classified by *who*?"

"The US Government."

"Which part?"

"All of it."

"Well, I guess Colonel Johnson is saying, Agent Forrester, that we'd better go through the 'appropriate channels' at the Air Force Office of Special Investigations in Washington. Seems Colonel Johnson isn't prepared to take advantage of the glorious opportunity we're offering him. Too bad, eh Scott?"

Scott Forrester wasn't sure what game Caulfield was playing. Or even what the rules were. But Caulfield seemed to know what he was doing, so Scott decided to play along, "Yeah, Lance. It's a tough call, buddy. But we're just going to have to do… what we're going to have to do. And damn the consequences, right?"

Scott then looked at Caulfield again with eyes that said, 'What the hell are you doing, Lance?'

"Right," Caulfield replied. "Then let's go. Don't want to waste any more of the Colonel's time."

Once again, Lance Caulfield picked up his cowboy hat and rose to leave. Once again, Colonel Johnson stopped them.

"What did you mean by 'goat'?" he asked.

Caulfield's cowpoke playfulness disappeared. He looked the Colonel square in the eyes. He produced another photo from the file in his hand and dropped it on Colonel Johnson's desk. "This is what I mean, Colonel!"

The photo was just a small sampling of Chester Franklin's extensive collection of child pornography.

Colonel Bradley Johnson's office was decorated with pictures of his wife and children on their summer vacations. There were framed Bible quotations on every wall. And Lance Caulfield had a pretty good idea how a God-fearing, straight-laced career Colonel in the US Air Force would react when confronted with hardcore child pornography. And Lance Caulfield was right.

The Colonel turned pale. *Very, very* pale.

"You see, Colonel..." Caulfield explained, his voice returning to its down-home, gather-round-the-campfire tone, "Sure... we can do it *your* way. The *Air Force* way. We can launch an investigation through the 'appropriate channels' just like you said. With the Air Force Office of Special Investigations. In *Washington*." He plopped the rest of the fat file on Colonel Johnson's desk. "And I'm sure they would be extremely interested in coming to some 'amicable course of action', given the overwhelming evidence the FBI has..."

As Colonel Johnson thumbed through the file, his eyes widened in disbelief.

Caulfield continued, Colonel Johnson's balls firmly in his grasp, "That a member of the Colonel's 73rd Space Wing has been distributing this grotesque smut throughout the western United States, and that so far, the evidence suggests it was smuggled into the United States on military aircraft from the Far East. By members of the good Colonel's staff."

Caulfield turned around. "What do you think, Scott? Is the Air Force Office of Special Investigations the right place to go with this *shit*?"

"It's hard to argue with your logic, Agent Caulfield."

"And if you did, you'd probably be wrong."

"And if I did, I *definitely* would be wrong," Scott replied.

Caulfield put the squeeze on, "You see, Colonel - this is why we came to *you* first. Where the *goat* and *hero* part comes in. Because if we launched an investigation through the 'appropriate' Air Force bigwigs in Washington - just like you said we should - you would probably end up lookin' like some little horned animal all gussied up in a fancy uniform, bleating for his mommy! Questions would be asked, Colonel. That's what good investigators do. Ask questions. Questions about *command* and *control*. Control of *everything* that goes on at this base. After all, if the good Colonel can't control what goes in and out on his military transports, how can the Colonel be *trusted* with the care of a hundred and fifty intercontinental ballistic missiles? Right, Scott?"

Scott Forrester finally understood the game Lance Caulfield was playing. And he just *loved* the rules. "God help us, Lance, if one of those suckers got loose without the good Colonel knowing it. There'd be hell to pay!"

"That's right, Agent Forrester. Hard to argue with him, Colonel, isn't it?"

Johnson's face turned from pale to beet red. There was a familiar name in the FBI's report. It was one of his closest aides. He let out a cross between a bleat and a shriek, "No! It can't be. Not *him*!"

"I think the good Colonel's starting to see things *our* way, Special Agent Forrester. He's such a decent kinda fella. I just knew he would come around. He seems that kinda guy, don't he?"

Lance put the cigar back in his mouth. "Now, let's talk about the 'hero' part of this story, Colonel Johnson. You see, there's more than just this one file that's in your hands. Much more. And the 'much more' contains pretty damning evidence about several other officers under your command." He turned to Scott. "But it seems - I'm such an idiot, Agent Forrester - I've left most of it back at the Denver Field Office. Never mind. We can always send it on to Washington."

"Wait a sec, Lance," Scott said. "What would a 'hero' do in a situation like this?"

"Good question, Agent Forrester. I think a 'hero' is someone who works aggressively with the relevant agencies-"

"Like the FBI, Lance."

"Like the FBI, Scott. To root out any notion that these kinds of perverts are populating the Armed Forces of these United States of America. And - this is where the 'hero' part *really* kicks in - through *immediate* and *decisive* leadership action begins his *own* investigation-"

"Which would uncover surprisingly *similar* evidence?" Scott added.

"Of course it would. Our 'hero' would root out the perpetrators. Isn't that right, Scott?"

"That's what a 'hero' would do, Lance. *Definitely.* That's what a *hero* would do."

Colonel Johnson picked up his phone, "Tell the Warrant Officer at 22nd Helicopter to bring me his logbooks. Immediately!"

Lance Caulfield chewed on his cigar and wandered over to the bookcase, "Nice picture, Colonel. Grand Canyon? Did you take this? She's a pretty little girl, isn't she? Wouldn't want her to end up in one of those photos, Colonel. No, sir."

• • •

"It says here the crew transported a payload called 'SS-1' into the Bridger-Teton National Forest on the 20th of September. What is this SS-1, Colonel?" Lance Caulfield asked. "Some kind of bomb?"

Scott found another notation of interest in the logbook of the 22nd Helicopter Squadron. "Agent Caulfield, did you know that Utah's Hill Air Force Base has a recreation camp on the other side of Deadman Mountain?"

"No shit."

"And this logbook says this camp was the pickup point for SS-1 on the day Deuce Meredith and Charlie MacNabb were killed?"

Caulfield chewed on his cigar. "SS-1, Colonel?"

Johnson walked over to the bookcase, placed his hands on a shelf and put his head down. Sweat was forming on his forehead. What was worse? Triggering a Pentagon investigation into child pornography at Harry S. Truman Air Force Base? Or telling the FBI who 'SS-1' was?

Lance Caulfield wouldn't let up. "The Colonel still wants to be a *hero*, doesn't he, Scott?"

"Well, Lance… I sure hope he does. For his sake."

The Colonel turned around and said, "C'mon guys, you know I can't give you classified information without the proper authorization."

"Scott, how many more photos we got back at the office?"

"Don't know Lance. Too many to count, I think."

"That's what I thought."

Colonel Johnson wiped the sweat off his face. "Okay. Okay. Enough. All we do - and I stress *all* we do - is drop them in. Then pick them up. That's our mission. Just *drop in*. And *pick up*."

"Why?"

"Survival training. Four days. No food. No shelter."

"Well, Agent Forrester…" Caulfield said, chuckling. He took the cigar out of his mouth and walked up to the Colonel. "I don't know about the Colonel's idea of 'no food', do you? Because, it seems to me - as the simple country boy I am – that if somebody gave me an SR-25 sniper rifle, and then dropped me in the Bridger-Teton Forest – a forest teeming with tasty wildlife - I'd sure as hell have me some food, pretty darn quick! Not much of a survival exercise, whatcha think?"

Scott Forrester had finished with the logbook. He had all the notes he needed. "Why should there be such a problem in telling us about a survival training exercise, Colonel? Sounds pretty routine. The Air Force does it all the time. Regular training for pilots, right? So what's so special about these particular trainees, Colonel? Who are they? Who do they work for? They don't work for the Air Force, do they?"

Colonel Johnson paced behind his chair, in silence.

"Oh, I get it, Scott!" Lance said. "The Colonel here wants to play a guessing game. You know - like in the movies. We ask a question. He just nods. So he can deny to the 'appropriate channels' he ever told us anything. We just figured it out by ourselves. That way he doesn't have to admit he revealed classified information without *proper authorization*."

"No Lance - I have a better idea. Let's say we just go to Washington like he told us, and see if we can get someone else to play games with us."

"You mean with a file full of kiddie porn?"

"Exactly," Scott replied. "Well, Colonel?"

Colonel Johnson was still sweating. He sat down, leaned back in his chair and looked anxiously at the ceiling.

"C'mon, Colonel Johnson. It shouldn't be this hard to be a hero," Scott said.

Johnson fidgeted, swallowed hard, and finally admitted, "The Central Intelligence Agency. We do it... for the CIA."

Lance Caulfield stopped chewing on his cigar.

Scott Forrester opened his notebook. "Names, Colonel. 'SS-1' is a covert operative, isn't he? I *want* his name."

"I can't give you a *goddamn name!*"

Lance picked up his cowboy hat. It was the signal. All rise. "Let's go, Scott-"

"I can't give you names!" Colonel Johnson said, distraught. This whole process was getting out of control. "I don't know any names! We *never* know any names!"

Caulfield wasn't impressed. "What the hell *do* you know, Colonel? Two men were killed by someone with a CIA-issued SR-25 sniper rifle in the middle of the Bridger-Teton National Forest! And you're telling us that someone hasn't got a name? Someone *your* aircrew dropped into the forest and picked up again. On *your* orders. Goddamn it, Colonel! We need a name! *Who is SS-1?*"

"I'm telling you... *I don't know!* All I know... is *they* come here undercover."

"Undercover? As what?"

"Maintenance contractors. For the base's security system."

"And the name of that contractor, Colonel?"

Colonel Johnson pulled a sales brochure out of his desk drawer and tossed it on the desk. Its cover said, 'Sapphire Systems – A Member of The Portland Group'.

Scott Forrester's heart stopped. He put his pen down and picked up the brochure. "The Portland Group?"

They were done.

At least they had some kind of name.

That name was Michael Wayne Portland.

Chapter Forty-Six

"Passengers arriving on Frontier Airlines Flight 724 from Denver can collect their baggage on Carousel #4. Once again Frontier Airlines would like to apologize for the delay in the arrival of Flight 724…"

The calendar had clicked over into December. His separation from Christienne Duval was nearly over. He'd received a text message that said her trip to Moscow had been a success and she was flying back via Paris in three days time. But her association with Michael Wayne Portland and The Portland Group was disturbing. It meant she was firmly inside the widening circle of danger that surrounded the reclusive billionaire and his connection with the Temple of Dvaipa.

The concourse in Terminal C at Washington's Reagan National Airport was crowded with political staff returning to Washington after being with family over the Thanksgiving recess, and with businessmen flying into town for one last effort to lobby their Congressmen ahead of the Christmas break. But one of the nation's busiest airports was not so busy that Scott Forrester couldn't tell he was being followed from the moment he left the plane.

A man in a Redskins shirt and jeans had dumped his coffee in the trash only seconds after Scott had passed by. No one dumps a coffee he's just bought. Not with a lineup that long. At Baggage Claim, the man in the Redskins shirt stumbled through a crowd of limousine drivers holding placards to get their customers' attention. He wasn't interested in a limo.

And there was a second tail – a woman in a business suit, wearing a Hermes scarf and carrying a thin leather briefcase. Scott breezed past Baggage Claim on his way out of the terminal. His garment bag had come with him as a carry-on. She looked at her watch without even a hint of a purpose, then moved quickly away from the baggage carousel where she'd been standing, without collecting the bags she was supposed to be waiting for.

Scott Forrester walked briskly out of the terminal, checking his phone for messages. It was 6:45PM. There were two messages. Lance Caulfield had called. And the second message was from someone calling from the Washington Marriott.

Scott made his way across the taxi rank into the parking garage. He dialed the Denver Field Office. "Lance? Yeah, yeah… cut the pleasantries, I've got a tail. Hold the line a minute."

The two people that were trailing him were pros. The man in the Redskins shirt approached a cab, chatted something apparently incomprehensible, then abandoned it and dodged the traffic to keep pace with Scott. The woman opened her cell phone and went into a 'Hi, honey. I'm home' fake smile, while making eye contact with the man in the Redskins shirt. It was a brief contact. But it was definitely contact.

Inside the parking garage, his tails dissolved into the concrete. No doubt there were others waiting for him inside. The first two would have done their job and passed the message on, 'The mark has arrived'.

Scott entered the elevator and selected a floor two levels above where his car was parked. When the elevator doors opened, he ducked down the stairwell, checking the signal strength on his cell phone. Caulfield was still on the line. "What's up, Lance? Why did you call?"

"I thought you might be missing my sweet voice. Why do you think? You know the only two people who can give us an eye witness description of 'SS-1'?"

"The pilots from the 22nd Helicopter Squadron?"

"Correct. Well, guess where they are now? Afghanistan."

"Shit!"

"Transferred. Can you believe it? It was just a few days after they dropped a highly skilled, CIA-trained assassin into the Bridger-Teton National Forest. Call that coincidence?"

"Now what? Oh no, don't tell me…"

"Yeah, the dreaded Air Force Office of Special Investigations. I contacted them just after you left. It's going to be at least two weeks for my request to be processed through the FBI to the Air Force bureaucracy in Washington. Then another week to get it to the pilots' squadron in Afghanistan and Lord knows how long to get their statements back. That is… if they aren't killed in action first."

"Three to four *weeks*? Great! And I've got to shake off Titus Griffin, Internal Affairs, the CIA and Lord knows who else is tailing me. For three to four *weeks*?"

"What can I say, Forrester? I'm real sorry. Just be careful, buddy. And keep a low profile."

"Yeah, right. That's easy for you to say!" He thanked Lance for the information on the chopper pilots and ended the call. *Keep a low profile Lance said? Shit!*

But at least his time in Wyoming's snowy mountains had proven more than worthwhile. It was now clear how the Tiger Paw Killer had acquired his skills in evasion and concealment, how he could access weapons and black ops technology. How he had moved across the countryside undetected. What they had learned explained the 'physics' of their killer, as Inspector Billings would say. But it was still short of explaining his motives. And who was his real sponsor? The Temple of Dvaipa? Or the CIA?

And then there was Michael Wayne Portland and Sapphire Systems.

And with The Portland Group, there was Christienne Duval.

A voice inside him said, *Don't do it, Scott. Don't get her more involved. Think of the risk. Think of what you might lose with Christienne.*

He walked down the stairwell to his parking level. There were a few people walking to their cars but no man in a Redskins shirt, or a woman with a Hermes scarf.

7:30PM. He dialed his voicemail from his car on the way into Washington. The message from the Marriott was from Winston Billings. Scott called the hotel and was redirected to Billings' room.

Winston Billings answered with his baritone island optimism, "Mr. Forrester, so glad you returned my call. I have good news-"

"Inspector, this phone may be compromised. And I'm being followed. I can't talk-"

"But I have to meet you. At Dr. Chandra's?"

"No. They're probably watching."

"Who's watching?"

"Go for a walk, Inspector. I'll find you."

"Go for a walk?"

"Get out of the hotel. Walk anywhere. Give me about an hour. I'll find you. Trust me."

• • •

Scott left his midnight black sedan several blocks from Dr. Chandra's redbrick townhouse in Scholar's Circle. A blue Ford Taurus had followed him from the airport. It was parked around the corner, its headlights going out before the car had come to a full stop.

Let them think we're meeting with Dr. Chandra, Scott thought, as he walked between the brownstones, meandering through the labyrinth of back alleys until he surfaced opposite the Watergate complex where taxicabs were always trolling for business. The cab deposited him a block from the Washington Marriott, north of DuPont Circle on 22nd Street. It was now 8:30PM. He hoped Inspector Billings was still on his walk.

Scott Forrester stood silently on the empty sidewalk, carrying a bulging brown envelope; the cold rain beating against his face. Washington's night air was tainted by a deep chill, and still smelt of a sniper's bullet. He couldn't enter the Marriott through the hotel's main entrance. They knew where Winston Billings was staying, whoever *they* were and were likely watching. He entered at the rear. If Billings had done as Scott asked, he wouldn't be in his room. Scott found a house phone and made a call to the desk. He waited by the elevators until a room service attendant arrived with the tray Scott had ordered.

He slipped into the elevator after the attendant, just before the door closed. The attendant pressed the floor where the tray was to be delivered. Scott selected the floor above it. On cue, the attendant left with the tray. Scott rode up the extra floor and got off. He waited two minutes before walking down. Scott searched the hallways until he found the room that had a tray sitting on the floor outside its door. He confirmed the tray's contents – it was the sandwich he had ordered - then stuck a note under the tray's dome.

Scott left the hotel via the stairs, followed 21st Street up to P Street, and found the Starbucks on the corner. A bulging brown envelope kept his coffee company as he waited.

Winston Billings returned to the Marriott, fed up with Washington's less than tropical climate. Inspector Billings had given up his lonely walk without any sign of Scott Forrester and - as Scott had hoped – he had returned to his room, where a tray containing a stale sandwich and a cold pot of Darjeeling tea was waiting at the door. With a note.

Billings read the note and opened the door to his room to retrieve his briefcase. The instructions in the note were very specific, and although Billings didn't know why Scott had chosen to contact him this way, he trusted Scott's judgment explicitly. Billings checked the map in the guestbook on the desk to confirm the location in Scott's note and left the Marriott.

The Starbucks at 21st and P St. was a building with a curious architecture - a German castle on the Rhine deposited in the middle of metropolitan Washington. Its advantage was a fairly private second floor where bookish university students could hang out with their lattés and pumpkin muffins, reading Kissinger and Mandela, Galbraith and Bernanke. Quiet enough. But busy enough. And away from prying eyes.

Billings found Scott Forrester exactly where the note said he would be, on the second floor, warming his hands on a frothy cappuccino.

Billings ordered a coffee and waited until the waitress delivered the drink. Then he reached into his black leather attaché and took out a thick report with the seal of the Commonwealth of the Bahamas on its front cover.

"It wasn't easy, Mr. Forrester, but I managed to convince the Bahamian banking authorities…" Billings said, "that maintaining the Islands' reputation for banking secrecy must take a back seat to murder."

His sun-wrinkled hands patted the report's surface, his smile as persuasive as a Caribbean night sky. "It's all in here. This was a con game on the grandest of scales, Mr. Forrester. The Bahamian banking regulators wouldn't have known where to start without your brother's help."

Scott Forrester opened the cover and studied the pages. It contained the blueprint for the greatest stock scam in Wall Street history.

"Small investors didn't stand a chance," Billings explained. "But here's the irony – the so-called savvy insiders? The ones who had invested in Carleton's private placements? They weren't any better off. Matthew Carleton siphoned off their money before any of them even noticed. The fraud was done because he had control of bogus companies that owned preferred stock, engineered to extract exorbitant default interest if dividends fell in arrears. And at the right moment, just after the IPO's were issued, he made sure the IPO companies defaulted on their dividend payments. And when they did, the punitive interest sucked the company's cash flow dry. Right into his offshore trusts."

"So the venture capitalists were sucked down with it, along with the general public?"

"Correct. Michael Wayne Portland. Sudhir Narayan. Dominic Sant'Angello. They were the biggest losers of all. But it wasn't just Carleton involved in scamming the investors. Liang Wong, Deuce Meredith, DeAndre Antoin, Bryan and Nicole Riverton - they all had a part to play in Carleton's greed machine. Their complicity and silence was bought off with obscene director's salaries and fat consulting contracts. And just before their companies collapsed, they were tipped-off to sell their shares and profit handsomely."

"So the killer made them all pay for their involvement with Carleton. With the Devil's blessing and guidance. Have you sent this report to the FBI, Inspector?"

"What the Royal Bahamas Police chooses to share with the FBI, Mr. Forrester, is at the discretion of the Bahamas Minister of the Interior. And he happens to be a lifelong friend of mine. And so - now that I have something the FBI really needs - it seems the Bureau has been much more co-operative. In fact, there's a new piece of information the FBI shared with me yesterday, Mr. Forrester," Inspector Billings offered. "Did you know that Lexi Carleton was having an affair with Dominic Sant'Angello?"

"Sant'Angello?"

"That was the real reason she made so many trips to Chicago. She was not attending board meetings. In fact, her board meeting the day before her husband was murdered had been cancelled. She went to Chicago to be with Dominic Sant'Angello. What's her game, Mr. Forrester? Now she's courting Sudhir Narayan."

"Follow the Yellow Brick Road, Inspector."

"The Yellow Brick Road?"

"The money. Matthew Carleton's illicit fortune. Who controls it now? Lexi Carleton. Who wants to get his money back? Narayan. The trail is leading us back to Matthew Carleton's money. To his widow, Lexi. Her narcissistic personality, and desire for glamour and fame, has driven her into the arms of Ambassador Narayan. But it's a trap. His true intention is to marry into the fortune her husband had stolen from him."

"In which case, Mr. Forrester, Lexi Carleton may be his next victim."

"*Their* next victim, Inspector. Physics. This murderous rampage is beyond the capabilities of a solitary predator acting alone. The ritual harvesting of blood. The indulgence of sadistic fantasies. The insatiable desire to destroy the victims' karma. It was never *only* about that. It was also about the systematic dismantling of Matthew Carleton's financial empire, for a greater and more evil purpose."

Scott then produced the bulging brown envelope he'd been carefully guarding. "I have something for you, Inspector," he said, passing it across the table. "But don't open it here."

Scott told Billings what the envelope contained. Photographs of Chester Franklin slumped over his computer keyboard. The evil that wallpapered Franklin's secret room. The altar and its leather-bound book. The connection between a Temple coven in Baltimore and a child pornography ring in Wyoming. Bitter tasting images of a cancer that had spread from the Indian subcontinent to the foothills of the Grand Tetons.

Scott then explained the two hunters and the Black Hawk helicopter hovering in the clear blue sky. The CIA training exercises that left regularly from an air base in Cheyenne into the Grand Teton Mountains. And finally, Sapphire Systems - one of the world's largest security firms - a subsidiary of The Portland Group, and a front operation for the CIA. Pine Ridge Lodge. The Carleton Mansion. Harry S. Truman Air Force Base. All of their security systems installed by Sapphire Systems.

"Matthew Carleton thought he had the best protection money could buy," Scott said, remembering the fog-shrouded mansion buried deep in The Hamptons. "But the killer was able to skirt The Carleton Estate's perimeter unnoticed, cross its guarded grounds, and bypass its laser entry alarms, undetected. How? The system had been turned off. Matthew Carleton's security system had been turned against him."

Scott sank back in his chair, the months and months of following a trail of evil finally leading to this, "Think of the potential, Inspector. Security systems that are designed not to protect their wealthy clients but to monitor them, and gather information about them. Extremely valuable information. About the most important and influential people at the top of our society's power structure. Their comings and goings. Their private conversations. Lawyers. Judges. Bankers. Politicians. The government. The judiciary. The military. Wall Street moguls like Matthew Carleton. Information that can be used against them. Against their families. Their friends. Their business associates."

"To blackmail them?"

"Or to recruit them for a higher purpose, perhaps? It's a chilling thought, Inspector. It's almost inconceivable for me to believe the Temple of Dvaipa and Sapphire Systems are not connected in some evil way."

"If, as you say, Mr. Forrester, that Michael Wayne Portland is one of the leaders of the Temple of Dvaipa," Billings paused as he thought out the implications, "and has been using his company's power to further the Temple's aims, then this alliance of technology and religious fanaticism could be... I struggle for the word..."

"Toxic," Scott said. "It would be, Inspector Billings... *toxic*."

"Where is the proof that Michael Wayne Portland controls this killer, Mr. Forrester? How can you be so sure that what happened in Wyoming leads directly to him? That he ordered these murders? That he even belongs to this cult? It could be anyone inside The Portland Group."

Billings was right. They had no direct evidence. It was guilt by association.

"And the question remains..." Billings continued. "How does the CIA fit into all of this?"

"God, I wish I knew. We have a suspect, Lexi Carleton, who's being watched night and day by the FBI. We have a reclusive billionaire, Michael Wayne Portland, who as far as I know is rarely seen in public. Then, there's Sudhir Narayan - a high-ranking diplomat cloaked in official secrecy, and who, no doubt, is surrounded by the private army of the Temple of Dvaipa. I'm being followed by God only knows. My own organization, the FBI. The

CIA. The Temple. Or any combination of the above. How can I possibly expect to penetrate through all of this on my own?"

"You're not alone in this investigation, Mr. Forrester."

"Inspector... you've done enough for me. That package in your hands is my safeguard that if anything happens to me - or heaven forbid, to Lance Caulfield - someone is still able to get that evidence into the right hands. I don't know why I'm still alive. When I was standing in Archie's parking lot, I was just a hair trigger away from having a bullet enter one side of my heart and exit out the other. They killed DeAndre Antoin in broad daylight. They tortured Matthew Carleton for two days. They can choose *when*. They can choose *where*. They can choose *how*. Why am I not *already* dead?"

Winston Billings sat back in deep thought. "I can't answer that question, Mr. Forrester. But I might be able to help you answer other ones. But it means I must return to Nassau."

"Nassau?"

"A lot of Brits retire to the Bahamas. One of those Brits owes me some favors. And he used to work for MI-6."

"MI-6? British Intelligence?"

"You see, an intelligence officer – especially a senior one – never really retires. Threats are global. Threats are eternal. I'm sure he's never too far away from what's going on. In a consulting capacity. And I'm sure he still maintains his contacts within the CIA."

Billings placed his hand on the brown padded envelope Scott had given him. "I will take this to him. As if I had uncovered the CIA connection in the course of my own investigation of Jiri Kostelic's murder. He will never know it came from you. There is no love lost between MI-6 and the CIA, even though the agencies are technically allies. He will help me. I know he will. I will leave for Nassau in the morning."

"Before you go, Inspector, I need you to do one more thing for me."

"Name it."

"I need to engage someone who isn't afraid to give up information about Lexi Carleton. Someone who isn't afraid to put themselves in the crosshairs of an assassin's sniper rifle. I need you to contact Dr. Chandra. Then I need him to contact Pradesh Bhandari for me."

"Bhandari? And you think Bhandari is that 'someone' you speak of?"

"No. But Bhandari can help me. It's not Bhandari. It's someone else. Let me explain…"

• • •

It was 10:45PM. The streets were quiet. Inspector Billings and Scott Forrester had left Starbucks at different times, and in opposite directions. Scott was looking for a taxi to take him back to his car when his cell phone rang.

It was a New York number. Trish Van Cleyburn.

"Someone I know at the Denver Field Office," Trish said, searching for Titus Griffin's bull's eye, "told me he saw you with Lance Caulfield at Denver Airport. But Caulfield then denied seeing you. Why would he do that? And what were you doing so far away from Washington, Forrester?"

"Remember that child porn case, Trish? The suspected distributor in Wyoming? Caulfield was doing some follow up work in Jackson Hole. I was doing some skiing. We met by pure coincidence."

"Bullshit! You're both lying. You hate cold weather. You particularly hate snow. And as for Caulfield-"

"He's got nothing to do with this."

"Do with what? Don't tell me… you crashed into a tree while skiing and some information just dropped into your lap? You met a mysterious stranger at an après ski party who just happened to be a missing link in your theories? Like Sue Lee Chen? This time, Scott… I hope you kept the witness alive."

"Something like that."

"Give me a break, Forrester. You know something. And I want to know what you know."

Trish Van Cleyburn was not the only one who could aim for Titus Griffin's bull's eye. "Okay, Van Cleyburn," Scott said. "How about this… Sapphire Systems."

There was silence at the other end of the line. Then Trish replied, "What have you got on Michael Wayne Portland that we wouldn't be able to find out on our own?"

That was strange, Scott thought. *She connected Michael Wayne Portland with Sapphire Systems without missing a beat.*

Time for dart #2.

"How about Sapphire Systems and the CIA, Trish?"

More silence. He could hear Trish's breathing and footsteps. He could hear a door close.

"The CIA?" she asked.

"Yes, Trish. The Central Intelligence Agency. Headquarters… Langley, Virginia. And Sapphire Systems. Headquarters… Alexandria, Virginia."

"Where did you get this information, Scott?"

"Scratch the CIA and you'll find it bleeds dark blue gemstones."

"You don't just *scratch* the CIA, Forrester."

"The Bureau's got contacts in the CIA, Trish. Use them."

"And who are the contacts that gave *you* this information, Scott?"

"Let's just say… it fell out of a tree."

"Keep going down that slope, Agent Forrester… and you might just ski right off the edge of a cliff."

Dart #2 had landed in the center circle.

"Is that a threat, Trish?"

"It's my way of telling you, Forrester, that if you're serious about getting yourself out of trouble, you'll turn around and ski right back in the other direction."

"You don't want me to go there, do you?"

"No, that's not it. I'm just afraid that when you get there... you might not be coming back."

On that note, she abruptly ended the call.

A taxi splish-splashed up to the curb in front of him.

Twenty minutes later and the cab arrived in the Scholar's Circle neighborhood where he'd parked his black sedan. As he left the cab and proceeded on foot, a faint sound – a distinct chirp of an engine's drive belt - was lost in the sounds of the taxicab as it drove off.

Scott got inside his car and decided to check his phone. The emails had piled up. The days had passed like minutes since the uncomfortable exchange with Titus Griffin and Corey Hamilton from Internal Affairs - his first meeting with Winston Billings; the discovery of Anna Bhandari in Baltimore; the hidden altar in Pine Ridge Lodge; Harry S. Truman Air Force Base. Clearing out his emails had been the last thing on his mind.

Most of the recent emails were from Jamie. His bro was working overtime on his legal defense and had copied Scott on everything. Scott found what he was looking for. Christienne Duval had sent him her flight details. If Winston Billings and Dr. Chandra could get through to Pradesh Bhandari, he just needed the few days between now and her return to take the next step in his plan. After that, he knew a big decision had to be made to ensure Christienne's safety. A decision he was not looking forward to making.

Scott's concentration had wandered and he was tired. As his car moved off and headed home, a black van pulled out of hiding, unnoticed, and followed him.

The caffeine fix from Starbucks was wearing off. It had started to rain again. With his car's wipers beating time on the windshield, Scott Forrester was fighting a losing battle with jetlag for control of his eyelids.

It had been a very long day.

Chapter Forty-Seven

"It must have been a tough decision, Mrs. Stavros. Choosing Palm Springs over West Palm Beach?"

"Teddy insisted. It had to be Palm Springs. It's the air. So much drier in the desert. Better for his rheumatism. More tea, Mr. Grant?"

"No thank you, Mrs. Stavros. When do you leave for Palm Springs?"

"Next week. Or is it the week after? I'm never very good at remembering dates. Or faces for that matter. You sound so familiar. Are you sure I haven't met you before, Mr. Grant?"

"I don't think so, Mrs. Stavros."

A fake press pass hung around Scott Forrester's neck.

He placed the empty teacup on the side table. The two-day-old stubble on his chin was coarse and rasping, and itched unmercifully. His clunky glasses were uncomfortable. But the disguise succeeded in fooling the elderly mother of Lexi Carleton. She had failed to recognize the FBI agent who had interviewed her daughter only two months earlier in this very house in Southampton, Long Island.

Pradesh Bhandari's credentials as a freelance photographer for 'International Explorer' magazine had gained Scott Forrester the access he sought. Access to the *someone* who was unafraid of a sniper's bullet. That someone was Anastasia Stavros - a benign and highly malleable informant, an open book just waiting to be read.

Hopefully, Pradesh Bhandari would play his part in this ruse and be just as successful. It was a risk, but one Scott Forrester had to take. In the adjacent study, Bhandari was conducting a phony interview with the octogenarian statesman of the Stavros clan: Anastasia's husband Theodore Stavros, or as she affectionately called him, 'Teddy'.

Despite the lavish attention they both would pay the elderly couple - the camera Scott had borrowed from Bhandari was only pretending to document the lifestyle of Teddy and Anastasia Stavros - this was an interview 'International Explorer' would never print.

The old bat headed towards the kitchen through the Great Room, tottering on unsteady legs, her head wobbling with a slight shake. "More tea, Mr. Grant?" she asked, forgetting he had already said no.

The Great Room, a vulgar monument to the Stavros' extensive world travels, was darker in decor than the bright, floral morning room where Scott and Tricia Van Cleyburn had interviewed Lexi Carleton the day after her husband Matthew had been murdered. It was the day the tennis pro had a smug look on his face and Lexi Carleton had arrived with flushed cheeks; the day Tricia Van Cleyburn had asked Anastasia Stavros to withdraw to the conservatory while they probed her daughter's sex life.

The Great Room was a Stavros family showcase. Primarily Teddy's treasures. Hunting trophies - South Africa, Botswana. Expeditions - the Amazon, Borneo. It was also an art gallery, with artwork collected over a generation of grand tours of Europe. A Monet pastoral hung next to a Da Vinci etching; a Picasso, rendered in the Spanish artist's colorful but angular cubist style, looked awkwardly at the flair of a Degas; the surrealism of a Dali clashed with Teddy's collection of tropical butterflies and African tribal masks. The Great Room was an eclectic mix of far-flung tastes epitomizing the travels of a pair of individualists whose only sole shared bond after forty-five years of marriage appeared to be their lust for grandeur, wealth and social recognition.

Anastasia's contribution to the room was a large oil painting that eclipsed the others, a full length portrait with a brass inscription that read, 'Anastasia Stavros, New York, 1948'. In her portrait, she was dressed in royal blue satin and wore a large necklace of diamonds.

"It's Coco Chanel," Mrs. Stavros said, returning with a tray of lemon tea. "The dress. It's Coco Chanel. The diamonds of course are Cartier."

"Of course. Do you mind," Scott asked. "If I take a picture of you beside this portrait?"

"Why, I'd be delighted, Mr. Grant!"

Anastasia Stavros was very obliging, and with every pose, she regressed back to the day when she had been a stunning, elegant young New York socialite. Scott understood where Anastasia's daughter Lexi had developed her sense of style and her lust for all things rare and fine. Lexi Carleton's sociopathic tendencies must have come from her father.

"You don't mind if I look around the rest of the house? Background material. For the article?"

Anastasia Stavros was flattered. "Please... go ahead, Mr. Grant. Consider this house to be yours!"

On the walls of the hallway that stretched for what seemed like miles from the Great Room to the library, there was a profusion of family photographs that documented the Stavros clan as far back as time recorded. The library itself was a memorial to the Stavros' children's transition from pampered little brats to aristocratic young bores. The most photographed of the Stavros children was Lexi, clearly her mother's favorite, perhaps because Lexi's demonstrated superiority at reigning like royalty had developed at a very young age.

Mrs. Stavros noticed Scott's particular interest in photographs of Lexi and her friends during her college days at Princeton. "I called them 'my girls'," she said.

"Your girls, Mrs. Stavros?"

"Of course they weren't 'my' girls, Mr. Grant. But as Lexi's sorority sisters, they all felt so much a part of our family at the time. And these young men? Oh, yes..." she crooned. "To be young again! They all had so many boyfriends. Lexi invited them to come here for their summers, for Christmas, for all the holidays. They never missed a season. Glorious hot days by the pool. The garden parties. I can smell the strawberries and cream! When are 'my girls' coming to see me next? I would ask Lexi. They were like my own daughters."

Scott found a photo of Lexi and her friends in tennis whites and asked, "Do you remember any of their names, Mrs. Stavros?"

"Let me take a closer look, Mr. Grant. It's been such a long time." Mrs. Stavros approached the photograph. "As I said, I'm terrible with names. Oh yes... that's Nicole. What a terrible business, Mr. Grant. She was such a beautiful girl. And such a sharp mind. That fire... how dreadful! How utterly horrible! I was devastated when I heard."

"You mean Nicole Riverton. And who's this? The girl with the sunglasses?" Scott pointed to a girl who was petit, had flat black hair tied back in a ponytail, and was much shorter in height than the rest of the group.

"Let me see. Hmm... That's Suzy - well, Lexi called her Suzy. That wasn't her proper name. I'm sure of that. She was a stuffy girl, Mr. Grant. Chinese, you know. I think her name was Sue May... no, no, let me think... not Sue May. It was such a long time ago..."

"Sue Lee?"

"Yes, Sue Lee! Sue Lee Chang."

"You mean Sue Lee *Chen*?"

"That's right, Mr. Grant! Sue Lee Chen. Do you know her?"

"Just a lucky guess."

Scott lingered by the photo gallery looking intently at the faces. He captured them with his camera. Taking pictures of photographs was a strange thing to do but he explained to Mrs. Stavros that it was for the article and in her heightened state of self-absorption, she didn't know any better.

There were photographs of Lexi and her friends sailing off to Montauk; down by the beach, with picnic baskets and champagne. One particular photo at her Princeton graduation ball showed a devilishly handsome young man, dark complexion, his arm clamped tightly around Lexi's waist. And by her smile, Lexi was returning his affection.

He thought he recognized him. "This young man, Mrs. Stavros? Who is he?"

"Ah..." she tutted. "Well, Mr. Grant... if it weren't for me, Teddy would have taken *that* picture down a long time ago. Isn't it strange that after all these years... he's back in her life? But I think it's much too soon, Mr. Grant, don't you?"

"Too soon? Too soon for what, Mrs. Stavros?"

"Charming chap. He was at Princeton too, you know."

Scott Forrester looked again at the photograph. "Who is he, Mrs. Stavros?"

"She called him 'Suds'. Funny nickname for such a well bred young man, don't you think? So rich. Such an aristocrat. I always liked him."

"His name, Mrs. Stavros?"

"Sudhir. Sudhir Narayan. He was the love of her life, Mr. Grant. Her first fiancé. But Teddy wouldn't have it. My Teddy's a bit old-fashioned, you see, Mr. Grant."

Sudhir Narayan?

In his twenties. At Princeton.

A fiancé to the future Lexi Carleton?

"Old-fashioned, Mrs. Stavros? You're saying your husband wouldn't let Lexi marry him because... he was a man of color?"

"Yes, Mr. Grant. Teddy didn't approve at all. And if Teddy didn't approve, there was no way around it. Sudhir returned to India shortly after this picture was taken. Teddy may be an old fool... but this time... what choice does he have now?"

"Choice?"

"My Lexi's put her foot down. And with Matthew gone, she doesn't need her trust fund. She'll get it anyway, of course."

"I'm not sure I understand."

"Lexi told her father he must give his blessing this time or he won't see his grandchildren ever again. Well, Mr. Grant... there's not many years left for the old fool, is there? Not seeing his grandchildren? Now, that would have broken his heart. He had to give his blessing this time, didn't he?"

"Your daughter's marrying Sudhir Narayan?"

"I know it seems too soon. So soon after Matthew's death. But my Lexi is so resilient. So strong. She always has been, Mr. Grant."

Resilient? Strong? Was that what it was called? Scott thought. He would add that observation to his files. Resilience. Strength. File under: Sociopathic.

"There will be two weddings, of course. New York society would not allow it any other way, Mr. Grant."

"Two weddings?"

"There has to be a traditional one of course. In a Greek Orthodox Church in New York. Very traditional. But we've also agreed to a second one. A Hindu ceremony, I believe. In something Lexi called... the Great Temple. I can't wait to see it. They speak so much about it. It sounds so grand!"

"Great Temple? Where is this Great Temple, Mrs. Stavros?"

"Oh, somewhere in the Caribbean. Where else? It's so romantic, don't you think, Mr. Grant?"

Chapter Forty-Eight

A heavy snowfall was wreaking havoc on air traffic along the East Coast. Scott's flight from New York LaGuardia to Washington's Reagan National was the last one to land before poor visibility and snowbound runways forced the airport to close.

Christienne Duval's flight from Moscow via Paris was scheduled to arrive at Dulles International two hours later. Scott had decided to undertake the twenty-six-mile cab ride between Reagan and Dulles to see her, perhaps for the last time.

Meeting at her townhouse near DuPont Circle was out of the question. The events in Wyoming had produced a deep conviction that was more chilling than the devilishly cold weather. *Someone* knew every step he took. Hooded strangers. Mysterious vans. The fictitious Jacob Weinberg. *Someone* had put Sue Lee Chen in their crosshairs. *Someone* showed Chester Franklin no mercy; owed him no loyalty. *Someone* had discredited his brother Jamie with trumped up charges of insider trading. *Someone* was listening. *Someone* was following him. Watching, waiting.

Meeting her at the airport seemed the only way to warn her. Afterwards, separation far away from him would be essential for her safety. Dark shadows had birthed a killing spree fueled by demonic intent and spread with a sociopathic rage. He could no longer make her a part of that.

The journey turned out to be a wearisome crawl on slippery, snow-covered highways at the height of rush hour traffic. By the time his cab reached Dulles International, the airport was in the process of shutting down. Its terminals were nearly empty of people. Departing passengers were giving up, stranded, and offered hotels for the night. Airport check-in counters were closing down. Luggage carousels were grinding to a halt. Airport workers crammed shuttle buses to take them to the parking lots, and home.

At 8:30PM, Air France finally announced that, due to low fuel, Christienne's flight was unable to remain in its holding pattern over Washington and would land in Philadelphia instead. Scott's anxious and final reunion with Christienne Duval would have to wait.

Air France told him to go home.

Home? But Scott was effectively homeless.

Scott carried a thumbdrive inside his leather jacket. It contained the pictures he had taken at the estate of Lexi Carleton's parents on Long Island. Pictures of warm sunny days. Of Lexi Carleton and Nicole Riverton. Sue Lee Chen playing tennis. Happy beach parties with Anastasia's 'girls' and, because of her failing memory, a retinue of unidentified boyfriends. Had Scott Forrester stood in front of one of these pictures of innocence and joy, and stared straight into the face of the Tiger Paw Killer?

He looked nervously around the vacant space that was the normally busy Arrival Hall at Washington's Dulles International Airport. A few lingering passengers had stretched across the hard seats to sleep, to be the first in line for flights out of Washington in the morning.

Did he recognize any of them?

Had they been following him?

A sickly acid crept up Scott Forrester's throat. He had worked undercover before, alone and in danger. Fear was an occupational hazard. But there was always that security of knowing a SWAT team was in position, the might of the FBI was watching his back.

Not this time. Not here. Not now.

This gnawing in the pit of his stomach was a new, a foreign, and an unwelcome feeling. A feeling of hollowness. Of weakness. A feeling of being disconnected. From all things *safe*.

The air itself seemed to have eyes and ears.

The custodian emptying the wastebaskets. Or was he?

The airport security guard locking up. Or was he?

The fear was real. The fear was justified.

A devil-cult. The Tiger Paw Killer. What was the *true* depth and breadth of this conspiracy? Had the world's most powerful intelligence agency fathered it all? And if so, *why*?

Trust was a scarce commodity, as precious as gold. In truth, he had only one lifeline. Not his bungalow in Georgetown. That was definitely off limits. It was sure to be bugged and watched. Jamie had moved out of his basement apartment and was staying with Sarah Vaughn at the townhouse she shared with her university girlfriends. At Scott's insistence, Jamie had one of his geeky friends sweep the rooms for listening devices. His friends were weird. But this one had a particularly useful knowledge of electronic devices and their electromagnetic signatures. The townhouse was declared clean. For now.

It was Scott Forrester's last remaining lifeline.

He called. Not from his cell phone. But from a pay phone in an isolated corner of the Arrivals Hall. At the other end of the line, Sarah Vaughn perked up at the sound of his voice. Their conversation was short and to the point - talking in a code of 'computerese' and hip-hop slang - a hybrid code that Jamie had invented to disguise where Scott was calling from, and why he was calling.

It was an awkward, choppy exchange.

But Sarah understood the message.

He hung up the phone and walked carefully away, watching over his shoulder to see if there was any movement that meant he was being followed.

Outside the terminal, a line of taxis inched forward in the snow, consuming the last of the disenchanted travelers. Scott joined them. He shivered in line, fidgeting with the thumbdrive in his pocket as he tried to stay warm.

Opening the cab door was like opening an oven. He crawled inside and handed the driver a note with Sarah's address. No words could be spoken. No chances could be taken with lives other than his own.

The road back into the city was long and slow. The cab picked its way through a tortuous route of bumpy snowdrifts, sliding nervously at every red light, barely capable of finding enough traction to keep moving forward in a straight line. Eventually, familiar street signs emerged from the haze of the blinding snow.

It was close to midnight when he told the cabbie to stop five blocks from Sarah's townhouse. Scott Forrester would finish the trip on foot.

Alone again, he zigzagged through the neighborhood, ducking into doorways, backtracking through alleys, waiting for headlights to pass, watching for any shadow to appear behind him. He trudged through drifting snow that had piled up on the sidewalks, the wind biting the back of his neck, its grains of sleet stinging his exposed flesh, the cold air tingling inside his nostrils.

Finally, the windows of Sarah's townhouse glowed through the sleety air with the inviting warmth of a Christmas card.

He waited.

The streets *appeared* to be deserted.

With the doorbell's ring, a friendly, porcelain face – Sarah Vaughn's face - peered through the crack of the door and ushered him into the townhouse's narrow front corridor.

"I'll put a fresh pot of coffee on," she said sleepily, as Scott brushed the snow out of his hair. "Jamie's in the living room."

The small room at the front of the townhouse had been converted into Jamie's office and bedroom. As usual, Jamie Forrester was at his computer, and a layer of Doritos bags and printouts littered every available surface and carpeted the floor. Jamie's cat had almost disappeared in the mess, eventually appearing on the lumpy sofa from under the sweatshirt where she'd been sleeping.

Scott opened his hand. It held the thumbdrive. "We're not going to get a return invitation," he said.

Jamie uploaded Scott's photos into the computer.

"We really need to identify *these* faces..." Scott said, pointing to the boyfriends. "If we can get these jpeg files to Inspector Billings, he'll have Interpol run them through their computers."

"Not a problem, Bro. I'll sharpen them up. Let's hope Interpol's facial recognition software is as good as the FBI's."

"Should be the same. It'll just take longer. But there's nothing we can do about that," Scott said, as he ran his fingers through his matted, wet hair. If this was Quantico, a facial recognition search would be done in a matter of minutes. But they were relaying the photos to Winston Billings of the Royal Bahamas Police. And then onwards to Interpol's database in Geneva.

"If Interpol draws a blank, is there any chance Inspector Billings can get these pictures to MI-6?"

"That Jamie... is a big unknown. These photos may take us somewhere. Or then again, they may not. It's just the nature of the game. An arrow, shot in the dark."

Jamie started the digital surgery on the photos from the Stavros estate. Scott's pacing was getting on his nerves. "Chill out, Big Bro. Sarah's freshening up the pot. Get a cup. Bring me one too, and by the time you come back, I should be done."

As Scott walked anxiously towards the kitchen, Jamie stopped editing and looked up. "Oh... I bet you haven't heard the news, have you?"

"What news?"

"The painting. It sold."

"What painting? You mean 'The Revenge of Dvaipa'?"

"Do you know any other butt-ugly Indian painting for sale in Washington?"

"Who bought it?"

"Don't know. Telephone bid. Anonymous buyer."

"Michael Wayne Portland?"

"Who knows? That's why it's called *anonymous*."

"Is there any way we can find out who bought that painting?" Scott asked, his voice straining with a sense of urgency that bordered on desperation. "Because I know the reason someone wants to buy it."

Jamie thought for a few seconds then nodded. "Yeah, Bro. I can find out. It could be a little tricky. But there's always a way."

"You're not going to do anything illegal, are you?"

"Me? Illegal, Scott? You mean the same kind of illegal as faking press documents to impersonate a photographer? Or trespassing with the intent to fuckup two old geezers? That kind of illegal? No, I'm not going to do *anything* like that, Scott. Well, nothing that can be traced anyway."

A smile crept across Scott's face; a fleeting respite, the only relief Scott Forrester would allow himself.

He followed the welcome aroma that was floating out of the kitchen. Sarah had been studying at the kitchen table, books and notes scattered about. She had made the coffee and fallen asleep.

There was a ghostly calm. It was now 1:00AM.

Scott poured two coffees. He didn't really need the caffeine. His mind was racing without it. Like a rat trying to navigate through a maze. *This way? That way? Which way now?* Even if he could predict the killer's next move, where would it lead him? His throat felt as if a noose was tightening around it. *Was his sanity crossing the line?*

His cell phone rang.

Caller-ID said it was Christienne.

From Philadelphia?

The rat stopped suddenly in the maze - confused and unsure. If he answered, their conversation would likely be monitored. There was no way to warn Christienne.

But what harm would be done if he answered her call?

Just a quick hello?

If the rat made a move, would the tiger follow?

I shouldn't answer it.

He answered the call. "Christienne?"

"Chéri? I'm here... in Washington! Finally!"

"I thought your plane was landing in Philadelphia?"

"Mais non. The captain said he had to make an emergency landing... low fuel. We got down okay but it was frightening, chéri. I'm standing in line. I'll be through Immigration soon. I can't wait to see you!"

"I'm not there at the airport to meet you, Christienne. I'm at-" He checked himself. *No Scott. Don't say where you are!*

"Chéri... it doesn't matter." She was talking fast, hardly taking a breath. "I'll take a cab. I'll see you at my place. We have so much to talk about. I'm dying to see you, chéri! You have a key, n'est-ce pas?"

The rat in the maze - froze.

No, Christienne! Don't say that. Not on this line!

It was a slip-up. It wasn't her fault. It was his fault, for answering the call in the first place.

"Scott... Scott... are you still there?"

The rat tried to backtrack down the maze. "Christienne, I can't let you-" An announcement in the background drowned out his words.

"It's noisy in here, chéri. I have to go now. I'm just about to go through Immigration. See you soon-"

The call ended.

A stupid mental error!

The rat turned another corner inside the maze.

A murderous hooded stranger.

The stranger in Scott's nightmare.

Would she walk into his grasp?

Scott looked at his watch. If he got a cab to Christienne's townhouse, her journey from Dulles would take longer than his and he would get there before her. But he must act fast. Scott raced into the living room, a man possessed. The rat's next move had been decided.

"They're done, Bro," Jamie said. He had just finished editing the pictures.

"E-mail them to Billings in Nassau."

"Don't you want to see them first?"

"I've got to go."

"*What*? Where? In this horrendous snowstorm?"

"No choice, Little Bro." Scott said. He rushed into the corridor to get his jacket. As he turned the doorknob, about to walk into the cold snowy street – and a potential rendezvous with a killer - he realized he had no weapon. Internal Affairs had taken care of that.

Scott hurried back into the kitchen. He began pulling drawers open at random. Sarah Vaughn, sleeping on a pile of books, lifted her head. "Scott? What are you doing?"

He rummaged frantically through a cutlery drawer and found a large cook's knife - the kind of knife big enough to chop a whole cabbage in half. He wrapped its naked blade in a dishtowel then stuffed the bundle inside his jacket.

The sight of the knife in Scott's hand jolted Sarah Vaughn out of her sleep-induced daze. She gasped, eyes wide open, frightened.

Jamie Forrester had wheeled himself into the corridor to see what was going on.

Scott ran past him to the front door.

"Scott... what are you doing? Where are you going? What do you need that knife for? *What the hell is wrong!"*

As Scott stumbled outside, he could say just one word, "Christienne."

The wicked chill hit Scott Forrester in the face.

A cold stiff blade was clutched close to his heart.

The rat was back in the maze.

Chapter Forty-Nine

An illusion of tranquility hung over the streets. The snow had stopped falling and the wind had subsided. The inside of Christienne Duval's townhouse was in darkness. A few wisps of white blew off the mansard roof.

As Christienne's taxicab pulled up in front, its bright headlights shone directly in Scott's face. All he could see in their glare was a woman's silhouette, a man carrying her luggage to the front door, then the silhouette slipping inside. The cab did a sloppy U-turn on the empty street and pulled away.

The knife tucked inside Scott's jacket pressed hard against his chest as he ran towards her front door. He struggled for air, his lungs stinging from the cold.

Scott had searched the alleyways behind Christienne's townhouse. They *appeared* harmless and vacant. He'd found nothing but shadows - heard nothing but his own crunching of snow underfoot, and the pounding rush of blood through his temples.

The door to Christienne's townhouse was slightly ajar. He caught it before it closed; his black, leather-clad figure bursting through the entrance, grabbing her by the shoulders. She shuddered, her mouth open, but no sound came out as she gasped in fright.

"Christienne…" Scott whispered, as he held her trembling body close to him. "It's *me!*"

The circular foyer was lit by a small table lamp. As his face caught the light, her fright melted away and she dissolved into his arms.

"Oh *Mon Dieu*, chéri! You *scared* me!"

Her cheeks were tinged with pink. Her face, her lips, were fresh and natural. They held each other tightly and kissed. The seconds seemed like hours, but as their warmth grew, so did the reality. Scott Forrester's reality.

The corridor in front of them was dark and brooding. He hugged her again - as if he never wanted to let her go - and whispered gently in her ear, "Say something, Christienne. Anything. Just talk normally. In a casual voice. Don't be afraid. Say anything - about your trip, about your flight. Anything. But promise me…" His grip loosened. "That you'll stay right here, by the door."

She pulled back, alarmed. Her eyes anxious, questioning.

He nodded - his expression telling her to start talking. He took his shoes off to deaden the sound of his footsteps across the hardwood floor, then crept carefully down the hallway.

Christienne shuddered again. Something was wrong. Like that night of terror. With that hooded stranger. *Say anything he said?* Her voice wavered as she scrambled for any kind of thought, "Chéri… it was such an awful flight. So long. And umm… tedious." She stumbled over her words. Her mind was nearly blank with fear. Scott signaled, *louder*. She raised her voice, "But the shopping in… umm… Geneva. It… it was marvelous…"

Scott pulled something out of his jacket - something long and pointed. A lump formed in her throat, her mouth was dry. She began to shake. "I bought you a sweater, chéri… I hope you like it…"

He disappeared around the corner.

The hallway led directly into the living room - high ceilings; a glass-fronted fireplace; a deep cushioned sofa.

There was a long silence, several agonizing minutes.

Christienne waited, shivering in the foyer.

Suddenly, the lights came on. Scott reappeared, exhausted, holding a large knife in his hand as he walked down the corridor towards her. Scott put the knife down on the small table and took her into his arms. "It's safe, Christienne. There's no-one here."

She collapsed in his embrace, sobbing.

"Sshh… there's no-one here," he repeated. "There's no-one here."

• • •

A snowplow rumbled by their window, its whirling blue lights bouncing off the fronts of the buildings, flickering through the curtains. Her hair fell like a veil around his face. The full weight of her warm, moist body, her heaving breasts, pressed down on his chest. Christienne moaned, quivered, and then relaxed on top of him. His heart was pounding, this time for a good reason, the right reason.

They lay together as one, the feather duvet enveloping them like a giant cocoon, safe and warm. He could hear her drift off to sleep, curled up on top of him like a newborn.

Christienne stirred and rolled away. Scott slid his arm around her waist and pulled her close, letting the heat of their love take him into a dream.

The phone by the bedside rang.

Scott glanced over at the clock. The digits said 4:00AM.

He was only half-awake.

Christienne groaned. "Don't answer it…"

The phone kept ringing.

The answering machine came on.

But there was silence.

The silence yielded to breathing. Then Scott Forrester's reality propelled him out of his dream… and back into his nightmare. A dark voice said, "Special Agent Scott Forrester?" The voice was electronically garbled. "I know you're there, Agent Forrester."

Scott jumped out of bed and grabbed the phone.

Christienne put the light on. "Who is it, Scott?"

"Turn it off! Turn the light off!" he said, with his hand over the receiver.

The caller was brief.

Christienne's voice faltered, "Who was it, Scott?"

Scott put the phone back in its cradle. A cold sweat replaced the warmth of their afterglow. "He said he was Michael Wayne Portland. And he wants to meet me."

"Michael Wayne Portland? He's back in Washington? He never told me. And he wants to meet you? When?"

"Now. At his apartment. Above the Bijouterie."

"Michael Wayne Portland? But he doesn't even know you."

"He knows me, Christienne. Oh, yes. He knows me. I need your help. Then I need you to find a safe place to hide and stay there. Under no circumstances are you to leave it! Do you understand?"

"Mon Dieu, Scott! What is going on?"

• • •

The moonlight scrawled its icy fingers across Le Roux-Berg's Bijouterie Washington, its breath frosting the storefront glass. The apartment windows above La Bijouterie were dark. Scott stood at street level, looking up at the building's expressionless face; its balconies and iron railings painted with the lurid gray of a lunar brush.

Suddenly, a yellow dot broke the monotony of the building's façade - a candle. A single candle had been lit in the middle window on the top floor. Behind the light, was a figure - a silhouette pulsing as the candle flickered. The figure retreated into the room, leaving only the candle's orange glow behind.

Scott Forrester took out the keys he'd been given by Christienne. They would unlock the boutique's back door and give access to Michael Wayne Portland's private suite above the store. He crossed the street and withdrew the knife from his jacket. There would be no SWAT team snipers training their scopes on the candlelit window. No FBI backup surrounding the building. It was just Scott Forrester. A creaky set of stairs. And a knife.

The backstairs led up to the second floor. There was a landing at the top of the stairs that was circled by an ornate iron balustrade that looked down upon the shop's interior below. There were two doors on the landing. One of them led into the boutique's business office. The other opened into another flight of stairs that led up to Portland's third floor apartment.

He put the key in and turned the knob gently. There was a metallic clunk as the latch released the pressure of the door's antique wood. The door opened with a groan, and as he climbed up, the old oak of the stairway squeaked under his weight. He paused and listened, clenching the knife tightly; a burning sensation returning to his throat.

Faint candlelight reflected off the walls at the top of the stairs - the haunting candlelight of his nightmare. A light that embodied his fears. A light whose life could so easily be snuffed out.

Christienne had described the layout of the apartment. The walls of its original nineteenth century interior had been knocked down to increase the size of the living room. It was now an open concept, with the kitchen at one end. The kitchen had a breakfast bar, and to its side, French doors led into a large dining room. Down the hall was a guest bedroom and bathroom, and further along, the master suite. From there, a small staircase led to a fourth floor loft, which had been converted into a study.

Scott Forrester stood motionless in the foyer at the top of the stairs. Under his feet, a rich wooden pattern of inlaid cherry and maple was designed into the floor. It represented the points of a compass. Michael Wayne Portland was an avid sailor Christienne had said - an experienced offshore racer that would have been very comfortable navigating the shark-infested waters off the Bahamas.

For at least a minute, Scott let the silence descend around him, so his ears could search the stillness for the faintest sound. But he could only hear the pulse in his head, and the beating of his heart.

He peered into the living room. A U-shaped sectional sofa lay before a black, glass-fronted fireplace. The gas fire was lit; its artificial embers glowing dull red. Across the room, the single candle that he'd seen from the street sat alone in the middle of three windowsills, its light dancing in an ephemeral draft.

In the semi-darkness of the candle's light, he could see an odd pattern running towards him across the living room's cream-colored carpet.

He reached for a light switch.

When the floor lamps came on, the nature of this dark pattern became clear.

It was blood.

A huge swath of blood.

It ran in an S-shaped curve, starting at the windowsill, then crossing the living room until it ran through the compass on the foyer floor. Scott Forrester looked down and realized he was standing in a river of blood; its tackiness sucking at his feet; its gummy surface leading all the way down the stairs that he'd just climbed. His footprints were clearly visible in the trail of blood he'd unwittingly stepped in.

A body had been dragged down the stairs.

Just then, a phone rang.

Not the phone in the apartment.

The phone inside his jacket.

He answered it. The voice was familiar.

It was the voice of Sue Lee Chen.

But Sue Lee Chen was dead. He'd seen her body slump onto the yellowed linoleum floor of Archie's Diner, her temple shattered by a sniper's bullet.

"Are you afraid to die?" she asked him, the electronically generated masquerade hiding the speaker's true voice.

"We all have to die, someday," he replied.

"The question for you, Scott Forrester…" the voice asked. "Is that day, today?"

Voice synthesis - technology perfected by the CIA. The voice of Sue Lee Chen wasn't real, but the evil behind it surely was.

The voice spoke again. And it had changed again.

He'd heard this voice in a TV interview taken from the FBI's video archives. A voice that was unforgettable. Conceited. And pompous. An audio portrait of the Tiger Paw Killer's most famous victim. It was the voice of Matthew Carleton.

The voice of the dead financier read from a carefully prepared script - a script of deception that had been used to hide the killer on that murderous night in Long Island. A deception that had bought him the necessary time to complete his manic work.

"I'm sorry Lexi," the voice began. "I'm busy right now. This bond deal. The Estonian shipyard. I'm in the middle of something that could take *hours*."

There was a pause in the evil discourse and then the voice continued, "Did the children like the movie?"

Another pause. "Put them to bed, Lexi, and give them hugs and kisses from Daddy. I'll see them tomorrow."

A tomorrow that for Matthew Carleton... never arrived.

Scott looked down at the trail of blood and asked the voice, "Who died here tonight?"

"Michael Wayne Portland, of course."

"Why *of course*?"

"Go to the bedroom. Look out the window and you will understand."

As Scott Forrester walked down the hall, he left a trail of bloody footprints behind him.

The master bedroom spanned the width of the apartment from front to back, with windows at both ends – a pair that overlooked the street in front of La Bijouterie, and a single one at the opposite end, that overlooked the courtyard and alleys behind the building.

Scott's feet left red imprints on the bedroom's plush carpet. "Front window or back?" he said into the phone.

"Back."

The back window's velvet drapes were tied open. Through its glass, the pale moon, high in the sky, cast its ice-cool light down into the courtyards below. Two alleys defined the property line between La Bijouterie and the buildings behind it. One alley ran across the back wall of La Bijouterie, the other perpendicular to it, the two alleys intersecting to form an inverted 'T'.

Scott looked down at the snow-laden courtyards. There was a trail in the virgin blanket of white. It led out of the shadows and down the length of the alley between the buildings. The trail ended where a figure stood, a figure in a hooded sweatshirt, his head covered. Beside him, a motorcycle was propped up against the alley's brick wall. In one hand was a motorcycle helmet; in the other, a cell phone.

The hooded figure spoke to Scott again. This time in the voice of Dr. Rajeev Chandra. The words had the same musical lilt of Chandra's East Indian accent, but were tainted by a demon's tongue, "You have run out of options, Special Agent Forrester. Look around you. At your footprints. He struggled briefly, didn't he? Before you sank your knife into him. Look down at the foot of the bed."

There was a suitcase opened on the floor, its contents tipped haphazardly around the room.

"Was your search in vain? Were you angry? You killed him without finding what you'd been looking for, then dragged his body down the stairs."

It was a macabre play, re-enacted in the horror of a winter's moonlight.

"You're thinking, Agent Forrester... how can I escape this hell? Where can I run? Take a bucket if you want to – there's one waiting for you in the kitchen – and, clean up. Like you did in East Hampton, remember? But it will make little difference what you do. Forensics will detect the slightest remnant of your footprints. Your fingerprints on the light switch and doorknobs. The staircase banister. The science of the very police forces that you once served, will find you, and then they will condemn you. Because, FBI Special Agent Scott Forrester, you have now run out of that most precious of commodities... time. And, as you can see with your own eyes... I am the energy of *Her* divine anger."

He was toying with Scott Forrester's karma. His intentions could not be any clearer. But Scott Forrester would not surrender. "It's *you*..." he stuttered in anger, "*You*... that has run out... of *lies!*"

The voice laughed. This time the voice was that of Christienne Duval - her bright, sugary laugh. And what the voice said next turned Scott's rage into a damp, clammy sweat. "I have tasted her blood, Scott Forrester," the voice mocked. "And it was sweet."

Christienne?

The scream started deep inside his mind and then tore open his throat, "No... *No!*"

"Yes, Mr. Forrester. Yes. She was... so *sweet*, under my tongue. So... *perfect*." There was an evil pause. The figure in the courtyard pulled something from a duffel bag nestled in the snow beside his feet. Even in the gray moonlight, Scott could tell he was holding... a bloodstained nightdress. The figure let it drop to the snow. "So... *sweet*."

Scott collapsed on the carpet and screamed, "*No! No!*"

"It has been such a pleasure talking to you, Mr. Forrester."

"*No!* No... it can't be! Christienne? It *mustn't* be!"

"Good-bye, Special Agent Scott Forrester..."

The rat's maze had reached its deadly... and lonely... end.

Chapter Fifty

Scott Forrester leapt onto the fire escape and cascaded down its rickety metal stairs. He jumped, landing awkwardly in the snow, and felt a sharp pain stinging his forearm. Blood oozed out of a tear in his jacket. He had landed on his knife, the tip piercing his bicep.

Ahead of him, in the shadows, a motorcycle's engine was revving up, taunting him. Scott struggled to his feet and stumbled up the alley. The phantom rider shot forward, then cut sideways like an expert skier schussing down an alpine hill. The bike's stubby, heavily treaded tires had been chosen for maximum traction.

Planning. Preparation. Attention to detail.

Scott slipped, and crashed into a row of trashcans, falling face down into a mixture of snow and garbage. He'd twisted his ankle. He winced as he tried to get up, and slumped backwards in the snow; his hands and feet quickly becoming numb; his shoes stuffed with coarse white lumps of ice. A raw chill gripped his tired muscles and his weary mind. But even though his body was weak, he was not ready to concede the fight.

The rider stopped at the end of the alleyway, just short of the exit onto Connecticut Avenue. He cut the engine and straddled the bike; his face... this evil... hidden beneath the Plexiglas visor of a glossy black helmet. He was teasing Scott – building a layer of frustration over a foundation of defeat and despair.

Scott Forrester stumbled again, the ankle giving way. "Why don't you get it over with..." he yelled, on his knees, "and just *kill* me!"

The figure remained silent.

Scott's screams reverberated off the alley's tall canyon of bricks. "I know about Sudhir Narayan! And his twisted cult! About Sapphire Systems... and the CIA!"

The figure remained silent, barely twenty yards away. A simple flick of the bike's ignition switch and it would end all hope of pursuit. But that's not what the faceless killer wanted. The cell phone appeared again. Numbers were punched with a gloved finger. Another synthetic voice was chosen, this time the sound coming from a speaker on the side of his motorcycle helmet.

"Why don't you silence me for good? Why don't you just kill me?" Scott repeated.

The killer's answer was like an echo from Hell. In a voice Scott Forrester knew intimately. Because the voice was... his own.

"Kill you?" it asked. "That would be too easy, Agent Forrester. Yes, you *are* looking into the abyss. The abyss of your own death. You *are* at that gate. But we can stop this. We don't want to kill you. We want to *deliver* you from this misery."

"Deliver me? What do you mean... *deliver* me?"

"Souls are not destroyed, Mr. Forrester. They are simply reborn in another form."

"Forged in *Hell*, you mean!" Scott bellowed, standing his ground in the face of an evil that had raped his world. "End it *now*, you bastard! Go ahead! End my life! But *this* soul..." he hissed back, "*This* soul...is *not* for sale!"

The voice inside the glossy black helmet laughed, "You're running, Mr. Forrester. You don't know *why*. And you don't know *where*. But when there is no place left for you to go, you *will* return. You will return... to *me*."

Was this his fate? To join this degenerate cult and become one of *them*? Was Scott Forrester still alive because - in the perverse logic of a demented mind – the killer believed he could make Scott succumb to his will?

Scott growled back, "You have *no* power! Not over *me*! I will not betray every value; everything I believe is right, and is good. Not for *you*... not for *anyone*!"

"Everything you have believed in, Scott Forrester... *everything...* has already betrayed *you*. I offer you the *only* salvation you have left."

"I would rather eat my own *shit*!"

The helmeted figure reached for the ignition, "You already have, Scott Forrester. You already have."

The bike's engine roared to life. The throttle raced. The clutch slipped into gear. The motorcycle accelerated with a spray of brown slush, fishtailing in a semi-circle as it lunged onto the street.

Scott scrambled to his feet and limped down the alley.

Connecticut Avenue yawned open and swallowed the Tiger Paw Killer into its dark shadows.

Once more, Scott Forrester found himself cold and alone.

Chapter Fifty-One

Headlights approached from behind. A vehicle slowed and pulled up to the curb. The window lowered and the driver called out. "Scott! They're looking for you! Get in! You need to get off the streets!"

It was Jamie, in his van.

"Scott... for Christ's sake, what have you *done*?"

Police sirens wailed in the distance, approaching fast.

In between the front bucket seats, a portable radio blared chatter from the police band, "Reporting a 10-54, possible dead-body... Roger that... All units, APB, white male, black leather jacket, blue jeans... Code 6AD, armed and dangerous..."

Jamie was frantic. Police lights appeared in his rear view mirror. "Didn't you hear me, Scott? Get in, *idiot*!"

Scott's gaze was fixed on some distant object Jamie could not see.

"We don't have much time! Are you getting in or not?"

Scott opened the door and climbed in.

The van's V8 screamed. Jamie drove two blocks and turned off Connecticut Avenue. The side street he turned down was crammed with parked cars half-buried in unplowed snow and the street quickly came to a dead end. Jamie pulled over and killed the engine, and with it, the headlights.

They sat in silence as two police cars passed by on the main road. Scott's mind was a nauseous fusion of sorrow and anger. Something he cherished so dearly, that mattered so much, had been snatched from him by a monster, and could *never* be replaced. He let the tension out and cried.

The warmth of the heater was melting the snow on Scott's jacket, but it couldn't melt away the discomfort, the anxiety, his sadness and hatred. Scott Forrester felt like he was floating above the van, looking down on his own doom. *Christienne Duval. The candle... snuffed out.* Darkness was descending on him. He was entering the realm of the killer's victims. He thought he could see their faces peering out of the shadows in the alley. His soul sought refuge from this intense pain. *Was he crossing the line between delirium and reality? Was he going... insane?*

"Bro? Scott? Snap out of it!" Jamie yelled, prodding him. He noticed blood on Scott's jacket and arm. "You killed somebody, didn't you, Bro?"

Jamie's accusation was enough to bring Scott back. "No. No!" he said. "I didn't!" The intense cold had numbed the sting of his wound but as he thawed in the van, the hurt returned. "I just fell. Cut myself... on the knife."

"It looks nasty. We need to get you to a doctor."

"No. No doctors, Jamie!" Scott's sense of place and time had returned. So had his sanity. "We've got to disappear. They'll be after us. And I don't mean just the police. How did you know where to find me?"

"What are you talking about, Bro? You don't remember? *You* called me. *You* told me to pick you up."

"I didn't call you."

"What are you on, Scott? I should know your voice. I'm your brother. *You...* called me."

"I didn't call you."

"Then who did, smart ass? Elmer Fudd? Oh, *shit...*"

A police car turned the corner and was heading straight towards them. Its searchlight scanned the parked cars and started to probe the back of Jamie's van.

"Shit! We're *fucked*!"

"Play it cool, Jamie."

The police radio between the seats came back to life, "Code 30, officers need assistance..." The police car's searchlight turned off, the car backed up quickly and its blue roof lights twisted into action. "Proceed to Connecticut and R Street. Black van…"

Black van?

"Jamie, let's go! We need to get out of here! *Now!*"

"What are you talking about?"

"The police have been tipped off by someone. But they're going to be disappointed."

"Scott, you're not making any sense."

"Nothing on the surface of this hell makes sense, Jamie. It's like looking at the surface of the ocean… from above, it's gray and shapeless. You need to dive *below* the surface to truly understand what's lurking underneath. And I think I'm beginning to understand why this madness is happening to me…"

"I'd love to chat with you about it, Bro. Over a latté. But what the *fuck* do we do now?"

"They've given us a lifeline, Jamie. Let's take it. The police will be drawn northbound to check out a black van. Take Connecticut Avenue. Head south."

"Then what?"

"We get out of the city."

"And go where?"

"I don't know."

"Well… that's sounds like a brilliant plan, Scott."

Jamie restarted the van and backed it up a delivery ramp. He hurried onto Connecticut Avenue going south, clipping a parked BMW on the way out. "I'm going to turn at DuPont Circle. But then we're going to head northeast," Jamie said. "I know someone who rents storage units near the Amtrak terminal. We can hide there for a little while. I need to make some calls. There's a pay phone in the terminal. And by the way, Scott… we need a better plan than just 'get the fuck out of Dodge'."

"Yeah, Jamie. I guess you're right. We do."

***

Across the cracked parking lot was a 7-11 store. Sarah Vaughn hurried in, her breath blowing mini-clouds of moisture as she ran. In her jeans was a list and three hundred dollars in crisp bills.

Ten minutes later, she returned, her shopping completed. Everything fit in one large paper bag. "Here's your change, Jamie. Fifty-three cents."

Inside Jamie's van, the heater was struggling to pump out hot air. "A few more stops and then we'll get back." The van wheeled in a circle and headed for a nearby strip mall. They were hunting for another ATM.

Sarah opened the glove box and pulled out an envelope stuffed with money and ATM cards.

"How much have we got so far?" Jamie asked.

"Twelve hundred dollars," she said, counting the money in the envelope. "But we've max'ed out four cards. And we only have two more left. Will that be enough?"

"It's got to be enough." When they were done, Jamie would write her a check and she would return the cards to her friends and reimburse them. From this point on, Jamie and Scott couldn't be traced through ATM withdrawals or credit card purchases. As long as this wad of cash held out.

The last withdrawals were made and they returned to Capital District Mini-Storage - a collection of decrepit, garage-sized storerooms with rust-drizzled corrugated doors.

Scott Forrester was huddled inside Unit #53 around a portable gas heater loaned to them by Jamie's friend, the owner of the storage units. The rear seat of the van had been removed to form a put-up bed while Jamie and Sarah had gone on their errand. He was dozing, his eyes crusted with dried tears.

Sarah woke him with a large cup of steaming takeout coffee. "They didn't have French vanilla, so I got you toffee-caramel instead."

Scott sat up slowly. He moved as if in a trance. His voice was monotone and lifeless. His mind searched its dark corners for the light from a candle. But there was no light. "It's hot," he finally said, recognizing the female figure bending down to comfort him. "It's caffeinated. It's perfect, Sarah. Thanks."

The electric lift on the side door of the van lowered Jamie to the ground. He handed Sarah the keys. In return, she gave him the keys to her Jeep Wrangler. It was Christmas break at the end of the week and Jamie's van was the ideal people mover for cash-strapped students on a budget. "Are you going to Florida with them?" Jamie asked.

"What? And leave you on your own, God knows where, doing God knows what, running out of money? Are you crazy?" She knelt beside his wheelchair and kissed him. "I love you, Jamie. I want to go with you."

"You can't, Sarah. It's going to be too dangerous."

"Then I'm not leaving Washington. Whatever happens, I'm going to be here for you." She kissed him again, tears streaming down her face.

Jamie Forrester put his hands on Sarah Vaughn's porcelain cheeks and cradled her soft face. He tried to fight back the sadness. It wasn't working. "It's time we got moving, Scott," he said, lingering in Sarah's disheartened embrace.

Scott was hunched over the warm curls of coffee vapor that were floating up into his grizzled face, his eyes red and bloodshot. His arm was tied with a makeshift bandage. It was 11:30AM. The day was gray and overcast with a temperature of forty degrees F, cold enough to feel it, warm enough for the previous night's snow to melt.

"We're going to have to risk the daylight, Bro," Jamie said. "If we don't leave now, it'll be dark by the time we get there. It's a rough road, with few landmarks. The woods have probably changed. The trails may have overgrown. There may be trees down. We could easily get lost. I've been there only once before."

'There' was the mountains of West Virginia and a hidden cabin of a reclusive hacker whose Internet call sign was I_H8_Brokers. In Jamie's lap was a brown paper bag with an envelope of cash, two hundred and fifty dollars of untraceable phone cards, and three multi-packs of pornographic magazines - a present for the cabin's owner. It was lonely in those woods.

Scott helped Sarah put the bench seat back into Jamie's van. Then Scott carried Jamie to Sarah's Jeep and loaded the wheelchair in the back. The Jeep already contained Jamie's laptop and gadgets, and a small case of clothes Sarah had brought for him. Scott only had the grubby leather jacket he was wearing; his faded blue jeans; the shirt on his back. And a heart heavy with vengeance, and fear.

Scott gave his cell phone to Sarah. "Remember Sarah... tell your friends to use this phone at least a couple of times on the way down to Florida. But they shouldn't hang on to it for too long after that. Ditch it out the window on the side of the highway. If they don't get rid of it, they'll be in danger."

"Yes, yes. I know," she said. "And do it with Jamie's too. And change the plates on the van. We've gone over this plan a hundred times..."

Scott climbed into the Jeep. Its engine squealed alive.

Sarah gave Jamie a long kiss through the passenger window, then ran to the other side. She hugged Scott tightly, crying. "You bring him back to me, you hear? Or I'll never forgive you!"

"Don't worry. I will."

"Call me... just to say he's okay. That's all I want to know."

"I can't promise anything, Sarah. You know we have no option. We *have* to take this fight underground. And we've got to win. But it's not guaranteed."

"I know."

Sarah stepped back from the car. The window rolled up.

She waved them good-bye.

And then they were gone.

Chapter Fifty-Two

It was cruel to name him Elvis. But how could his parents have known how damaging it would be to grow up in rural West Virginia, as a fat boy named Elvis?

Elvis Arnold Prendergast.

It didn't get any easier when he dropped his first name, Elvis, in favor of Arnie, and went off to college in Kentucky. Somehow 'Arnie' - and its connotation of tree limb sized biceps and tight washboard abs - never meshed with the reality of Elvis Prendergast's bulbous three hundred and eighty pound, five-foot-seven inch body.

When Arnie Prendergast dropped out of college, he needed a job where social interaction wasn't required but highly developed programming skills were deemed invaluable. In the tech boom of the last decade, that wasn't really a problem.

That's when he and Jamie Forrester first met. They'd worked together on several big projects – Jamie, the freelance programmer; Arnie, his team leader from the software company that had negotiated lucrative subcontracts, then outsourced the heavy lifting to disposable temps like Jamie.

Projects like 'Lightning Strike'.

'Lightning Strike' was the reason Arnie Prendergast went underground. Deep underground. *Untraceably* underground.

'Lightning Strike' was the reason Jamie had brought Scott to this ramshackle hunting cabin in West Virginia, a decaying structure of pine logs and old carpets that was overrun with spiders and - if the wind was blowing in the wrong direction - had a disgusting smell coming from the septic system.

'Lightning Strike' had been tested with mixed success, then abandoned. There were only two known copies of its source code: the original held in a top-secret vault in a basement in Langley, Virginia - the basement of the Central Intelligence Agency; and the other – a bootleg copy on a smudged CD – currently being held in the chubby fingers of a three hundred and eighty pound, beady-eyed hacker who resembled a punk version of Jabba the Hutt, and was known outside the confines of his West Virginia shack as 'I_H8_Brokers'.

To the FBI and the CIA, Elvis Arnold Prendergast was a 'person of interest'. An unspecified national security threat that had disappeared off the face of the Earth. That was just fine with Arnie. He didn't like government. Didn't pay taxes. And he *never* had visitors. The last visitor he'd had was Jamie Forrester. Jamie had helped him buy the shack in the woods, and had been the other half of its two-person house warming party just after the CIA's 'person of interest' had moved in.

Like Jamie Forrester, Arnie Prendergast survived by day trading. He used offshore accounts to hide his identity and had other equally underground miscreants mail him the profits, in cash, to a numbered post office box on the outskirts of Charleston, West Virginia.

Arnie made a regular run for money and supplies into Charleston in the only vehicle known to be large enough and capable enough of trekking the undulating deep wood trails and carry its three hundred and eighty pounds of human cargo… a Hummer H1. A vehicle he appropriately named the 'Arnie-mobile'.

Arnie *never* had visitors.

Never, until now.

Whether online or in person, Jamie Forrester had always treated Arnie Prendergast with the professional and personal respect he deserved. So when Jamie Forrester said he needed Arnie's help, that he had a challenge of grave importance, and it involved 'Lightning Strike', Arnie Prendergast made an exception to a rule he hadn't broken since the day he quit his contract with the CIA - the day he walked out of a top secret facility with a bootleg CD of highly classified source code jammed up his gigantic butt crack.

"Your brother looks pretty bummed out," Arnie whispered in Jamie's ear. "Guess I would be too, after what you've told me, his girlfriend and all. And I know what it's like having the CIA probing your ass. Ain't a nice feelin'."

"My brother will be alright. He's strong. And he's itching for a fight."

"Well, he's come to the right place."

Scott pushed another log into the woodstove, sending a burst of sparks up the flue. The kettle on the stovetop began to sing. "You guys want a coffee?"

"Hell no..." Arnie said, pulling a bottle of Jack Daniels out of a paper bag. "It's after six, and we've got shit to do..." Shot glasses were never far away from Arnie's reach – they were on top of a humongous stack of computer servers, on bookcases stuffed with sci-fi paperbacks, on a coffee table that had seen better days, on a kitchen table that looked like it had been carved from a single slab of wood, under chairs, on window ledges. The trick was to find a glass that was clean.

Three glasses emerged from a cupboard. "After tonight, I gotta do some dishes," Arnie said, as he slopped whiskey until the glasses overflowed. He wobbled the dribbling shot glass in the air and toasted, "To 'Lightning Strike'. Let's fuck those devils..."

Arnie slugged the shot back, picked up the bottle, and staggered over to his massive workstation, an assortment of four interlinked 'big irons'- top of the line computers with flat panel screens – that ran six high-speed file servers, each with ten terabytes of storage.

Serious multi-tasking.

"So Jamie, where do we start, boy?"

"I've got a list."

"You got a *list*? Let me see it..." Arnie poured another shot. "Is this *all*? Hell, this is easy. You won't need 'Lightning Strike' for this shit."

"Save the big gun for later, Arnie. Start at the top."

"*Lee-Roy* Berg Switzerland?"

"Le Roux… Roo, Arnie. Like kanga-roo."

"That's what I said, Lee-Roy." Arnie Prendergast plopped his ass into his swivel chair and brought his flatscreens to life like a virtuoso pianist at the New York Philharmonic. The screens soon filled with lines of code scrolling at a speed faster than the eye could read. He was war-dialing – running a computer routine that hacked a back door pass into the target network. Then Arnie's homebrew of ping sweeping and password grinding software probed the network's vulnerabilities to unlock whatever part of the network he wanted to interrogate further. "So what specifically do you want to find, Jamie?"

"I want shipping instructions for a painting called 'The Revenge of Dvaipa'."

Scott grabbed the bottle of Jack from the desk and tipped it into their shot glasses. Arnie looked up approvingly. "Your bro's getting in the spirit."

"He's not the dick smack you think he is."

"He's a Fed. They're all dick smacks and bakebrains. They're trained to be."

"Hey, dude, I ain't arguing with you. But he's my bro, okay? And without him, I'm shit!"

"I'm cool with that, Jamie. I'm cool."

A dialogue box flashed madly on the screen: *Access Denied… Access Denied.* Then after a few more attempts… *Login Successful.* Arnie had broken into Le Roux-Berg's accounting system.

He navigated through the menus and found the shipping invoice. "Here it is… yer paintin' departs the Port of Baltimore, the day after tomorrow. On somethin' called the 'Princess of Goa'. Say, why'd you'd come up here for this? You could've done this from home."

"We don't have a home," Scott replied.

"Join the fuckin' club, sunshine! None of us has a home. See that?" Arnie said, pointing at his computer screens. "*That's* my home, you dumb shit."

"Okay, Arnie. Okay. Settle down. Have another shot." Jamie said. "You wanna kick ass? Let's kick some ass. We need the ship's registry and ownership, its ports of call, manifest, stuff like that."

"Look at the screen, dude! I'm way ahead of you!" Arnie had hacked into the Port of Baltimore's shipping records. His printer kicked into action. "Come to Pappa…"

The 'Princess of Goa', a bulk cargo freighter, owner: Narayan Holdings of India. Destinations, ex-port of Baltimore: Jacksonville, Florida; Nassau, Bahamas; Turquoise Cay, the Turks and Caicos Islands. Manifest: construction materials – cement blocks, paving stones, electrical conduit and switches, lumber, custom windows… and a painting. The cargo had insurance, paid by a Cayman Islands registered company with the name, MWP International Construction.

"MWP International Construction? Who wants to bet a bottle of Jack that MWP stands for Michael Wayne Portland?" Scott said. "A shitload of construction supplies? Michael Wayne Portland must be building something *big*. In the Caribbean, somewhere near the Turks and Caicos Islands. And I can guess exactly what that something is… a temple. The Great Temple. And that temple needs an altarpiece. And that altarpiece is the painting."

Arnie burped. "So what's next on the list?"

"What do you think, Bro?" Jamie asked Scott, as he refilled the three shot glasses. "Let's see if our photos have been processed. We're expecting an e-mail from Interpol, Arnie. But we need a back door hack into my e-mail account. If I access it directly with my own password, the spooks will know it's me. And if they trace it back here, we're screwed."

"Jamie…" Arnie snorted. "Just when the fuck are we goin' to do somethin' hard?"

"Patience, Arnie. Drink your JD like a good little boy... and we'll get there soon enough."

"You're the boss, Jamie."

Arnie's program broke into Jamie's e-mail account without wasting any more than a nanowatt of energy in the effort. Jamie was impressed. "Hey, can I get a copy of that?"

"It'll cost you," Arnie said, slurping down another shot. "Hot damn... that stuff's good."

Jamie looked through his mailbox and found the e-mail from Interpol, forwarded with a simple note - "Wherever this leads you, tread carefully... Billings."

No doubt this e-mail had already been intercepted. It was an assumption they had to make. Whatever information was contained in its attachments, whatever conclusions the Interpol analysis had made, it likely meant both predator and prey were on equal footing.

Was it too much to hope they could gain some small advantage? Scott thought. *Was it too unrealistic to expect that an overweight hacker and two penniless fugitives, in a shack in West Virginia, could wage war on a monolithic intelligence agency, a super-secretive cult, and their horrific spawn? On anything resembling an equal footing?*

Maybe not, Scott concluded. *But I will die trying.*

Arnie printed the pdf files and other attachments.

Scott's hastily taken photos from the Stavros Estate were now the faces that occupied the top right-hand corner of Interpol's background checks - data culled from Interpol's member organizations, including US law enforcement agencies. With its member states' permission, Interpol had access to government and criminal records, APBs, most wanted lists, passport information, terrorist watch lists. There were a few gaps, but on the whole, there was more background information on the subjects in his photos than Scott Forrester had dreamt of getting. Inspector Winston Billings had pulled it off.

Scott tipped the bottle of Jack Daniels and filled Arnie's shot glass again. "If I survive this nightmare, I owe you a case of this stuff. You aren't going to let me forget that, are you?"

"Forget?" Arnie said. He pointed to the electronic colossus that was his workstation. "You can run, Scott Forrester... but you can't hide."

"I kinda thought that. I'll add you to the list."

Interpol's files were more than they had hoped for. The faces on the beach, at the tennis club - the entourage of friends surrounding Lexi Stavros; and their names, the ones that had escaped Anastasia Stavros' aging memory - had been brought back to life by facial recognition software.

Scott shuffled through the printouts. Nicole Riverton and Sue Lee Chen: the progress of their lives all the way from Princeton to their untimely deaths. A file on the young man in many of the photos: Lexi Stavros' future husband, Matthew Carleton. But most of Interpol's information about him wasn't new to Scott. Carleton had no criminal record. What was contained in his Interpol file was a result of his celebrity status and well-publicized murder.

As expected, there was a file on Sudhir Narayan. But his college tryst with the young debutante, Lexi Stavros, was a nuance absent from Interpol's analysis of the future Indian Ambassador to the US. It appeared that the details of their short-lived engagement at Princeton had been kept private within the family.

The profile that caught Scott Forrester's attention was of a young man that appeared in several of Anastasia's snapshots. A young man whose identity was now confirmed to be that of Michael Wayne Portland. The college connection between the brilliant student from Massachusetts and the Indian blueblood from New Delhi became more and more apparent as Scott read through Portland's dossier.

"Portland attended Princeton's Woodrow Wilson School of Public and International Affairs in the same years as Narayan and the others," Scott explained, as Arnie opened a fresh bottle of Jack Daniels. "Then after graduation, Michael Wayne Portland got a job with the US Embassy in New Delhi, India. As Assistant Attaché for Regional Security Affairs.'"

"Regional Security Affairs?" Arnie said, smirking, as he rocked in his chair. The chair looked like it would break at any moment. He laughed. "Shit. Anyone who's read enough spy novels knows - that's just a cover for the damn CIA!"

"You're right on the money with that, friend," Jamie said. "So Michael Wayne Portland was CIA."

"And still is," Scott said.

"But in India? Doing what? Does it say?"

"No, it doesn't. That's not something Interpol would have access to. But it sure would be nice to find out. What it *does* tell us… is that Michael Wayne Portland and Sudhir Narayan attended Princeton together, and they socialized in Lexi's circle of friends. A friendship was formed - a college kinship that is never forgotten and rarely broken." Scott poured himself a shot. "They were both intelligent, rich kids. From influential families. With bright, promising futures. I'd bet they shared the same desire: to be movers and shakers within their respective countries. They were ambitious, well connected, and power hungry. With the speed of Michael Wayne Portland's overseas posting, coming as it did just after he finished his studies, I'd bet he was recruited by the Agency even *before* he graduated. And Sudhir Narayan? I think there was more than one kind of recruiting going on at Princeton."

"The cult?"

"That would be my guess, Jamie. I think Sudhir Narayan has been involved with the Temple of Dvaipa since birth. It would take a particularly intense kind of religious brainwashing to preserve his satanic beliefs in the middle of such a foreign, Western lifestyle. And I think he would have been conditioned by the cult to accept everything around him as a chance to propagate his religion at every opportunity. I think he was pre-ordained at an early age to be a spiritual leader in the cult. I've seen him in action – how he manipulates his surroundings, and the people in them. Lexi Stavros and her impressionable college friends were innocent and benign, and ripe for recruitment. They were ideal candidates for indoctrination into a deviate religion that offered them the carnal thrills that were absent from their stuffy privileged upbringings."

The shot quickly disappeared.

"What do you think of the bakebrain now, Arnie?" Jamie said.

"Not bad, Joker. I'm impressed. How's his keyboarding skills?"

Scott filled Arnie's glass again. "Both Michael Wayne Portland and Sudhir Narayan knew how to exploit the vulnerabilities of youthful idealism. If Michael Wayne Portland and Sudhir Narayan had anywhere near the friendship I think they had, they found many ways to support each other's goals and objectives. Why else would Michael Wayne Portland end up in such a high profile post in India, fresh out of college? Michael Wayne Portland - the young, ambitious CIA agent on his first foreign posting - would have been given a tremendous career advantage with Sudhir Narayan as his conduit into Indian society. The CIA loves people who exploit advantages. They knew who Narayan was. And how useful he could be to the Agency in the Indian subcontinent, on the doorstep of Afghanistan and Pakistan. The CIA recruited Portland and he in turn recruited Narayan. I'm sure of it."

"And what if Narayan recruited Portland in reverse?" Jamie asked.

"The cult? *That*, Jamie is the trail we're on."

The printer continued to spit out pages. "You got more e-mail from Interpol," Arnie said.

Jamie took the fresh sheets, looked them over and handed them to Scott, saying, "Do you know these guys?"

The sheets contained three more profiles. More of Lexi's male friends from college. But their names had never surfaced before. Scott looked at their faces. *What connection did these guys have with Portland and Narayan?* "They mean nothing to me, Jamie. The only time I've seen these faces was on the wall at the Stavros estate. The only time I've come across these names is now."

"And there's no Dominic Sant'Angello, Bro?"

"No. There's no Dominic Sant'Angello." Scott poured another whiskey and backed it down. "Shit, Jamie! Where does Sant'Angello fit in with all this?"

One last set of pages emerged from the printer.

"That's it. That's all of them," Arnie announced.

Jamie scanned the last profile and within seconds understood its meaning. "*Oh, shit...* is right, Bro! Take a look at this..."

Jamie handed over the final pages from Interpol. Scott Forrester looked at the photograph in the top right-hand corner on the first page and grew very pale. The sickly acid taste returned. He put his shot glass on the computer table, slunk over to the tatty sofa in the middle of the room, and put his head into his hands. He was sweating. A cold sweat. He looked at the photograph again to be sure. His mind ran back into the maze. *This way was a dead-end. That way... was too.* But now, a face in the background of a group portrait with Lexi Stavros - the only time that face was present among Anastasia Stavros' entire wall of memorabilia - was staring up at him with shocking familiarity.

The maze ran left and right, back through time. Back to the night when a hooded stranger left a sinister calling card. Forward to a snow-covered alley, whose echoes came from Hell itself. The hooded sweatshirt and glossy black helmet hid the face and body of a predator whose deception was genius, whose preparation was incomparable, and whose horrific identity was now deposited onto a piece of paper inside a hacker's shack in the West Virginia woods.

"We've found the killer, haven't we Bro?"

"Deception, Jamie. This whole thing has been about *deception*." Scott tried to compose himself. "*Jesus*, how could I have been so, so *stupid*?" He took a long, deep breath and pointed to the stack of computers. "Arnie?" he asked. "Can you access US military recruiting records with that thing?"

"What the fuck do you think?"

"I think you can."

"Then give me a name and let's find out."

Scott gave Arnie the name from Interpol's last dossier, the name connected to a face on a photograph from the Stavros Estate on Long Island. A photograph from Lexi's college days at Princeton. A photograph that had been sliced and diced, enhanced and crosschecked, by Interpol's facial recognition software. A photograph that Scott Forrester now knew, after experiencing *so much* pain and terror, was the face of… the Tiger Paw Killer.

The engine of Arnie Prendergast's monster computer fired up once again and went into warp drive. In a few short minutes, the Pentagon's records of every serviceman recruited into the US military were unlocked by the Grand Hacker of the West Virginia woodlands.

The computer printed out the service record they had requested. Arnie looked over at the two brothers huddled on the sofa. "So, do you guys want this? Or are you just going to sit there and mope? Would somebody please tell me what the *hell* is going on?"

Scott read over the new information. It confirmed his suspicions about the killer. He passed the Interpol report and service record to Jamie. "You know where we need to go next, don't you, Little Bro?"

"Yeah. I do." Jamie wheeled himself over to the computers. "Arnie, time for the *big gun*, dude."

"What we need to do now, Arnie…" Scott said, "is break into the CIA's Top Secret case files. We need to connect some dots. Getting into the CIA's computer system - is that even a possibility?"

Arnie took the half-empty bottle of Jack Daniels, placed his fat lips around the bottle's mouth, and glugged a face full of bourbon. As the liquor hit the back of his throat, he shook his head and said with great satisfaction,

"So you guys are finally gonna give me a reason to get back at those mothers, aren't you? Connecting dots is what 'Lightning Strike' is all about, friends. You got dots? Let Arnie connect them. But know this, Joker. Once I crank up 'Lightning Strike', we'll all be brothers. Because once I do, there won't be *any* way back. We need to know exactly what we're gonna do. Because when I get in, we won't have much time."

Jamie looked concerned. "And it's old code, Arnie. They must have countermeasures for it by now."

"Countermeasures? Maybe. But not with this version, Jamie. It's not the same program." Arnie loaded the smudged disk into his computer. A message box quickly launched. "It's taken me a long time, but I knew it could be done. I knew I could make 'Lightning Strike' better, Jamie. I fixed it. I fixed it good!"

"What is 'Lightning Strike', Arnie?" Scott asked.

"Better to show you. Gimme some search terms, dude. Keep 'em simple."

Scott took a blank sheet of paper from the printer and wrote down two sets of words he wanted to find in the CIA's files. The first set was… 'Sapphire Systems'. The second: the name from Interpol's facial recognition analysis - the name of a covert operative that Arnie's hack of military records said belonged at one time to a unit of Special Operations Command. A covert unit they believed was controlled by the CIA. The name they now knew to be… the Tiger Paw Killer.

Arnie looked the search terms over and typed them into the dialogue box. The box dissolved, and a new one appeared. 'Lightning Strike' asked him for the target network. "Okay, dudes. This is it. When I press the next button, 'Lightning Strike' will crank up in all its fuckin' glory. You guys ready?"

Jamie seemed to know what that meant. But Scott's Jack-fueled curiosity could no longer be contained. "Just exactly *what* is going to happen, Arnie?"

"He is a bakebrain, isn't he, Joker?"

"Tell him, Arnie. Just think of him as a kid at a science museum or at a games arcade. A kid who is mesmerized by the bright flashing lights and fake explosions, but can't possibly understand how difficult it was to create them."

"You mean the Reader's Digest version?"

"No, too much. Think comic book, Arnie."

"I can dig that. I like comic books." He turned to Scott. "Okay, Mr. Federal Agent, here's the comic book version - it'll start with a massive denial of service attack-"

Scott looked a little blank.

"That's a deluge of pings routed through a network of slave computers, dude. These computers, located all around the world, operate as my surrogates."

"This doesn't sound legal," Scott said.

Jamie laughed. "We left 'legal' when we turned off the highway and entered these woods, Bro."

"Yeah. No kidding," Arnie said. "So… where was I? Oh, yeah. They're mostly porn servers. In places like Latvia and the Ukraine. The pings will never be traced back here."

Arnie typed the final target into 'Lightning Strike': an IP address that came back onto the screen as a verified link into the network of a certain federal agency in Langley, Virginia.

"How do you know the CIA's network access protocol?" Scott asked.

"Scott…" Jamie said. "That's gotta be the dumbest question you've asked so far, Bro."

"Yeah, dude," Arnie said. "How do I know? 'Cos I programmed it, *asshole*!"

"Make that *two* cases of Jack," Scott said.

"Yeah. Too right." Arnie swigged from the bottle again. "When the CIA commissioned me to develop 'Lightning Strike', they wanted a program that would penetrate the impenetrable. Hack into the unhackable. Anywhere in the world. Now *that* was difficult. When it was tested, every advance in programming science kept defeating it. Then the Agency wimped out. They gave up the idea. But me? *Never.* I left with the only other copy of the source code. And *I* didn't give up, dude."

"Arnie's a genius, Bro."

"It's going to take a genius to find a genius. That's why we're here."

"Arnie…" Jamie asked, "what's so different about your new version of 'Lightning Strike'?"

"That's the cool part, dude. It's the Trojan of all Trojans! With some *kickass* horsepower!"

"A Trojan?" Scott said. "Now I know what a Trojan is."

"This one does way more than just open a backdoor into a network," Arnie explained. "And this is where it gets *suh-weet*! During the attack, this Trojan actually activates the network's anti-viral defenses before they do."

"You're *shitting* me," Scott said.

Arnie let off a deep, guttural burp. "Do I look like the kinda guy that would shit about somethin' like *this*? 'Lightning Strike' locates the account of a System Administrator then lulls the system into a false sense of security – that's the proprietary part. Basically, it makes the network think it's being helped, rather than being hacked. Then 'Lightning Strike' initiates our search inquiry in parallel with its own bogus anti-virus check - like it's just tryin' to help fight the attack - but in the meantime, it's tearing through their files like one crazy mother!"

Jamie gave his buddy a high-five. "That's *brilliant*, dude!"

"I knew you'd like it."

Scott was uneasy. He didn't understand the programming science behind Arnie's magic, but it sounded too simple. "You mean 'Lightning Strike' will give us unlimited access to the entire CIA database?"

Arnie detected the skepticism and poured another shot, just in case Scott riled him enough that he would need it to calm his nerves. "Our access is unlimited in *scope*, dude. But limited in *time*."

"What do you mean?"

"It will only last as long as the network is still searchin' for my Trojan. With current software technology? That could be thirty seconds, or it could be three seconds... or it could be three *nano*seconds. It depends on the computin' speed of the network. If it's a corporation, we would get a pretty decent amount of time to look up their skirts. But this is the *C*... *I*... *fuckin' A*... dude. It's gonna be a *whole* lot different with that system. So basically, we'll only get *one* shot at it. Once the CIA's network figures out what's happenin'... it'll be time's up! And *fast!*"

Scott Forrester now understood why his brother had brought him to a shack in West Virginia. This rundown hovel would be Ground Zero for the most ambitious computer hack in history. "Three *nano*seconds? That's not a lot of time, Arnie to get the information we need."

"That's why we need to be sure that *this* particular name..." Arnie pointed to the paper in his hands, "is really the one you want to go after. You've got a barn full of downloadin' horsepower sittin' right next to you. But once we're in, we need to make sure we're searchin' for the right thing. *Capiche?*"

Jamie asked, "Arnie, so what if we set up some kind of priority? Find and download only those files that contain both Sapphire Systems *and* this name?"

"I can program that. No sweat."

"Then... let's do it," Scott agreed.

"Yeah, what the *fuck*, Twinkies!" Arnie replied, as he glugged down the last drops from the bottle of Jack Daniels. "*Let's roll!*"

Chapter Fifty-Three

At 9:45 PM, Eastern Standard Time, the main computers at CIA Headquarters, Langley, Virginia detected a port scanning attack emanating from multiple computers located in countries formerly behind the Iron Curtain.

At five nanoseconds past 9:45 PM, the CIA's firewall software took remedial action - first by blocking all new users from logging on; then by suspending sessions for current users; and finally, initiating anti-viral software to search for a nasty Trojan that was leaving teasing markers throughout the CIA's network.

At two full seconds past 9:45 PM, the CIA's automated hacker defenses had restored order. System Administrators had been alerted and permission was granted to access the network to examine it for residual damage. One of those System Administrators had been locked out of the network. His password and ID were not accessible. Because they were already in use.

At three seconds past 9:45 PM - three seconds after the first ping had opened the portal - the attack was officially over. Unbeknownst to the CIA's IT managers, in those three seconds, 4,834,000 files had been interrogated and 2.8 GB of data had been downloaded. This data now resided on semi-public servers in Latvia and the Ukraine.

At 9:45 PM and fifteen seconds, the files disappeared from the remote servers, and shredder programs eliminated any trace of their previous existence.

An hour later, at 10:45 PM, Arnie Prendergast was snoozing in his oversized La-Z-Boy chair like a fat, drunken Cheshire cat that had eaten the entire rodent population of the New York City sewer system in one gluttonous meal. The smile on his face would have to be surgically removed. A third bottle of Jack Daniels lay at his feet, a testament to the fact that Arnie's mission had been completed successfully.

"Michael Wayne Portland isn't dead," Scott said. "Like everything else, Jamie, it's just another illusion. From what I see in these files, we have every reason to believe he's very much alive."

While Arnie slept, Scott and Jamie Forrester had mined a rich seam of top-secret intelligence data from Arnie's phalanx of hard drives. It spewed out of his printer like tailings from a gold shaft; the coarse raw material sorted first, then the resultant treasure trove of precious metal piled neatly on the floor.

Scott's suspicions were quickly confirmed. Conjecture became alloyed with fact. He read through the data with the enthusiasm of a California prospector who had struck the mother lode, "Boy genius Michael Wayne Portland graduates summa cum laude from MIT at the age of eighteen. At the age of twenty-two, his Sapphire Systems is a thriving, growing international business tailored to the security and privacy of corporations and wealthy individuals. His surveillance technology was second to none. Needing a new challenge, he enrolls in graduate school at Princeton, finishing his PhD in record time. And just as we thought, he was a CIA operative well before he graduated from Princeton. In fact, his case file shows he became the CIA's most successful recruiter of undergrads. Then his posting to India - where he and Sudhir Narayan partnered to build their sinister enterprise."

The enormity of what Scott and Jamie Forrester had obtained was hard to absorb. The information that lay in front of them was adrenaline-producing, but at the same time, paralyzing; fascinating, yet repulsive.

It was knowledge.

It was understanding.

But it was also shock.

There were no longer any secrets. Sapphire Systems and the CIA. The identity of the Tiger Paw Killer. And that identity - that reality - chilled Scott Forrester to the bone.

The printer finally stopped printing. As Scott Forrester finished reading the last piece of data, he stretched out on the floor, his bloodshot eyes staring into the naked bulb dangling below the shack's bare rafters. "It's pretty clear, Jamie, that Michael Wayne Portland had a zeal for the CIA's game. Like an addict, he became hooked on it. The danger. The deception. It was exhilarating, electrifying. And the more he accomplished within the CIA, the more the CIA demanded of him. They became mutually addicted to each other."

"He must have been devastated when the CIA pulled the plug on his project."

"I don't see Michael Wayne Portland like that, Jamie. I think by that time, he and Sudhir Narayan had already reached the conclusion that the capabilities they had developed together – their ability to infiltrate corporations, blackmail politicians, even control elements within a country's military – was a wasted talent in the CIA. I think they began to believe they had superhuman abilities. History is full of people like them. Megalomaniacs like Adolph Hitler and Saddam Hussein. People who believe they have a pre-ordained right to rule over others. It's just a question of getting in a position to do something about it. They simply *outgrew* the CIA. And now with Michael Wayne Portland as the mastermind, and Sudhir Narayan, the charismatic prophet, marrying into Matthew Carleton's billions, the disease they control - the Temple of Dvaipa - is ready to step up its claim to be the next totalitarian superpower. A superpower without borders."

"So, what do we do now, Bro? While we sit here, we're being hunted by this superpower. Like deer being hunted by an Abrams M-1 tank. It's not a fair contest."

"It's more than just the two of us being hunted. The FBI's investigation has been sabotaged from the very beginning, misled into dead-ends. What do *we* do next? That's a question I don't have an answer for right now."

A moth flew aimlessly in a circle towards the naked light dangling from the ceiling. Jamie followed Scott's eyes as he stared at the insect's movements. "Both of us are in your nightmare now, Scott. A nightmare that's no longer a dream. Yeah, for sure... it's real. The FBI won't help us. We're fugitives. Even in police custody, we won't be safe from the Temple. We're like that candle flame... the one flickering in the dark, ready to be snuffed out. We're like that moth circling endlessly without hope..."

Another moth joined the first. They orbited the warm light bulb in an erratic pattern of confused flight. Their movements were mesmerizing. "You're right, Jamie. About the flame. And the moth that has no choice but to be drawn to it." Scott paused, rethinking what he had just said. "Jamie! The moth! That's it!"

"What's *it*?"

Scott sat up. "Despite what Michael Wayne Portland and Sudhir Narayan may believe, we're fighting a natural force, not a supernatural one. The *painting*, Jamie. The painting can be our flame. And all of them... the Tiger Paw Killer included... will be our *moths*."

"That sounds like the Jack Daniels doing the talking now, Bro."

"Jamie... the Princess of Goa will be departing with the painting for Michael Wayne Portland's private island. I'll bet even money the killer will use the ship as a way to leave the United States. It's the perfect escape route. And that painting can be the perfect flame. We need to draw as many moths to it as possible."

"Moths? The perfect flame? What are you suggesting, Bro?"

"We can't run any more. Because we have no place to hide. And if we die... *this* knowledge..." Scott pointed to the pile of paper on the floor, "will die with us."

"You don't need to ask for my help, Bro. You know you've got it. So what do we do?"

"We start by leaving a message for the Tiger Paw Killer in your chat room."

"The BuzzBoard? For Gabriel?"

"I'm going to accept the killer's invitation."

"Invitation? To what? Your own funeral?"

"If it comes to that, yes."

"Let me get this straight, Scott. You want to put yourself in a position to become bait for this predator? That we come out of hiding - with only the shirts on our backs - and go toe-to-toe with the deadliest assassin on the planet?"

"We've got plenty of resources, Jamie. You just have to know where to look."

"We can't trust the FBI. Or the police."

"We'll use what the Tiger Paw Killer uses - *deception*."

"Bro... you're fucking *insane*!"

Scott Forrester picked up several documents from the pile on the floor. Documents they'd hacked from the cold digital vaults below CIA Headquarters. "This... is the birth record of a monster. *This...* is a chronology of death. Underneath it all... the truth has been smothered by an *avalanche* of lies and deception. No, Jamie. I'm not insane. This... and *this...* this is really *insane*. And it's time we stopped it... or died trying!"

Chapter Fifty-Four

Midnight on the Patapsco River, the inland estuary that forms the Port of Baltimore. The South Locust Point Marine Terminal. Eighty acres of wharves, cargo yards and warehouses.

The Princess of Goa lay placidly in its berth at South Locust Point, resting its tired, rusty hull; waiting for the last item on its manifest to be delivered before setting sail for the warmer waters of the Caribbean.

A Jeep Wrangler parked opposite the chain link fence on the Marine Terminal's southern perimeter. A man got out of the car, crossed the road, and proceeded to carve a hole in the fence with a pair of heavy gauge wire cutters. He then slipped inside the grounds, unnoticed.

Scott Forrester picked his way through the slushy snow between the stacks of sea containers; slinking catlike in the shadows past large transit sheds full of zinc ingots and Japanese earthmovers, slabs of raw latex and rolls of Polish steel. But it wasn't these detached, soulless commodities that Scott Forrester had come to find at South Locust Point. A more malignant cargo would soon arrive. The Devil's export. It had already unleashed an epidemic of death in the United States and once it left these shores, it was sure to multiply – like an infection of the mind, a modern day plague.

Scott hugged the rough, redbrick wall of the U.S. Customs warehouse. The night was cold, the sky was clear and the air was still. Above him, innumerable white sparkles wove their starry magic on a velvet blackness.

On a similar night in 1814, nearby Fort McHenry was besieged by the British, bombarded from the sea. That night, under the rockets' red glare, the defense of Baltimore inspired a nation's anthem. Two hundred years later, the ghosts of those brave soldiers stood silent watch, praying for Scott Forrester's success.

He reached the corner of the Customs warehouse. Breaking through the darkness were the lights on the bridge of the Princess of Goa. Beside the ship, a one-hundred-ton revolving gantry crane stood like a giant metal Hercules. Adjacent to the ship's berth were two more buildings with a roadway between them - the corridor the truck that was carrying 'The Revenge of Dvaipa' would have to take once it entered the terminal from Interstate 95.

The Customs warehouse had a massive rolling door, two-stories high. A freighter, which had left its berth further upstream en route to Chesapeake Bay and the Atlantic, passed by South Locust Point. As it did, a light shone from the freighter's deck towards the wharf, shining into the warehouse entrance. The transient light crept slowly by. The entrance was open... open wide enough to fit... a black van. As the freighter's ray of wandering light moved away, the black van disappeared back into hiding.

Scott Forrester knew... it was time.

He closed his eyes and prayed.

The same prayer brave soldiers prayed that clear and still night two hundred years ago: *Yea, though I walk through the valley of the shadow of death, I fear no evil...*

A thin sliver of moon cast just enough light to define the way forward. As he neared the open warehouse door, he heard the faint chirp of a drive belt. The same chirp he'd heard on another clear and still night; the night he'd ran naked from his house in pursuit of a nightmare.

He crept within sight of the van. It sat like a resting panther - a singular black form listening in the darkness for the faint heartbeat of its prey.

Scott fell to his stomach and crawled through the grit and snow to the warehouse entrance. He could feel the warmth of the van's engine; he could smell its sulfurous exhaust.

He knew exactly what he had to do.

When he reached the rear of the van, he grabbed the door's handle... and pulled.

The response from inside the vehicle was precise and instantaneous. With a rapid arm movement, the long steel barrel of a silenced Sig-Sauer pistol pressed into Scott's forehead. The arm that held it belonged to a man with a military buzzcut wearing a com-set. The man who'd called himself Jacob Weinberg, now stripped of his makeup and wispy-gray fake hair. Even an A-list actor couldn't mask the sourness in Weinberg's face – the arrogance, the air of superiority.

Behind him, basking in the electronic glow from a bank of surveillance equipment, was the man with eyes as cold as polar ice – 'Special Agent' Spencer Brant. 'Assigned' by the FBI to the SEC. The agent who'd confiscated Jamie's computer to build the 'case' against him. The agent who declared Jacob Weinberg a dead man - the lie that reinforced the other lies, in order to forge the 'truth'. The CIA played that game as well as anyone on Earth.

Spencer Brant frisked Scott and declared him clean.

"This is some stunt you're pulling, Forrester," Weinberg said, pushing the silencer into Scott's forehead. "I've got to admit... you've got some balls. But you're lucky you still have them. Takes guts to come here unarmed, alone, unsure whose bullet – ours, or the Tiger Paw Killer's - will end all of this. Is this the act of a desperate hero? Or can you finally admit what a *fool* you've been?"

"You won't pull that trigger... because you don't know who the Tiger Paw Killer is, do you? And you know... I do."

There was a click behind Scott Forrester's back; a trigger had been cocked. A female voice came out of the darkness of the warehouse, "You may be intelligent, Forrester, but you're not very smart."

"So when did you sell out, Trish? At what moment did you realize that the FBI's investigation was hopelessly outclassed? When the bullet entered Sue Lee Chen's head? Or when the Rivertons' home exploded in flames?

You found yourself on a losing team, and it didn't sit well with you, did it? You needed help. And glory. And the CIA obligingly offered you both."

"They had the resources to close this case."

"And once they offered you their 'resources', what was the price *you* had to pay to subordinate to *their* rules, *their* methods? Or was it simply the fact that Weinberg here - whatever his real name is - convinced you that bending the rules was not just a tactical necessity, but a golden prerequisite. For job-hopping out of the FBI and into the CIA? One small step backwards for justice; one giant leap forward for Tricia Van Cleyburn?"

"It's called career management, Scott," Trish replied. "A concept you *never* grasped."

"You've always been the perfect subordinate, Trish. But would you really pull that trigger... if the CIA told you to?"

"You're a murder suspect, Forrester. I don't need anyone to tell me what I need to do. Michael Wayne Portland's dead. And your face is in every sheriff's office in this country."

"Michael Wayne Portland is *dead*, you say? Are you sure? That's *exactly* what both of them want you to believe."

"Both of *who*?"

"Michael Wayne Portland... and the CIA."

"You're crazy. What are you talking about?"

"The CIA knows I didn't kill Michael Wayne Portland. Because he's *not* dead. There's a lot your new friends aren't about to tell you, Trish. You're just too new and naïve to be trusted with the dirtiest of their little secrets. Let's start with the fact that Portland's murder was staged. For the benefit of the police and the FBI. Staged not by the CIA - even though they're more than willing to play along – but by Michael Wayne Portland himself."

"You're hallucinating, Forrester! Portland's apartment is covered in his blood! Forensics has identified it as his!"

"Blood can be drawn in advance and saved. So where's the body, Trish? They haven't found a body yet, have they? I was there in the apartment, remember? And so was the Tiger Paw Killer. But, no body. You see, Trish, it's *always* been about deception, illusion... and then reincarnation. About the unintended consequences when someone ventures further into Hell than they should. And it's those consequences that the CIA has been desperately trying to cover up."

"You're a manipulative sociopath, Scott Forrester! You're squirming, trying to find a way out of a murder rap!"

Scott was still looking straight ahead, his back turned to Van Cleyburn, straight into the eyes of the phony Jacob Weinberg. "She really doesn't know, does she, Weinberg? Hasn't got a clue? Ask yourself, Trish. Why *am* I here? Why would a manipulative sociopath walk up and surrender like this? What psychological purpose would that serve? You know full well that if I were truly born to keep killing, then I wouldn't just give myself up! Not without a serious fight."

Van Cleyburn's trigger finger was getting nervous. "You obviously have the answers. So let's hear them!"

"If the CIA *knew* who the killer was, then I'd be face down in a ditch somewhere. Murder suspect: dead. Case: closed. Credit and gold stars to Special Agent Tricia Van Cleyburn of the FBI. Don't ask *me* for answers. Ask *them*. Ask your new 'friends'. Ask them why they're sitting in a van on a pier in Baltimore harbor. To arrest *me*? An unarmed psycho? The CIA needs all *this* equipment to do *that*? I can hardly believe they would. And neither should you!"

Trish's gun bit into his back.

Scott stared into Weinberg's menacing face. "Who is the Tiger Paw Killer, Weinberg? Come on... if you *know*, tell her! Then tell Van Cleyburn to pull the trigger! That's what you ultimately want, isn't it? That would be your perfect ending. But you can't tell her, can you? Because you don't *know* who the Tiger Paw Killer is, and you've been hoping all along... that I would find out for you. That's why you've been following me. Bugging my house. But they're smarter than the CIA. One step ahead of you, all the time. Playing your game even better than you play it. And guess what, Trish?... I *do* know who the killer is! And as long as I'm the only one who knows, Weinberg's not going to let you put a bullet in my head. In fact, be careful, Trish. Someone in those shadows has *you* in their crosshairs!"

"Weinberg... can you please tell me what the *hell* this idiot is talking about!"

Weinberg's eyes weren't giving anything away. "You have no idea who you're messing with, Forrester, do you?"

"Yes. I think I do. In fact, I'm *certain* I do. Michael Wayne Portland had a special talent didn't he, Weinberg? A kind of *magic* that could discriminate between a lethal killer that can be controlled... and one that can't. He's very much in control of this one. And it scares the living crap out of you, doesn't it? Go ahead, Weinberg... tell Van Cleyburn why you want the Tiger Paw Killer shut down. Tell her about India. Tell her about 'UNIT 7'. And its botched mission!"

"UNIT 7?" The gun in Scott's back relaxed its pressure.

"You see, Trish, Michael Wayne Portland was an astute judge of talent. And his company, Sapphire Systems - contracted by the CIA for its cutting edge spy technology - was also skilled at something far less easy to produce... deep cover assassins. Seven of them, to be precise."

"The Tiger Paw Killer is a CIA agent?"

"*Was* CIA, Trish. The CIA supplied Portland with handpicked recruits from U.S. Special Forces. He trained them, in the US and then in India, to standards beyond the CIA's highest expectations. Their mission: to penetrate the most hostile of hostile, unfriendly countries. Afghanistan, Iraq; then Iran, Syria."

"Deep cover assassins hunting al-Qaeda leaders?"

"That was their initial mission. And they were very successful. No headlines or they would blow their cover. Just results. But the more successful UNIT 7 became, the bolder Michael Wayne Portland got, targeting government officials, religious leaders – I mean *high-ranking* officials. Regime change, the old-fashioned way. From the inside. One corpse at a time. Working his way up the chain of command."

"What do you mean? Heads of state?"

"Why not? Michael Wayne Portland could do it. Michael Wayne Portland thinks he can do anything. Absolute power corrupts absolutely."

"But assassinating heads of state is against US government policy. By Executive Order of the President. It's been a policy since John F. Kennedy. Since the CIA's failed attempts on Fidel Castro."

"Sure. Because of the potential embarrassment. Not to mention retaliation in kind. You know your history, Trish. Yes, there's an Executive Order. And yes, it applies to the CIA. But it doesn't apply to an assassination squad operated by a foreign government, does it?"

"A foreign government?"

"India. Sudhir Narayan. Officially, UNIT 7 didn't exist. Officially, its operatives weren't CIA. They were a part of India's own covert operations. Why do you think Sudhir Narayan was made Ambassador to the United States? Why do you think he's been allowed so much freedom to flaunt his privileges in this country? The United States' worst nightmare… is nuclear weapons in the hands of Islamic extremists. And just how fragile is the ruling party that protects Pakistan's nuclear arsenal? What happens if a fundamentalist Islamic revolution replaces the military rulers of Pakistan? It's a disaster for everyone. For the USA. For India. A rapid global escalation of the terrorist threat, de-stabilizing more than just the Middle East. It would destabilize the Indian sub-continent, the fragile peace between India and Pakistan. India has as much reason to fear an Islamic revolution in Pakistan as the US does. So Sudhir Narayan and the Indian government became the CIA's willing partners. By sponsoring UNIT 7. But it all came unglued when the CIA forced India to pull the plug."

"What?"

"UNIT 7 was compromised. Its deep cover assassins were hunted down and executed. All of them... or so the CIA thought. The CIA and India had to train more recruits... or shut UNIT 7 down. But the political pressure from Washington was too great. The CIA had stonewalled the Congressional Intelligence Committee about the existence of UNIT 7. The President concluded that if the truth about UNIT 7 came out in the open, it could bring down the Presidency, a scandal potentially bigger than Iran-Contra. And once Osama Bin Laden had been found and killed in Pakistan, the stakes had grown even higher. It could escalate tensions with Pakistan and start a full-scale regional war. UNIT 7 *had* to be shut down."

"You said the CIA *thought* all the assassins were executed. But they weren't?"

"One of them had survived. Rescued in a daring raid by Indian commandos. Then hidden by Sudhir Narayan. The CIA didn't know about this operation. Because by the time UNIT 7 was ordered shut down, Michael Wayne Portland and Sudhir Narayan had developed an even *bigger* agenda. Michael Wayne Portland had been initiated by Narayan into the Temple of Dvaipa while they were both at Princeton. The Temple was growing in strength and numbers. It just needed that little *extra something* to give it that final edge. And that little *extra something* was a person we called the Tiger Paw Killer - an assassin who unexpectedly crossed the Pakistani border back into India, an assassin who unexpectedly survived. Now, the genie is out of the bottle, no longer controlled by the CIA, and as deadly as ever."

"How did the CIA find out that the Tiger Paw Killer was one of their ex-UNIT 7 assassins?"

"The CIA had a mole in the Indian Embassy. He told them that Michael Wayne Portland and Sudhir Narayan had lost millions in Matthew Carleton's stock scams. Money that was supposed to finance the expansion of the Temple. It wasn't long before the CIA made the connection between the Temple and the killers."

"Killers? But you said just *one* assassin survived."

"Think, Trish. Was it really possible there was only one person doing all this killing? Someone had to help carry all those bottles. Someone had to pilot the boat off the Florida coast. Check Ambassador Narayan's movements. Do your homework, Trish. Then think. Master and apprentice. Ask the CIA. Ask Weinberg. He knows."

Trish Van Cleyburn removed the gun from Scott's back. Scott Forrester was not a dangerous sociopath on the run, the deception Jacob Weinberg and the CIA wanted her to believe. "Is he right?" she asked.

Before an answer could come, Spencer Brant leapt out of the van, grabbed her wrist, turned her arm behind her back, and stuffed the end of his Sig-Sauer under her chin. Weinberg's pistol pressed into Scott's forehead, "I think this is the point in the evening where you and I, Mr. Forrester, have a nice little chat."

A red dot appeared suddenly on Jacob Weinberg's chest.

Another dot appeared just as quickly on Spencer Brant's temple. More red dots followed the first ones.

Many, many more.

Spencer Brant felt cold steel press against the back of his head.

"*Now* it's a fair contest. Wouldn't you agree, Scott?"

The voice belonged to Lance Caulfield.

Another voice said, "Drop your weapons." It was Titus Griffin. "And don't tempt us, Weinberg!" Red laser beams crawled out of the crevices between the bales and boxes behind the van. FBI sharpshooters with laser-sighted assault weapons advanced. "Because they can, and will, follow orders. *My* orders!"

Weinberg grabbed a headset from the surveillance panel. A message was sent before Titus Griffin could stop him, "Abort! Repeat… abort! Walk away!"

Griffin ripped the pistol from Weinberg's hand, reached in with his massive arms, and pulled Weinberg out of the van by his coat. He then raised Weinberg like a sack of feathers high in the air and slammed him hard against the van's roof rail, the metal frame cutting into his back. "*Abort*, you shithead? That's right… crawl back into your holes!"

Griffin relaxed his grip and dropped Weinberg to the ground. Weinberg was handcuffed and hauled back to his feet.

"I guess you got my files?" Scott said.

"Colonel Johnson sends his regards," Lance Caulfield replied, pulling a photo and an FBI identity sketch out of his jacket.

Scott had seen the photo before. It was the Tiger Paw Killer's file photo from UNIT 7 – the same photo they had downloaded from the CIA's central computers via Arnie Prendergast and 'Lightning Strike'. But the FBI identity sketch? This was something new. Scott was handed a flashlight to take a closer look. "The photo and the sketch… they're the same person," he said.

"Funny what you can accomplish… with a little motivation," Caulfield said.

Scott understood. "Colonel Johnson got to those chopper pilots."

"In world record time, Scott. The pilots gave an FBI sketch artist a pretty good description of the person they dropped into the Bridger-Teton Forest. So, when we got the stuff you e-mailed us with that CIA file photo, we had a positive match. I'm not going to ask, Scott, how you obtained top-secret CIA files. Just let me get this straight… the CIA *doesn't know* who the Tiger Paw Killer is?"

"We can fix that, Lance. Right here. Right now." Scott pushed the photo and sketch into the bleeding Jacob Weinberg's face, "You're right, you scumbag. I guess it's time for our 'little chat'. This is what you came for, isn't it? Take a good long look, Weinberg. Because this… is the face of your killer. Surprised?"

Chapter Fifty-Five

Through the night vision scope of Griffin's HK assault rifle, ghostly shapes of yellow and green could be seen patrolling the decks of The Princess of Goa. They were the ship's deckhands, their weapons brandished in full view.

Scott Forrester was crouched behind the warehouse door tucking a wafer-thin microphone into the lining of his jacket. Titus Griffin lifted his eye from the sight and asked, "Are you sure you want to take this kind of risk? You've done enough already. We'll close this trap, one way or another."

"How does anyone know if they've done enough, Titus?" Scott replied, slipping the receiver into his ear. "This killer has made a profession out of escaping traps like this."

Griffin loaded a clip into his assault rifle, looked one more time at The Princess of Goa, and took the safety off. "This terminal is locked down tight. I have snipers on the roof. Police boats and Coast Guard vessels have sealed the harbor. There's *nowhere* for this killer to go, Forrester. This is one big cat that's about to run out of lives."

"It's not just about shutting down a *single* killer, Titus. It's about shutting down... a whole organization of killers."

"Yeah, sure... but no-one's saying *you're* the one that has to do it."

"You're not wimping out on me, are you Titus? Who told me to make a choice - just pick a case, and solve it? Well? Who was it?" There was no reply. "That day, Titus, I made my choice. *This* case was the one I chose to solve. And walking across that pier... is a part of that choice. It is *exactly* what I have to do."

"Understood."

A message came through Titus Griffin's com-set, "Gate 4. Target arriving." Griffin put a hand on Scott's shoulder. "Okay, Forrester, you got the ball. And so far - for a skinny white guy - I'd say you've been running pretty good with it. No coach I know pulls a running back from a game when he's making good yardage. Especially when there's still a lot to play for. Guess you're telling me... I shouldn't either. But remember Forrester..." Griffin said, squeezing Scott's arm, "this ain't football."

A stretched limousine passed through the corridor between the buildings, its headlights cutting through the night, illuminating the words 'The Princess of Goa' on the ship's rusty bow. The limousine slowed. Its lights went out. And the pier returned to silence.

Griffin gave Scott Forrester the thumbs up. Scott rose from his knees and walked out of the warehouse. The vehicle was fifty yards away, but it might as well have been fifty miles. The walk was painfully slow; Scott trying to appear in control, and unhurried.

The limousine's door opened. A man got out.

Scott was frisked. The hidden microphone was not detected. Then Scott waited - the stars shining brightly in the cloudless sky above him; a weirdly peaceful sensation, a tense expectation, an uneasy calm. Amidst the tranquility of the starry night, raw nervous energy percolated in his veins. He was like a coiled spring.

The bodyguard opened the limousine's rear door. A man in a long, black fur coat stepped out. It was Sudhir Narayan. He moved with a powerful defiance into Scott's space. His eyes locked quickly on Scott; his chiseled face and tall frame holding dominion over him, like a monarch over his subject. He was god-like. But it wasn't a charisma born from a god's generosity of spirit; a king's grace; a reverent hope. No. Far from it.

Narayan exhaled a cloud of scented breath. "One night, a few days ago, Mr. Forrester, you looked down into a snowy courtyard and said you were not afraid to die."

"I wasn't."

"So... what *are* you afraid of, Mr. Forrester? What will bring that fear to the surface?"

"I'm not afraid of shadows."

"Your fears are not shadows, Mr. Forrester. They are real. Am I a shadow? No." Narayan's face stiffened. "You intrigue me, Mr. Forrester. Even though we come from opposite sides of a spiritual divide, we have much in common."

"What could we possibly have in common?"

"Our insights into the human mind. Its frailties. Its malleability. That is why I am here tonight. That is why I hope *you* are here tonight. To see how malleable *your* mind is. The Temple made you an offer in that snowy courtyard. Is that the reason you returned the invitation? Could it be... that you are ready to cross that divide?"

"I came here seeking... finality."

"Finality?" Narayan asked, pondering the meaning. "Finality? Are you sure that is what you want, Mr. Forrester?"

"What will be destroyed, will be reborn," Scott replied, quoting one of the opening verses in the Asura Ghita, the book he and Lance Caulfield had found in Chester Franklin's apartment in Wyoming - a book designed to lure wayward souls with its illusory vision of demonic power and immortality.

Sudhir Narayan looked scornfully down at Scott from his imaginary height, "You talk of rebirth? And how would you accomplish that, Mr. Forrester?"

Scott answered, as many willing inductees would have answered before him, "Strike thine enemies hard... and sever them from their hearts. And with their blood, you will be reborn."

"Very Good, Mr. Forrester. But what does that prove? Why should the Temple - why should *I* - invite you into my protection? Just from knowledge of *Her* scriptures? It just proves you are a scholar. But actions... not words... will prove if you are ready to take... the next step. Are you ready for that next step, Mr. Forrester?"

Oh yes, Scott thought. *I'm definitely ready to take the next step with you, Narayan.*

A grinding of gears and a screech of brakes echoed between the buildings as a flatbed 18-wheeler arrived at South Locust Point's Gate #4. The group and the limousine were bathed in its oncoming lights.

The flatbed rolled past the limousine and stopped beneath the gantry crane. Strapped to its back with thick chain was a tall wooden crate, reinforced with heavy metal bracing. The painting, 'The Revenge of Dvaipa', was taking its last steps on American soil.

Behind the flatbed truck, a solitary motorcycle rider advanced slowly - the same motorcycle that had vanished down a snowbound Connecticut Avenue. The bike circled the limousine, then grumbled to a stop; its rider clad in black leather, face hidden behind the same glossy black helmet.

"I think you've met my protégé, Mr. Forrester?"

The helmet came off. Long nut-brown hair tumbled out.

Two sets of eyes met.

Scott Forrester felt the pain. The chill.

This time as the killer spoke, the voice was real. Pure, but not clean. Unadulterated, but not uncorrupted. "Aren't you going to say hello?" she asked.

"She has broken men much stronger than you, Mr. Forrester. I have seen them scream in pain until their lungs are empty. She can squash their souls in the palm of her hand."

"Yes, I know," Scott said, his eyes filling with tears. "But can she... love?"

The rider abandoned the motorcycle and walked towards him. She slipped her arms around Scott Forrester's waist, and kissed him.

Her lips were cold. Her heart was cold.

Scott did not respond, resisting any notion of warmth.

She withdrew her lips, "Was this not love, Scott Forrester?"

"No," he replied.

"Then... what was it?"

"It was evil."

Christienne Duval smiled.

"The bottle on my dining room table? The one you took from Carleton's wine cellar?"

She smiled again.

"You placed it there. When I went outside to chase the CIA van that was spying on me."

Christienne Duval circled Scott like a shiny black leopard contemplating its next move, never once letting her eyes stray from his. He felt her breath against his cheek, smelt the intoxication of her deceit.

"The welt on your arm. I noticed it at lunch, at the Bistro Fermette. You said you had burnt yourself on a kettle. That was a jellyfish sting. Did you get that before or after the Rivertons were incinerated?"

"After," she purred.

"You were never on a flight from Paris. There was no business trip to Geneva or Moscow. No emergency landing." Scott continued. "You followed me from Dulles Airport. Knew that I had gone to Sarah Vaughn's townhouse. You were in Washington watching my every step all the time. Luring me ever closer to the trap: the bogus murder scene inside Michael Wayne Portland's apartment. The perfect opportunity for Portland to disappear - to begin another identity - just like *you* have done so many times before."

Christienne Duval walked over to Sudhir Narayan. She placed her head on his shoulder. Narayan drew her into the warmth of his coat. "The Temple holds many secrets, Scott Forrester," Christienne said, as she stroked the black fur. "The next step is trust. Trust in our beliefs. That is the divide you must cross... if you are to be accepted."

"*Trust*? Would your brother, Dominic Sant'Angello, *trust* the sister he once adored, if he knew the legacy of death that has followed her every step?"

Scott did not expect a reply. "The genesis of lies…" he continued. "Started the day Gina Sant'Angello, a Princeton student invited by Lexi Stavros into her exclusive circle, was recruited into the CIA by Michael Wayne Portland. You were the ideal candidate, weren't you? Your athleticism. Your language skills. Your dark Arabesque looks. The lies have no end, do they, Gina? You were never a weapons officer in the Air Force. You were never missing in action. More lies. But what made you cross that final divide? The betrayal you felt? When the CIA abandoned you in the souks of Kabul? Thinking they had buried UNIT 7 in the Afghan dust? And with it, Gina Sant'Angello - the assassin the CIA discarded without a second thought?"

"I am *no longer* Gina Sant'Angello! Gina Sant'Angello died with UNIT 7!" she replied with venom. "And *then*…" she said, looking deeply into Narayan's satanic eyes, "I was reborn."

"Sadly, yes. Reborn as Christienne Duval – the instrument of death we named the Tiger Paw Killer."

"You know nothing of *who* I am now. How *powerful* I have become."

"*You*… are the daughter of horror and deception. That, I *do* know."

Narayan broke her embrace and pointed at Scott. "*And you,* Mr. Forrester… you know too much."

"You're right, Narayan. We *do* have things in common. We are both cunning. Because a secret that is shared with others is no longer a secret. With the information I have provided to the FBI, I doubt, Ambassador Narayan… that you will be welcome to stay in the United States. After tonight, the bonds of your influence will be broken. Michael Wayne Portland's assets will be frozen. It is the Temple's heart that will be severed… and will stop beating. Strike thine enemies *hard*."

Barely able to contain his rage, Narayan motioned to his bodyguard. A pistol came out of the thug's jacket and a silencer was applied. Two more bodyguards exited the limousine, carrying Uzi's. Narayan turned to Christienne Duval. "I think you two lovers should get reacquainted," Narayan said. "Take him to the ship, Christienne. Show him how the energy of *Her* divine anger can bring his fears to the surface. Show him... *finality*."

A gang of Indian stevedores had descended from The Princess of Goa to prepare the crate to be lifted. A hook was guided into place. The crane began to accept the tension. Scott watched the flatbed's evil cargo rise slowly into the air. He raised his arm, rocking it back and forth over his head. It was a signal. A signal the crane's operator, Pradesh Bhandari understood. The painting stopped its ascent. The cab at the top of the crane opened and a road flare was lit. It was tossed to the ground.

Another signal... that was understood.

Doors rolled open from the building next to Gate #4. An intense spotlight emerged. A crowd of East Indian men and women rushed forward, carrying placards and banners. At the front of the crowd was a television van with a TV camera perched on top. The dazzling TV lights struck Narayan and his bodyguards in the face. They turned away and hid their weapons.

The crowd was shouting, "Let Vishnu's tears consume you, evil Dvaipa!"

"What is the meaning of *this*?!" Narayan screamed.

The crowd began throwing what looked like eggs at the crate, wobbling as they flew through the air. When the objects landed, they burst open, wetting the crate's side.

"A comet will descend from *His* Heaven..." Scott recited to Narayan from Hindu legend. "And *His* blazing fire will destroy you!"

Narayan turned to Scott, "What will this *pitiful* demonstration accomplish? Water balloons? The acts of children, Mr. Forrester! Like children... their words are *meaningless*!"

"Then do not trust their *words*, Narayan. Trust their *actions*. Trust their *beliefs*."

He laughed. "Is this why you came here? To parade this infantile display of weak-minded *fools* in front of me? What did you expect this *feeble* mockery to accomplish?"

The crate was soaked. A storm of water balloons had rained down upon it. The crate hung twenty feet off the flatbed, liquid dripping down its sides.

Scott spread his arms out and looked up into the starry night, "I call on Shri Rama's bow to bend. Bring Kalki's flaming sword... and strike Her *evil* down!"

Narayan laughed again. "That, Mr. Forrester... is the pathetic wish... of Hindu *dreamers*!"

"Really?" Scott replied, as he pointed to the building the crowd had come out from.

Narayan looked over and saw a flame burning on the roof. And then another.

"Those, Ambassador Narayan... are indeed Shri Rama's bows."

A silhouette of an archer appeared on the roof. And then another. And another.

"And *that*..." Scott said, pointing back to the crate, as a flaming arrow soared high in the air, "isn't water. It's... *gasoline*!"

A flurry of arrows descended through the starry blackness like the comets of Hindu legend. Some missed their target. But it only took one to strike the crate – and one did – to cause the night sky to explode in flame.

"It looks like *my* dream... is now *your* nightmare, Narayan!"

Narayan glared at his bodyguard. *"Kill him!"*

A hand moved into a jacket.

A red dot appeared.

The silenced pistol was only halfway out when the impact of an FBI bullet threw the bodyguard onto the limo's hood. The other bodyguards made similar mistakes. Their Uzi's never felt the cold night air. FBI snipers placed their bullets with surgical precision.

Sudhir Narayan, stunned and wide-eyed, stood amid the carnage, watching the blood of his entourage paint his limousine... and the defiant, angry Hindu crowd turn his precious altarpiece into a blazing wall of flame.

Christienne Duval saw more red dots appear, this time on her chest. She pulled on Narayan's coat to use him as a shield and as he toppled sideways towards her, the bullets - intended for her - hit him squarely in the chest.

"The painting!" Narayan wheezed, as he fell. "You must not let it burn!"

Christienne, straining with his dying weight, dragged Narayan for cover until she was beside her motorcycle.

"Leave me! Get to the crane," Narayan said. "Drop the crate in the water! It must not burn!"

The painting inside the box was packaged for its overseas journey in waterproof wrapping. Although the crate was now a complete fireball, the flames were only burning an outer layer of rough chipboard. There was a good chance that if the crate were submerged in the harbor, the painting, inside its waterproof wrap, would survive intact.

Christienne Duval revved the motorcycle. Narayan's lifeless body, in his blood-soaked fur coat, dropped to the ground. She tucked her head below the handlebars and accelerated; the bike reaching full speed as its front wheel lifted off the ground.

Scott grabbed the pistol that had fallen from the bodyguard's hand and started running. He could see red dots appear on Christienne's back.

The motorcycle weaved.

Shots bounced off the ground.

The motorcycle headed straight for the crowd, a crowd that was dispersing as bullets flew.

An armored posse of FBI agents sprinted out of the Customs warehouse towards Narayan's limousine. "Hold your fire!" Griffin yelled into his com-set. The FBI's snipers had no clear shot at Christienne Duval without endangering the fleeing crowd. She knew that.

Scott Forrester ran between the ship and the flatbed truck, towards the gantry crane and its dangling ball of fire. *The moth was coming to the flame.* He stopped, took out a cell phone and speed-dialed. The call was answered in the gantry crane's cabin by Pradesh Bhandari.

"Pradesh…" Scott panted. "Pradesh… drop it! Drop the crate! *Now!*"

The motorcycle swerved, on a collision course with the gantry crane's base. The bike wasn't slowing down. Just before impact, Christienne Duval rose from its seat, let go of the handlebars, and leapt up at an overhead girder. The bike skidded, smashing violently into the crane's base, twisting in the air as its momentum spun it forward. The bike slid off the pier and hit the water with a loud splash.

Christienne swung from the girder like a gymnast.

Scott Forrester had reached the base of the crane. He was twenty yards away from her. He looked up and fired, but his bullets missed and ricocheted off the girders. More shots rained through the steel as FBI snipers tried to find a clean line of sight. The black leather-clad figure was darting in and out of the crane's legs. As she climbed, the shots kept getting closer - sparks flying around her head - but the bullets still missed their target.

Suddenly, the mass of flame dangling from the crane hook fell from the air. The burning crate landed heavily on the back of the flatbed truck and disintegrated on impact. Cinders ascended into the night sky like an exploding firework. The crowd cheered. The painting – 'The Revenge of Dvaipa' - was exposed, then quickly became engulfed by the fiery kindling, and caught light.

For a brief moment, as its wrapping burned away, Dvaipa's demonic gaze appeared through the licking flames. A creeping black stain - the burning silk's last breath of life - reached the Demon-Goddess's face. And then, the image that had inspired centuries of evil… was gone. Consumed.

Christienne Duval looked down at the blazing painting - her beloved Temple's altar-piece - and froze. That one split-second of inaction was more than enough. An FBI sniper's bullet ripped through her motorcycle leather and entered her thigh. Her leg lost strength. She lost her balance and tumbled down the scaffold-like girders, awkwardly grasping at the beams to break her fall.

Christienne Duval dropped heavily to the pier.

A pool of blood seeped onto the ground from the bullet wound in her thigh.

Scott approached cautiously, his pistol held out in front of him in both hands.

Christienne's body lay motionless, bent in a fetal position, her knees drawn up into her stomach.

This doesn't feel right, Scott thought, as he crept forward. *This doesn't look right.*

Her hand moved.

Chapter Fifty-Six

The knife was drawn from a scabbard strapped to Christienne's calf - a stiletto... razor sharp, and as thin as a pencil. She threw it with a fluid backward motion and it entered Scott's stomach with a needle-like pain that grew and grew. Christienne cried out in pain, the effort torturing her wounded leg.

Scott released one hand from the gun and looked down at the red stain creeping through his shirt. Christienne sliced her leg through the air and knocked Scott's gun out of his hand. With another rapid but painful move, she then cut Scott's legs from under him. He fell backwards onto the hard concrete.

Christienne pounced on top of him and grabbed the dagger that was protruding from his stomach. Her weight began to press down on the knife. Scott clamped his hands over hers, to prevent the blade from sinking even deeper into his abdomen.

Christienne's face - lit by the flames of her Temple's burning icon - was knotted in a wild, angry grimace as she struggled to break through Scott's resistance; grunting in frustration like a child with a broken toy.

Adrenaline locked his arms and prevented her from driving the dagger even deeper.

It was a stalemate.

At that very moment, as the knife stung deeply inside him, as her viciousness controlled her and the sociopathic rage reached its peak, Scott Forrester understood *what* Christienne Duval had become. Gone was the soft warmth against his bare chest; the sweet smell of her nut-brown hair; the caress of her sugary laugh; the breathless perfection he wanted to keep locked up in his heart.

That was *his* Christienne. *This* was *another* Christienne.

A beast. A rabid *wild* beast.

A red dot appeared on her forehead.

She looked up as Titus Griffin took aim.

The anger that was fueling her suddenly drained from her face, and was replaced by fear. And defeat.

Unexpectedly, her grip went limp.

She knew it was time.

She knew it was her turn.

"No!" Scott cried out, as he saw the red dot on her forehead - the dot that marked her for death. "No!"

He pulled her to one side.

The bullet whizzed past her ear.

Scott began to cough up blood; the grip he had on the knife weakening, as shock seized his body.

He let go of her hands. He was hers now.

Finality.

Christienne looked down at his face, her tears glistening in the light of the painting's fire. She hesitated, then bent towards him… and kissed him on his bloodied lips. She retracted the knife… and tossed it away.

Griffin's second bullet sank into her shoulder, spinning her around. She rolled towards the ship and then struggled to her knees. Once again she was hit, this time in the chest. She landed heavily, the bottom half of her body sliding over the edge of the pier; her hands barely maintaining their grip on the concrete.

She looked one last time into Scott's eyes, her lips trembling, her cheeks wet with fright.

The red dot reappeared on her head.

Christienne released her grip before the fourth bullet could find its mark… and fell into the darkness between the ship and the wharf.

A few seconds later, a body hit the water with a splash.

Scott heard footsteps in his ear. He tried to lift himself up, but the pain in his stomach punched him back.

A sickly cold spread in a rush to his limbs. The blackness of the starry sky descended from above like a blanket.

One nightmare had ended. Had another one begun?

He lost consciousness.

His thoughts drifted upwards, towards a bright white light.

The pain in his stomach was gone.

Finality.

Chapter Fifty-Seven

A pale white light removed the darkness. Scott felt a gentle touch on his hand. His eyelids were heavy and stuck together. He looked up and saw a blood red plastic bag hanging from a metal stand. He felt uncomfortable. Something, a long plastic tube, was poking him in the nose.

"Sshh!" a voice said, as he tried to speak.

Pink lips kissed him gently.

He turned towards them and saw her soft freckled face.

"Sshh, Scott… sleep."

• • •

He heard them talking quite clearly – a broad-shouldered black man and an angel with softly sculpted red hair.

The man said, "Give this to him when he wakes up." And then he left the room.

The angel put the small package on the bedside table. It was wrapped in bright colors and a ribbon. She sat in the chair beside the bed and picked up a magazine.

"What are you reading?" Scott asked.

The angel's face grew into a big wide smile. She put the magazine down, placed her warm hands on his cheeks, and kissed him – a long, luscious soft kiss; a feeling he thought he would never feel again.

Kelly Whelan rubbed the tears from her eyes.

"How long?" he asked. "I've heard your voice whispering to me so many times."

"Three weeks. You've been in a coma. I've been here every day."

Scott spoke slowly, "No wonder I'm starving. I'll have the Hungry Man's Special."

She giggled. "French toast?"

"With red wine, Kelly. And yes, I do know the difference."

"Sure, hon," she said, kissing his cheek.

Scott's eyes wandered over to the gift-wrapped box. "What is it?"

"A present, silly. From Titus Griffin."

"But it's not my birthday."

"No, hon. Today is Christmas Day."

"Titus Griffin gave *me* a present?" Scott tried to sit up but a twinge in his stomach stopped him cold. "Can I open it?"

Kelly put the present in his hand. But he was still too weak to unwrap it. "Here, hon… let me help you," she said.

Inside the gift-wrap was a small box, and as she lifted its lid, there was a note. Kelly mouthed the words in silence, looking puzzled, then said, "I don't understand what it means, Scott, do you?"

She passed him the note and the box.

He read it and smiled. "Yes, Kelly. I do."

The box contained two darts.

The note said, "I think these belong to you."

Made in the USA
Charleston, SC
03 March 2012